Past Historic

Future Perfect

Marie Leprêtre

This novel is entirely a work of fiction and except in the case of historical fact, the names, characters and incidents portrayed in it are the work of the author's imagination. Any resemblance to actual persons, living or dead, is purely coincidental.

Copyright © Marie Leprêtre 2021
All rights reserved
ISBN : 9798773880837

Author's note

Anyone who has studied languages, including English, will be familiar with the Past Historic tense and the Future Perfect tense and possibly the difficulties of getting one's head around them.

So here is a story about a past and a future that I hope will be much easier to understand.

Also by the same author

Worlds Apart series
Book 1 : Forget-me-not
Book 2 : French Leave
Book 3 : The Casket
Book 4 : Past Historic, Future Perfect
Book 5 : Renaissance

The Château of Tressandre

The French Island Hotel

Let me dedicate this one to
Madeleine, Jane & Christine,
friends from the past,
the present and for the future.

And to my sister Josephine Quinn
for painting the book cover.

Chapter One

The Solicitor

Clare stood looking around her with interest at the stately old house that rose up before her, thinking rather smugly to herself that is was not unlike her own home-to-be in the heart of Brittany. Built more than a century ago, one in Ireland, the other in France, both buildings were imposing, squatting in a proprietorial way, graciously indicating that they would be around for generations to come, long after their current occupants had played their part.

Still thinking of the manor house in France, she went up the stone steps and rang the bell. A metal plate announced 'Damien Murray & Sons, Solicitors. By appointment only. Please ring and enter'.

She was shown into the familiar waiting-room by a bright young assistant that Clare had not met before.

She wondered briefly what had happened to Mrs O'Donnell. The waiting-room was elegantly attired, a showpiece, with its beautiful bow window and original 19th century fireplace. A large mahogany dining table sported a variety of magazines and an assortment of cosy armchairs flanked the walls.

A full twenty minutes later, when Clare had finally lost herself in a fascinating article from Country Life, the door opened and Damien Murray himself came quickly over to greet her.

"Clare, my dear. How lovely to see you! It's been, what? A year? Two? You're looking well, I must say. How's that Nursing Home of yours? Are you keeping me a place there, like I asked you to?" His eyes twinkled in merriment at his own joke.

"Oh, Damien, where have you been this last while? I'm not the manageress of Oak Lodge any more. Sharon Murphy is. Or Sharon Harrison, to be exact. Just got married last Saturday, to Paul Harrison." And she gave his arm a gentle nudge.

"What? But you were manageress there for ages! You'll have to tell me all about it. What on earth are you doing with yourself? You're far too young to retire, surely. No, wait. I'll get Sophie to make us a nice cup of tea first. Let's go into my office. Go on ahead; you know the way... Sophie?"

And out he went to organize refreshments with the young assistant.

He was back within minutes. "It's good to see you Clare. So many new faces these days. Most of my clients seem to be just out of school. Sobering thought…"

"Where's Mrs O'Donnell, Damien? She hasn't left you, has she?" began Clare, starting with what was uppermost in her mind.

"Ah, Mrs O'Donnell" said Damien, sighing, "that paragon of virtue, champion of filing systems and terror of solicitors, old and young. Yes, she finally decided to retire. I do regret her, you know, in spite of her domineering ways. But my sons were heartily relieved when she left. No client, however difficult, was as difficult as Mrs O'Donnell. She kept us all on our toes."

He smiled. "Sophie, now, she's sweet. A word I would never have equated with her predecessor. And we've got Amanda; she's a fully trained solicitor. Been with us for two years. And my younger son, Declan, remember him? Same class as your Owen at Saint Brendan's. Just qualified and come to join the practice too. Still got the learner plates on him but he's not doing so bad."

"Wow, you've really expanded, haven't you? Congratulations, Damien. Last time I was here, you were away, resting, if I remember. It was Vincent who saw to me then," said Clare.

"Ah, that explains it. I've been semi-retired these last three years. Had to. All those cholesterol-filled lunches, and late hours, and stress. Had a bit of a heart attack. Flora put her foot down and made me leave the business. That's when we took on Amanda. And now young Declan's caught the bug. Only just started. So I bribed Flora to let me come back part-time, for six months or so, till he got on his feet. And here I am. Going to cost me a holiday in Italy, I fear, but I'm enjoying being back in the driver's seat, so to speak."

"Oh, Damien. I'm sorry you had that attack. You're still quite young. Why, if I remember rightly, you're only two years older than me," said Clare, concerned.

"I know. Fifty-four. Big wake-up call. Now I'm not allowed to take life seriously anymore. And I have to stick to a diet. And I had to give up the cigs. That was the hardest part. And, you know Clare, it's damn difficult to hand the business over to the younger generation, however well trained they are."

"I imagine it is."

Clare tried to envisage her son Owen stepping in to take over from her at the holiday homes in France and rejected the idea outright.

"Here, Clare, be mother," said Damien as Sophie brought in a laden tray. "Pour us out a cuppa and have some of those nice biscuits." He watched happily as she sorted out milk and sugar, thanked Sophie, who left discretely, and settled back comfortably to enjoy a good catching up.

"Now, tell me what you're doing in the world. How's that Frank of yours?" he asked.

"We're fine, really fine," began Clare. "But we had a rough time of it back in 2012-2013. Frank found out at the beginning of that school year that he was going to be made redundant the following June, because of the cutbacks. I know, Damien, such a scandal! And He'd been teaching in that school for over twenty years! Well, he went through a bad time, keeping this all to himself and trying to find another job and being rejected everywhere, until finally he was forced to tell me what was happening and, to cut a long story short, I convinced him to move to France and open a business there! It's what we'd intended doing all long but when we were nearer retirement age, you know?"

"Ye Gods, Clare. What's the world coming to? Frank was one of the best teachers at St. Brendan's. Even my boys enjoyed French when he taught them. And they're hopeless at languages."

Clare could see that Damien was furious on Frank's behalf and she couldn't help but warm to him all the more so for that.

"Thanks, Damien. That's really kind of you. Well, as I say, in the end we upped it to France. We sold the house, took the plunge and bought a gîte complex in Brittany. Imagine! I never thought we'd ever do anything like that. Not at this point in our lives, anyhow." Clare sighed and continued, smiling. "We haven't done too badly, actually. It's a large complex, eight gîtes, all year round swimming-pool, games room, etc. And in the winter months, when the holiday rentals are quieter, we run courses. Frank teaches French and my brother, Ian, remember him? He runs computer classes, mainly for retired people wanting to get to grips with all this new technology that's floating about."

"So Ian's in France too? How did your mother react to that? I'm sure she wasn't pleased that both her children had moved away."

"Well, actually, she's taken it better than any of us would've thought. Dad's been wonderful, but then he always is. But, yes, you're right. Mum's always been the problem. She's so full of herself, I don't know how Dad puts up with her." Clare frowned, visions of her mother's domineering ways clouding her thoughts.

She dismissed them abruptly. "But anyway, getting back to Ian, he met this French girl, Céline, who came as a French assistant to St Brendan's and... well... the rest is history, as the saying goes. She's now teaching English in France and Ian has managed to negotiate working for his old company on a free-lance basis, travelling back and forth between the head office in Belfast and their subsidiary in Rennes. And as it's free-lance he can spare a week here and there to do the IT courses for us. They're really popular, both courses, but we're going to have to find someone to help Ian out. I want to increase their number and he's just not free." Clare paused, her thoughts going back to this particular problem. Then she brightened. "But getting back to Mum and Dad, they see more of Ian than when he lived in Ireland, actually. And they come out to us about twice a year. Every Christmas so far."

"Good for them! I'm sincerely delighted things are going so well for you Clare. I love a happy ending." Damien smiled, a wide, satisfied smile. "Now, is there anything I can do for you, while you're here? I love hearing how you are getting on but I imagine you have a reason for coming to see me?"

"I do, Damien, actually. You see, we've done so well in our first two years in France, that I've managed to persuade Frank to purchase a lovely old manor house that's only half a mile from the gîte complex and we're going to do it up and live in it ourselves. So I thought it was a good time to get our wills and stuff sorted out and I wanted to put things in motion while I was home for Sharon's wedding. I can send you all the details by email and either Frank or I, or both, will be home regularly for any signing that needs to be done but our lives have changed so much in the last three years, we need to stop and take stock, so to speak."

"So-oo... my dear Clare, if I surmise correctly, you've managed to badger poor Frank into purchasing a manor house on *top* of what you've already taken on as a huge holiday gîte project after only two years of activity? Clare, are you sure you haven't caught the Oak Lodge Alzheimer bug or something? Aren't you biting off more than you can chew?"

Damien was now looking at her shrewdly, his hands joined in a semblance of prayer, the finger tips touching his mouth.

"Oh Damien, don't look at me like that! I'll make it work, I promise," protested Clare. "And really, we're not over-stretching it. The gîtes are funded, okay, by me and Frank, and a huge bank loan but Ian has invested in the project and so have our two lovely French friends, Laura and Nathan. Nathan is a bank manager and he's ever so pleased with the way things are going. Really! And in order to finance the manor house, which was going for a song actually, we've just finished having the attic converted in the gîte that we were living in ourselves and it's become a four-bedroomed, two bath affair and I *know* we'll get it rented out for the summer months. I had to turn away ever so many people last year. I could've been doing with that extra gîte and now I'll have it!"

"Clare Hunter, you always did bulldozer people, ever since I've known you," began Damien. "You fought for that big extension to Oak Lodge and you got your way and, I'll admit, you made it pay. I suppose you're doing exactly the same in France and you'll not stop till you get what you want there, either. God, you make me tired just looking at you. How does Frank keep up?"

"Now, Damien.," said Clare, "You know Frank as well as I do. He'd not let me do anything suicidal, would he? Trust me. Or even better still, come out and visit us. Why don't you and Flora come for a week in the off season? It's extremely reasonable, I assure you. Or better still, take one of our courses. I can see you're still not very computer-minded. You've no work-station or lap-top or anything. Have you even a got an I-phone?"

"A), no I haven't and I don't know how to use the damn things, and b), it's none of your business, young lady." He looked at her sternly.

"So you'll give some thought to doing one of our courses? They're great fun, I assure you. Ian's a hoot. Bring Flora. She'd love it." Clare smiled, certain she was getting the upper hand.

"Oh, alright," said Damien with an exaggerated sigh. "I'll talk to her about it, as a favour to you. No promises, mind."

"Lovely! Here's my card. It's got the website and my email address on it. That way we can keep in touch. And I can send you our wills, even if they are all higgledy piggledy at present. And you can sort them out for us into legal language and get us the best deals to minimize inheritance tax and things. Things like that can be quite hefty in France."

"Yes, yes of course. I'll do what I can."

"Thanks Damien. Much appreciated." Clare beamed and made to get to her feet.

"Umm… wait a moment, Clare. There's something I'd like to ask you. I was actually going to visit you at Oak Lodge, which, in hindsight, would've been a waste of time, now wouldn't it?"

Clare sat down again, her interest aroused.

"Fire away, Damien. Anything to help. But if it's Oak Lodge business, it's Sharon you'll have to see or Paul her deputy, and since Saturday, her husband. I can advise you, but they're running the place now and making a darned good job of it, I must admit."

"Well, it's about George Hamilton, really. I'm his solicitor."

"Don't tell me George has died? I knew he'd had a few bad spells of health but he always seemed to pull through. I really like George. Such a gentleman!" Clare was immediately distressed.

"No, nothing like that. George is still alive and kicking. No, that's not right. He's in a wheel-chair now but the rest of him is doing quite well. The dementia has progressed, as you know it would, but he left me instructions, years ago, before I took my heart-attack, actually, and it's only now I'm getting around to doing something serious about it. I'd like to get all my old files up to date before I leave here for good. So Clare, will you help?"

"Sure, Damien. I'd love to," said Clare. "But you haven't even said what this is about. Something to do with his estate, I imagine. A will? A donation after his death?"

"Indeed. But it's a tricky one. However, now that I know you've moved to France, it's like Providence giving me a shove in the back and telling me to get a move on. And you're just the person I need." He smiled.

"So what can I do for you? Or for George, to be precise. If it's at all in my power, you know I'd be willing to help." Clare looked at him and waited.

Damien took a deep breath. Then he looked hard at Clare and said: "Just what do you know about George's past, Clare?"

"Well," said Clare, thinking hard. "I remember that he never married. His only visitors seemed to be his cleaning lady, Mrs… Mrs… oh, what was her name now? And her daughter Rosie. And some friend who used to come and play chess with him at the start. They all came quite regularly and seemed to be very fond of him. Now, what else was there? He was not receiving subsidies for his care at Oak Lodge, so that means that he must be fairly well off. He was a private patient, yes, that's right. He was… is… very polite. A kind man, really. I remember he liked to do the rounds of the home at night to make sure everything was locked up and everyone safe. He told me that Oak Lodge was his responsibility. We all knew he'd been a foreman at some point in his life so we just played along. That's all I can say, really. That's all I know."

"Well there's a lot more to our George than what you know", began Damien quietly. He sighed. "Let me tell you the story of his life. It's an interesting tale, you'd be surprised."

Clare looked at him expectantly.

"But I'm going to need your help to bring him closure, Clare. And now that you're living in France, I know of no-one more qualified for the job."

-oOo-

Chapter Two

George's Story

Damien sat back in his leather armchair and gathered his thoughts. Then, abruptly, he got to his feet and began to search in the filing cabinets that stood against one wall of the office. Clare watched him while he took out one file after another and rejected them.

"Times like this I still need Mrs O'Donnell," he muttered. "Just a moment Clare, I'll see if Sophie has the file. Pour yourself another cup of tea. I'll not bother, thanks."

He went out to find his assistant while Clare helped herself to tea.

Sophie came back with him within seconds and went straight to the same filing cabinet, pulling out George's file almost immediately.

"There you are, Mr Murray. That's Mr Hamilton's file. I've put in everything we know about him and I'll print you out a copy of his will, if you like."

"Ah, thank you, Sophie. But no need. I've already got the original will. Took it out the other day."

"Very well, Mr Murray." And out she went.

Clare waited patiently while Damien perused the documents and re-read George's will.

"Yes, yes," he muttered to himself. "Yes, indeed. Umm... ah, here it is! Ah... indeed."

Finally, he looked up at Clare, took off his glasses, and began.

"Well, Clare, I'll start at the beginning. Our George was born and bred on a farm in Co. Fermanagh. He had two brothers, no sisters. The eldest brother ran the farm when their dad got too old. He never married. The younger brother, George was in the middle you understand, was a bit of a wild one and was killed in a motor-bike accident in Cookstown. That was towards the end of the Second World War. Now, for some years already, George had been living in England, helping with the war effort in an armaments factory. He'd been in London at the start of the blitz in September/October 1940, got out of London and went to Coventry, only to live through the Germans bombing Coventry a month later." Damien paused to let all this sink in.

"Goodness," said Clare. "I never knew he'd been through all that."

"Well, according to George, he told me all this about five years ago now and only because he had to, when he was in Coventry, some two years later, in late 1942 it was, he met this French girl called Meira. She had fled France some weeks previously, shortly after the Nazis had sent her husband to Germany, to work for them. He was an electrician, and starting to specialize in radars etc. All very new at that time and just what the Germans needed. He tried to get out of it but was forced to leave."

"I've heard of that. It was called the STO - *Le Service de Travail Obligatoire*," said Clare.

"Exactly. But before he left, Meira's husband made her promise to leave France. They hadn't been married long and he knew she was of Jewish descent, and they'd already been cut off from her parents, who had been living in the "free" zone in the south of the country. Communications were not all that good, nor safe. The Nazis were starting to organize the concentration camps and Jews were having to wear the Star of David. Meira managed to escape by boat from Bordeaux with the help of friends of her parents and headed to Coventry, where she had distant relatives, or thought she had. Turned out they had left for Wales at the start of the war and she never did manage to find them." He paused.

"The war was a strange and difficult time, Clare. The rules were not the same, or so George tried to explain it to me. When he met Meira, in 1942, she had been living by her wits, trying to find work, no ration card or anything. She spoke a little English and, well, they just took to each other, friends, or survivors , for want of a better word. He befriended her. Passed her off as his wife, got her to change her name to Moira, less Jewish and more Irish, got her a ration card and they found work and a little place to live. She tried to get news of her husband but it was impossible, as you can imagine. And by the end of the war, Meira and George had become lovers and Meira was expecting his baby."

"Oh!... complicated," said Clare, trying to equate the George she knew with this other George and the young woman he had helped.

"Indeed," sighed Damien.

"So what happened, then? Did she go back to her husband?"

"She tried to. She made George realize that she had to find out. Go back to where they had been living in Paris and wait for him, even though she was expecting someone else's child. She felt it was the least she could do for him, he who had spent most of the war in such difficult conditions. Also, she was worried about her parents. She'd had no news of them for years now but stories of the concentration camps were filtering through and she feared that they might have been deported."

Clare sighed. "God, we've had our troubles in Northern Ireland, but what happened to those poor Jews in the Second World War was genocide. You know, Damien, living in France, I realize just how very present it all is, even to this day. They've recently been celebrating the 70th anniversary of the landings on the Normandy coast and this year, they'll be celebrating the 70th anniversary of the end of the war. It's been on the news, lots of media coverage and many people are coming to France to be there for it. And you only have to talk to anyone over eighty to know that they've never forgotten those times."

"I don't think we can imagine the hardships all those people endured, even when they weren't Jews. It must've been a terrible time. But we digress, Clare. Getting back to George..."

"Please..."

"Well, Meira went back to France without him. I think he was heart-broken, poor man. Then, some months later, he had a letter from her to say that she had been told her husband had been killed in an Allied air-raid on Germany. She was sad for him but, as I say, they had not been married long and she had now fallen in love with George. Her letter was full of hope of a better life together, actually I've got a copy of it here, and she talked about coming back to England to live, once she'd had confirmation about what had happened to her parents. She was leaving for the south of France, a little village in the Landes region, where she hoped there would be news of their whereabouts." He paused.

"And so, what happened then?" asked Clare.

"Nothing."

"Nothing?"

"Nothing! No more letters, no news of Meira or what happened to her. Did she make it to the village where her parents lived? Did she have her baby? We don't know. George didn't know. It must've been awful for him."

"Oh my God! Poor George! Didn't he make enquiries? Or follow her to France or something?" Clare was suitably aghast at this ending to the story.

"Of course he did. He followed her to France a month or so after receiving her letter, worried that she was getting near her time for the baby to be born and anxious because he'd had no further news. That was towards the end of 1945. He went to Paris and then to the village in the south of France, following the trail she had left him. He couldn't find her. He did find out, however, that her parents *had* been deported, sometime in 1943, and had died at Auschwitz, both of them. But of Meira there was no news at all."

"That's so sad. Poor George!"

"He went back the following year 1946, twice, I think, and again in 1947. He made enquiries with the French authorities but France was one unholy bureaucratic mess in those days and he never did find out what happened to poor Meira."

"So that's what you want me to do? Find out what happened to this woman, or her child, and try and get them reunited with George before he dies?"

"Well, yes, there's that. And it's important, too. But there's more to it than that, Clare."

"Good Lord, Damien, isn't that enough for one life?"

Damien smiled, a sad little smile. "Did you ever stop to think about George's surname?"

"Hamilton? What about it?"

"Aren't the original owners of Oak Lodge called the same?"

"No!" Clare gasped. "Damien, you're surely not suggesting that George is related to the Hamilton's that own Oak Lodge?"

"I am. Even George didn't know that, to be honest. Not until about fifteen years ago. After all, he was reared on a farm, nothing pretentious, and all his family are dead now, as you can imagine. But he is a descendant of Ellen and Henry Hamilton, the couple that went to America in the 1860's and made their fortune in the textile trade. Henry was originally from Lancashire, and was already quite well off. But it was Ellen that had Oak Lodge built, as a family seat, so to speak, as she came from this part of Ireland originally, and George, our George, is a direct descent of one of their sons."

Clare sat back in her chair, flabbergasted. "You know, Damien, George was always saying that Oak Lodge was his home. Was quite insistent, actually. It was one of the reasons he always wanted to make sure it was closed and locked up properly at night. I had put that down to the fact he had worked as a foreman once, but if he really does part-own Oak Lodge, well that explains it, doesn't it? Do the other heirs know?"

"Well, they do now. But then they always knew that they had cousins in America. Ellen and Henry are buried out there. And so are their children and most of their grandchildren. But George is a direct descendant of their first born, their son George as it happens, whose own son came back to Ireland, bought the farm and incidentally was George's father. And when you had that extension made to Oak Lodge, the American attorneys hunted out the Hamilton descendants to see if they wanted to invest or sell their shares, or whatever. That's when they pulled George out of the hat and contacted me. He actually owns 15% of the place. He was left 5% in his own right and has inherited the 5% from each of his brothers, now deceased."

"So, Damien, let me get this straight. Are you saying that George is actually quite rich and Meira, or her child, would be entitled to it all?"

"Yes, I am. Not only that, they would also have a say in the running of Oak Lodge. With a 15% share, they could logically claim a seat on the Board of Governors. George always felt he was too old to sit on the board himself, but his descendants might think differently."

Clare exhaled. "Wow! I can see now why you thought I'd be the right person for the job. I've only just resigned from the Board of Governors myself. But I never knew about George. I suppose his voting rights were lumped in with those of the other Hamilton heirs, sleeping partners for the most part. "

"Indeed, Clare, that is so. So you can see why I thought of you, even before I knew you'd moved to France. I knew you'd want the best for George."

"Of course I do."

"And that you can't resist a good challenge, when you see one."

This made Clare laugh. "Oh Damien, you know me so well! But it's one hell of a challenge seventy years on."

"I acknowledge that, Clare. But you're my only hope. Will you help me then?"

"I will, Damien, of course I will. But after all these years, the chances of me being successful are very slim, as you know. I'm going to need time to research this. And I do get so busy with the gîtes and the courses. But I'll do my best, my very best. At least my French is now up to scratch. If you'd asked me this time last year, I was still struggling with the lingo."

"Clare, you're an angel. I can't thank you enough. And George, I'm sure, would be happy to know that his secret love is safe in your hands. If anyone can find trace of Meira, or her child, it'll be you. And I'll reimburse you any expenses incurred, of course."

"I'll have to get my skates on, though," said Clare. "He might not be with us for much longer. Or he might have forgotten Meira by now."

"I know."

They looked at each other, understanding. Even if Clare did succeed in finding George's heirs, would

Alzheimer's disease have beaten her to it? It would be just too sad if he never got a chance to meet them and tell them good-bye.

-oOo-

Chapter Three

Owen

In the Queen's university Speakeasy bar, Owen sat glumly staring at his pint of beer, while his friend Pete looked on. There didn't seem to be much to say and Pete certainly didn't feel equipped to help Owen out. This last year or so, both lads had drifted apart as Judith gradually became the centre of Owen's love life and since the couple had moved into a flat together eight or nine months ago, Pete had hardly seen Owen at all.

"How can she do that, Pete?" said Owen, for the third time in half an hour. "I thought... I really thought... this was *it*, you know what I mean?"

"Umm... not really," said an unhelpful Pete. "But I can imagine," he added hurriedly, seeing his friend's tortured look.

"And now she's accepted this work placement in San Francisco! I mean, how can she *do* that to me? She'll be gone for a year... at least."

"Has she said it's over?" asked Pete, secretly hoping that it was.

He did like Judith. She was a nice girl. But she'd certainly curtailed his mate's propensity to having fun. Gone were the days when they got through girlfriends by the week-end load. Gone were the parties, the booze, the good times together. Meeting Judith had been disastrous for Owen in that sense. Christ, he'd become domesticated! It was 'Judith' this and 'Judith' that. Not good for a guy's reputation. Big 'hands off' sign all over him.

"No. She hasn't said it's over. But she's adamant she's going. Taking the full year out. She's leaving on Monday, Pete. Says she'll never get such an opportunity to study architecture in those kind of conditions. Says she wants to specialize in the construction of buildings in earthquake zones."

"And there's nowhere else she could do that?"

"Yeah. Japan."

"Ah... tough."

"I mean, Pete, we've been living together for ages. She's been with me to France several times. My parents love her to bits. And I'll be lost without her. I always knew she had a year to go after you and I qualified but I thought I'd just take a year out, visit Europe, or Australia... or something."

"Did you say this to her?"

"Of course I did, I don't have secrets from Judith."

"So... let me get this straight. While Judith did her final year and qualified, you intended to bugger off to Australia? And now you're broken-hearted that *she's* accepted this placement in San Francisco?"

"That's not the same thing."

"Oh yeah?"

"And of all times to break up! It's our Masters finals in two weeks. God, Pete, I'll mess them up!"

"Don't be an eejit, Owen. You're one of the best in our year. There's no way on earth you're going to mess them up. For God's sake, get a grip on yourself. And if it's really over between you and Judith, well, I'll help you celebrate being an architect, even if she won't."

In spite of his self-pity, Owen had to smile. He was going to have to rethink his priorities, though, and fast. He loved architecture; had loved doing this course. And he'd taken it for granted that Judith would always put him first, not herself. He looked deep into his beer. Was he suffering from a broken heart or wounded pride? Both probably, if he were honest.

He took a deep swig. Still, it was good to be with Pete again, just the two of them, a good pint of beer, and some really nice, uncomplicated females just waiting to be chatted up. He grinned and looked around him.

"See what I mean?" said Pete, capable of reading his friend like a book.

"Yeah, well, no harm in window shopping, is there?"

"Now you're talking." And off went Pete to order two more pints.

Later that evening, a less-than-sober Owen sat watching unhappily as Judith put the finishing touches to her packing. She was flying out to San Francisco on the Monday but had decided to spend all day Sunday at her parents' house and leave from there. This would be their last night together.

Ever since Judith had been accepted for the earthquake programme some ten days previously, they'd done nothing but bicker and sulk. She'd told him about her plans ages ago; it's just that he'd never taken her seriously, never thought she'd actually go through with it. And when she'd had that interview via Skype, he'd never imagined for one second that she'd get the job.

So it had been a terrible shock to him to learn that she was actually going. Judith, *his* Judith, was going to America for a full year, leaving him all on his own. Christ!

"Judith, you shure about all this? Really shure?" he articulated with care.

"Owen, we've been over this and over this. I'm going. This is a once-in-a-lifetime opportunity that I just can't miss out on. You *know* that," said Judith with patience.

"And what about me? You'll be gallivanting off to the Schtates for a year. Then you'll be coming back to Queen's for your Master II year. Shat's two whole years, Judith. Two whole bloody years! What am I shupposed to do during that time? What about me?"

"Owen," began Judith, seriously exasperated now. "There's lots of things you can do. You can get a job in San Francisco if you want. Or go off on that tour of the world you've been bragging about. We don't have to break up if you don't want to. I'm not doing this so as to leave you, Owen. I'm doing this for my career."

"And why now? Itch's my finals soon. You should be helping me get through them, Judith, not leaving me all on my own." He belched, rather loudly.

"From all accounts, you're far from being on your own, Owen," snapped Judith crossly. "You're just in from a boozy night out with Pete and by the smell of perfume on you, you're already looking to replace me. Jesus, can't you even wait till I get out the door?"

"Judith, that was nothing! You know you've always been the one. I'm juss so miserable at you going, shat's all. Those girls, tonight, that was just a bit of fun... honestly! Shwear ta God."

"Huh!"

And Judith flounced out, leaving Owen to wallow in his misery and fall asleep soon after on the sofa.

She was already gone the next morning when he woke up, with a sore head and a raging thirst. He could've kicked himself for letting Pete talk him into a

27

quick drink the night before. He wanted to die, quietly, painlessly, here on the sofa... their sofa. He got up stiffly, went to the loo, took a few paracetamol and downed them with a pint of water. Then he headed to the bedroom which was looking all tidy, and empty, and Judith-less. She'd left her key on the bedside table. No letter, just her key.

Awash with remorse and longing, he flung himself down on the bed and instantly fell back asleep.

For the next fortnight, Owen buried his pain in an orgy of studying and exam-taking. He'd had contact with Judith on several occasions, first on that Sunday, to apologize and wish her well, and several times after to know that she had arrived safely, and was settling in, finding her feet, meeting new colleagues, sorting out accommodation. She was bubbly and enthusiastic and he had forced himself to sound happy for her. But inside he was crumbling, desperately drawing on all his reserves to cope with her parting and his final exams.

When at last they were over, he went slowly home, letting himself wearily into their little flat. He hadn't known it was possible to be so exhausted. Physically and emotionally, he was an empty shell, numbed by all that had happened in the past few weeks. It was as if his future had been played out, fast forward, with no chance of escape. And now it was over, out of his hands. He couldn't even begin to worry if he'd passed or failed. He just didn't have the energy.

He looked around their little flat with its faded furniture and air of dejection. In the two weeks since she'd left, it had lost its soul. Judith's presence had made it home, made it cheerful, a haven for the two of them where the rest of the world could be shut out and forgotten about.

And now Judith was gone. What a bloody awful way to finish at Queen's! Nothing would ever be the same. He lay down on their bed, where her perfume no longer tormented him, a torment in itself, closed his eyes and tried to forget.

He woke up several hours later to the sound of someone banging on his door. He turned over on his side intending to let them hammer away. He was not in the mood for celebrating the end of his exams and was certainly not going to let himself be talked into going out.

But the banging didn't stop. In the end, he got up and went wearily to open the door.

It was Ian, standing there, arms out, his habitual grin fading at the sight of this world-weary Owen. With only about twelve years or so between them, they were more like brothers than uncle and nephew; they'd always been the best of mates.

"Christ, Owen, what's wrong? You look terrible," he began. "Mucked up your finals? It's not the end of the world, mate. You can always take them again."

"Nah, Ian. Don't know how I did. Can't even remember the questions. But I don't think I've messed up too bad. I did my best."

"So? What's up? Where's Judith?" Ian looked around him at the all-too-obvious mess in the sitting-room, at the un-made bed and clothes strewn all over the place that he could make out through the open door to the bedroom.

"Where's Judith, Owen?" he repeated softly.

"She's gone, Ian. Off to America, a fortnight ago."

"What's she doing in America?"

"Got this work-placement in San Francisco. She'll be gone all year. Never thought she'd do it. Said she couldn't miss the opportunity."

He gulped, realizing all over again that Judith was really gone. "Miss her like hell," he added, unnecessarily.

Ian looked at his nephew; saw the misery in his eyes.

"Course you do. She's a great kid," he said with conviction.

It was hard not to put his arm round Owen's shoulders, ruffle his hair and tell him that everything would be alright, like when he was a child limping home with a bloody knee. Those days were long gone and

Owen certainly would not appreciate a dose of pity on top of all his other problems.

"Chinese or Indian?" said Ian. "Pub or off-licence?"

Owen looked back at him and gave a lung-splitting sigh.

"Chinese and a couple of six-packs. You doing the honours?"

"Okay," said Ian cheerfully. "I earn more than you do. Not for much longer, I know."

He again looked around the flat.

"Right. I'll nip out and get the goods on the sole condition that when I get back this place no longer resembles the local tip. No rats yet? Yeah, it's probably too dirty for them. Get cracking, mate. No clear-up, no Chinese… and no beer. See ya."

One reasonably efficient tidy-up, two full stomachs and a couple of beers later, Ian turned to Owen and said:

"Well? What's the plan, then? What'll you do now?"

"No idea, Ian. Took me all I had to get this far. Haven't even begun to think about what I'll do next. Thought I'd take a year out. That's before Judith got the offer of this job in San Francisco."

"When's the lease up on the flat?"

"In two weeks' time. End of March."

"Right. Think you can get your act together and come back with me to France on Saturday? I'm heading straight to the gîtes. I'm giving an IT course there on Monday for a week. We could share the gîte I usually have. Céline won't be coming this time. She has to teach next week."

"Run home to Mum, you mean?" said Owen with a hint of sarcasm in his voice.

"Worse places to run to, you know," replied Ian. "Plus I know she needs all the help she can get at the moment. The garden's woken up after the winter months and is threatening to run riot. Even Jean-Christophe can't keep up with it at this time of year. The pool needs an overhaul once my course is over. And your parents have bought this manor house which Clare wants to show me. Needs a lot doing to it by all accounts. You could help her there. Save them the expense of hiring an architect, for a start. Get your hands dirty for a change. What about it?"

Owen sat sipping his beer, thinking hard. Now that Judith had left Belfast, and his course was over, there wasn't much point in staying in Northern Ireland. He hadn't given it much thought before, but it wouldn't do any harm to head to France for a couple of weeks, dump his books and stuff off at the gîtes, give himself time to decide what he wanted to do.

"Yeah. Why not? No point in hanging around here. And Judith can always find me at the gîtes, if she needs to. A bit of gardening won't do me any harm. Think my mum will take any advice I give her about the house?"

"If your advice happens to coincide exactly with what Clare thinks needs doing, you've got your chances. Just mind you let her think she's the boss, though," said Ian, grinning.

"Been doing that since I was five. Shouldn't be too hard," said Owen wryly.

"Cheers, Owen, welcome to the first day of the rest of your life," said Ian.

"I'll drink to that," said his nephew, smiling for the first time in weeks.

-oOo-

Chapter Four

Oak Lodge

Sharon wiped her mouth and flushed the toilet, her stomach still heaving. So this was morning sickness... except this was early afternoon. She'd never been queasy before, never had anything like this when she had been expecting Kieran. So why now, eighteen years on? Perhaps this time it was a girl. Paul would love a little girl. They'd never really discussed it much but she just knew that he would be besotted by a little girl.

Well, he'd better be, she thought bitterly, as she leant over the toilet to be sick again, *cos I'm certainly not going through this another time.*

She gave herself another five minutes and then made her way slowly back to the office. She felt really tired and she wasn't even showing yet. Perhaps they'd better start advertising for a new nurse, just in case she wasn't fit to keep up with all that managing Oak Lodge entailed. Paul would step in as Manager for the three or four months she would be absent on maternity leave, he was more than capable of doing the job. And Catriona would be given the post of deputy, they'd already talked to her about it, and she'd agreed.

But there was no getting away from the fact that the management of a residence specializing in dementia in the elderly was difficult and time-consuming and the nursing side was equally important, even more so. Carmel was still working nights and Beatrice was only part-time. A new nurse was needed, if only temporarily. There was only so much the care-workers could do without supervision. And if Sharon continued to spend half her working-day in the loo, a new nurse would be needed sooner rather than later. She just hoped they would find someone with knowledge of Alzheimer's disease and senile dementia. This was a world within a world and the newcomer would need to adapt as of day one.

At that point, Paul came into the office to start his shift. They often worked different shifts, not only so as to have a manager present on the premises all day, but also from a personal point of view, so as not to be with each other 24/7.

He came over to kiss her hello.

"Um… you smell of toothpaste. And… oh you don't look well." He peered at her closely. "You been sick again, my love?"

"Ten out of ten for observation," sighed Sharon. "Thank God we got through our holiday before all this began. I'm exhausted throwing up, Paul. I never had these problems when I was expecting Kieran."

"Ah… my fault then, I suppose. Looks like I'm going to have to get used to a lot of abuse before this little baby is born. By the time we get to the birth, I'll be a battered husband!" And he put his arms lovingly around his wife and gently touched her tummy. "Little baby, don't make your mummy sick. Please? We still want to be friends by the time you come along."

"I think we should start advertising for a nurse straight away, Paul. I can't really take medication and I just feel so weak. If we have an extra nurse on hand, I won't feel so bad if I have to go and lie down from time to time." Sharon's face was greenish-white and she could feel the incipient nausea rising in her throat.

"Well, I'm a nurse, too, Mrs Harrison. And I'm ordering you to go and lie down right now. Use that wee room I go to when I help Carmel on night duty. It's fairly quiet at the moment and I promise I'll let you know if we need you." Paul looked at her with compassion. "Come on, sweetheart, you look terrible. Let's get you to bed. I'll give Beatrice a call and see if she can't do a bit of overtime for a few weeks till you get on your feet. Knowing Bea, she'll jump at the chance."

He put his arms gently around Sharon and led her to the sleep-over room where she could lie down and rest. He put a basin by her bed, and a jug of water with a glass, and some tissues. Then he drew the curtains so that the room was in semi-darkness and quietly let himself out.

Back in the office, he rang Beatrice and was lucky to find her at home. She willingly agreed to do some extra hours, thrilled to learn that Sharon was expecting. Paul wondered briefly if Sharon had wanted to keep things a secret for much longer. Too late now, the cat was out of the bag. By dinner-time, the whole of Oak Lodge would know.

Shrugging this off as unimportant, he next went to do his rounds and have a chat to Catriona. Catriona already knew of the pregnancy as she had been at their wedding some two weeks previously when they had told her. But Paul secretly appreciated the fact that she had said nothing to anyone else. It was a nice show of trust. This gruff, no-nonsense, fifty-something matron was a goldmine and they had been lucky to get her. Paul wondered briefly if the next nurse they took on would be as good.

He shook his head. Catriona was going to be a hard act to follow but they'd certainly get no-one if he didn't get the advertisement written out and published. He sat down to get this done and start on the paperwork that his pretty wife had not been able to do that morning. He felt a pang of anxiety for her. She must be feeling really unwell, if she'd had to leave all this. It wasn't like Sharon at all.

He got the ad made out and sent off, then worked non-stop for two hours at his desk before deciding to take a break. He was glad that he had not been interrupted. Early afternoon was a time when most of the residents took a nap and in general, things quietened down. Even the phone had left him in peace.

He took off his glasses and ran his fingers through his hair, stretched his arms and stood up. He was putting a few files away when he heard a light tap on the door. He glanced at the secret mirror he had rigged up there, back in Clare's time, when a certain nasty cleaning-lady had been the bane of her life, spreading rumours about Clare and her husband and revelling in causing strife. Unfortunately the self-same cleaning lady was still at Oak Lodge and standing just outside his door.

The two years or so Paul had worked in Oak Lodge had taught him to be careful of what he said and did. Not everyone was as honest and discrete as Catriona, and being the only (formerly) eligible male on the premises that was under seventy-five, he'd had, on more than one occasion, found himself the target of playful bantering, serious flirting, or worse, from several of the all-female care-worker population and one or two female residents to boot. That he could deal with. Had learnt very quickly to deal with.

Malicious gossip was something else.

So when he saw the distorted face of Mrs O'Neill in the hidden mirror, he groaned. This middle-aged, po-faced, smarmy individual loved to cause trouble and Paul was not at all pleased to see her. But he was the boss and it was his job to find out what she wanted now. With a quickly swallowed sigh, he yanked open the door.

"Yes, Mrs O'Neill?"

"Oh, Mr Harrison! You made me start."

Hand on heart, big sigh, eyes rolled to heaven, he thought briefly that Mrs O'Neill should've been on the stage.

"What can I do for you?" said Paul, taking absolutely no notice. "I'm busy."

"Of course you're busy. All that work Mrs Murphy... sorry... Mrs Harrison couldn't get done this morning."

Paul tried to hide his surprise. Surely she hadn't been snooping up here? He wouldn't put it past her but she wasn't allowed to clean this floor, wasn't allowed anywhere near their office. She'd been caught prying before and had been banned. Catriona had seen to that.

"Just why have you come to see me, Mrs O'Neill?" said Paul evenly.

"Well... it's a bit difficult for me to say, really, Mr Harrison. I'm not one to go spreading gossip but I thought as what you should know, like, given that it concerns yourself and Mrs Murphy, and it's what people are *saying*."

She leaned forward, looking up into his face, dark malevolent eyes staring gleefully. He automatically took a step back.

"And what are people saying about my wife and I, Mrs O'Neill?" Paul was dangerously calm now.

"They're saying that Mrs Harrison doesn't look a bit well. Very off colour and the like. Ever since yous got back from that honeymoon of yours. So she must've got food poisoning or something. That Myxomatosis, what it's called. You get it from eating meat that's not been cooked properly. All those foreigners, got stomachs like iron, so they have."

"Thank you Mrs O'Neill," said Paul coldly, "but my wife is not suffering from Toxoplasmosis. Now, if you've nothing else to say, I need to get on."

"Yes, Mr Harrison. Just wanted you to know. It's wrong when people spread gossip. Downright spiteful, if you ask me."

This was rich, coming from Mrs O'Neill. In ordinary circumstances, her effrontery would have made Paul want to laugh. But he stood there, in silence, indicating that the interview was over and that he was waiting for her to go. Reluctantly, she did so, smiling, no doubt congratulating herself on getting one over the boss.

When he could see that she had gone down the stairs, Paul went silently along the corridor to the little room where Sharon was resting. She stirred as he came in and he could immediately tell she was over the worst. The colour had come back into her face and she had obviously been sleeping.

"Hi Paul," she whispered.

"Hi, darling. Feeling better?"

"Much. That sleep did me good. But you're right to wake me. Otherwise I wouldn't sleep tonight at all."

"Do you want me to run you home?"

"No. Not at all. I can drive. Thanks anyway. I'll just slip away. I *am* feeling a lot better. Really." Sharon was by now on her feet and leaning over to make the bed up again.

"Beatrice is coming back full-time for the next two weeks. I told her why we needed her so you know it'll be all over the place very soon. Mrs O'Neill already has you down as having caught Myxomatosis," said Paul, starting to chuckle.

"Well, that'll be a first," said Sharon, joining in, her good humour restored now that the sickness had left her.

"Here's your mobile. I took it away to let you rest. You've a message from Kieran," said Paul.

"Oh, it's just to let me know he has a driving lesson after school and won't be home for dinner till about half past seven."

"Didn't know driving lessons took three hours these days," muttered Paul.

"Ah but his lordship has it planned so as to spend two hours with Elizabeth beforehand when he should be revising for his A levels."

"Umm… perhaps they're revising together?"

"You really think so? Come on, Paul, don't tell me you think they're just holding hands. Since you moved into my house and Kieran took over your flat, I get the impression that Elizabeth spends more time there than at her own home."

Paul digested this information. Wondered just how much Sharon knew. Better not probe too far. Paul had kept on the rental of the flat until the end of the summer, hoping that their new house would be completed by then. It was somewhere to keep his stuff and Kieran used it now as a place to stop-over most nights. It let Paul and Sharon be on their own and gave Kieran an insight into being independent, which he would be anyway as of September when he went to Queen's. He still went back to Sharon's or, when she was on duty, Eileen's place for dinner, but inevitably returned to the flat afterwards to sleep.

"Been up to the new house this week?" Paul asked, adroitly changing the subject.

Sharon often took a tour up there on her way home from work. Their future house was in the final stages of construction on a new estate that was only a few hundred yards from where they currently lived. And between the two were the pensioner cottages, where Kieran's grandmother, Eileen, lived.

Of the three of them, it was Eileen who missed Kieran the most when he went to Paul's flat to stay. She had got used to having him stop over regularly in her spare room when his mother was on a late shift. Tall, dark-haired, irrepressibly cheeky, Kieran reminded her so much of what her own son had looked like at that age.

Matt was dead nine years now, wrenched from them all in a stupid car accident, the pain of which Eileen had never quite recovered from. But she was happy that Sharon had found a new love at last, and Kieran and Paul got on so well together. Kieran's imminent going away to university was not to be thought of but would be softened, to some extent, by the arrival of the new baby.

"The house is coming along just great." Sharon's eyes lit up at the thought. "They say it'll be ready by the end of July! I can't wait to move in and decorate the baby's room."

"Perhaps we'd better put your house on the market then," mused Paul.

"Yes, you're right. This pregnancy is going to be a busy time for all of us. Here's hoping the morning sickness clears up soon. I'm really glad Beatrice is coming back full-time for the next two weeks. It'll give me a chance to get on with things like that."

Paul took her in his arms. "I can imagine. And Myxomatosis can be terribly tiring... especially in the early stages..."

-oOo-

Chapter Five

Alzheimer's Disease

After Sharon had left, Paul went back to the office to put in another hour's paper-work and answer a few calls. There was always a demand for beds in Elderly Mentally Infirm units like Oak Lodge and all too few places available. Beds cost money. And the Government needed to cut-back in order to save money. Social workers now had the added complication of trying to persuade overwrought, bewildered families that it was best to keep their loved ones at home, trying to cope with the increasingly exhausting demands that Alzheimer's disease and other forms of old-age dementia imposed on them. It saddened and angered Paul. Another ten years like this, with Alzheimer's on the increase and less and less establishments to deal with it, soon it would be the fifty-year-olds that would be burning out *before* their parents.

He went along to help Catriona with the evening rounds, starting with those residents that were confined to bed, living out their twilight years in a haze of memories and medication. Some did recover, physically, and get back on their feet and some would never go outdoors again.

Families and friends of the residents would come and go, watching with dismay as the disease took hold. Sometimes the illness catapulted the person into dementia in a frighteningly fast way and sometimes it took years, stripping them of their memory, their personality, their very essence, leaving them naked and empty. Tired eyes that would look at him, searching for answers to questions that eluded them, families that had learnt the hard way how every day widened the gap to their loved ones and that one day, death would prove to be a friend.

And then there were those residents whose personalities had not yet been destroyed, who fought back, who bantered, who held on to good old Irish craic when their bearings had become distorted. Many of these patients were well enough to spend part of their day in the large common-room, with its floor to ceiling windows overlooking the grounds. Each had their own armchair, their own place to sit. Those that could might go for a walk down the corridor, or into the conservatory or outside to the walled remembrance garden with its vestiges of times gone by. On good days care-workers would be commissioned to take as many residents as possible out into the grounds, to sit beneath the oak trees that gave the home its name, or stroll down by the lake and drink in the beauty and quietude of the scenery. Workshops were organized by an occupational therapist who came in four times a week, ecumenical services were held once a fortnight and everybody's birthdays were celebrated in style.

When he first came to Oak Lodge, Paul had found it difficult to play along, to enter into the spirit of dementia and see that often life was not as sad as he thought. In his own life, he was still smarting from a difficult divorce and the come-on he was getting from staff and residents was, to put it mildly, overwhelming. It had taken Clare to point out to him that the only young-ish male to grace Oak Lodge before Paul came along was Ben, the gardener, and even he was over fifty. Clare had encouraged him to loosen up, not to take life so seriously, to observe the care-workers, see how they all found time to enjoy themselves, bringing laughter and happiness, however fleetingly, to those old people in their charge.

Now he joked and cajoled with the rest of them. Now the quirky banter had become a second nature and he loved his job, so much more satisfying that being on a geriatric ward, which was where he had worked previously. Here he could forge relationships that lasted over months, years even, with residents and their families and the staff that cared for them. Here he finally felt at home.

And he had met Sharon, and her son Kieran, become friends with them both before realizing that he had met the woman he wanted to spend the rest of his life with. And now this woman had married him and was carrying his baby and Kieran had called him a 'Dad'.

Once the bed-ridden patients had been checked over and given their medication, Paul turned to those who were in the common-room. The care-workers were now gathering everyone together there for toileting purposes before going into the dining-room for dinner. Most of the residents needed some form of help to move around, whether it be wheel-chair, zimmer-frame or walking stick but a few could walk without any aid and, while this was a blessing in itself, it was good to know that none of them could work out the code to leave the building. An Alzheimer patient wandering unaccompanied around the grounds or out onto the road was not to be envisaged and here the little walled remembrance garden came into its own. Dotted with a plough, an old bicycle, a red phone-box, a hand-pump and other relicts of bygone days, it served the dual purpose of letting the residents wander freely outdoors in safety while enjoying reminders of the past.

Paul worked his way round the residents, dosing out medication to those that needed to take it at this time of day, taking blood pressures and checking temperatures. Then he began helping the care-workers in the multitude of tasks that needed doing as dinner-time approached. Apart from toileting, and getting residents seated in the dining-room, meal-times could rapidly become something of a Mad Hatter's tea-party if not carefully supervised. Helping to feed two old ladies at once, was a job in itself, being accosted by at least two others while doing this made the operation something of a marathon. Finally, he let everyone look after their own desserts and took one of the trays to spoon-feed Maggie, whose dementia was exacerbated by the complication of Parkinson's disease and where meal-times had become something of a trial.

He knocked gently on her door and went into her room.

"Oh, Fred. How are you dear?" she began.

"It's Paul, Maggie. I'm Paul. I've come to give you your dinner. It looks appetizing. Are you hungry?"

"Hungry? No, I'm not hungry. But where's Fred? He usually helps me with my food. He's very good to me, you know. Just like when we were courting." And she smiled at the memory. "He was very handsome then, just like you."

"And you must've been the prettiest girl he'd ever seen, Maggie. Sure you could still break any man's heart if you wanted to," replied Paul, grinning.

"Get away with you!" Maggie went to dig Paul in the ribs but the movement was jerky and uncontrolled and she nearly sent the tray flying.

"Steady, Maggie, steady. Here why don't you rest your hands in your lap," said Paul, matching actions to words. "There. Like that. That's perfect."

He began to feed her slowly, gently, giving her time to drink a little between mouthfuls and digest. About a quarter of the residents needed feeding this way, often because their overall health had deteriorated as their mental health had failed. Some got to the point where they would put food into their mouths and forget to swallow it. Some could no longer chew properly and needed their food to be mixed like a baby. Some, towards the end, did no longer know what food was...

And while he was feeding her, Paul kept up a running chatter about anything and everything, often things they had talked about the day before but to Maggie, it was as if she were hearing them for the first time... again. They talked a lot about Fred, Maggie's long-dead husband, but whom Alzheimer's disease had brought back to life some years ago in her mind and was now living an ethereal existence through Paul, especially when he spent fifteen or twenty minutes alone with her for the feeding process.

Pushing the food away, she now said: "Do you remember when we went to Naples, Fred?"

"Tell me about Naples, I can't remember." said Paul, a spoonful of mashed potato suspended half-way to her mouth.

"Well, really, sweetheart! Your memory is getting terribly bad, you know."

"Must be..." said Paul.

"It was a lovely time," began Maggie, wistfully. "Just you and me and all that sunshine. And we were young and free. No wee-uns to worry about. We went by train; no, we flew to Rome and *then* we went by train. In the 1950's it was. Don't you remember?"

"I'm sure it was a great holiday," said Paul quietly, trying without success to get Maggie to eat a little more.

"It was. It was. All those lovely memories. Remember how hot it was at night?"

"Maggie," said Paul. "Don't you want to eat any more? Look, there's lemon meringue for dessert."

"No thank you, dear. I'm quite full up and we'll be going out to the restaurant tonight. If I eat that dessert it will only spoil my appetite."

"Okay," sighed Paul, "but I'll leave it here on your table just in case you change your mind."

He started to gather up the dinner plate, the cutlery and the tray, but left her the large napkin and a spoon. As he made to go, she beckoned him over and planted a watery kiss on his cheek.

"'Bye, Fred, see you tonight," she whispered and shut her eyes to revel in the memories of Naples and Rome.

This wasn't the first time, by any means, that Paul had been mistaken for someone else. He was actually quite used to it by now. He was rubbing his cheek with the back of his hand when he ran into

Geraldine, one of the older care-workers, who had seen him come out of Maggie's room.

"Shame on you, Paul Harrison, you're a married man now," she began.

"Geraldine, it's not my fault. Maggie thinks I'm her husband, and I can't go breaking her heart saying Fred snuffed it ages ago."

"Oh no?"

"No, it would be cruel. You surely know that."

"It's just that I bet her 50p this morning that she'd not get to kiss you before the day was out. And it looks like I've lost. Maggie knows perfectly well where her husband is, Paul. She's taking you for a ride."

And Paul stood there open-mouthed as he watched Geraldine go into Maggie's room and heard them both burst out laughing.

Later that evening when most of the residents had been prepared for bed, Paul went along to see how George Hamilton was doing. He liked George, had seen him through some pretty rough bouts of ill-health over the last two years and was pleased to see how well he was doing lately. Plus George, in spite of his dementia and being confined to a wheel-chair, was a man's man. No silly bets about getting one over the male-nurse here. With George, Paul just liked to sit down and chat, or not, as the mood took them. On his good days George was an interesting companion and that always made the visit worthwhile.

Paul and Sharon had been made aware of Clare's quest to find George's heirs. Clare had been to see George before leaving for France and had told him quietly what she was trying to do. George's short-term memory was failing fast but the war, Meira and all that had happened during those years in Coventry were still for the most part intact. He couldn't help Clare any further than what Damien had already told her but she had obtained his permission to take a copy of Meira's letter back to France to begin her investigations.

Now Paul sat in the visitor's chair after helping one of the care-workers get the old man into his pyjamas and plumped up comfortably in his arm-chair to sit for an hour or two before going to bed. He could just see George, in the days before he went into Oak Lodge, sitting in his study at home, sipping a whisky and smoking a cigar. He was that kind of man.

George was clearly thinking along the same lines as he now asked Paul to serve him a dram from a bottle hidden away at the bottom of his wardrobe. All the staff knew that George's housekeeper kept him supplied with whisky and this situation was tolerated inasmuch as he kept his consumption of it to small glass in the evening. George himself was convinced it was a big secret that only he and Paul knew of, which made the taste of it all the more special.

Paul duly brought out the bottle which this time was a bottle of Bushmills 1608 anniversary edition whiskey, not yet opened. He poured George out a small measure and, on his insistence, a tot for himself. They clinked their glasses and wished each other good health.

To Paul, the fiery liquid was an explosion of flavours that slid with panache down his throat. Never had he tasted a whiskey that had so much to say for itself. It was not something he drank regularly but what he wouldn't give right now to be a taster at Bushmills. He said as much to George.

"Yep, young man," as George was wont to call him, "know that this is one of the best whiskeys in Ireland, made right here on our doorstep. Taste that oakiness? And how sweet it is? Just hope the Good Lord has stocked up before I pop my clogs. No use going to heaven if you can't get a drop of this." And he put his nose into the beaker to sniff the aroma.

"The Good Lord will have to wait a while longer, George. You're as fit as a fiddle," said Paul.

"Ah, there's no use getting round it. I'm getting nearer to Him every day. Just a spot of unfinished business to sort out from the war and I'll be on my way."

"Unfinished business?"

"Yep. That young lass came to see me about it the other day. She's living in France now. She's going to help me find her."

It took Paul a few seconds to realize that George was talking about Clare. 'Young lass' did not quite equate with the fifty-something ex-Manageress of Oak Lodge that Paul knew.

"It must have been difficult for you all during the war. It's hard for us to imagine when food was rationed, and when the bombs fell, and everyone took refuge in the shelters," he said.

George looked deep into his whiskey, as if all his memories of the war lay there.

"Aye, I remember the war," he said. "I was over working in England then. All those German war-planes flying low over the cities, the lull before the sirens sounded, the noise and the shuddering when they dropped their bombs..." He trailed off, his eyes far away, unseeing, memories of those terrible times engulfing him. Then he went on: "We listened to Churchill on the radio, you know, tried to imagine what was happening in Europe. We were hungry and we were frightened and we worried that it would never end. And that bastard, Hitler. Why did no-one stop him? Tell me that, eh? Why wasn't he stopped?"

"Is that when you met Meira?"

"It was. The only girl I ever loved. She was French, you know, French. But she went back. Told me she had to go back... and I never saw her again."

"I'm sorry, George. You must've missed her a lot," said Paul quietly.

"I survived. I had to survive. We were all in the same boat, y'see? If you didn't get up and put one foot in front of the other, you were a goner. You had to bury the dead, and clean up the mess and start rebuilding the country." He sighed. "And all the time I waited for Meira. And she never came back."

Both men were silent for a few minutes, gently sipping their whiskies.

"Bet she was pretty, George," said Paul.

"Aye, she was that. Prettiest lass I'd ever seen. French, you know. She was French. Had to go back. Never saw her again."

"What was she like then?"

"Eh?"

"Was she blond, dark-haired, what age was she? Tell me what she was like, George."

"Ah, she was the cutest, kindest, bossiest little woman I ever came across. Want to see a photo?"

"A photo? You've got a photo of Meira?"

"Yep. Got several. Here, hand me that wallet of mine and if you give me another wee dram, I'll show you my Meira."

"Okay, George, but only a tiny one. That's your limit for today," said Paul laughing.

"Have another wee drop yourself."

"No. No thanks George. I'm supposed to be at work, you know. You're a bad influence on me. Now, here's your wallet."

With trembling fingers, George slowly took out three small black-and-white photos and laid them side by side on the bedside table. Paul got up to have a better look. The first two photos showed a pretty woman, somewhere in her early twenties, with long dark hair hanging over her shoulder in a plat and laughing at the camera in a pert, even provocative way. Clearly it was George who was taking the photos. The third photo showed her in a more sober attitude, standing beside a young, handsome man who had his arm around her. On close inspection, Paul could see that she was pregnant. The young man was George. He studied the photos for a while until he could see that George was getting tearful, the combination of whiskey and pictures of Meira just too much to take.

"George, would you let me scan these photos and send them to Clare?" he asked. "She's trying to find traces of Meira and the photos would certainly help her. Would you mind? I'll do it now and bring them back to you straight away."

"I... I don't like letting them out of my sight. They're all I have left of her. They're all I have..."

"Well, why don't you come up with me to the office and we'll scan them together? I'll just be taking photocopies. I'll give you back the originals, George. You okay with that?"

George hesitated, not knowing what to do.

"We're trying to find her for you, George. We're trying to find Meira," said Paul, gently. "And Clare needs to start somewhere. It would be good if we could give her copies of these photos."

"I'll get them back, won't I? I'll get them back?" pleaded the old man.

"We'll do it now. It'll only take a few minutes and you can watch me every step of the way."

"Alright, alright. If it helps you find Meira, I'll let you take the photos."

"Great. Now let's get a rug over you and I'll wheel you up to the office. Ever been in the lift yet?"

The whole operation didn't take more than ten minutes, including Paul sending them by email to Clare in France. This done, he handed the photographs to George who put them carefully back into his wallet, where they had lain for many years…

-oOo-

Chapter Six

At the Gîtes

Clare was looking forward to Saturday evening. Not only was Ian due to arrive, and it was always a treat to have her brother around even if Céline could not be with him this time, but her son Owen was coming too. No Judith, apparently, but Judith was probably off to stay with her parents. The boys were travelling on the same plane and what's more, Ian had left his car at Nantes airport which meant that Frank had got out of a four-hour round-trip to pick them up.

This visit by Owen was unexpected, even though Clare was aware that he had been taking his finals. She knew the rent was paid on the little flat until the end of the month, as it was she and Frank that helped pay the rent, but she had expected that her son and his girlfriend would be making the most of the post-exam celebrations for a while yet. Still, it was a nice surprise and Clare was looking forward to a cosy family evening before it was all hands to the fray for the week-long IT course ahead.

All the students, for want of a better word, were due to arrive on the Sunday and Clare had spent the week preparing the gîtes for their arrival, cleaning the classrooms that made up part of the games-room area and making out menus and shopping for food, as she personally did the catering when the courses took place, as opposed to the holiday rentals when the guests looked after themselves. This time, it was only an IT course, which meant a maximum of eight guests. Frank would be continuing to teach English at the language school in Lorient for the coming week before hosting a two-week long course at the gîtes teaching French after Ian had finished.

This was the time of year, from March to early June, when the demand for the courses was at its highest. From June onwards the holiday rentals took over and this lasted until the end of September, at least. One or two courses were then programmed for the autumn and again in the winter months, the indoor swimming-pool being an attraction even when the weather was not, and a smattering of holiday rentals were always to be had at Easter and Christmas-time and during the bank holidays in May.

All in all, there were not that many weeks in the year when the gîtes did not pay for themselves. More often than not, they made a hefty profit, and this lead

Clare's thoughts inevitably on to the manor house that she had recently acquired with Frank.

Clare loved to think about the manor house, her head full of all the improvements she would make there. It had belonged to the English couple in their seventies who had sold them the gîtes and, at that time, there had been no question of stretching finances even further so as to buy the manor on top of everything else. Besides, even though the price had been attractive, there was still a lot of work needing doing on the house and Clare had taken Frank and Nathans' advice and said no.

But eighteen months further on, the manor house had still been on the market for the third year running and now reduced to the ridiculous price of €120,000. Although habitable, and with a new roof and electrics, it was far from luxurious inside and Clare and Frank would be camping there until such times as money and time allowed them to do it up. As with the gîtes, they had negotiated with the owners to include some fixtures and furnishings in the price, it being more of a hassle for them to have everything brought back to England, and their new abode there, much down-sized, could not cope with huge antique armoires, pine dressers and even a mahogany dining-table that the manor house had inherited from way back.

Clare could not wait to show it to Ian and now to Owen too. After all, it was her and Frank's new home, something the gîtes could never really be called. She hoped they would have time to go there this evening before it got too dark.

A loud cacophony of tooting horns around four pm announced the arrival of the boys. Clare had yet to know Ian arrive any other way. She ran out to meet them, with a big hug to each before stepping aside so that Frank could say hello too.

"Oh, my darlings. So good to see you," she began.

"Mum, it's only been a couple of weeks since you were home for Paul and Sharon's wedding. You'll squeeze the life out of me," replied her son, laughing.

"Good Lord, Ian, where's the kitchen sink?" said Frank, peering into Ian's car which was pretty full.

"I know," agreed Ian. "All Owen's stuff. He had to pay extra, we even bought another case."

"Really, love? You going to stay a while?" asked Clare hopefully. "Judith joining you later, then?"

"No Judith, Mum," said her son, his face momentarily clouded, "she's gone to San Francisco for a year."

"Oh sweetheart, I *am* sorry," said Clare. "This is all rather unexpected."

"Yeah. And not only for you, Mum."

"Oh, dear! Come on in, I'll make you a nice cup of tea or something. Ian, Frank, will you take the cases to the gîte you usually stay in Ian?"

And she ushered Owen into the gatehouse gîte to hear all about Judith.

Frank and Ian stood outside looking at each other.

"Motherly love," said Frank rolling his eyes. "Now Clare'll get all the time she wants to smother that boy. God help us all..."

"Dead right, Frank. This is the last favour I'm doing him," said Ian as they got into the car to drive the 150 yards or so to Ian's habitual gîte.

"So what happened?" asked Frank, as they dumped the cases unceremoniously on the kitchen floor.

"Just what he said. Judith got the offer of a year's placement in America and left, just before his finals, from what I gather. So he's been having a pretty rough two or three weeks of it," said Ian. "But he thinks he's got through," he added, seeing the look of fear Frank gave him at this news.

"So that explains the luggage, I suppose? He's brought all his stuff to France?"

"Yep, needed somewhere to run to and I suggested he come back here. Keep him busy, Frank; get him to help you both out. A bit of pay-back time won't hurt him and I know you could be doing with it."

"Be the makings of him, probably. All that studying's over now, at least till he gets a proper job in architecture. He needs to clear his head. I agree," said Frank.

"In a way, I'm glad Céline's not here this week. It'll be good just to have this gîte for Owen and me. Give us time to get him sorted."

"Well, we're intending to move out of the gîtes in a few weeks when the holiday lets get going and stay in the manor house even though it'll be a bit rough and ready. We're starting to transfer our things there in bits and bobs."

"There you are, Frank. Get Romeo to help you with that, put his talents to use for the manor house. He should be able to tell you what needs doing and when."

"I'd already thought of that. Wanted to ask his advice."

"That'll be a first. He'll be chuffed," said Ian, smiling. "Really," he added for measure.

"And get him to help you out with the IT course," suggested Frank in turn. "He's as computer literate as they get, without actually being a programmer."

"Good idea. There's times I could do with an assistant on those courses."

"Well, got your keys? Let's head back to the gatehouse gîte before Clare mollycoddles him to death."

As it happened, Clare had already obtained all the information about Judith that Owen was prepared to tell her and was in the act of suggesting a walk to the new house to stretch everyone's legs. Ian readily agreed, having been sitting far too long that day already and Frank decided to come too.

The manor house was situated at about half a mile from the gîtes, close enough to be on call if needed, yet far enough away from the complex to feel that they could leave work behind once they had shut the door.

From the outside it did indeed look splendid with its grey stonework and its tall, imposing structure and the new slate roof did it proud. Stone steps lead up to an entrance porch with a balustrade and a small outdoor reception area. From this vantage position, it was possible to see most of the garden which, although not huge, was mature, wrapping itself around the house and providing the privacy the former owners had obviously tried to achieve. Although tended to by a gardener from time to time, it was clear that the trees and bushes needed a serious hacking back if the grounds were not to be swamped before the spring was out.

Clare took out an old-fashioned wrought-iron key and opened the door. They found themselves immediately in a stately hall with a wide wooden stairway winding itself upwards and out of sight. To the right of the hall was the main drawing-room with panelled walls to waist-height, parquet flooring, a huge tiled fireplace and double aspect windows letting in tons of light, once the shutters had been opened. To the rear of the room were double doors leading on to a rather faded dining-room with french windows opening on to the garden beyond. Behind the stairwell, was an old-fashioned kitchen with units that had seen better days and various pantries and utility-rooms. To the left of the entrance hall was a rather dark fully-panelled study, relatively small, and behind that a cosy sitting-room leading out on to an old conservatory, which smelt rather dank. Before them, to the right of the staircase was what turned out to be a cloak-room and toilet and a door leading down to more stairs and the basement.

Upstairs there were four bedrooms in all, rather disproportionately huge, and a bathroom that had seen better days and a separate toilet. A door in the corridor lead up to the attic which was suitably full of cobwebs and dust, some bits of old furniture, and not much else.

The basement turned out to be not as damp as had been feared as most of the rooms there had small windows letting in a minimum of light and air. There was a wine-cellar, a large workshop, the boiler-room, some storage-rooms and a garage.

Clare took them from room to room, bubbling with enthusiasm, chatting about how she would like to see it all refurbished. Ian was suitably impressed by the whole building and readily agreed that Clare and Frank had got it at a bargain price. But where his parents were enthusiastic, Owen was cautious, his well-trained architect's eye seeing necessary expensive renovation where Clare could only see a lick of paint.

But he did not have the heart to dampen her obvious thrill of purchasing such a house and wisely said nothing to that effect just yet.

It was getting dark by the time they got back to the gîtes and Frank poured them all out a pre-dinner drink while Clare heated up the meal she had prepared earlier in the day. The talk during the meal was all about the manor house, how it could be improved, how long that would take, Frank noting with interest that his son was rather reticent about putting forward his opinion.

Finally, he turned to Owen and asked him outright what he thought of the place and what would need to be done sooner rather than later, and what could wait.

"I don't want to be a wet blanket, Dad, and the house is really lovely with bags of character," began Owen.

"But…" prompted his father.

"I'd need to go back and have a proper look at it but I'm estimating that it's going to cost a pretty penny to bring it into the twenty-first century."

"Surely not, Owen", said Clare frowning. "The roof's been re-done and so has the electrics. That's two of the most expensive things."

"Yes, yes of course. But that's just the beginning, Mum."

"Well, I can see it needs redecorating throughout and the garden needs overhauled and the bathroom and kitchen need ripped out and replaced…" began Clare.

"All cosmetic, Mum. I agree the bathroom and kitchen need redoing, and probably all the plumbing while they're at it, and possibly add an en-suite in the master bedroom and things like that. But there are more serious items to be addressed and without delay."

"Such as, Son?" said Frank.

Owen took a breath, looked at his parent's expectant faces and said: "The boiler is old and probably not working or dangerously out of date. A new heating system needs installing and possibly those old cast-iron radiators replaced. Perhaps not but whatever happens, they'll have to be checked out by a specialist. The whole place needs proper insulating, which can be expensive, but it's an investment that you cannot do without. Some of the brick-work needs reappointing and all the windows need replacing with double-glazing. Not just your run-of-the-mill white PVC stuff, either. I suggest aluminium frames for their durability and look, or even wood, and we'll have to work out a way of keeping those windows that have stained glass, such as in the stairwell and the drawing-room. Obviously all the windows will have to be specially made, as none look standard size to me." He paused for breath. Then continued: "Now, most of the floors look fairly solid but will need special attention, particularly those that are old parquet, such as the study, the drawing-room and the dining-room. There are cracks in the ceilings in some of the bedrooms and a large crack over the main fireplace. Now, if we want to keep the character of the house..."

"Owen, Owen, stop. Please!" said Clare, her voice betraying her growing anxiety at all that her son could see was necessary after just one short visit. "How much is this all going to cost?"

Owen looked at her stricken face and faltered.

"Probably as much as you paid for the house, Mum," he said finally. "But... if you like, I could help you out, oversee operations, make sure you don't get taken for a ride, that sort of thing. Plus when I stay at the gîtes, I can help with the work, too... if you want. That would reduce the bill."

"Well, you've certainly given us food for thought, Owen," said Frank. "I appreciate your offer of help. And it would be good to have you around for a while, wouldn't it Clare?"

"Umm... that's not exactly what I meant, Dad..."

"Yes, yes of course, darling; you know I'd be delighted," said Clare faintly, her mind still on all the work her dear manor house needed doing to it.

"Look," said Ian. "It's late and we're all tired. I suggest we call it a day and we'll talk about this tomorrow if we can. Personally, I think Owen's suggestion of help on the manor house is a grand one but if you want to get the gatehouse gîte rented out for July and August you're going to need the workmen in straight away. So that's one urgent job for you, Owen, deciding what needs done and getting quotes for the work. Plus I'll be needing you elsewhere this week also. I want to show you the ropes of my IT class. And you'll also be needed in the garden and for helping out at meal-times. And for cleaning the gîtes on Saturday in time for the next round of students for the French course."

"God, Ian, I'm on holiday!" protested Owen. "I've just spent the last three weeks swotting and taking my finals. Aren't I even allowed a few days' break to get over them?"

"Well of course, love…" began Clare.

"Absolutely not," said Ian cutting across her. "This is a busy time for your parents and for me. And the manor house refurbishment can't wait. So there'll be no slacking. If you wanted a break, you should've stayed in Belfast. Now you're here, we need your help."

"Mum, is he allowed to talk to me like that?" said Owen.

"Welcome to my world, Son" said his father. "I used to be a French teacher, just minding my own business, and getting lovely, long school holidays every six weeks. Now your mother has my days mapped out from morning to night. And once she realizes what a good help you're going to be to us, she'll have you cornered as well."

"So glad you've decided to stay with us, sweetheart," said Clare, joining in, patting his arm.

"I think I must've missed a page. When did I decide that?" said a genuinely bewildered Owen, to laughter from the other three.

-oOo-

Chapter Seven

Eileen

"Oh my God, a baby boy! Oh that's wonderful," cried Eileen, her heart going all fluttery at the thought. "Oh, Margaret, isn't that just great?" And she cradled the phone closer to her ear so as not to miss a word.

"It is Eileen; he was born at four this morning and from what Dan says, Sandra and the baby are both doing fine."

"Poor lass. I'm sure she's exhausted. They all say that the 'mother and baby are doing fine' but you and I both know it'll be a day or two before Sandra will be up to calling herself fine."

"Well, Dan's over the moon. He told me he's already been holding the baby and he says that there's not a more handsome looking baby in the whole world. Between you and me, I think he's a tad prejudiced but there you go. My very first grandson. Oh! I can't wait to see him, Eileen."

"I'm so happy for you all, Margaret. Isn't life a wonderful thing?"

"It is. It is, indeed. And in another six months or so, you'll be a granny again too!"

"Well, technically speaking, I'm only the stand-in grandmother. I'm not even related to the poor wee mite. But Sharon and Paul have made it clear that they want me to think of myself as its granny and they didn't have to ask me twice."

"I'm sure Kieran can't wait till he has a brother or sister. He's been on his own for so long, with just his mother, until you came along. Now he has his grandmother, a new Dad, and a sibling on the way. It's all happening for him, isn't it?"

"You're right. I can't keep up to him, Margaret. Did you know he'll soon be taking his driving test? And he's head over heels about that nice wee girl, Elizabeth O'Neill, and before you know it their 'A' levels will be over and they'll both be away to Queen's university and I'll hardly ever see him again." Eileen's voice was getting higher and higher as she envisaged what she had been dreading most these last few months.

"Hey, Eileen, that's life," said Margaret kindly, "this time next year we'll be wheeling the prams together, you and I. You'll be up to your eyes in baby-food and nappy-changing and Sharon will be so glad to have you around, like she has been for Kieran. Why do you think they've chosen to purchase one of those new-builds just round the corner from you? You'll be even closer to where they live now."

"You're right, Margaret, course you are. It's just that since I moved to Kilmore, Kieran has been the light of my life. He's the spitting image of what Matt was like at that age. But he's growing up so fast. He's slipping through my fingers, you know?" She sighed. "It's hard, sometimes; I get so sad, all over again."

"I know, sweetheart, but you're doing just great. Sharon, and Paul, and Kieran, they all need you in one way or another, even if they do lead busy lives. And the baby, when it's born, will be someone else who needs you. So just you hang on to that. Think of the positive things! And don't forget me. I need you too," she added.

"Get away with you! Sure you're the apple of John's eye. He dotes on you, anyone can see that. He's a good man, is your John," said Eileen with conviction.

"And guess what, Eileen? He's nuts about the new baby too. Got all tearful when we heard the news. And John's already been a granddad for ages now. He's got four grandchildren already!"

"Ah but this is your first, Margaret. And he's delighted that he's with you to share the joy. Just you wait and see. He'll be spoiling that wee baby just as if it were one of his own children that were the parents. Oh! Do you know what Dan and Sandra intend to call it?"

"David Daniel. Isn't that a great name for a boy?" said Margaret with pride.

"It is indeed. They've chosen well. Oh, I'm so happy for you Margaret! When are you going to see it?"

"Day after tomorrow, just before they let Sandra out of hospital. That way she'll be feeling a bit stronger, hopefully, and I prefer to see her at the hospital 'cos I don't want to be arriving on her doorstep as soon as she gets home. Her mum is coming to help, though, which I'm sure she'll appreciate."

"Well, now that I know it's a wee boy, I can thread some blue ribbon through the little jackets and bootees I knitted in white. You can take them along to her when you go," said Eileen.

"Nonsense, you'll take them yourself in a week or two. I'm sure Sandra will be delighted at all the work you've put in. They're gorgeous, that wool is really soft and fine. Tell you what, we'll both go together. We could have lunch in Newry one Thursday, say, and call in to Dan's place to see Sandra and the baby, spend an hour there, and finish up like we usually do at Oak Lodge around five."

"That's a grand idea! Just keep me posted as to which Thursday it'll be."

"I will, dear. Now, I'll have to go. Give my love to the family and a big hug to Whisky. See you soon."

"Bye Margaret… and oh! Congratulations on becoming a granny!"

Eileen put the phone down gently, her smile still lighting up her face. As soon as her lap was free, her little white Westie dog, Whisky, seized the opportunity to

73

jump up and lick her face. Eileen was quite besotted with this little dog. He had been her lifeline in the dark times after Matt's death when she had felt so alone, providing the company and consolation that she had so badly needed. And when the fire in her old flat in Newry had caused Eileen to seek refuge with Sharon, it had been Whisky who had helped her break the ice and get to know and love her estranged daughter-in-law. It had been Whisky that had led her to meet and make friends with Margaret. And Kieran had been so delighted to have both his gran and her little dog living with them, it had brought their little family unit together where sorrow had previously torn it apart. When the time had come for Eileen to go back to her flat, Sharon had been all for her staying in Kilmore and continuing to look after Kieran. And Eileen had found a little pensioner's cottage to rent and *really* begun to live once again.

The arrival of Paul into this equation had provided not only male company for Kieran, but eventually a new love for his mother. When it became apparent that Paul was going to ask Sharon to marry him, Eileen at first feared that she would lose, all over again, what little of Matt she had left. But it had proved not to be the case. Matt's memory would always remain in their lives, in Sharon's as she put her wedding bouquet on his grave, in Kieran's when he listened untiringly to the stories his grandmother would tell him about his father, and forever in Eileen's, particularly each time she opened the little battered case of mementos she had kept all these years.

That Thursday afternoon, some two weeks after the birth of baby David, Margaret had called for Eileen and together they had shopped and lunched in Newry, a real girly treat for them both, before calling in with Sandra to 'ooh' and 'ahh' over the baby. By this time Margaret was almost smugly efficient in bottle-feeding, putting the baby over her shoulder to burp after his meal.

He would never be called dainty or sweet, he was far too big a baby for that. His shoulders were very wide for a new-born and his hands were relatively huge. This was a little boy and no mistaking, but he was nonetheless beautiful, quite perfect in every way.

Sandra was delighted with what Eileen had knitted, saying that she would be using the little garments straight away. She was already dressing David in clothes for a 3-month child and he was putting on weight at an alarming rate.

She dressed the baby in one of the little white knitted jackets and bootees and gave him to Eileen to hold. Then she took out her phone to take a photo. Margaret stood behind Eileen and both ladies smiled and tried not to cry. Sandra promised to send the photo to Margaret via WhatsApp.

On the way back from Newry to Kilmore, Eileen kept up a happy chatter about the baby and how lovely he looked; how strong, too, for a child so young.

Margaret concentrated on the driving and smiled happy smiles of pride and contentment. They were still on the subject when they drove up the wooded avenue into Oak Lodge.

For the last three years, Margaret and Eileen, with Whisky, had been visiting Oak Lodge as voluntary helpers on Thursday afternoons. Margaret also went along on a Monday, glad to be back in the home that had looked after her parents in their last years. Both of Margaret's parents had succumbed to Alzheimer's disease, first her mother and then her beloved dad. Whereas her mother had had a more traditional form of the disease, for want of a better word, her father had had vascular dementia with Transient Ischemic Attacks propelling him dramatically further and further into the illness until there was no-one left. The support and care both her parents had received over the years had been a godsend to Margaret and after their deaths, she had missed the institution in more ways than one. It was Sharon who had persuaded her to come back as a voluntary helper and eventually bring Eileen as well, and Clare, who was still manageress there at the time, had taken the unprecedented step of letting Whisky accompany them, the little dog quickly becoming a great favourite with patients and staff alike.

Today was no exception to their weekly routine. Whisky was permitted into the common-room to visit each resident in turn and revel in all the attention and patting he received. Margaret automatically went into care-worker mode, helping the staff with whatever needed doing and Eileen sat down to do what she was best at, chatting away.

First person on the agenda was Maud, a rather plump, happy-faced lady who sat in the armchair nearest to the door. Maud loved to fuss over Whisky and Eileen would look on fondly at this display of affection. The next old lady was Mary, Maud's other half, as when you saw one of them, you automatically saw the other. Mary was small, thin, and sharp-tongued, but she loved Maud like a sister. Many a complot to create mischief had been hatched between these two and the staff were always wary when both had disappeared.

After the terrible twins, as they were affectionately known, Eileen went on to talk to William, a gruff old man whose eyes came alight as soon as Whisky trotted in. Eileen enjoyed talking to William; they had found common ground in that he, too, had lost a son a long time ago, and of course, he just loved to play with the little dog, telling Eileen he'd had a wee terrier dog of his own before going into the home. It was generally known that this was not true but it was true to William, so that was all that mattered.

As Eileen left William, she noticed that the next resident was not asleep, as she had initially thought, just sitting, staring into space, her mind far away. This was Rita, who had lost her dear friend Sally only some months previously, and who now wandered aimlessly around trying to find her. Sharon had repeatedly explained to Rita that Sally was now gone forever, but this was not something that Rita was prepared to accept and in her dementia, she missed her friend so badly it was wearing her out. Eileen decided to take her for a little walk, not far, just out into the remembrance garden, as it was a lovely spring day, quite warm for April, just the thing to brighten her up.

"Well, Rita, isn't this just lovely?" she said, as they wandered slowly round the little garden admiring the flowers, Whisky trotting on ahead to explore the sights and smells.

"Sally loves this garden. We always sit out here when we can. And we talk. Yes, we talk," said Rita.

"And what do you talk about, Rita, or is that a secret?" asked Eileen, entering into the way of dementia as smoothly as any trained care-worker.

"Sally's my friend. The best friend I've ever had in the whole world."

"It's lovely to have a friend like that. I know just what you mean," agreed Eileen fervently.

They walked on for a while, round the little path, past a red pillar-box and a little seating area, Whisky never far.

"She's my best friend and I lent it to her 'cos she thought it was so pretty and she said she'd give it back. She's my best friend and I don't know why she doesn't give it back," said Rita suddenly.

"Oh! And is that why you're looking for her, so that she can give it back?" asked Eileen, knowing a good mystery when she saw one.

"Of course. Sally's my best friend. She'd never steal anything from me." Rita looked sadly into Eileen's eyes. "I can't find her. She's not here. I've already looked here. Why would she go away when she's got something that belongs to me?"

"Oh, Rita. I'm so sorry," said Eileen kindly, sensing the old lady's unhappiness. "What was it that you gave to Sally? Tell me what it was."

But Rita just continued to mutter 'best friend I ever had' and Eileen could not get her to elaborate more.

They returned to the common-room soon after that, Rita apparently appeased for now, and Eileen and Whisky continued their tour of the residents. It was getting near the time for the evening meal and most of the care-workers were busy organizing this. George was next in line for Eileen to talk to but he had no sooner begun to pat the little dog, than he was whisked away by an over-zealous member of staff to get him settled at the head of a table, where his wheel-chair had the most room. That left Caroline, who suffered from early-onset Alzheimer's. She was only in her sixties, a year or so younger that Eileen. She picked up the little dog.

"Aren't you a lovely little dog?" she said, "What do they call you, eh?"

"He's Whisky, Caroline," said Eileen, who'd had this conversation many times before.

Whisky, loving the attention as always, licked Caroline's face.

"Oh! Wet!" she said, the lick taking her by surprise. "Aren't you a lovely little dog? What do they call you, eh? What do they call you?"

"Whisky. His name's Whisky, Caroline," repeated Eileen. "Tell me, how are you keeping today?"

"Oh, I'm fine. I have a few classes to take this afternoon, and I haven't had the time to prepare them. I'll just have to wing it. I do that sometimes," she added confidentially. She put Whisky back down on his feet and ruffled his head and ears. "Aren't you a lovely little dog?"

Eileen knew that Caroline had been a teacher and indeed had been teaching until about four years ago when her illness became apparent. What a tragedy to get to sixty and fall ill to dementia and lose all those dreams of retirement. Her poor husband, Edgar, had tried to cope on his own for so long, he had quite worn himself out in the process. Eileen continued to ask Caroline about Edgar and her life at school until Beatrice came along to let them know that dinner was being served. This was Eileen's cue to help feed those residents that couldn't do it themselves and she went to join Margaret who was also helping out with this time-consuming task.

Once the meal was over, the care-workers started getting the residents washed and into their night-things and Eileen and Margaret prepared to leave. On their way out, they ran into Paul:

"Evening, ladies!" he began, "just off then?"

"Done for today, Paul," said Margaret. "Tell me, how's Sharon keeping?"

"Still suffering from morning sickness, I'm afraid. We're advertising for a temporary nurse to replace her and Beatrice has stepped up her hours meantime."

"Oh, the poor woman! Tell her I was asking for her, won't you?"

"Sure will, Margaret. She'll be pleased to know you're thinking of her."

"Paul, can I ask you something?" said Eileen, her thoughts on what Rita had said this afternoon.

"Fire away, Eileen," said Paul smiling.

"Remember Sally who died last year on New Year's Eve, Rita's friend, you know?"

"Of course I remember Sally. Rita's lost without her."

"Well, I found out today, when Rita and I were taking a wee turn around the remembrance garden, that she had lent something to Sally and is now fretting because Sally has gone off and never returned it to her."

"And what was it she lent her, do you know?"

"No, when I tried to get more information, she wouldn't say. I've no idea what it was."

"Umm… tricky one, that. I'll try and talk to Rita myself. Perhaps she'll tell me what it was. Then we can contact Charlotte, Sally's daughter, and take it from there, okay?"

"Thanks, Paul. You'll let me know how you get on, won't you?" said Eileen.

"Sure will, grandma," he said smiling. "I know you just love to get those false teeth of yours into a nice juicy mystery, when you see one."

"Oh, you're a bad article, Paul Harrison!" retorted Eileen. "If it hadn't been for me, you'd still be wondering why your flat was burgled last year and Ian Maher got attacked. I'm very good at solving mysteries, so I am! Just remember that Japanese casket!"

Paul gave her a quick hug. "I'm only winding you up, Eileen, I'll always be grateful for your interfering... for your help," he added quickly.

"And I don't have false teeth," came the righteous reply.

They were still laughing as Margaret punched in the code to let them out of Oak Lodge.

"Eileen, you're telling falsehoods, now," she said, shaking her finger at her friend.

"Only a half-truth, dear. The bottom teeth are all my own," said Eileen, grinning.

-oOo-

Chapter Eight

Past Historic

It was hard for Clare to find time to get to grips with the quest concerning George's descendants and the IT and French courses always made for extra work. Doing the catering was all very well, and Clare loved to cook, but it *was* time-consuming and that plus making sure all the guests were happy and contented, and managing the summer bookings that were now coming in thick and fast, generally left little time for finding a long-lost heir dating back to the Second World War.

But a month after her interview with Damien, Clare began her search in earnest. She had received the photos of Meira from Paul, which at least showed her what Meira had looked like at that time and also confirmed that she had been pregnant and that George's story was not just a figment of his imagination, all too common in someone suffering from dementia.

It was all very well to go on the Internet, thought Clare, so long as you knew what you were looking for. All she had were the photos plus Meira's letter, which although cheerfully poignant, only mentioned that she was writing from Paris, where no doubt she had lived with her husband, and the fact that she was on her way to Saint Avit des Landes where her parents had lived before what turned out to be their deportation. George, himself, had been able to find out Meira's parent's names when he made extensive enquiries into the Jewish people that had been living in Saint Avit during the war, so she had that information via Damien. Their surname was Leblang, Jaron and Ayla Leblang (which they had changed to Leblanc in the 1930's when they obtained French nationality). They had named their daughter Meira, meaning 'ray of light'.

Clare began looking at the websites but it was a mammoth and discouraging task, firstly, selecting those websites that might have lists of what happened to the Jews in France after the end of the Second World War. Here there were several official lists including those of the Red Cross and various Jewish-run memorials to the Shoah and after much searching and cross-referencing, she was able to confirm that Jaron and Ayla Leblang had indeed been handed over to the Germans in October 1943, first being sent together to the French Camp at Drancy and from there to Auschwitz where Ayla was sent to the gas chamber on arrival and Jaron some four months later, when he could no longer provide the work output demanded, weaken by the rigors of appalling conditions, lack of food, and the exceptionally cold winter.

Sickened by trawling through website after website depicting the worst kind of human suffering, coping with intolerably sad images that chased themselves round and round in her brain, plus the frustration of a search that only seemed to meet with dead ends, Clare decided to back off for a day or two. She had so far established confirmation that Meira's parents were both dead in Auschwitz, that Meira's husband was also dead and that Meira had been en route from Paris to Saint Avit des Landes when she disappeared. Perhaps she got as far as Saint Avit and it was there that she learnt of the awful fate that had befallen her parents. If George was able to find out this information some months later, perhaps Meira had previously found that out too.

But why had she not contacted George who waited for her in Coventry? Why this silence after writing him a happy letter full of promises of a 'better life to come'?

Clare decided to concentrate her search on the village of Saint Avit des Landes, and start with the house the Leblang, or Leblanc, family had lived in. This involved more Internet searching to locate previous owners or renters of a house in or around the Saint Avit area. The task was enormous. She decided to seek help.

First she asked Paul to question George to see if Meira had told him anything about her house in Saint Avit : where it was located, what kind of house it was, did her parents own it, where her father had worked. This might prove to be a dead end, as Clare knew all too well, but every little lead had to be followed up.

Then she contacted the Town Hall in Saint Avit to see if they could provide some help in tracing the house where this Jewish family had lived. Had Mr and Mrs Leblang owned it? Did the *Mairie** know where Mr Leblang had worked? When Clare explained that they were trying to trace a descendant of Mr Leblang's daughter Meira, the town hall also put her in touch with the local *notaire**. Research was undertaken on both fronts. All Clare could do now was wait, secretly glad to relinquish the quest for a few days and concentrate on the gîtes and her new manor house and having her son back home.

Spring was the time of year when the large gardens of the gîtes needed the most attention. Jean-Christophe the gardener, who normally came only on Fridays, now came for a fortnight non-stop to tackle the most urgent tasks. Every spare minute that was not taken up with plans for the manor house and catering for the courses, Owen and Clare helped him and all three would mow, and weed, and sew flowers and vegetables for the summer. Then they moved on to the manor-house garden where she gave Jean-Christophe a free-reign. Although not huge, the garden now needed a good deal of pruning and several trees had branches that needed cutting in order to let the rest of the grounds breathe. While the boys cut back branches, communicating in a version of Franglais all of their own, Clare began a serious pruning of bushes and flowers that had all but overrun the pathways and Frank would come and help on his days off by sawing the cut branches into logs and stocking up for the winter fires.

Once the courses were over, Clare had organized for the pool to be overhauled by a professional company, something that was necessary to ensure that the water was clean, the pumps and the heating system checked out, and that the water was at the proper level of ph, did not smell of chlorine and was, in general, fit for the holiday-maker season that was soon to start. The previous year, Frank had looked after all this himself but this year, they had decided to drain the pool completely, and as so much needed to be done elsewhere in the gardens, it was better to call in the professionals.

And every evening, when Jean-Christophe packed up his gear and trundled off to the local dump with a trailer-load of weeds, grass, and general debris, Clare would take time to revisit the interior of the manor-house with Owen, trying to clarify what she would like doing and what was essential to have completed before the winter months. Very often it was there that Frank found them after his day's teaching.

This was Clare's favourite time of day, listening to her son, asking advice and marvelling at all he knew. In the space of just a few years, he'd become all grown up, she hadn't noticed the transition from student to professional, from cosseted teenager to independent man. And every minute with this new person was a treat, a new adventure, as he filled her head with ideas for the house and her heart with quiet pride.

The general consensus had been that they needed to tackle the insulation, change the boiler and the windows, and get the radiators overhauled as a very first step. Bathrooms, kitchens and decorating could wait until there was more money but the gîtes would be booked out in six weeks from now and Clare did not see herself sharing a tent with Frank in the manor house garden, even if it *were* just for the summer months.

And so, while the courses were still being held, Owen had begun the round of artisans who were called in for quotes.

Clare had learnt to her cost that France was still a country where women implicitly, though not unkindly, were thought of as never knowing as much as a man, at least as far as the artisans were concerned. She found that when the professionals came to look at the house, her role as interpreter was tolerated but her opinion as to what needed doing, ignored. After one or two blood-pressure-raising interviews, she decided that it was best only to get these guys out at times when Frank was at home, as his French was perfect, Owen's knowledge a godsend, and she could be relegated to the role of making coffee and ignore them. It was just after one of these extremely frustrating episodes that they had had a visit from her good friend, Laura.

"*Clare, tu es là?*" came Laura's voice from somewhere to the front of the house.

"Oh, Laura, that's nice of you to drop in. How are you?" said Clare, going quickly from the back garden to where Laura was standing looking up at the house. "Come and have a coffee with us. Frank and Owen are both here. We've just been having someone look at the house with a view to replacing the windows."

"*Frank, quel plaisir! Tu vas bien?*" began Laura kissing Frank on both cheeks. "*Et Owen! On ne s'est pas vu depuis Noël. Comment ça va ?* " And she kissed him too.

"*Er... très bien, merci, Laura.*"

"Coffee? Tea? Or lemonade, Laura? I'm afraid I don't have much in the way of refreshments at the manor house," said Clare.

"Coffee is fine, thank you," said Laura in perfect English. She looked around her appreciatively. "Every time I visit your *maison de maître** I like it even more, if that were possible. You have done much work in the garden, I see."

"Yes," said Frank. "Jean-Christophe has been doing wonders and we've all been lending a hand, especially Owen, here."

"That is good. It will keep you fit and strong," said Laura unashamedly putting her hand on Owen's arm to feel the muscles beneath his tee-shirt. "You must come to Lanester and meet my daughters, Owen. My youngest daughter, she has just finished university, like you, and she is quite lost. She tells me she is looking for work but I do not see many signs of it."

"Er… yeah, sure," said Owen, somewhat taken aback by this less-than-subtle hint of matchmaking.

"How's Nathan?" said Frank, adroitly changing the subject.

"Oh, you know… the usual. He is so busy, always so busy. If Gwenaëlle was not living at home at present, I would have no company at all!" protested Laura, dramatically. "But he will be pleased to hear I have stopped to see you. He will want to know all your news."

"Well, we're in the throes of having the professionals in and quotes getting done for things like insulation and new windows and a new boiler," said Clare. "All quite time consuming. And dreadfully expensive, from what I gather."

"But it will be worth it, dear Clare, on your next tax return," affirmed Laura immediately. "You will have tax relief on your revenue because you are carrying out much needed work to reduce heating costs! And you may be entitled to subsidiaries… how do you say? Grants? From government bodies such as the ANAH or the Conseil Général. But you must get a professional artisan to carry out these jobs. Do not attempt to do them yourself." Laura, being an insurance agent, knew something about the subject.

"The guys that were here this morning wanted us to install solar panels on the roof," said Owen.

"Well, yes, that can be interesting in the long term," said Laura dubiously. "But they are very expensive as an investment and if you have a fire, it is difficult for the *pompiers,* the firemen, to use water to put the fire out. They do not like solar panels, I know that is true."

"Really?" said Clare, "those people this morning never said anything about that."

"It is not in their sales arguments, you see," said Laura smoothly.

"Laura," said Frank, "you might know something about the artisans in this area. Here are the brochures from the people we have seen already. Have you met any of these companies before?" And he gave her the documents to study.

Laura took her time, sipping her coffee in silence, while the other three looked on expectantly. Finally, she raised her head and took off the glasses she had put on to read the small print.

"This double-glazing company are quite good. I have heard of their reputation. If their quote is acceptable, you can work with them in confidence. Ah, I see you already have several quotes. That is good. You must get several quotes for every job that needs doing." She took another sip of coffee. "Now, this company for the heating-system is very small. I have heard that they have had problems in the past. You need them to guarantee the work for ten years. Do not use this company. I think they will not be around for much longer. But this, here, this insulation company is the best locally. They will do you a good job, but they are not cheap." She tapped her glasses on one of the brochures. "If you wish, for the heating-system, I can recommend you someone I trust. I have worked with him in the past and he will give you a good rate."

"Oh, would you, Laura?" said Clare, gratefully. "That would make all the difference. Owen here will be overseeing the work, but it is good to have someone who knows the artisans, at least by reputation. It's a lot of money, when all is said and done."

"Yes, thanks Laura," said Owen. "Glad of the help. Oh, and could you tell them it's urgent? We need to get the work started right away."

"Yes, of course. I will do that. Now, you must all come and dine with us one week-end, before the season gets too busy," she said, gathering her handbag and taking a last sip of coffee. Then, as if having a revelation, she exclaimed: "How about this Friday? I do not work Fridays. Are you free?"

"Sorry, not this Friday, Laura. I'm still taking my French classes," said Frank. "Actually, I'll have to get back there now. I just popped out during the break to see this latest artisan."

"The Friday after?" persisted Laura.

"Frank?" asked Clare. "What time do you finish up on Friday week?"

"Umm... not before seven, unfortunately, or even half-past. But that's no problem. I'll go directly to Laura and Nathan's house from work. If that's okay, Laura?"

"That is perfect, Frank. And why not stay over for the night? How do you say? Let the hair down? Before your big season gets underway." She smiled. Then because neither of his parents had thought to ask him, said to Owen. "And you, Owen, will you be free that day?"

"Okay. I'd love to, Laura," he replied. And then before he could stop himself added: "But no matchmaking, now!"

"Oh... spoilsport!" she laughed. "But I shall be so very discrete. You will not notice!"

-oOo-

Mairie = The town hall and local administration

Notaire = A French solicitor

Maison de maître = A French manor house

Chapter Nine

Driving Ambitions

Kieran executed the three-point turn with practiced precision and drove off towards Newcastle as requested. The one-way system there was not particularly difficult to negotiate but summer was not far away and the holiday makers were out in force every time the weather showed signs of improving. It meant that you had to keep your wits about you and be on the lookout for cars pulling away from the kerb or children chasing beach-balls across the road.

Kieran's test was in two weeks' time. But he was fairly confident that he'd pass. Like in most things, Kieran was a fast learner and the faster he learned, the more at ease he felt behind the wheel. Then there was the incentive of the car. If he got through his test, he would be allowed to use some of the money from the sale of the Japanese casket to purchase a second-hand car. There'd be no stopping him then. And once the 'A' level exams were out of the way, he'd be turning his thoughts towards Belfast and Queen's university and leaving Kilmore for good.

He wondered for the umpteenth time if he could coax his mum into letting him lease a flat rather than spend the first year in a hall of residence. Elizabeth's mother had already put her foot down and was insisting on a hall of residence for her. And Kieran wanted Beth all to himself, in a little flat where they could make love whenever they wanted, and not be held to mealtimes and rules and sharing with other people. He'd already starting a campaign about how grown-up he now was, how independent and dependable. But his mother continued to extoll the virtues of residential life for first year students, a totally unreasonable attitude as far as Kieran was concerned. And Paul, his eternal ally, was refusing to take part in this discussion, declaring it to be between Sharon and Kieran alone.

Kieran sighed and brought his thoughts back to the driving lesson. Now they were heading up King's Street, a sharp incline to a plateau that overlooked Dundrum Bay. Here they stopped and the instructor asked Kieran to start the car on the hill. It took him several goes to master the moment when he could feel the car rising and it was time to let the handbrake off and raise the clutch while pressing the accelerator pedal. And all this had to be done while indicating and pulling out into the road and making sure no other car was coming. Far from being intimidated, Kieran thought this the best part of the lesson and after the third or fourth go, felt he had mastered the manoeuvre completely. Then at the end of King's Street, there was a difficult blind corner junction to turn left back towards Newcastle but all went well and soon he was pulling up in front of the little house in Kilmore which he had shared with Sharon these last nine years and where Paul had now come to live. The instructor organized four more lessons in the next two weeks, all of them in Downpatrick, where the test would take place. Kieran, not in the least nervous, was filling his head not so much with thoughts of passing or failing his test but rather in choosing the car that would be his.

He bounded into the kitchen to be greeted by Eileen and Whisky. Of his mother there was no sign.

"Hi, Gran! How's life?" said Kieran, giving her a quick hug. "Where's mum? Still at work?"

"Hello, Son. No, your mother's upstairs. She's not feeling well again. *Morning sickness*," she mouthed. "I've come round with some soup. She has to eat something. Here, have a bowl yourself and you can have some of this lasagne I've made for afterwards."

Eileen busied herself serving out bowls of soup to Kieran and making up a tray for Sharon. She was about to go upstairs with it but Kieran stopped her.

"I'll take it up, Gran. Haven't seen Mum all day."

"Alright, but mind you don't spill any. I'll put yours back in the pot."

Kieran balanced the tray on one hand, climbed the stairs and knocked on his mother's bedroom door.

Sharon was lying on her side and looking very pale. The curtains were drawn and in the gloomy light, he could see that she was not well.

"Hi Mum, soup? Eileen made it," he began.

"Thanks, Kieran. That's good of her. I'll try and take some. I'm hungry, actually. But everything I eat just comes back up at the moment. It's exhausting."

"Aw, poor Mum! Was it like this… before… with me?"

"No, my love. Never had morning sickness before now. Strange, isn't it?"

"All Paul's fault," said Kieran cheerfully. "Make him pay, Mum."

"Make me pay for what?" said a familiar voice from the doorway.

"Hello, darling," said Sharon, smiling.

"For making my Mum ill with morning sickness. Or evening sickness, as *is*."

"Takes two to tango, Kieran," said Paul philosophically. "And it won't last. Hopefully in a week or two, your mum will be as right as rain."

"Typical," said Sharon, sitting up and pulling the tray on to her lap. "If there's ever another baby after this, you'll be doing the carrying of it, Paul Harrison, not me."

"Well, that'll be a first," said the culprit, laughing. "See? You're looking better already. Now, I'll leave you to talk to Kieran and I'll go back down with Eileen. That soup smells good."

"I'll be right down," said Kieran, calling after him.

"Well, tell me, how did the driving lesson go then?" said Sharon.

"Really well. I think we've covered more or less everything now. Just four more lessons in Downpatrick and then the test. Won't be difficult."

"Don't be so sure of yourself. You'll need all your wits about you on the day. Many people fail the first time, you know," said Sharon, sipping her soup.

"Not me, Mum. I'll be fine, don't worry."

"And how's the studying going? You're not neglecting it, are you? In that flat?" queried his mother, frowning, still not convinced that she was doing right by letting Kieran live on his own.

"*Mu-um*. We've been over this a hundred times. I'm working hard. I promise. I really want to get these 'A' levels and get into Queen's. And I really want to pass my driving test and get a car. I'm studying, Mum. Believe me. In fact, staying in Paul's flat gives me all the peace and quiet I need right now." He took her free hand. "Now, you have to get better, and look after yourself and my little brother or sister. I'm fine, really. Don't be worrying about me."

"Okay, sweetheart, I'll try not to. Now off you go and have your dinner with Paul. It's Eileen's bingo night. She'll be away any minute now."

Eileen was indeed putting on her coat when Kieran came back down the stairs. Margaret was due to call for her and she didn't want to keep her waiting. Paul had elected to look after Whisky till she came back.

With Eileen gone, and the soup eaten, Paul and Kieran settled down to partake of the big dish of Lasagne that Eileen had prepared. They were both hungry and ate in companionable silence for a few minutes, Kieran resting one hand on the little dog's head.

"God, this is good," said Kieran between mouthfuls.

"It is, that," said Paul. "Driving lesson went okay?"

"Yeah. Easy. Hey, Paul, will you help me chose my car?"

"Sure, but aren't you putting the cart before the horse? Or the car before the driving test, to be precise? When *is* the test?"

"In two weeks. A doddle, don't worry." *Why does everyone worry so much?*

"Who said I'm worrying? Just being practical, that's all. Once you get the car, you'll have to start paying insurance. And that costs a bomb for restricted drivers."

"Insurance? Hadn't thought about that, to be honest."

"See? Someone's got to pay it. And even if your university fees will be paid from the money the casket brought in, you'll still need your mum to help pay for your accommodation and other things."

"I'll have a grant, though."

"Which won't go very far."

"I can take out a student loan."

"And start your working life owing thousands."

Kieran sat silent, thinking this over. He could see that his money wouldn't cover all his needs but surely living away from home and running a car wouldn't be all that expensive. He would be careful, economize, and continue working in Tesco's in the holidays. He'd be fine. No need to worry. None at all. Now if he had a wee flat all to himself...

"Paul, do you think Mum'll let me get a flat of my own when I go to Queen's? Or a bedsit, or something? Don't really fancy a hall of residence. Beth has been told she has no choice. Her parents are saying it's a hall of residence for the first year, or nothing."

"Wise decision on their part," said Paul nodding. "But why don't you want to do the same? Why a flat? Surely it'll be more fun being with other students. And less expensive too."

"But what if we're not in the same hall of residence? What if some other guy comes along and... and she leaves me?"

Paul looked at this teenager, so sure of himself one minute, so scared the next. He knew that Kieran would never confide like this in anyone else. It was important to take him seriously. He was in the flush of first love with all the ups and downs and joys and torments that inevitably tag along.

"Kieran, it's not by keeping Elizabeth all to yourself that you can prevent her meeting someone else. You're not even doing the same courses. She's bound to meet other guys just like you'll meet other girls. Sometimes that can break a relationship and sometimes it can strengthen it. If you both continue to love each other very much, no amount of separation will change that."

"But she's beautiful, Paul, and I know she's been asked out by other guys in my year at school. And she's generous and wonderful and… and…"

"Yeah. She's all those things," said Paul gently. "But she's young. And so are you. There's a whole lot of things for you to do, and feel, and be afraid of, and enjoy, before you start talking about settling down together. Make the most of freedom, Kieran, before tying yourself in knots. University is all about that too, you know, not just the studying."

"Did you have girlfriends before going out with your first wife?"

"Sure. When you're a man doing a nursing degree, there aren't many other men on the course. So, yeah, I was popular. Had girlfriends that were nurses, mostly. Then Anita came along. She was different. And I fell hook, line and sinker." His face clouded at the thought of Anita and how badly things had turned out.

"She wasn't nice, Anita," said Kieran.

"No, she *was*. At the start, she was lovely. Then she changed her job and met other people, had affairs that I knew nothing about. And... and before I knew it, she was asking for a divorce and turfing me out of our flat in order to sell it. Not good for the ego, believe me."

"Beth would never do anything like that."

"I surely hope not. Wouldn't wish it on a dog."

"So do you think Mum'll come round to letting me have my own place then? She's allowing me use your flat."

"Kieran, you haven't listened to a word I've said! "said Paul exasperated, "My flat is a temporary arrangement here in Kilmore, for a few months at the most. And I think your mum already regrets letting you stay there 'cos she thinks you're too young. So no. I don't hold out much hope of your getting permission for a place of your own in Belfast." He sighed. "Why not apply to the same halls of residence as Elizabeth? You never know. Could be the answer, couldn't it?"

"I suppose so."

"It is. Believe me. And even if you don't get into the same hall, they're all more or less close together." He smiled. "And you'll have your car."

"Yeah! I'll have my car, won't I?"

"Not many students have that in their first year."

"Yeah. Cool!"

After dinner, Kieran took Whisky out for a short run before handing him back to Paul and heading for the flat. The little dog was not quite as energetic as before, the accident he'd had the previous year having left its mark. But he trotted along quite happily with Kieran and by the time they got back to Sharon's house, he could see Eileen and Margaret pulling up in the car.

It was nearly eleven when Kieran finally got back to the flat, made himself a hot drink and settled down to cram in half hour's revision before going to bed. It was the first time he'd opened a book all evening, the two hours before the driving lesson having been spent in a much more satisfying way with Beth. Lying in Paul's bed, in Paul's flat, his last thoughts were crowded with her, the sight and the smell of her, and why, oh why, would his mother not let him have his own place at Queen's?

-oOo-

Chapter Ten

A Breakthrough of Sorts

The next day at Oak Lodge, Paul saw that Rita was looking as lost and forlorn as ever and decided it was time he tried to find out what was wrong. It was late afternoon and the time of day when there was a lull of sorts before the evening meal got underway. She was wandering the corridors, searching no doubt for Sally, and Paul had no trouble finding a quiet moment to accompany her. He deftly steered her into the library area with its view over the conservatory and was glad to find it empty.

"Now, Rita, tell me, how are you today?" he began, taking her hand in his. It was immediately snatched back.

Rita didn't answer.

He tried again. "Are you unhappy, Rita?"

Her look said it all although she remained stubbornly silent.

"Is it Sally?" he asked gently.

"She's my best friend. My best friend in the whole world," she chanted. "Where's Sally? Where's Sally gone?" Rita looked at him properly for the first time.

"I'm sorry, Rita. Sally has gone away for good," said Paul. "She won't be coming back."

"Where has she gone to? Tell me where she is. I want to see her. She's wearing my brooch. It's *my* brooch. I chose that brooch. Sally said she would give it back to me."

"Was... is it a nice brooch?" asked Paul quietly.

"It's *my* brooch. Sally said she would give it back. Where's Sally?"

"Tell me about the brooch. What was it like?"

"Why has she kept it? Why won't she give it back?" cried Rita, her voice becoming shrill with annoyance. Paul knew it was time to put an end to the conversation. At least now he knew what it was that Rita was searching for.

"It's okay. It's okay, Rita. We'll try and find your brooch," he said soothingly. "Now don't worry about it anymore. We'll do our best."

"Sally. Where's Sally?"

"Rita, come, I'll get you a nice cup of tea. Come with me into the kitchens. It'll be alright. Don't you worry. Here, come and have a cup of tea."

And Paul adroitly led Rita off to the kitchens where he asked the staff there to get her a cup of tea. Only when she was calmer did he go quietly away.

He immediately set off to see if Geraldine was on duty. Geraldine and Rita were friends. It was Geraldine who had helped Rita settle into Oak Lodge at the beginning of her stay there and it was Geraldine who had introduced Rita to Sally. To Geraldine, Rita was special inasmuch as she reminded her of her own grandmother, now dead for many years, but never quite out of sight when Rita was around.

He found her with another patient, having just helped him get to the toilet after the afternoon nap. Paul waited till they were on their own and said:

"Geraldine, do you know anything about a brooch that Rita gave to Sally at some point? She's still pining for Sally but she's now focusing on this brooch saying it was hers to start with and that she lent it to Sally but Sally never gave it back."

"That rings a bell, Paul," said Geraldine. "There's something about a brooch but I can't remember what it was. Have you looked in the safe?"

"The safe?"

"Yes. That's where we put jewellery that gets left behind. Sometimes one of the residents loses something in the remembrance garden, or in the grounds, or it gets overlooked when we're clearing out their room after they've gone. Not often mind, the girls are fairly thorough, but it has been known to happen."

"I see," said Paul.

"But if it's not in the safe, there's a wee box there for trinkets if you look, well, the only thing to do is to contact Charlotte, Sally's daughter. She might have taken it away with her."

The brooch was not in the safe so Paul hunted out Charlotte's number and gave her a call. He asked her how she was coping now that her mother was gone, and how her brother Benedict was faring too. Charlotte explained, hesitantly, how it had been hard at first and how it had taken many months to pick up the threads of her life. Paul understood only too well. The death of a parent was always hard to cope with, but a parent who needed as much care and attention as an Alzheimer patient required, must leave a huge hole in their family's universe when they died.

"It does, Paul," agreed Charlotte. "It's been hard to get back to normality, so to speak. I'm only now starting to sort Mum's stuff out. It was just too difficult, too sad, before. Benedict's not interested in anything like that, so it's all left to me. But I don't want to simply give everything into the charity shop. It'll be like she never existed after that."

Paul could feel that Charlotte was near to tears. He hastened to come to the point. "Charlotte, have you come across a brooch in your mother's possessions, something that would have been brought back from Oak Lodge?"

"Well, she had several brooches. She liked wearing brooches. I'm sure they're around somewhere. I know I haven't thrown anything out. Not jewellery, anyway. Why do you ask?"

"Actually, it's for Rita. Remember Rita?"

"Oh, I do! 'Course I do. How is she coping? They were quite close, Mum and Rita. She must miss Mum as much as I do," she finished thoughtfully.

"Yes, Charlotte. She does. She spends a good deal of time asking where Sally has gone, even after all these months. We've tried to explain but she doesn't understand. And to make matters worse, she's now focusing on a brooch that she says she gave to Sally and that Sally has taken away with her."

"Oh, poor Rita! God love her!" Charlotte gulped, all the memories flooding back.

"So I was wondering if you could have a look in your mother's jewellery, if you've still got it, and bring us in anything that might not have belonged to Sally?"

"'Course I will. I'd be only too happy to do so. I'll call in to see you next week. Will Wednesday afternoon be okay?"

"Sure, no problem. I'm on duty… let me see… from two onwards. I'll look forward to seeing you again."

"Me too. It's not going to be easy going back but I can't leave Rita like that. She and Mum had such good times together."

"Thanks Charlotte," said Paul, glad that one problem might be getting solved. Here's hoping she would bring the right brooch.

When Charlotte drove up to Oak Lodge the following Wednesday afternoon, she sat for a few moments in the car-park, just taking it all in. From the floor-to-ceiling windows of the common-room, she could make out some faces that were familiar although the names escaped her now. She marvelled at how little she had thought of the home since her mother had died on New Year's Eve, how quickly she had been to forget the place where Sally had been so lovingly cared for in the last year of her life.

The years she had spent coping with her mother's dementia had left Charlotte physically exhausted and mentally drained. And when Sally had been accepted into Oak Lodge, it had been a longed-for blessing, the knowledge that she now had round-the-clock supervision and care had been an enormous relief to them all. And when she had died, a huge part of the time Charlotte had spent in coming to visit her had been eaten up in grieving and missing her presence.

She went up to the front door and tried the code. It opened first time, just like all those other times before. Charlotte went in to stand hesitantly in the hall. From there she could see into the common-room and those faces she remembered now took on names. George was sitting there in the same spot, reading the paper, trying to focus. Maud and Mary were sitting side by side mumbling to each other. One or two new faces stared at her from various points in the room. Careworkers were coming or going, some nodding to her with a smile as they passed. She could make out Paul, further down the corridor, his tall frame easy to spot among the patients and staff. She went straight up to him.

"Ah, Charlotte," he said pleasantly as soon as he spotted her. "Nice to see you again. Come with me. We'll go up to the office, it'll be quieter there."

"Hi Paul," said Charlotte shyly. It was strange being back in Oak Lodge, different from when she used to come every day, but just the same too. She couldn't quite explain it. They went up the stairs and along the corridor and Paul held the office door open for her.

"Would you like a cup of tea, coffee?" he asked.

"Er... no. No thanks. I'm fine. But it does seem weird being back in Oak Lodge."

"I'm sure it does. Been a few changes, too, since Sally died."

"Really? New faces, you mean?"

"Well, yes, of course. We have some new faces. Inevitable," began Paul, hesitantly.

"Changes in the staff?" suggested Charlotte.

"No. Well, we're all still here but we're taking on another nurse very soon. Sharon is reducing her hours at the moment and will be on maternity leave as of October or November."

"Wow! I didn't know she was married. That's lovely."

"It is," said Paul, blushing, wishing he hadn't started this conversation. "Actually, she's married to me."

"Oh! Really? Congratulations to you both! I hadn't heard." Charlotte beamed, tickled to see Paul blush. It was so out of character with the Paul she had been accustomed to deal with.

"Thanks, Charlotte. I'm a lucky man." He changed the subject. "Now, down to business. Did you find anything that might correspond to what Rita is searching for? A brooch that didn't belong to Sally?"

"Actually, no, Paul. All the brooches I have belonged to Mum. There's four of them. I brought them all with me. Perhaps one of them will mean something to Rita? I don't mind if she keeps it. In fact, I'd be happy to give Rita something of Mum's."

She took out a black velvet pouch and placed the brooches on the desk. They were, for the most part, old-fashioned, flower-bedecked creations that were of no monetary value whatsoever. One brooch, though, was solid silver, with pretty red stones and mother-of-pearls, quite an intricate work of art. It was in a different category to the other three and was probably quite valuable. It came in its own special box.

"This one looks expensive, Charlotte. Are you sure you don't mind if Rita picks this? We can't show her anything that we can't let her keep, you understand."

"Yes, I know, Paul. But I don't need it. Mum loved it because it was Dad who had given it to her for their last wedding anniversary together before he died. She wore it all the time. But obviously, when she became bedridden, we had to take it off."

"Well," said Paul. "Let's go and see if we can find Rita. She'll not be far. And we'll show the brooches to her and see what happens."

They found Rita, for once, sitting alone quietly in her room. She didn't greet them when they came in and didn't seem to recognize Charlotte, with whom she had spent many hours together with Sally. Paul gently laid out the four brooches on the tray-table and wheeled it over to where Rita was sitting.

"Look, Rita," was all he said. Charlotte watched closely and said nothing.

Slowly Rita turned her attention to the jewellery. Then she put out a boney hand to the silver brooch and gently picked it up. She turned it this way and that to capture the light and her face suddenly lit up. "My brooch," she said. "Sally's brought back my brooch."

Paul looked at Charlotte who nodded. He silently took the other three brooches away and gave them back to her.

"It's a lovely brooch, Rita," he said softly. "Sally would want you to have it."

"Lovely brooch," chanted Rita, "lovely brooch. Sally's brought back my brooch."

"Shall I fasten it on to your cardigan?" asked Paul, making to take the brooch from her hands. She immediately grabbed it and turned away. "No," she cried. "My brooch."

"Okay, Rita, no problem," said Paul, holding his hands up. "Look, it has its own box. You can keep it in the box. Look? The box."

Rita slowly put the brooch back in the box and cupped her hands around it. Paul signalled to Charlotte that it was time to go.

"Nice to see you again, Rita," said Charlotte, "'bye, now."

Rita didn't answer but they left her, eyes riveted on the brooch, with a tender smile that Paul had not seen since Sally's death.

When they were outside her room, Paul began to thank Charlotte sincerely, convinced that this was the brooch Rita had been looking for and which she took to be her own.

"Please, Paul, don't mention it. If Mum's brooch can give pleasure to Rita, then I'm happy to let her keep it."

"She'll be carrying it around in her pocket from now on," said Paul. "You've been a marvellous help. Thank you so much."

"Great!" said Charlotte, pleased. "Now, I'd like to call in on Carmel, if I may. She sat with me last New Year's Eve and helped me... helped me be with Mum when she died. I never thanked her properly at the time."

"Sure, come back upstairs with me and I'll show you where Carmel's quarters are. She'll be about at this time of day."

They said good-bye outside Carmel's flat. Paul was pleased that things had gone so well. Now, he thought, time to tackle that other problem - George. He needed more information from George. He looked at his watch. No, it would have to wait. Not enough time before dinner. He'd try again later that evening when things were quieter.

-oOo-

Chapter Eleven

Hidden Memories

Paul did indeed go to see George that evening but George was not inclined to talk. He was stubborn and morose and nothing Paul could do would cheer him up. He decided to let things lie for the time being.

It was a quiet evening and once all the residents were in bed, and checked over and medication given, Paul found himself with time on his hands before Carmel came to take over from him at ten pm. He decided to find out more about the Second World War and the bombings in Coventry so that he could best bring up the subject with George the next time they talked. He spent a fruitful, though depressing, half hour surfing the net, wondering if Clare was doing the same thing on her computer in France.

The following day, Paul was once again on an afternoon/evening shift. He intended to try and get George to remember the details that Clare had asked him to find out, if possible. This time George was more receptive and inevitably asked Paul to bring out the whiskey bottle and serve them both a tot.

Thus settled, Paul brought the subject round to Meira.

"George," he said at length, "remember Clare? She's trying to find trace of Meira or her family in France. Meira; that you met in Coventry during the war?"

"Grey. Everything was grey after the war. No other paint, see? Only grey, from the factories," said George.

"And Coventry was all but bombed out, wasn't it?"

"Aye, it was that. But she wasn't in Coventry. She was in France. I went there. I went and searched. But I couldn't find her. Even in the village, there was no trace of her anywhere."

"In Saint Avit."

"Aye, that was the name. No sign of her. I searched everywhere. Bloody mess."

"Mr and Mrs Leblang, Meira's parents; they lived in Saint Avit, didn't they?"

"They were long gone. Sent to Germany, or Poland, to one of those camps. Never came back. None of them came back. Meira didn't come back," said George sadly.

"And what did her parents do before they were deported... before they were sent away? Do you know what her dad worked at? What did he do for a living?"

"Jewellery. Had a shop. Mended jewellery. Aye. She had a wee locket. Her father made it. She put our photos in it when she left. Never came back. I searched for her but she never came back." George looked sadly into his glass as if by doing so he could find Meira there.

"And what happened to the shop, George? Was it still there?"

"Gone, all gone. They were all gone." He sighed. "I asked. They said they never came back."

"Okay, George. Thanks. I'll tell Clare. It might help to find a trace of Meira."

Paul stayed a while longer talking to George about the war but got no further information that he thought would be of help. He left shortly after and did his rounds but all continued calm and he decided to send a quick email to Clare with the information he had collected before leaving for home.

Back at Sharon's house later that evening, he could see that she was looking better than she had been for several days.

"Wow, welcome back, love," he said taking her into his arms and planting a long kiss on her lips. "You look great."

"Haven't been sick not even once today! God, the relief of having food stay down, Paul. You can't imagine."

"Um… probably not, in the circumstances. Where's Kieran. Has he left already?"

"Just. It's a wonder you didn't see him go."

"My mind was on other things, probably. I've been playing detective all week. Certainly adds a new dimension to being a geriatric nurse."

"Detective?"

"Yep. Found out why Rita was so upset and might have solved that particular problem. Now all we can do is wait and see." And he proceeded to tell Sharon all about the brooch.

"And what Clare asked you to find out from George. Any luck there?" said Sharon.

"Well, I found out two more pieces of information. They might help her, you never know."

"Go on. Tell me," said Sharon eagerly.

"Meira's parents had a jewellery shop in Saint Avit. I believe her mother was behind the counter and her father mended. He made Meira a locket and Meira put photos of George and her in it when she left for France after the war. I sent Clare an email this evening before I left."

"Well, that's sure to give her a start as to where to look. She was a bit discouraged when I spoke to her last week."

"It's a needle in a haystack, really. I mean it's been seventy years! If somehow Meira survived to give birth to their baby, that 'baby' is seventy years old today.

And Meira would be over ninety, like George, if she were alive still."

"What I can't understand," said Sharon, "is why the silence? Her husband was dead, she was free to be with George, *wanted* to be with him as her letter attests. Her parents were also dead. What on earth could have happened for her to break contact? Did she ever make it to her home town? And, how on earth is Clare going to find out *anything* after all this time?"

"Well," said Paul, sighing. "You know Clare. She'll not stop one way or the other. I hope, for George's sake, she does find out the information he's wanting to hear. Can you imagine what he went through all those years ago? Poor man."

"I know. He's had it hard. It's the not knowing which is the worst, I believe. Not knowing whether she survived or not; not knowing whether he had a son or a daughter."

"You know, Sharon," said Paul thoughtfully, "when Anita left me and we got divorced, I kind of had to come to terms with the fact that I'd never have a son or daughter of my own. I think… even though I knew she didn't want kids… I think I'd always hoped for a miracle of sorts. I was willing to put up with a helluva lot from her in that respect." He looked down fondly at Sharon and kissed the top of her head. "And now I *will* be a dad, thanks to you. And you're the most wonderful mother, all ready-made, who's done a great job bringing up her son in difficult circumstances and is now willing to go through the whole rigmarole again, just for me. I don't deserve you, Sharon, my sweetheart, I really don't."

"You daft eejit, Paul Harrison," said Sharon cuddling up to him. "Are you forgetting all you've given to me? How you've changed my life, not to mention Kieran's. We'd be lost without you. We're so lucky, *I'm* so lucky, it's even worth the morning sickness! Or nearly," she added honestly.

In France, Clare was indeed sitting in front of her computer digesting the information in Paul's email of earlier that evening. Finding out that the Leblang family owned a jeweller's was indeed a step forward and she could now go back to the Mairie in Saint Avit with this information and make further enquiries. A trip to the south of France was needed as soon as possible and she only had a short time-frame in which to carry this out. The gîtes were getting booked up, it was May with all the bank holidays and long week-ends that so tempted the French to use up their *RTT** leave to take a week off work and have a foretaste of summer. In fact this really was her last chance before the season got too busy. She said as much to Frank and Owen that evening.

"Two or three days, is that wise, Clare?" came Frank's inevitable response.

"What about all that's going on in the manor house, Mum?" added Owen for good measure.

Clare knew they were right. But it was now or never. The last IT and French classes were over till the end of October. Everything was clean and ready for the rentals. The manor house was indeed an unholy mess with the insulation being carried out and a new boiler being installed but she would only be away for a few days. Surely her menfolk could cope without her for that? After all, only three of the gîtes were rented out this week. Clare remained firm.

"No, I'll not get another chance like this until after the season. And I can't guarantee George will be around for many years longer. He's ninety two. I owe it to the old man to try. Can't you both see how important this is?"

"Yeah, Mum, I know it is but Dad's going to be at the language school and I'll be all on my own here. And I hardly speak any French at all."

"Owen, I'll leave my mobile on. Call me if you think it's necessary. Now there's only three gîtes rented out at the moment. Two of those are to Dutch people who speak perfect English. All you have to do is make sure they're okay during the day. And the third one's rented to a French couple and Frank will be here in the evenings if you really need him for them. As for the house, you're doing a great job, much more hands on that either of us two would be. And I'll get Solange to start the season a day early, on Friday, so that she can bring the website up to date and check out the gîtes."

"Solange, who's Solange?"

Clare looked at Owen, exasperated. "I've *told* you who Solange is. She's part of our set-up here, like Jean-Christophe."

"Solange comes in during the season on Saturdays to help with the changeovers," said Frank. "She's been with us since the start and she can now do the websites and order supplies. She's our good fairy, actually. You'll like her, she's a nice girl." he concluded.

"Now don't you start, Dad," said Owen, "It was bad enough Laura playing matchmaker last Friday when we went to their house for dinner. That daughter of hers, Gwenaëlle, was coming on a bit strong. I mean, I don't mind," he added, "but I'm not really looking for that kind of attention right now. I'm still with Judith."

"Heard anything from Judith lately, then?" said his mother, as innocently as possible.

"We Skype. That's all we can do. She's really wrapped up in her new life in San Francisco, loves the job and all."

"Ah!" said Clare, her mind leaping to all sorts of conclusions following the divulging of this meagre information.

"Well, getting back to Solange, she'll be here Friday," concluded Frank "and Clare, if you're leaving tomorrow, will you be back by Friday evening then?"

"I'll do my best. And I'll be in touch every day. Now I must get on the Internet and book myself a hotel as close to Saint Avit as possible. I reckon it's going to take me six or seven hours to get down there. I'll need to take breaks from the driving."

"It's a long way to go on your own, Clare, you be careful now," said Frank.

"I will, darling, I will. I'll start early and try and get to the *Mairie* of Saint Avit before it closes tomorrow evening. They might have some information for me already. And now I know what Meira's parents did for a living, they can surely point out where the old shop stood. The *notaire* might be able to help me there." She sighed. "There must be *someone* who knows what happened to Meira, if she got as far as Saint Avit. She can't just have vanished into thin air."

Clare set off early the next day, with her file on George and a small suitcase of clothes. She had made herself up a picnic and brought it in a freezer box with several bottles of cool water. Being mid-week, the motorways and dual carriageways were fairly clear, more lorries than cars really, and her journey, although somewhat boring, went by quite quickly. She found herself listening to the radio, the 'Nostalgie' station mainly, as it specialized in songs from twenty, thirty or even forty years ago, some in French and some in English, which she could now sing along to in either language... albeit slightly off-key.

Her I-pad also served as a SatNav and the smooth feminine voice guided her firmly to her destination. It was just after three pm when she pulled up into the forecourt of Saint Avit's Town Hall.

Just being in Saint Avit felt strange, and Clare stood looking around her trying to recapture what it must have looked like all those years ago. Most of the buildings in the town centre had not changed. Renovated or repainted possibly, they had not been replaced with modern concrete blocks or glass-fronted architectural creations. And if you obliterated a satellite dish or two, it was possible to imagine Saint Avit how it was in Meira's time. Clare drank it all in.

The town centre was just off a pretty, geranium-lined street that led directly to the train station, now no longer in use. A river gurgled somewhere close and, as she crossed the square, she could glimpse the main bridge and the small pedestrian bridge behind it that linked the two sides of the town. She decided to put off exploring as she knew that the *Mairie* might close any time from four pm onwards and she wished to initiate her quest by getting to talk to the right person or people. She went up the steps and, not without a little trepidation, pushed open the door.

-oOo-

RTT* = Récupération du Temps de Travail = Any hours worked above the standard 35 hour working-week are generally considered to be time that can be taken off work at a later date.

Chapter Twelve

Solange

Back at the gîtes, Owen was beginning to wonder why on earth he ever let himself get talked into coming to live in France. He'd have been much better off trying to save his relationship with Judith by going to work in San Francisco, even if it meant spending a year washing dishes. The two Dutch families were nice, uncomplicated people but they intended to get the most out of their holiday and plied Owen with questions about what to do and where to go, local information that he was poorly equipped to give them until he discovered Clare's file on the subject, built up over the two years she had been in the area, and gratefully handed it over. The French couple were more discrete but Owen dreaded having to make conversation with them at all, as he had little confidence in his capability to talk French.

Then there were the artisans. Keeping an eye on professional people, when one did not speak the lingo, was complicated, and Owen's youth was against him. Even though it had been explained to them that he was the *Maître d'Oeuvre** and an (almost) qualified architect, they did not consider him to be an expert in any of their own particular fields and tended not to take him seriously. After a particularly frustrating run-in with the insulation people, Owen found himself storming off to the gîtes for coffee and calm.

In fact, he forego the coffee for a swim, having found that he had the pool all to himself and nearly half a mile later, climbed out refreshed and ready to take on the world again, feeling that perhaps life wasn't quite so bad after all.

Apart from the guests and the workmen, Owen dreaded answering the phone. Email enquiries he could deal with, as most of them were on the English version of the website anyway and those that were in French he left for Frank to reply to after work, but enquiries by phone in French were a nightmare, leaving him feeling guilty and stupid.

By the time Friday came around he was counting the hours till Clare's return.

On Friday morning at precisely nine o'clock, there was a knock on the door of the office in the gatehouse gîte and Owen went to answer it, thinking it was the Dutch people wanting some other piece of information he was in no position to give them. A pretty young girl stood there smiling, her head to the one side. She had grey-blue eyes fringed with dark eyelashes and long curly brown hair that bounced gently on her shoulders.

"*Er... Bonjour?*" said Owen.

"*Bonjour. Je suis Solange,*" she said.

"Solange... oh yes!... Solange... *oui. Entrez s'il vous plaît,*" said Owen, somewhat flustered at her presence and cursing himself for having forgotten, once again, that she was coming today.

"*Vous voulez café?*" he ventured, not knowing where to start, his Irish breeding taking over, making the offer of refreshments automatic.

"*Oui, merci, c'est gentil,*" said Solange, watching him closely, her smile never faltering.

Owen stumbled out of the office to the kitchen to busy himself heating up the coffee that Frank had made that morning before leaving for work. He didn't know how he was going to deal with Solange, nor what work he could give her to do, had no idea how to communicate with her even. The day suddenly seemed to stretch out unending before him. He fought down an unreasonable urge to panic.

When he got back to the office, Solange was already seated at the computer and dealing with an enquiry on the French version of the gîte website. She smiled her thanks and continued working away, while Owen drank his coffee and tried to look busy while in fact doing nothing. Finally, she pressed the send button and turned to face him.

"*Vous êtes Owen, n'est-ce pas?*"

"*Er... oui. Moi, Owen,*" he said.

"*Et vous êtes architecte. Clare m'a parlé de vous. M'a beaucoup parlé de vous, au fait. Et vous allez vous occuper de leur nouvelle maison.*"

"*Er... oui.*"

"*Ne vous inquiétez pas pour moi. Je sais ce qu'il y a à faire ici. Si vous avez besoin de vous absenter, n'hésitez-pas.*"

Owen was still trying to work this one out when the phone rang. Solange automatically picked it up.

"*Allo. Les Gîtes de Plurviel, bonjour,*" she said, then listened for a few seconds before saying smoothly, "Yes, of course, how can I help you?" And proceeded to deal with the query in perfect English, her lilting French accent, as much as the fact she spoke English at all, music to Owen's ears. She had hardly put the phone down when he burst out. "I didn't know you spoke English, Solange. This is great!"

"Do not be so surprised, Owen. Clare and Frank are very good teachers. And my parents made us speak some English as children. I like to speak it as often as I can."

"But *my* parents never said anything about that. I thought you only spoke French. And my French is rubbish."

"It will come, if you stay here long enough. You will speak French quite well soon."

"You're very optimistic. Try telling that to the insulating company that's doing up the manor house. We're at loggerheads at the moment and I can't get them to understand what I mean."

"Where is loggerheads? Are they not working at the house?"

Owen laughed, in spite of himself.

"Loggerheads is an expression. It means stalemate." He looked at her. "Stalemate? Ah, let me try something else. We are in an impasse, we cannot move forward because we don't understand each other."

"Ah, je comprends."

"In *fact*," said Owen, the advantages of this new situation dawning on him, "you could help me a lot, Solange, if you would come with me to the manor house and be interpreter. Would you do that?"

"Yes, I will help you if I can. But first, I must check the gîtes to see what needs doing for tomorrow. I see from the website there are several bookings for next week. And you have three gîtes rented out at the moment."

"Okay. I'll come with you. You can show me what needs doing."

"Clare did not do this already?"

"Umm… I wasn't free that day."

He was suitably rewarded with a look that spoke volumes.

From that moment onwards, Solange took over the running of the gîtes. While she finished bringing the website up to date, she suggested gently but firmly that Owen clear up the office which seemed to have got into a very disorganized state since Clare departure only three days previously. Only when he had complied did she get up to reach for the keys and they headed out to make their inspection.

The cottages due to be let out for the following week were clean and the beds made up, as Solange knew they would be. But she nevertheless opened windows and dusted every room, sending Owen out to wipe down the garden furniture and make sure the barbeques were well stocked with charcoal and check the outdoors generally. She plugged in the fridges so that they would be ready for the following day and joined Owen in the garden when she was finished.

"All set?" he asked her.

"I shall put a bouquet of spring flowers from the garden into each gîte. But I will do that tomorrow," she replied. "So I am 'all set' as you Irish say."

"Great! I'm done here too. Want a coffee before we head to the manor house?"

"Yes, please. Or tea. I like tea."

"You've been corrupted by my mother, Solange, she lives on tea."

"From what I gather, so does everyone in Ireland."

They walked back companionably to the gatehouse gîte where the office was situated. Solange asked him about Ireland and if he missed it, if he was now finished university and what he intended to do. Owen found himself telling her all about Judith and how she had gone off to San Francisco for a year, leaving him rudderless, washed up ashore in France.

"This girl Judith. She is your girlfriend, yes?" said Solange.

"Well, yes, I suppose so. But her going away has changed all that," said Owen sadly.

"You will live here. You will wait for her, no?"

"That's the plan."

"For how long?"

"A year in America. Then she still has another year to go at Uni in Belfast."

"You will not wait two years, Owen."

"Actually, I'm beginning to think that myself. I'm not sure what to do."

"That is easy. You must go to San Francisco as soon as you can."

"Really?"

"Of course."

"Perhaps." Suddenly, the idea of going to San Francisco was not as urgent as it should've been.

They entered the office and this time Solange made tea. When they were settled at the kitchen table, Owen brought up the subject of her studies. He learnt that Solange was in her Master 1 year at the UBS

University in Vannes, not that far from Lorient, studying something to do with the management of coastal resources. It all seemed complicated but very interesting and the environmental aspect of her course had echoes in his own studies, which gave them common ground.

Before they knew it, it was after eleven and Owen reluctantly suggested they head to the manor house before everyone stopped work at midday for lunch.

In fact, once Solange understood Owen's worries about the insulation materials, which had a lot to do with him coming across polystyrene-backed plaster boards, totally unsuitable for the outside walls given their low porous characteristics and their inability to let the walls absorb ambient moisture, she set about finding the foreman to explain the problem, making it clear that Owen would not stand for this type of corner-cutting on no account.

The foreman was as relieved as Owen was to have Solange interpret and it soon became clear that these plaster boards were not destined for the outside walls but for the insulation of the internal walls of the four bedrooms upstairs. Downstairs the wood panelling, although old, was of excellent quality and served as internal wall insulation on that front. The outside walls were destined to have compact wood-chipping insulation treated with borates for fire-resistance and protection against insects with a vapour retarder between the insulation and the plasterboard or wood panelling. The foreman wished to point out that he, too, knew his job. He'd been doing it for twenty years, Monsieur, and had worked on several *Maisons de Maître* over the years and he knew their specificities and how to bring their energy consummation down to under 100/kWh/m2/an. He was aiming for 50/kWh, Monsieur, but *his* problem was to know when the windows would arrive. It was not easy to do *his* job properly until the new windows were in. And that's why his team, after insulating the attic space, were now concentrating on the indoor walls and hence the polystyrene plasterboard. *Il n'était pas fou!*

When Solange had regenerated all this back into English, Owen nodded and smiled his relief. It explained everything. Now his priority was to get on to the double-glazing people to get them to deliver the specially-made windows as quickly as possible. He resolved to get Solange to help him with this phone call that same afternoon and got her to translate this back to the chef, who nodded and smiled his approval.

It was amazing how everyone's irritation evaporated and their attitude changed, once they knew they were all on the same side. The foreman shook Owen's hand vigorously and gave Solange his heartiest thanks. Owen was giddy with relief as they walked back to the gîtes and sincerely thanked Solange for her help.

As it was just after midday and too late to phone the double-glazing company, Owen suggested cycling to the local bakery for fresh baguettes and said that he would make up sandwiches for them both. Solange watched him go, smiling at this young man whose stubbornness made up for his youth and floundering self-confidence, watching him test his wings in the professional world, trying to compensate for lack of experience. Next year it would be her turn to affront the artisans, the professionals and the complacent know-it-all's and claw her way into their respect. There were some things that five years of university did not even come close to equipping a person for. She was intuitive enough to know she would find all this out for herself soon enough.

By two pm, they had eaten, dealt with another booking and a request for an IT course which they had had to turn down, the next one not programmed until October, and set about calling the double-glazing firm. Solange knew the score and also that Frank had negotiated a very short lead-time to coincide with the insulating work being done on the house. There was no two ways about it. The windows were overdue.

Taking her queue from Owen, Solange was courteous but insistent. When told that it was a specially made-to-measure order which took longer and more expertise than standard windows, she agreed, and continued to request delivery as per the contract. In the end, after translating the situation to Owen, and on his suggestion, she obtained immediate delivery of those windows already completed, with a second delivery as soon as possible to complete the order, at no extra charge. The first lot of windows would arrive and be installed in two days. She rang the foreman on his mobile to let him know.

The rest of the afternoon, it being Friday, Owen went to spend it with Jean-Christophe in the garden while Solange inspected the pool area and games room, did some cleaning in the kitchen and bar areas and finished up back in the office. At half past five, as Owen was helping Jean-Christophe tidy his tools away and load up the trailer with grass-cuttings, he saw her wave over to them to say good-bye. He was thoughtful as he watched her drive away.

"*Elle a déjà un copain, mec*," said Jean-Christophe, giving him a nudge.

"*Er... moi aussi*," said Owen, which led Jean-Christophe to look at him askance and prompted Owen to wonder why.

-oOo-

Maître d'Oeuvre = project manager

Chapter Thirteen

Saint Avit des Landes

Clare was lucky in that her contact at the Saint Avit town hall was the mayor himself, who was extremely interested in local history and in Clare's particular story. When she told him how many hours she had been driving, he immediately suggested they take a short walk so that he could show her Meira's parents' shop, which he was pleased to announce that he had eventually found after several hours of painstaking research. He thought the walk would do them both good.

He was a pleasant man in his early sixties, an ex-Maths teacher, as she found out. His hair was quite abundant, salt and pepper, flopping over his forehead when he got excited. He was excited now, his large hands gesticulating in the air, explaining to her how he had despaired of finding trace of this jewellery shop until he consulted his good friend, Marius, a historian and until recently Saint Avit's librarian, who trawled through the land registries and cross-referenced that with local accounts of the war years and finally came up with its whereabouts.

They walked on, crossing the main square and over the footbridge which spanned the river and separated, to some extent, the old town from the new. Once on the other side, the streets became narrower, and seedier, although it was clear that a renovation programme was underway. The mayor walked on, Clare thinking to herself she should've worn trainers, as they were now making their way down a pedestrian zone laid out with areas of cobbled stone, reminders of days gone past and not particularly conducive to high heels. Finally, he stopped at a small, narrow, glass-fronted establishment, which turned out to be a *Salon de Thé*.

Inside the air was perfumed with a hundred different essences of tea, coffee, chocolates, macaroons and patisseries that were to die for. The large counter ran all the way down one side of the shop. Lit up and carefully cooled, it displayed an array of wonderful things to eat that had Clare's mouth watering in seconds. Behind the counter, about fifty sorts of tea were kept in large metal canisters, all of the same size and model, the different varieties indicated clearly on tiny blackboards. Opposite the counter were a smattering of tables and chairs and it was here that the mayor invited Clare to take a seat.

"So this was Meira's parents' shop, Monsieur Joubert?" she said in French, taking it all in.

"Without a doubt. We have checked," he replied. "Although it was not easy at the start."

He was interrupted by a young woman who came to give them menus and Monsieur Joubert advised Clare to try the *thé gourmand,* a selection of tiny pastries and macaroons accompanied by the tea of her choice. He chose the same and asked the waitress to inform her boss that he had brought Madame Hunter to meet her. He then continued his story.

"After Monsieur and Madame Leblang had been deported in 1943, someone, the SS probably, had painted a yellow Star of David on the door of the building and no-one dared to touch it. It lay like that for a long time. Some say the resistance used the cellars in it to hide people, some said it was haunted by the spirits of Monsieur and Madame Leblang. After the war, the shop was boarded up and left to become derelict. In this it was not alone. Rumour has it that there was a small Jewish quarter here and many other premises met a similar fate. In the 1990's, the local authorities began a renovation project of the old part of Saint Avit and the shop was scheduled for realignment, along with the buildings on either side of it, all of them empty for decades." He paused.

"How very sad!" said Clare "So it looks like Meira never made it home. Surely there would be some trace of her, if she'd had."

"Let me explain." said Monsieur Joubert, holding up his hand. "First I must prove to you that this is… was… Meira's home." He broke off as the waitress brought them their teas and placed a three-coloured egg-timer in front of them, explaining that Clare's tea needed 3 minutes to infuse, the green egg-timer, and Monsieur Joubert's needed five, the black egg-timer. Clare smiled her thanks.

"So, where was I? Yes. Well about twenty years ago, the *mairie* refurbished the buildings, re-doing electrics, and plumbing and replacing rotten flooring and windows etc. We became, by default, the new owners of these properties and rented the shops out to different people. All three shops had some sort of accommodation above them although they were not very big, and these had also been part of the refurbishment programme. Since then, this particular building has been a shoe-shop, a bakery, and now, a rather select tea-shop. The current occupant, Madame Blot, applied for, and obtained, permission to re-do the whole place again, including the attic space and the cellar. That was about five years ago, when she set up in business."

Monsieur Joubert paused to pour out Clare's tea which was now ready and invited her to try a macaroon. It was, to Clare's practiced taste, quite simply a slice of heaven on earth. She resolved to get the recipe somehow and make her own. Just then, they were joined at the table by a tall, elegant lady, of about Clare's own age, who kissed the mayor hello and held out her hand in greeting to Clare.

"Madame Blot, Hélène, bonjour. Thank you for coming, please join us." began the mayor. "Let me introduce you to Madame Hunter, who has undertaken to research into the Leblang family. I spoke to you about her on the phone."

"Bonjour Madame Hunter. Welcome to our little town," said Hélène Blot, "I have heard a lot about your quest from our mayor. Such a tragedy! So many tragedies in that awful war!"

"Indeed. So many lives lost, so many families decimated," agreed Clare sadly. "I am trying to help an old man in Ireland who may have descendants in France. Any information you could possibly give me would be very welcome."

"Ah, my excellent tea is now ready," broke in Monsieur Joubert. "May I offer you a cup, Hélène?"

"No, no thank you, I must not stay long. But I am, of course, willing to share with you any knowledge I have, Madame. Did *Monsieur le Maire* tell you about my discovery when we were refurbishing the attic?"

Clare turned to Monsieur Joubert who hastened to say: "I was just getting to that point when you arrived. But please, go ahead. I will savour one of your delicious little cakes and you will explain to Madame Hunter why there is no doubt that this was the Leblang family home." And he smiled, whether from being able to help

Clare with her quest or simply the exquisite taste of the patisserie, she wasn't quite sure.

Madame Blot stood up and went to the back of the shop, unlocked one of the cupboards there and brought out a small red metal box. She placed it gently on their table. It looked quite incongruous, totally out of place among the cakes and the egg-timer and their pots of tea. It was rusting in places, Clare could see that, but she could still make out the faded Toile de Jouy figurines that ornamented the sides and the lid.

She turned to Clare. "When we decided to insulate the attic space some years ago, that was when we turned the bakery into a tea-room, we had to replace the existing insulation which was outdated and not very effective. The workmen, they found this, locked, but with its little key hidden not far away under a rafter. They brought me both and I opened them. I was very surprised when I saw what was inside. It did not make sense at the time but now, thanks to you, things are becoming clearer."

She took the key and opened the box. Inside there was a small jewellery box and a yellowish folded letter. She silently handed the letter to Clare, who put on her glasses to see it better.

"May I read it?" she asked.

"But of course," said Madame Blot.

Clare began to read. *"Ma chère Meira,"* it began. Clare caught her breath, and looked up at her two companions, who nodded their encouragement to read on:

"Sweetheart, time is running out. They will be coming for us tomorrow or Thursday, from what we hear. We cannot get away and even if we could, we have nowhere to run to. This is our destiny and we must accept it, like our forefathers did before us. Our only consolation is that you have been able to escape. When we are feeling sad, we think about you and are happy to know that you are safe and sound and no longer in France.

This war is unjust. We have done nothing wrong, nothing to warrant such persecution. But God, in His goodness, has not forsaken us. He has blessed us with so many good things: the love I have for your mother and her love for me, our little jewellery business that has been our livelihood all these years, the friends we have made in Saint Avit. Your husband is a kind man, and he gave you good advice when he made you flee to England. We hope that one day you will be reunited, in a world without war and hate.

In this little box, we have put some jewellery and all the money that we have left. It is not a lot, but if ever you come back home, it is there for you.

Dear Meira, you have been the light of our lives. We love you so much, your mother and I. The memory of you, your pretty smile, goes everywhere with us and will remain in our hearts till the end. May God bless you.

*Your father, Jaron"**

It was hard not to cry. Clare felt a lump rising in her throat. She couldn't speak. She took a sip of tea to steady herself while Monsieur Joubert and Madame Blot remained silent, giving her time to ponder on what she had read.

"So we are sure that this was the house then," she managed at last.

"Yes, we are sure," agreed Monsieur Joubert.

"But there is more," said Madame Blot, "if you feel up to it?"

Clare took another sip of tea. She should be pleased. Things were moving forward at last. But it was all so heart-breaking. She braced herself to hear more, nodding to Madame Blot, not trusting herself to speak.

Madame Blot showed Clare the rest of the contents in the box. Gone, though, were the money and the jewels. Clare's face mirrored her disappointment. It was only to be expected, after all. All that remained was the little jewellery box, which she gently took out and examined. It was the sort of box for putting earrings in, or even a ring. When Clare opened it, another letter, folded many times, fell out.

This time, it was just a note, hurriedly scribbled on a page from an old exercise book, yellowed with age and curling at the corners. Madame Blot helped Clare to spread it out taking precautions not to rip the fragile paper.

"To whom it may concern," began this note in French. *"The baby is a girl. We have called her Aurore, meaning Dawn. Her mother's name meant Ray of Light. It seemed a fitting thing to do. Before she died, she told us where to look and we found the box with the money and jewels. We will use them to help the baby. That is all we can do. It is better than the orphanage for a Jewish child in these troubled times. We are not thieves. We are good Christians and she will be brought up like one of us."*

It was dated Saint Avit, 21st November 1945.

So Meira was dead, after all. Clare sighed. It explained at lot, her silence and the fact that she never contacted George again. She must've died in childbirth, or shortly after, and her child taken in by someone else, someone kind enough not to want the baby to be brought up in an orphanage, but in a family.

"We think," said Monsieur Joubert, breaking into Clare's sombre thoughts," we think that Meira may have found the box and read her father's letter before she died. How else could she tell the people who adopted her daughter where to find it?"

"So she would have found out that her parents were deported, and dead," continued Madame Blot. "Perhaps the shock of this hastened her into labour. We can only make conjectures."

"But who are these people who adopted Aurore?" said Clare, anxious to piece together all the information she was receiving.

"Alas, we do not know," said Monsieur Joubert, shrugging his shoulders. "But we are trying to find out. You must be patient, Madame Hunter. French administration is complex and slow. And we have only just obtained this information. Do you not see? Your quest to find Meira's heirs is the missing link between the past and the present, the discovery of these letters five years ago meant nothing until now. But today all is different and I have every hope that we will succeed."

Clare looked from one to the other, these kind people that were trying their best to help her find George's heir.

"Of course," she said brightly. "You have already done so much. How can I ever thank you for your help?" And she smiled.

"You will perhaps stay for a few days, no?" said the mayor. "We have much to do. We will search for any births that are registered in Saint Avit, in November and December of 1945, for any little baby girls called Aurore. We do not have a surname, unfortunately, unless she was registered under Leblang or Hamilton, but we do have somewhere to start. I do not know how far back we can go with our local archives but if we come away empty-handed, we will then try Dax which holds the county archives for the whole of the Landes region."

"You are so kind, Monsieur Joubert. And you, too, Madame Blot." Clare folded both letters and put them back in the box. "May I keep this?" she asked. "If we find Meira's child, I will make sure she gets this, and if not, I would like her father to see it in Ireland before he dies. He is a very old man now and he is counting on me."

"But of course, you must keep it. You are the right person to have it. We have been waiting for you," insisted the mayor. And seeing the tears in Clare's eyes, gently suggested another cup of tea.

-oOo-

*"Ma Chère Meira,

Chérie, le temps nous est compté. Ils viendront demain, ou jeudi, selon les dires. Nous ne pouvons pas fuir et nous n'avons pas d'endroit où aller. C'est notre destin et nous devons l'accepter, tout comme nos pères l'ont fait avant nous. Notre seule consolation est que tu aies pu t'échapper. Lorsqu'il nous arrive d'être tristes, nous pensons à toi, heureux de savoir que tu es saine et sauve et hors de la France.

Cette guerre est injuste, nous n'avons rien fait de mal, rien qui ne justifie une telle persécution. Mais Dieu, dans sa bonté, ne nous a pas abandonnés. Il nous a bénis avec tant de bonnes choses, l'amour que j'ai pour ta mère, et son amour pour moi, notre petit commerce de bijouterie qui nous a fait vivre toutes ces années, les amis que nous avons fait ici à Saint Avit. Ton mari est un homme bien, qui t'a bien conseillée en te faisant fuir vers l'Angleterre. Puisse un jour vous pourriez être réunis de nouveau, dans un monde sans guerre et sans haine.

Dans cette petite boite, nous avons mis quelques bijoux et tout l'argent qu'il nous reste. Ce n'est pas grand 'chose, mais si jamais tu reviens à la maison, ils sont là pour toi.

Chère Meira, tu as été la lumière de nos vies. Ta mère et moi, nous t'aimons tant. Ton souvenir, ton joli sourire, nous accompagnent partout, et resteront gravés dans nos cœurs jusqu'à la fin. Que Dieu te bénisse.

Ton père, Jaron. "

Chapter Fourteen

Dax

Monsieur Joubert called for Clare at her hotel the following morning at half past nine. She was sitting in the lobby determined to be on time and not keep this kind man waiting. She wondered briefly why he was giving up so much of his time when he probably had quite a lot of administrative work to carry out but when she mentioned this to him, he dismissed his work at the *Mairie* with a wave of his hand, not unlike waving away a persistent fly.

"That is what assistants are for, Clare. I may call you Clare, may I?" he said smiling. "I feel I am getting to know you very well and if we do find Meira's baby, Aurore, I want to be there to say 'I, Marcel Joubert, had a hand in this!' It is all very good propaganda for the next local elections, you see."

Clare laughed. "Of course, please call me Clare and I shall call you Marcel. But only in private. If we are with your electors, you shall be *Monsieur le Maire*."

"Ah, I see that we shall get along perfectly, you and I. Now, I have brought my car because we will be going to Dax. Since yesterday afternoon, my staff have been searching for information about the registration of the birth of Aurore in Saint Avit and they tell me there is nothing to find here because our archives do not go back that far. Dax is about forty minutes away and the archives are enormous. But I have been pulling a few strings since this morning, and we have someone who is already bringing out the births, deaths and marriage registers of 1945 and 1946 for us at the town hall there. After that, we will have to go through them ourselves, by hand, starting with those registered in Saint Avit. But the child may not have been registered here, or not registered at all." He looked at Clare's stricken face. "It was a perfect time to get around administrative obligations, Clare, French bureaucracy was in tatters. Civil servants were trying desperately to pick up the threads of post-war France and it is likely that some errors and omissions may have occurred."

"Well, all we can do is hope, Marcel, and pray that this family who adopted Aurore gave her some sort of identity."

On the drive to Dax, Clare was fascinated by the amount of pine forest they were driving through. In fact, everywhere was forest, broken only by little towns and villages and the roads were Roman-road straight, no doubt to facilitate the control of forest fires. She shuddered.

Marcel rattled on about the Landes region, its wood industry, its bull-fights, its triumphs and occasional catastrophes. It was a region that could be affected by floods and storms, as well as fires, but these things were rare and most of the time their huge, beautiful forest, their wonderful climate and their long, un-spoilt beaches, made it one of the nicest regions of France. As they drove, Clare noticed the architecture of the typical Landes-region house, with its long sloping roof to one side and arched windows and all around, the pine trees that dominated the horizon.

Her thoughts went back to Aurore, this baby girl saved from a solitary, unloved life in a post-war orphanage by a family that was not Jewish. Would they have told her about her origins? Would she then have tried to find her father? Probably not, if Meira had not said anything about George. Perhaps this family thought the father was Meira's husband, now dead. Perhaps they thought she had been abused and this baby was the result.

Clare shook herself. This baby she kept envisaging was now seventy years old. A pensioner, some eighteen years older than Clare herself! How many seventy-year-olds were there in France with a first name Aurore? Hundreds of thousands, probably. A needle in a haystack! And what if she were already dead? Would they have to continue the hunt for *her* descendants? Would they have the energy, or the time? For the first time Clare was to admit to herself that she had embarked on an impossible task.

No, she chided, they must find some clue to the family that adopted Aurore. And the first place to start was the registration of her birth. Clare hoped fervently that Aurore had been brought up by a loving family. After all that her grandparents went through, and all that Meira went through, surely Aurore deserved a happy childhood.

There was the money and the jewels, of course. They would have gone a long way to help pay for the child's keep in those troubled, post-war years when everything, especially food, was scarce. But if Meira had told the family about the box with the money and the jewels, why had she not told them about George, the child's father? Was she ashamed to admit having conceived a child out of wedlock in front of this Christian family? Was she afraid? Or did the family know about George and chose to ignore that fact? He was a foreigner, this was an illegitimate child. Why would he be interested in a baby he was in no position to offer a home to? Perhaps the family thought they were protecting Aurore by not trying to contact George.

And perhaps they did and the letter got lost. Who was to say what could have happened? It was hard to pick up the threads after a gap of seventy years. God knows it would be a miracle if she succeeded.

Clare was delivered of these worrying thoughts by their entry into Dax, a large busy town and regional capital, bathed in the hot morning sun of late May. Clare wondered what it must be like in the summer with its tourists and its feria. Marcel pointed out to her some of the thermal bath establishments informing her that over 50,000 people came every year to take the waters and was a very important source of income to the town. Thermal baths had been in operation in Dax for over a thousand years, he said, and had the reputation of helping in particular those suffering from rheumatism. Clare thought privately that this was probably quite a lucrative business, given the number of people over-fifty concerned.

They drove on over the river Adour, past the Cathedral Notre Dame Sainte Marie, Marcel taking a roundabout way to show Clare as much of the town as possible. They stopped briefly at the Fontaine Chaude, this hot-water spring that symbolizes the importance of the thermal baths at Dax throughout the ages. Finally, they pulled up in front of the town hall.

Even though Saint Avit was only a small and rather insignificant satellite in the administration of Dax, Marcel Joubert was nonetheless known, and greeted with deference and ceremony. They were rapidly led into a small but brightly-lit office where registers of births, deaths and marriages for the years 1945 and 1946 had been laid out and were issued with plastic surgical gloves. A junior administrative assistant came to inform them that coffee was available in an adjoining room but must not be brought into contact with the ledgers. Both Clare and Marcel opted for a coffee first and perusal of the ledgers second and it was quite some ten minutes later that they sat down to begin their search.

After discussing with Marcel the best way to move forward, it was decided that Clare would concentrate on the months of November and December 1945 to start with, while Marcel would take the 1946 ledger and begin with January. Each birth entry contained an "Extrait d'Acte de Naissance", a full page long, with information about the child born, the names, dates of birth and professions of its parents, their address, the date and place of declaration of birth and the names, grades and ages of the officials who had made out the declaration. In fact, thought Clare, there was almost more information about the officials than the actual child. Still, it was a work of art, hand-written in beautiful, sloping italics, signed and stamped in several places. In the margin, the name of the child and its date of birth were underlined and any subsequent event such as marriage and death were added. All in all, it was a relatively well-documented piece of work. If only they had had Aurore's surname, they could have obtained all the information they were looking for immediately, even online. As it was, it was going to have to be done manually. Marcel had already had his staff try "Leblang", "Leblanc" and "Hamilton" with no result.

Clare sighed and began to scrutinize those entries from the 1st November onwards.

Some two hours later, she got up to pour herself another coffee. She was stiff from sitting and her eyes were sore. She had only come across three little girls called Aurore in all the month of November. These she had written down carefully as Marcel had asked her to. He now came to join her.

"Well, Clare, how is it going?" he asked. "Yes, thanks, I need a coffee too."

"Only three, so far. We're lucky in a way. 'Aurore' was not such a common name then as it is now. How about you?"

"Only one in all of January. I am going cross-eyed trying to skim down so many entries."

"The writing is beautiful, isn't it? So carefully done."

"Indeed. I am afraid we have lost all that with our computers these days. Why, even in primary school, children are learning to type faster than they learn to write. When I was a child we had to write with quills and ink and learn how not to make blots. It was quite a skill."

"Painstakingly beautiful, though, and now no longer taught in the same way."

"So what shall we do?" said Marcel, changing the subject. "It is almost mid-day and everything stops at the

Town Hall until half past one. Shall we look for somewhere nice to eat? We can take a walk along the banks of the Adour, if you like."

"Yes, I'd like that very much," said Clare. "Thank you. But lunch is on me, or rather on George. The solicitor who asked me to take on this research is handling expenses."

"In that case, I accept," said Marcel, smiling. "We will have a nice cold beer and raise our glasses to the good health of George."

The afternoon passed away in their continued search. By five pm, Clare had done December and also back-tracked two weeks of October. Marcel had got as far as the end of March. They decided that if the birth of Aurore had been registered in that region, she was surely among the eleven names they had singled out. If she had been registered elsewhere, the chances of being found were altogether too slim to take things much further. They decided to call it a day.

Clare fell asleep on the journey home, only waking when Marcel pulled up in front of her hotel. They agreed to meet up the following afternoon to study what they had come up with, Marcel having two meetings in the morning that he could not possibly postpone.

In a way, Clare was grateful for the break. After calling the gîtes and speaking to Frank and Owen, she dined at the hotel and had an early night.

The following day was Friday and Clare realized with dismay that she had less than seven or eight hours before she needed to be on the road back to Brittany. She decided not to wait for Marcel but began studying the eleven birth certificates to see if anything could distinguish 'her' Aurore from the others.

Only two of the Aurore's had been registered in Saint Avit. This was probably the best place to start, although in this, Clare knew that a phone call from a perfect stranger, and a foreigner at that, would be less likely to produce results than if it were a call from the mayor of Saint Avit himself. She set them aside and examined the others.

It was frustrating because all the birth certificates seemed perfectly straight forward with the names, professions and dates of birth of the parents clearly indicated. She decided to write out all eleven names, more for something to do than anything else. At the *Mairie* this afternoon, it would be easy to check up on these women online. Most of them were married and the names of their spouses had been added to the certificates. Two of the Aurore's were deceased, though not the ones registered in Saint Avit. She looked down the names again.

Suddenly, one of the names struck her as odd. This person had been registered as Aurore Amilta Delormeau and her parents were from Mont de Marsan. It was the Amilta that had Clare's skin beginning to tingle. Hamilton, Amilta, the French would not know that Hamilton was spelt with an 'H'. Could it be? Could it possibly be?

Chapter Fifteen

Ian & Céline

Céline was back to watching the post, or to be more precise, going on the Internet Academy website and waiting for her name to come up. She kept telling herself that there was very little chance that the schools she had selected would offer her a permanent posting so early on in her career but it was only human nature to hope.

And she really couldn't discuss it with Ian. He was already like a cat on a hot tin roof, berating the French education system whenever he got the chance, expostulating for all to hear (Céline) that it wasn't fair she could still be sent all over France, like some family in the military, that they couldn't put down roots, that their temporary accommodation in Laval, a nice, modern house, cost the earth in rent, that it was money out the window when they had a hefty deposit in the bank all ready for purchasing something. What was the point of having sold the Japanese casket and got all that money if they couldn't use it?

There were times, just sometimes, when Ian did Céline's head in.

Her thoughts wandered to the casket and all that had happened the previous year. Who would've thought that Kieran's little wedding present would be worth so much? One hundred and eighty-five thousand euros it had fetched at auction, over three times the price it had been estimated at! The casket was originally Paul's, having been given to him by his late godfather, donated to the Kilmore charity shop by Paul's mother, spotted by Eileen and set it aside for Kieran who had paid £15 for it as a wedding present for Céline and it had ended up in France. That was, until Paul's ex-wife Anita had shown up, suspecting its worth and wanting to get her hands on it.

Céline had never had the opportunity to meet Anita but to all intents and purposes, she was a nasty piece of work. She would never forget how Anita had had Paul's flat trashed; how Ian had ended up being mistaken for Paul and almost getting kidnapped by those awful thugs; how there had been a fight and even young Kieran was involved. She shuddered when she remembered the bruises on Ian's body after the attack. She had not wanted him to go to Ireland that time, she remembered, she had felt trouble in her bones.

But it had all worked out in the end. Anita had been fobbed off with an expensive imitation casket that Paul and Ian had gone to Paris for and the real casket had been sold in France and the money from it, by common assent, divided up among Paul, Kieran and Ian and Céline. It was helping Paul and Sharon buy a bigger house in Kilmore and Kieran would not have to take out a bank loan to pay for his university fees, and here in France it was also to be used as a deposit on a house, *if* and *when*, they could put down roots. Meanwhile, it was burning a hole in Ian's pocket and doing nothing to sweeten his temper.

Céline sighed. It was all so frustrating. She was now into the website and waiting for the results. The decisions were to be taken today or tomorrow, according to where the posting was requested, the current needs in that sector, the length of time the postulant had been in the education system (only one year for Céline), and all this conditioned by her getting through her probationary year (she was fairly confident about this as she had had good reviews by the education inspectors). But it was quite unheard of for someone in her position, after only a year's teaching, to obtain a permanent post in a town of her choice. She knew it and Ian knew it; the difference being that Ian refused to believe it. She was grateful he was working in Rennes today and that her last class of the day had finished at three pm. She could check the website in peace.

All evening she refreshed the page until it was obvious that her name was not going to come up. If it didn't come up today or tomorrow, then she would have to wait until July to see what temporary posting (or postings) she had been given. Oh dear!

Back in Ireland, Kieran got out of the car, shook hands with the inspector and got slowly into the driving instructor's car, passenger's side, to wait for him. He sat there, staring into space, letting the warm sensation of success sweep over his body before it finished up on his face, lighting it up into a wide grin. He'd passed! He'd passed his driving test and now he could drive! He could go wherever he wanted; no more depending on his mother, or Paul, to give him lifts. No more busing it to work in Tesco's. He was free, free as a bird. He squirmed with pleasure.

Now he could buy his car, the money from the casket was there to help him for that. He could take Beth out and they could do whatever they liked. Life was *good*!

He sat there smiling, his thoughts miles away, when the driving instructor opened the door and asked him what did he think he was doing in the passenger seat, when there was a perfectly good driver's seat waiting for him to occupy? Kieran laughed. He thought briefly that he would never be able to calm down enough to drive but once behind the wheel, all the automatic reflexes took over and he pulled away from the kerb with confidence.

When they got back to Kilmore, Kieran found Sharon and Eileen waiting for him with baited breath. No time to phone Beth, he was assailed with hugs of joy from his mother and grandmother. Then he had to sit down, have a cup of tea and tell them all about it, Eileen 'ooing' and 'ahhing' at every pause. He could see his mother was quietly pleased; it made him feel warm inside.

"Now, you'll be able to get that wee car you were wanting to buy," said Eileen, clasping her hands.

"Yes, gran. Paul's going to take me there on Saturday."

"Can't I come?" said Sharon, grinning.

"Mum, aren't you on duty that day?" said Kieran stalling. The last thing he wanted was his mother with him to help him buy a car.

"Luckily for you, I am," said Sharon, who knew exactly what her son was thinking.

"Aw Mum… it's a man's thing. You know?"

"Never been one, Kieran, but don't worry, I've no intention of cramping your style. Now, aren't you going to ring Beth to give her the good news?"

This was the escape Kieran was waiting for and he ran happily up the stairs to his old bedroom to ring Beth.

When he came down, some fifteen minutes later, Eileen was just about to leave and Sharon was dangling her car-keys, smiling.

"Well, even if you don't want your mother's help to choose a car, I've nonetheless put you on my insurance, Kieran."

"Oh Mum! That's really great!"

"So why don't you run Eileen home, get the feel of it?"

"God, yeah! Thanks Mum, thanks a million."

Eileen's smile was nearly as wide as Kieran's as they made their way out of the house and into Sharon's car. Kieran settled himself, adjusted the mirror, adjusted the seat, put his seatbelt on and reversed carefully out of the short drive. It only took two minutes to get to Eileen's cottage; Kieran never got past second gear. Still, it gave them both a thrill and when they got there, Kieran proudly got out of the car to open the passenger door for his gran.

On the way back, he couldn't resist having a quick drive round Kilmore town centre, telling himself that he wouldn't be long. The thrill of driving a car without having someone sitting beside him, ready to pounce on the dual controls, was intoxicating. Kieran took the car out of town and up into fifth gear. He put the radio on, found a station he liked and let the music blast out. God, this was *it*!

Racing along, the window open and the wind whipping his hair, Kieran was living the thrill of his life.

He thought dreamily that it was almost as thrilling as making love to Beth. After Saturday, he'd have his own car and be able to take Beth out wherever they wanted. He imagined them making love in his new car, out in the country somewhere, where no-one could see them. Oh, the freedom of it!

Kieran's thoughts ran happily along in this self-satisfied day-dream until he found himself, some twenty minutes later, back in Kilmore and sweeping into the drive of Sharon's house. His thoughts still on Beth, he realized he had misjudged the angle of the gateway and that he was parked all wrong. He decided to reverse out and take the car in again. He didn't want Sharon saying that he didn't do things right. Kieran put the car into gear and reversed.

A sickening crunch jolted the car to a stop and the engine conked out. Kieran looked behind him to see Paul getting out of his car with a look on his face that, even at this distance, boded no good.

"Kieran, you *eejit*! Look what you've done to my car!" he cried angrily. "Don't they teach you at that driving school to look behind you when you reverse?"

"But Paul," said Kieran, cringing, "I looked in the mirror but I was trying to straighten her up. If I'd known you'd be arriving at the same time, I'd never have reversed at all."

"The mirror isn't enough. You've to turn your head. And you've got to be prepared, Kieran, at all times and for all eventualities." He bent to get a closer look.

"Oh my God! That's your mother's car. Look at it! Just look at it!"

Kieran looked. For such a tiny accident, the damage was indeed impressive. His mother's car had a rear light broken and the fender was all bent. So was the number plate from what he could see. Paul's car also had a broken light, a buckled fender and even the wing was dented. How all that could happen in such a short space of time was beyond him. They weren't even going fast!

"I'm really sorry. I didn't mean it... I passed, Paul. I passed my test and Mum said I could take gran home. And I went for a spin and it was great and I wasn't thinking... I'm sorry," he finished lamely.

"Where's your 'R' plates, then, if you passed?" went on Paul, relentlessly.

"My 'R' plates? I haven't bought them yet. I've only just passed."

"So what were you doing out on the road without them, then? Eileen lives two minutes away, Kieran," shouted Paul, pointing in the general direction of Eileen's house. "I'm sure Sharon didn't mean for you to take her car any further."

Paul was so angry; Kieran had never seen him like that before. He didn't know what to say. He wanted to turn the clock back ten minutes and reverse out more carefully so that the accident would never have happened. If he'd been watching properly, he would not have damaged both Paul and Sharon's cars. God, what a *mess*!

"Paul, I'm sorry. I wasn't paying attention. I'll pay for the damage... to both cars, I promise."

"You're bloody right, you'll pay," said Paul. "Neither your mother nor I are going to lose our bonuses by making an insurance claim. And you'll not be using the casket money either. That's several hundred quid's worth of damage you've just caused. And I expect you to pay for it with the money you saved from Tesco's."

And he stormed off into the house, leaving Kieran looking helplessly at the damaged cars.

"Paul, what's happened? What's up?" said a seriously worried Sharon as Paul came into the kitchen.

"Oh, it's nothing serious," said Paul, sighing. "But I've just been teaching that son of yours a lesson. He's only gone and damaged both our cars! I've been reading him the riot act. He'll be more careful in the future, believe you me."

"Damaged the cars? Both of them? How did he do that? Is he hurt?" Sharon, anxious to know what had happened, nevertheless chided herself for putting this question last.

"Yep. Not paying attention. Did you know he'd been out on the main road without his 'R' plates?"

"*What?* He was only supposed to go as far as Eileen's. Just as a treat for passing his test."

"Well, Mister Kieran thinks he can do what he likes. He *did* take the car out on the road and he admits that he wasn't paying attention. I want him to remember the consequences of not paying attention, Sharon, even if he *did* only pass his test today. He's getting far too sure of himself, that lad. One of these days his not paying attention could end up getting himself, or worse, other people killed or injured."

"You're right, Paul," said Sharon, "I was starting to get really worried when he didn't come back at once. And him taking the car out on the road without my permission and without the 'R' plates!" She exhaled. "Yes, you're damned right to make a fuss. I'll play along too when he comes in."

"That's my girl," said Paul, kissing her on the nose. "Now, I'm going to take my car to Murray's to see when they can do the repairs. I'll book yours in too, but not at the same time. Mine's more serious because of the front light being broken. I can't use it after dark."

"And what's the damage to mine?"

"Fender, number plate, rear-light. Nothing that can't be fixed. Don't worry. But Mr Kieran's paying for the damage out of his savings. I'm not letting him use the casket money and anyway, he won't get that for another few months till he comes of age."

"Oh dear! And he was so looking forward to buying that car with you on Saturday."

"Yeah. I was going to lend him the money till he got his own. That's not going to happen now, unfortunately." He sighed. "If I don't make Kieran realize that what he did was serious, then I may as well pat him on the back and tell him not to worry. Now I'm going to stomp out there and pretend I'm still angry at him. I'll see you later, love."

And he was off, doing, Sharon thought, a pretty good imitation of a stomp.

"He was raging, Beth," said Kieran mournfully later that evening in Paul's flat. "Really, really, pissed off. I've never seen him so angry. God, I feel awful"

"He'll calm down, Kieran, you'll see," said Beth gently.

"We should've been out celebrating! And, instead of that, the last I saw of him, he just got back into his car without another word and drove off."

"So what did you do then?"

"Well, I got back into Mum's car and parked it properly. Then I went into the house to face *her*. She was none too pleased either. Said she was worried because I didn't come straight back from gran's, that she didn't know if she could trust me anymore. Oh, and other things I just want to forget. I felt wick, Beth. Then she handed me the broom and the dustpan and told me to make sure that I didn't leave any broken glass on the driveway. By the time I'd done that, she'd gone upstairs and she didn't come down again. She didn't even make the dinner. So I bought myself a carry-out at the chippy and came back here."

"Perhaps they're trying to teach you a lesson."

"Me? But I'll be eighteen in November! I'm not a child, Beth."

"Umm..."

"You don't sound convinced. Whose side are you on?"

"It's not a question of sides, Kieran. You messed things up and they're mad at you."

"So what would you do to make things right? I've already offered to pay for everything and Paul won't let me use the casket money... which, incidentally, I think is a bit mean."

"Why don't you do something nice like buying your Mum flowers and getting Paul something too? Show them you care? I'm sure they'd forgive you if you make a gesture of some sort."

"Like in 'grovel', you mean," said Kieran with sarcasm.

"Precisely! Look at all they do for you, Kieran. Your Mum hasn't always had it easy. And Paul lets us use his flat, which he doesn't have to." She smiled, coaxing. "And he knows perfectly well what we get up to here."

"Oh, alright. I'll grovel."

He grinned suddenly, back to his old cheeky self. "Now, after all that I need comforting, Beth. Any ideas?"

"A few."

"Me too! Come here."

"So what happened then?" said Margaret avidly when Eileen had finished telling her the whole tale.

"Well, he came back yesterday evening when he knew they'd both be finished work and apologized and presented them with a voucher to have dinner in that nice new restaurant in Kilmore. You know? The one that only opened a few months ago. 'The Lemon' or something like that. They say it's quite good."

"Oh, the Orangery. Yes, John took me there one Saturday night about a month ago. The food's good and the décor is really quite nice. It's not very well known yet but I think it's going to take off one of these days."

"Well, as I say, all's well that ends well. They both forgave him, it's hard to stay cross with our Kieran for long, and Paul's going to go with him to see about a car Saturday as originally planned."

"Well, I suppose it's been a lesson to him, Eileen, he'll drive more carefully from now on."

"He will at that. Sharon told me that she'd never seen our Kieran so downcast."

"I can't imagine Kieran eating humble pie. So very out of character, don't you think?"

"Sure it won't do him a bit of harm. God, he reminds me so much of his father at that age. Did I ever tell you what happened to him, when he took his driving test?"

"No! What happened?"

"Well, it was like this..."

-oOo-

Chapter Sixteen

Saturday at the gîtes

Friday evening brought a phone call from Clare to say that she couldn't possibly leave Saint Avit as they were on the point of an important breakthrough in the quest to find George's heirs. She promised to be home on Saturday evening but meantime could Owen continue to hold the fort?

Clare's arguments were that Frank would be there for the week-end and Solange would be around all day Saturday. With only three gîtes to clean and four rentals for the following week, she had every confidence that he could manage quite well.

She then went on to give him a list of instructions as long as your arm about all that had to be done, making sure he wrote it down so as to forget nothing. Owen put the phone down feeling put upon and out-of-sorts. Did his mother not realize all that he'd already done that week? He was working harder now than he'd ever done, even for his course. What kind of sabbatical was this?

He decided to go have a swim and forget that the gîtes and the manor house existed. The pool was already occupied with children from the Dutch families, having a last-minute splash around before leaving the next day. Still, he managed to get in quite a few lengths before being the last to climb out. Then he automatically set about tidying up the pool area and the games room to make them ready for the next day's flow of guests.

Thinking about the Saturday, and the changeovers, he logically got to thinking about Solange. He found himself looking forward to seeing her again, which was a strange feeling to have, given that he loved Judith. And what was it Jean-Christophe had said? She already had a boyfriend. Well, that was that, then, wasn't it?

When he got back, Frank was already home and doing the evening meal. Father and son ate early, as both were hungry, and then went to have their regular walk to the manor house to see how things were coming on. Owen explained what a good help Solange had been that day by translating for him and helping him clear up misunderstandings. He felt that they were all getting somewhere at last and was looking forward to Monday when the first batch of new windows was due to arrive. He was more confident now that before the end of June, they could all move into the manor house and free up the gatehouse gîte, even if it meant sharing a dingy bathroom and a seriously outdated kitchen. It would be better than camping in the garden at least.

Much later that evening, when Frank was watching the late night news in French, Owen went back to his own gîte to call Judith on Skype. He longed suddenly to be close to her, to feel her skin, smell her smell, revel in the good times they'd had together. He was pleased when she answered almost immediately.

"Oh, Owen, you've just caught me as I was going out. How's things?"

"Oh, you know, busy. Mum's away at the moment so I'm more or less managing the gîtes on my own. Plus supervising the refurbishment of the manor house; it's all go. And what about you Judy, how's it going for you?"

"Fantastic. I love it here. They're really nice people and my boss is giving me proper jobs to do, just as if I were qualified! Then we get together and talk about them and he gives me ideas and keeps me straight. It's such a good opportunity, Owen, I'd never get this in Ireland or England. I'm so glad I came."

"Oh... really?"

"Absolutely! And they don't leave me on my own at week-ends either. I've been invited to the boss's house. He's really nice, and so's his wife. And I'm just off now with Brad and Jenny and some of their friends for a few days. We're heading to Brad's parents' chalet near Carson City. It's gonna be awesome."

"Ah, well, if it's gonna be awesome..."

"Owen, now you're cross. You'll have to come over and see it all for yourself. You'd really like it too. There's times when I think I don't ever want to go home."

"Well, I can't get away in the foreseeable future, what with the house and the gîtes and the season about to start. They're counting on me here."

"I can see that. Never mind. Perhaps you'll get way after the summer? Hey, I'm sorry, Owen, but I really must go. They'll be here any minute. Say hello to your parents for me, won't you?"

"Yeah. Have a nice week-end."

"You bet! Bye, Owen."

And she disconnected.

Owen came away from the conversation, if anything, even more frustrated. Judith, with her '*awesomes*' and her '*you bets*' was already turning into an American. He could see that she was not missing him one little bit. He sat looking at the empty screen, then slowly closed the lap-top. What felt funny was the fact that he should be more upset. They'd been together for over a year. She'd been out to France twice, or was it three times?

He thought tenderly of the good times they'd spent together, her quirky sense of humour, setting up home in the flat, the sex which had been great. He still loved Judith in a sense but was he actually *in love* with her? He tried to analyse what was wrong. He missed her; that much was clear. But would he be willing to wait a year, or even two, for her to come back?

Suddenly it came to him that even if he did, Judith certainly wouldn't be hanging around that long. He was going to have to face the fact that it was over, he could see that now. She might not have started dating anyone else but it was just a question of time.

He put his head in his hands and thought. What could he do? What did he *want* to do? He knew he didn't want things to continue on in this limbo-land of maybes. Perhaps Judith was letting him down gently. It did look that way. So it was up to him to put a stop to it all. And sadly, there was no time like the present.

He re-opened his lap-top and went into email.

He was surprised to find that he had managed to sleep quite well in spite of the email he had prepared the night before. He hadn't sent it yet; he wanted to make sure that he still felt the same way in the cold light of day. Unfortunately, in the cold light of day, he was feeling even more lonely and abandoned than the night before. With a heavy heart, he re-read his email, took the only decision he could, and pressed the send button.

After a quick breakfast, which went a long way to cheering him up, he decided to head over to the office in the gatehouse gîte and be there for when Solange arrived. Frank had said he would be working on the manor house garden for most of the morning and would be leaving Owen and Solange to look after the website and take care of the changeover.

Solange was there on the dot of nine and greeted Owen the French way with a kiss on both cheeks. He was startled and pleased, not yet realizing that Solange would greet Frank and Clare in exactly the same way when they met up. He hastened to make her a coffee while she sat down at the computer to check the website.

"Solange, do you know how to add another gîte to the website?" he asked.

"Yes, it is not very complicated to do. Why do you ask?"

"This gîte here, the gatehouse, will be available for renting from July onwards. The manor house will be habitable in a few weeks, end of June at the latest, and I know Mum wants to put this place on the website so that we can start taking bookings. The other gîtes are all fairly booked up for the summer and she told me she was confident this gîte would get booked up too."

"I agree. Last year we turned down bookings for July and August. What is good is that some of the guests are coming back. After the first year, they book again the next year."

"So what do we need?"

"Well, pictures mainly. Photos of the exterior and the interior." She looked around at the office which was set up in one of the bedrooms and was rather small and cluttered. "Although not of this room. And a description in French and in English."

"We could do that, couldn't we?" said Owen, eager to spend time with Solange and not just for cleaning the gîtes.

She laughed. "Yes, we shall do that. That is what we shall do today."

Owen beamed.

"But first we have to put flowers in the four gîtes that are rented out for next week. We also have three gîtes to clean this afternoon when the current guests are gone. And this morning, we have to check the swimming-pool area and the games room. They are big. They take time to clean."

"I've already done the swimming-pool. Did it last night," said Owen proudly.

"So you have washed the floors and cleaned the toilets?"

"*What?*"

"That is what cleaning is, Owen," she answered, highly amused.

Solange kept Owen very busy all morning long. They spent over two hours working on the pool and games-room, vacuuming, washing floors, windows, making him clean the men's toilets while she did the ladies'.

Then it was time to say good-bye to the Dutch people and the French couple who thanked them for a lovely stay. Solange handed them a little goodies bag each with reminders of their stay in the form of a post-it block and pen with the name, phone number and website of the gîtes printed on them, a calendar for the following year with a picture of the gîtes and again, contact information, and finally some workbooks in English for the Dutch children to keep them occupied on the journey home. Owen was quietly amazed at how these little trinkets brought them all pleasure and admired his mother's marketing skills. Here were two families that were happy with their stay and might well come back. For that they had been given all they needed so as not to lose touch.

It was by now getting near lunchtime and Owen suggested nipping to the bakery to buy baguettes for lunch. Once again, he looked after the meal, calling Frank on his mobile who said he would join them. He came in looking dirty and tired, so different from the dapper-dressed Frank who went to the language school most days. But he was glad of the physical exercise, he said, and the garden was looking good. He went off to shower before lunch.

In the afternoon, while Frank manned the office, Solange took Owen out to clean the three gîtes that had been left vacant. To Owen, they weren't in a bad state, having been left, on inspection, quite clean. But that was without counting on the demands of Solange who made him help her vacuum, and clean bathrooms and kitchens, and make up beds, and defrost the fridges. Even the bar-b-cues had to be cleaned and stocked again with bags of charcoal and the little terrace areas washed down. Owen thought wryly no wonder his father had preferred to duck out of these particular tasks. What must it be like in the height of the season with eight gîtes to clean in the four-hour window between the guests leaving and the news ones arriving? It didn't bear thinking about.

In fact, by the time they had finished, the new guests were starting to arrive. Frank accompanied them to their gîte and introduced Owen and Solange as their paths crossed.

"Now, how about a coffee?" said Owen when they were on their own once again. "I'll make you one in my place, if you like," he suggested.

"Yes, I would like that," she replied smiling. "We have deserved a break for we have worked hard."

Owen secretly wondered if he hadn't shot himself in the foot. After all the cleaning they'd been doing, his little gîte was definitely lived-in. Books and CD's were strewn all around the sitting-room, the kitchen still had his breakfast things on the table and this was one time he was never going to let her see the bedroom, whatever happened.

But Solange seemed to like it. She looked through his CD's while he made the coffee and chose a Nora Jones, nice background music, very soothing.

"So, how long will you stay here with your parents?" she began in that direct way that was so typically French.

"Umm… not sure. At least for the summer season and to make sure the manor house is refurbished. I've no other plans for the present."

"And San Francisco, you have no plans there too?"

He took a breath. May as well say it. He would be saying it to other people soon enough.

"I broke up with Judith. It wasn't going to work out. You were right. I was not going to wait two years and she's almost forgotten me already. She seems very happy in her new life. There isn't room for me there anymore."

"Then you are free to come out tonight?" said Solange smiling, her head tilted to one side and looking at him closely.

"Christ, yeah. Is that an invitation?"

She laughed. "It is my boyfriend's birthday. We shall make the *fête*. He is thirty, so he is very old now. We shall celebrate with many friends and his parents and his family. It is in Pontivy so it is not far away. I shall go there after work to help them decorate the hall where it is being held. You can come with me, if you like, or join us later."

"I'd rather come with you, if that's okay. I'll help you decorate."

"That is perfect. Now shall we get back to the gatehouse and begin working on the website to add on the extra gîte? Have you got a camera? We will need to take photos."

The gatehouse gîte had been refurbished earlier in the year and now had four bedrooms and two bathrooms. By carefully selecting the new rooms where Clare had already made up beds and the new bathroom and a hastily-tidied sitting-room, and the exterior, they managed to put together a small selection of photos that would hopefully attract visitors. Owen, when she wasn't looking, even took a few of Solange.

They only had half an hour before leaving for Pontivy, so Solange showed him quickly how to put an extra gîte on the website. They did not have the time to write out the description in English and French but Frank assured them that he could do that on the Sunday.

Then Owen dashed home happily to shower and change; his thoughts, so downcast that morning, now buoyantly optimistic, looking forward as he was to the evening's festivities and spending more time in the company of Solange.

-oOo-

Chapter Seventeen

La Fête

The birthday party was different from any party that Owen had ever attended. If he had to sum it up, it was more like Ian and Céline's wedding than the habitual university parties he had been to in Belfast.

For a start, it wasn't just confined to people of his own age group. Solange's boyfriend, Antoine, had invited people of all generations. Even his grandmother was present, besides his parents, and a host of uncles and aunts. Then there were his siblings, his cousins and various partners thereof, plus their children, mostly babies, and a group of friends around the 30's mark and work-colleagues of all ages. Antoine did not seem at all put out that his girlfriend had brought along another man and welcomed Owen warmly.

At first Owen had felt awkward and shy as everyone who had come along to decorate the hall all seemed to know instinctively what to do. His French took a battering as he struggled to understand what was going on and more often than not, he ended up getting in the way. Finally, Solange took pity on him and teamed him up with a girl called Marina to blow up balloons and rig up a net to put them in. These would then be released in a shower at some point in the evening. Blowing up balloons was much easier than talking French and Marina was easy company to be with, giggling at his mistakes and even trying to help him out in English. Owen found himself sitting beside her at a table for the 25's - 35's where those within shouting distance all tried to make him feel at home.

As always in French get-together's, the food was the most important part of the evening and Owen found himself roped into helping out with serving and clearing away the dishes of those tables for the older generations, who tended to stay put. What he lacked for in speaking French, he made up for with his natural Irish charm and was always ready to join in a laugh, even when it was against himself, having been targeted, along with Antoine and other young people, including Solange, in a series of games that were funny or embarrassing, aimed at breaking the ice. By the time the meal was over, he was becoming quite popular.

By now it was after midnight and the crowd was thinning as grandmother and aunties were driven home.

Some young couples with children also left which meant that tables could be pushed back or folded up leaving room in the centre of the hall to let the dancing start.

And now a second party began, something more on the lines of what he was familiar with in Ireland. The lights were dipped down low, a DJ appeared out of nowhere, and Owen found himself grabbed by a girl who wanted to dance 'Le Rock'. This he was not trained to do but he hung in there, as she turned and swirled. Seeing that he was no expert, she stopped and put him through the basic steps so that their second dance together was much more successful.

The music continued to be a mixture of hits from the sixties to the present day, catering for all tastes, a lot of it in English. He hardly saw Solange at all, but didn't mind, as he was having such a good time. During a series of *Slows*, towards the end of the evening, he went at last to sit down and she joined him, pleased to see that he had integrated so well.

"So, Owen, how do you find our little French fête? Have you enjoyed it?" she began.

"Yeah, I have. It's been really good fun."

"That is good. I see that my friends have been looking after you very well. You are very popular with some of the girls."

"Jealous, then?" he laughed.

"Umm... perhaps. Just a little?" she countered, smiling.

"I like your Antoine. He's grand."

"Yes. I like him too."

And they laughed.

Before the evening was over, Owen found himself asked, on more than one occasion, for his mobile phone number and realized that it had never occurred to him to buy a French phone, something he would have to remedy as soon as possible if he weren't to spend the summer months watching TV with his parents every evening. It felt good to be free, good to have a life to himself after Judith. He wondered briefly if she had read his email by now but he did not feel guilty. After all, it was Judith who had left him, not the other way around, and the miserable eight weeks he'd spent since then were more than enough to atone for any mistakes he might have made. Yes! He was back in the circuit and ready to run again. Was looking forward to it.

And what a way to learn French!

Back in Saint Avit, on that Friday afternoon, Clare had waited impatiently for Marcel Joubert to free himself from his various meetings. She was convinced that she may have found 'her' Aurore. Amilta, Hamilton, it was just too much of a coincidence for it not to be true. For the umpteenth time, she perused the information that she had gathered from the French birth certificate, relishing the fact that this Aurore was still alive and was now married. It would be easy for Marcel to get his staff to check up on her whereabouts, whether she had children, or grandchildren even! Clare was dying to talk to her and every five minutes had her checking for signs of the arrival of the mayor.

He eventually turned up, apologizing for keeping her waiting, explaining that things had got complicated and that it was impossible to get away earlier. He listened attentively to what Clare had to say and agreed that her Aurore from Mont de Marsan was their best bet. They walked back to the *Mairie* to check on her current status, whether she was still living in Mont de Marsan and to make that all important phone call.

Their research led them quickly to as much information as the French legal system could provide. Aurore was now called Madame Aurore Gaudin, having married Pierre Gaudin in Mont de Marsan in 1965. It turned out that her husband had died some ten years ago and that she had moved to Rion des Landes in 2007. She had a son, Serge, and a daughter, Catherine, both married as well. And Catherine was living in Rion des Landes also.

Marcel Joubert picked up the phone and rang Madame Gaudin.

After four rings, the line went to voicemail, asking the caller to leave a message. Clare's heart sank. She felt she was getting so close to solving this mystery and that any little setback was disproportionately frustrating. They decided to look up any information they could gather on Catherine. And Marcel picked the phone up again.

This time they were in luck. Catherine was at home. She listened, quite astounded, at what Marcel was saying but although trying to be helpful, it was clear that she did not know a lot about her mother's childhood. She was able to confirm, however, that her mother had been adopted, which was a very good sign, but did not know who her original parents had been. She suggested that they call back in a few weeks when her mother would be home. She was currently on a cruise with a friend, a long awaited holiday of a lifetime to recover from a serious illness, and Catherine did not want to contact her unless it was absolutely necessary. She suggested, gently but firmly, that as Clare's quest had waited so long to get this far, it could wait another two or three weeks. Moreover, it would be so much more productive to talk to her mother face to face. Phone calls and emails would only serve to upset her. She was nearly seventy after all.

Bitterly disappointed, Clare could nonetheless see the logic of this and suggested coming back to the Landes region in three weeks' time. Marcel agreed that it was all for the best and meantime, he would get his staff to check out the ten other Aurore's they had found together in the ledgers in Dax and he would personally visit the two who lived in Saint Avit.

They spent the rest of the afternoon in a meeting with the local *notaire*, who had agreed to undertake research to help Clare out and was happy to be of service to the Mayor. But apart from a lot of waffle to justify the annexing of Meira's parents' house by the municipality back in the 1990's, he had no further information to impart that could reasonably help their cause.

It was now too late to envisage driving the long journey back up to Brittany, so Clare accepted an invitation to dine with Marcel and his wife. Madame Joubert was a kind, elegantly-dressed lady some ten years older than Clare, who was fascinated by what Clare was trying to do and delighted that they seemed to be moving forward at last.

When Clare finally arrived at the gîtes the following evening, she was stiff and tired from driving. The thought of doing the whole thing over again in three weeks' time was daunting but she knew she just couldn't let things stay the way they were, not when they had made so much progress. She only hoped George would be around to meet his daughter, if Aurore Gaudin really was his daughter, and that Alzheimer's disease, and the language barrier, would not prove too great an obstacle for them both to communicate.

She was surprised to find that Frank was on his own, and pleased to learn that Owen had been in invited by Solange to a party. As Frank could not provide any further details apart from the fact this was being held in Pontivy, she reluctantly let that topic go in favour of regaling Frank with all that had happened in Saint Avit.

Over in Ireland, on that Saturday night, Paul stood looking down at George as he slept. He'd been called back into work by Beatrice who was worried that George was taking another TIA attack. Thankfully, this had proven not to be the case. George was, however, a very tired old man. There was no doubt that he had entered into the last lap of his life. He was ninety-two, after all.

Paul sat down to spend an hour or so keeping him under observation. He was sleeping peacefully enough whereas he had been agitated and not well all day. Paul wondered to what extent George realized that Clare was trying to find Meira's child. He'd had an email from her the night before bringing him up to speed with all that had been happening in France and he was pleased that she was on to something serious at last. He hoped, for George's sake that Aurore would be found and brought to Ireland before it was too late.

His thoughts far away, he hadn't noticed that George was awake until the old man put out his hand to touch his own.

"Hello George," he said gently, "how's it going?"

"Not good. Ticker… not good," whispered the old man.

"Here, let me listen." And Paul put his stethoscope to his ears and listened to George's chest.

Then he took his pulse and temperature and sat down again beside him.

"You sound fine, George. You'll be alright for a while yet. Big, strong man like yourself. You're not going to give up on us now."

"Not long to go..."

"Nonsense. You can't go now when things are starting to move forward. Clare's been busy in France. I had word from her last night. She told me to tell you."

"Ah, France," said George, his eyes taking on a faraway look. "Meira went to France. Never came back."

And Paul was stricken to see tears in the old man's eyes.

"George," he said softly. "Meira never came back because she died. We think she may have died giving birth to your baby daughter."

"Meira's dead? Meira..."

"Yes, George, I'm very sorry, but yes, Meira's dead." Paul paused to let this sink in. Then he went on, gently. "But we know she had a baby girl and Clare's trying to find her. She's called Aurore. That means 'dawn' in French."

"A baby girl?"

"A baby girl called Aurore."

"If my Meira died, who's looking after the baby? Tell me, where is she?"

"Meira's daughter was brought up, it would seem, by a loving family. We don't know much more than that. But Clare thinks she may have found her. We won't know for a few weeks yet."

"But if Meira's dead…"

"It all happened a long time ago, George. Just after the war. That's why Meira never wrote to you again. That's why she didn't come back to England to be with you. I'm sure she loved you very much."

"The little baby, the little girl…"

"She survived. She was adopted and brought up by a nice family. Clare's trying to find her. But she's not a baby any more, George. She'd be seventy by now."

"*Seventy*?"

"Yep. Seventy. That's how long ago it was."

"Dear Lord. Seventy! She's not a baby any longer then."

Paul chuckled. "No, George. She's not a baby any longer."

George closed his eyes, no doubt memories of Meira swirling before them, trying to take on board all that Paul had told him. He lay like that for some time, saying nothing. Paul thought he had fallen asleep.

As he was finally getting up to leave, George fumbled for his hand and held it hard.

"Find her, please. Find my daughter," he said, his voice earnest with emotion.

"Clare's doing everything she can, George. If anyone can find her, she will," said Paul as reassuringly as he could.

On the drive back to Sharon's house, Paul pondered on George's life and all that had happened during the war. It must've been very hard to let Meira go back to France like that, to look for her husband when she was carrying George's child. He must've loved her very much to sacrifice all they had had between them, to let her go, to lose her. Then her letter, telling him she was free, that her husband was no more and that she would be returning to join him and live happily ever after. He must've been overjoyed, counting the days till she came back.

Then... nothing, no news from Meira and the growing worry that something had happened, the searching for her, the slow realization that she'd never come back. Paul sighed. He could not imagine the pain of losing Sharon, especially now that she was carrying *his* child. To have all that joy in the making and then to lose it; it was unthinkable.

And yet George had been through it, not once but twice. It must've been awful for him. And no-one else had taken her place, either. He had never married. Meira had been his sole love. And now at the end of his life, he was finding out what had happened to her all those years ago, that Meira was dead, that he had a daughter called Aurore and that he might get to see her before leaving this world.

-oOo-

Chapter Eighteeen

Making friends

Owen got home very late after Antoine's party, having stayed to help clear up the aftermath of the fête with Solange, Marina and about half a dozen of Antoine's friends. Between them they quickly took down the remaining decorations, cleared up the kitchen and swept the hall so that it was clean and ready for use for the following afternoon's senior citizens' *Belote** tournament. A couple of die-hards, drunk and sleepy, had to be got into someone's car to be ferried home but by four am, all was done and it was time to say good-bye.

Owen was perfectly sober, yet he'd had a grand time. On reflexion, this was probably due to the fact he'd ate a ginormous meal during the earlier part of the evening and then proceeded to dance well into the early hours. He'd eventually got the hang of the 'rock' and as for the rest, he was not a bad dancer and was sought after by the female population never shy at asking him to dance. He caught Solange smiling, watching his antics on more than one occasion when he tried to communicate in pigeon French, and grinned in reply. She had told him at the end of the evening that she and Antoine, and some other friends, were heading to a *Fest Noz** the following Saturday near Lorient and that if he was interested, to let her know. He was already looking forward to whatever a *Fest Noz* was, simply because Solange would be there. Life was looking up.

Dawn was breaking as he let himself into his little gîte but he was too hyped up to go to bed straight away. He opened his lap-top and went into his emails. And sure enough, there was an email from Judith.

So now it really *was* over.

In spite of the happy evening he'd just spent, he was once again struck with a pang of sadness. It had been good with Judith and fun too. She had been his first serious girlfriend and they'd been together for what seemed like a long time. She had been understanding, had written nice things in her email, had said she would never forget him. But underneath it all, her relief was all too obvious and deep down that hurt. The platitudes about remaining friends were all there but he knew that it would never be the same. And without deliberately setting out to find each other, there was every chance they might never meet again.

Losing Judith for good brought on a weariness that had him heading for bed soon after where he buried his sad thoughts in welcome sleep. It was after midday when he woke, feeling quite refreshed, thoughts of Judith banished and his main preoccupation being to know where to purchase a French mobile phone.

The week went by quickly enough. The first lot of customized windows arrived the following day, Monday, and their installation took till the following Thursday to complete. The exterior walls' insulation was now well under way and a new boiler had been put in and the original radiators serviced and pronounced fit for use. It was agreed with his parents that they would get a professional chimney-sweep in to clean the various chimneys, of which there were a surprising number, as Laura had warned them this was obligatory for their house insurance to kick in in case of fire. All in all, by the end of the week, the manor house was definitely a work in (advanced) progress. Another week or two like that and they could then move in.

Saturday came around eventually and, to Clare's undisguised surprise, Owen was already at the office before nine am, waiting for the arrival of Solange. Clare knew all about Antoine, of course, but she also knew her son. And his off-hand announcement during the week that he and Judith had officially broken up had all her matchmaking instincts on the alert, big-time. She settled down unashamedly to do a bit of discreet observation with a definite view to poking her nose into other people's business.

Solange was punctual, as usual, and Clare was amused to watch Owen fussing over her, suggesting a coffee, eager to show her the addition of the gatehouse gîte to the website which he had completed with the help of Frank. Clare was due to go shopping in Lorient, in the cash & carry warehouse exclusive to people in the food and beverage trade. She lingered over her coffee but eventually had to leave as she needed to get back in time for the weekly changeover. The gîtes were getting progressively booked up each week and by the following Saturday, middle of June, they were going to be fully booked out. The gatehouse gîte would indeed be a welcome addition in July. Before she took her leave, she was tickled to listen to Solange listing all that had to be done that day, sharing out the work-load to an (almost) grateful Owen! That, in itself, was a miracle, if ever there was one. Clare wondered where it all would lead.

By the time she got back, some two hours later, Solange and Owen were just finishing up the cleaning of the pool and games-room areas and were exchanging mobile phone numbers on Owen's new phone. Another little innocent gesture that had Clare's mind doing overtime.

She got to work to heat up some home-made soup and put out the fresh bread she had bought while in Lorient. Solange and Owen helped her put away the groceries and Frank came in from the manor house, where he had been, once again, chopping logs. They all ate together around the kitchen table in happy companionship.

Then it was a question of all hands to the fray, as guests began leaving and the four gîtes that had been rented out that week needed cleaning. They worked in pairs, Solange with Owen and Frank with Clare and by 4pm, all the available gîtes were ready for rental. Solange, as always, had put flowers from the garden in all the gîtes that would be rented out for the coming week, the two already empty gîtes along with the four others that had just been vacated. However, for the week after that, Owen would be called upon to vacate his gîte too and was hoping to transfer his stuff directly into one of the bedrooms at the manor house. Failing that, he would just move into the gatehouse gîte with his parents for a week or two.

They just had time for a quick cup of tea when the first of the guests arrived to take up residence. For the next hour and a half, they were all kept busy showing people around the complex, answering questions, pointing out the local tourist attractions and generally making sure that everything was just as it should be. By now, even Owen had got the hang of this task and was becoming quite sure of himself… so long as the guests spoke English.

With only one more family left to arrive that evening, Clare told Solange to finish up early for the day.

"Shall I collect you around six this evening, Owen?" she asked.

"Yeah. That's great, Solange. Thanks. So where's this Fest Nose, you're taking me to?"

"Ah hah. It is near Lorient. At Larmor-Plage. Can you bring a sleeping bag? We shall stay overnight at Léa's place."

Clare tried to busy herself while listening intently.

"Who's Léa then? A friend from Uni?"

"Oh, no. Léa, she is my sister. She is an artist and she has her studio in our parent's house by the sea."

"Really? Never met a real live artist before. Should be interesting."

"I do not think she has ever met a real live architect before. So you will have that in common at least," laughed Solange.

So that's what it was. Solange was introducing Owen to her sister. Clare breathed a sigh of relief. She liked Solange but she did not like the idea of Owen muscling in on Antoine when Solange and Antoine were an item. She wouldn't put it past her son. Ian had given her to understand that before Judith, he was something of a ladies man at Queen's, especially when that friend of his, Pete, was around.

"And we shall meet up with Marina, and Alain, and Françoise, and Logan and more of the people you met last week at Antoine's party. A lot of our friends are meeting us at the *Fest Noz*."

"And will everyone be staying at Léa's place?"

"Probably, most of them. It is a big house. But there are not many beds. You will be sleeping on the floor."

So, Clare thought to herself, it wasn't just a foursome. There was a whole crowd of them going to this *Fest Noz*.

"Mum?"

And this Léa, she probably had a boyfriend too. So it was all platonic, really. Still it was nice for Owen to make friends this way. Be good for his French too.

"Mu-*um*? Earth to Mother, do you read me?"

Owen's voice finally penetrated Clare's thoughts, bringing her back to reality with a start.

"Oh, sorry Owen. I was miles away."

"So we noticed! Mum, have you got a sleeping bag you could lend me for tonight? We're stopping over."

"Yes, yes of course. Here, there's several in that cupboard upstairs, in one of the new bedrooms, the one on the left, I think."

Owen, took the stairs two at a time to sort this out.

"Solange, do you need a sleeping bag too? I've got some extra," said Clare, solicitously.

"Thank you, Clare, but no. I still have my room at Léa's house with my bed and my pillows. I like my little comforts."

"Oh I know *exactly* how you feel."

"So, I shall leave now and get ready for the *Fest Noz*. Bye, Clare. See you next Saturday."

"Bye Solange, have a nice evening, now."

Just at this point Frank came in and helped himself to an ice-cold Perrier, asking Clare if she would like one too.

"No thanks, Frank. But I could murder a cup of tea. Owen, cup of tea?" called Clare.

"No thanks, Mum. I can't find the sleeping bags. No... sorry. Here they are." He came down the stairs with a neat little sleeping back in its own holder. "Hi Dad."

"Hi Son. How's it going?"

"Off to a Fest Nose this evening, whatever that is. Solange wouldn't tell me."

"It means a night-time feast. Usually there are cider and galettes, savoury crepes, and sweet crepes too. Plus traditional Breton music and dancing. And it's a *Fest Noz*, not Fest nose. *Noz*."

"Whatever. Looks like I'll be roped into dancing with every available female again. I'll have to start charging soon."

And he headed off happily in the direction of his gîte to shower and change.

"Gigolo," called Frank pleasantly, after him.

"Bighead," added his mother, for good measure.

"Don't think he's suffering from his break-up with Judith any longer, do you?" said Frank, wistfully. He'd liked Judith.

"I think it was more wounded pride than anything else. He never expected Judith to leave him. If anything, he assumed it would be the other way round," replied his wife.

"Well, at least he's getting out and about and not moping at home. Talking of which, fancy a stroll over to the manor house? It's coming on really well."

"We can't leave the gîtes until the last family arrives. They shouldn't be long. They said they'd be here around six."

An hour or so later saw them walking arm in arm towards the manor house and Clare duly congratulated Frank on all the wood he had cut. One more day should see the last of the branches cleared from the garden and enough logs in the house to keep them going for most of the winter, particularly as there would be central heating as well. Traces of the workmen could be seen at every twist and turn but they always had a clean-up before leaving for the week-end and Clare could now see the house clearly for what it was and start imagining how she would decorate the rooms and what furniture would go where. She was beginning to get really excited about it all as it got nearer the time to vacate their little gîte.

"We're going to have to buy two beds, Frank. We can't really avoid that. But there's still that big dresser in the kitchen and that lovely oak table in the dining room and that huge armoire in the hall and a second one upstairs. We'll pinch a few fold up chairs from the games room, if needs be, and the former owners have left a lot of bric and brac in the attic that needs sorting out. And removal boxes make excellent bedside tables with a cloth thrown over them. And we have that TV we were keeping. It'll be like when we first set up home together, remember? A glorified campsite."

"Yes, indeed," chuckled Frank, remembering fondly their very first bedsit, all those years ago. "We'll be okay for the office stuff, more or less. We've got that new desk and the book-shelves we bought at the very start. But we'll have to turn where the office currently is into a bedroom. So that's three beds we'll have to buy."

"We'll bargain for a discount then," countered Clare happily.

"And we'll need a wardrobe or two."

"For the gîte, yes. But for us, what about those metal frames on wheels? They're not expensive and we can use them in the cloakroom, once we get our proper furniture bought."

"Good idea. I've seen some for less than fifty euros each. They'll do meantime. No use buying expensive stuff until we've worked out exactly how we want the bedrooms."

"Oh Frank! It's really going to be ours! In a few weeks, we'll be moving in. And really, I don't care if it's not perfect. We have all winter to sort the house out. Just so long as we have insulation and heating and running water, that's fine by me."

"And an Internet and telephone connection. I must get on to that right away. I must admit, it had gone completely out of my mind."

"Oh yes. That's very important."

By this time, they were going up the stone steps to the front door, with its little seating area to the side, pretty now in the late spring evening, flowery trailing plants bringing a touch of colour to the grey stone walls.

"Shall we chose which bedroom shall be ours then?" asked Frank.

"I already have. Oh, didn't I mention it to you?"

"No, you didn't," sighed Frank, "but that's a technicality I've got used to over the years: what the lady wants, the lady gets. So show me what we've chosen together then."

"Oh Frank! You'll love it, I promise."

And she took his hand to show him their room.

Belote = A popular French card game similar to Whist
Fest Noz = Traditional Breton dances

-oOo-

Chapter Nineteen

Léa

She was just as pretty as her sister, more so, if anything. She had those lovely long eyelashes and rich auburn hair and she bubbled, kind of. Owen found himself suddenly shy, something he had not experienced in a long time. She jumped up now from where she had been working on a painting, hair scrunched up out of her eyes and smudges of paint on her hands and the protective smock she was wearing.

"*Chérie, ça me fait plaisir!*" she said brightly, coming over to kiss Solange hello. "*Qui c'est, ce beau jeune homme?*" And she proceeded to kiss Owen four times on the cheeks in the more traditional Breton greeting.

"Léa, meet Owen," began Solange. "You will have to speak in English with him, at least for now. His

French is still not quite fluent yet. He is the son of Clare and Frank, my bosses at the gîtes, you know?"

"*Ah, si!* Solange told me about you on the phone. You are the architect, no?"

"Nearly, Léa, I'm waiting for my exam results. If I've passed, well, yes, I'm an architect. Nice to meet you."

She turned to Solange: "And the others, they have come too?"

"No, we are the first. They will join us later."

"Perfect! Now we can have some coffee, and talk." She turned to Owen. "I have not seen my sister all week. And we do not live so far away from each other. We are always busy. Life goes by so fast, like that!" And she clicked her fingers.

Solange left them both to prepare the coffee.

"You speak excellent English, Léa. Just like Solange," began Owen.

"Ah, that is because we had English nurses... no... nannies, to look after us when we were children. It is difficult to forget the language, even when I do not speak it regularly."

"Nannies... really?"

"Oh yes. And they made us speak English. Our parents were both barristers. Very busy people. Solange and I, we did not see them very often. This was their house."

"It's a beautiful house. And the view over the see is breath-taking. I can see why you are using this room as your studio." Owen stood admiring the view.

"Yes, it was our parent's bedroom, before they died."

"Died, both of them? I'm really sorry."

"Thank you. But it was a long time ago. They were killed in a car crash, when Solange and I were seventeen. It was a... difficult time for us both. But we have each other."

"You are twins, then? Solange never said."

"Yes we are twins, but not identical twins. We are very good friends and that is what is important."

"It sure is."

"Now, shall we go and find my sister? I can smell the coffee."

She led him downstairs to a huge kitchen where coffee and *pains aux chocolat* awaited them.

"Let us have a *goûter** Léa, just like old times. I am fairly certain you have forgotten to eat today, as you always do, so I brought these," chided Solange.

Léa, laughing, admitted the truth in this. She fell on the *pains au chocolat* with relish.

"Owen, please," said Solange. "Do not be shy."

"Thanks, Solange," said Owen, suddenly hungry too.

Afterwards, he suggested taking a stroll down on the beach, refusing to let the girls accompany him as he knew they wanted to chat. It had been like that with

Judith, whenever her sisters were around, and these girls were no exception. Throughout the *goûter,* they had kept bursting into French, then stopping when they saw he couldn't follow. He would do some exploring to himself and let them get on with their natter without the hindrance of having to stop and translate.

Once outside he took time to study the house. It was what the French called a 'house from the thirties', quite similar to a Victorian villa really, and were now extremely popular because of their character, and no doubt extremely expensive too. Léa's house was big and rambling and very pretty with what looked like Virginia creeper covering most of the front and side of the building and bow windows overlooking the bay. He would ask her to show him round the rest of the house, if she did not object, his curiosity aroused from an architectural standpoint. But what gave this house its charm was undoubtedly its setting. The view over the Lorient estuary was wonderful and its generous garden with a few mature evergreen trees meant that the house itself would surely be protected from the worst of the high winds in the autumn and winter months. He wondered briefly if Léa lived alone here. It seemed an awful lot of house for one person to manage.

Then he turned on his heels and set off down a nearby coastal path that lead him to the beach. Taking off his trainers and socks, he rolled up his trouser legs and went for a paddle, enjoying the feel of the cold water as it lapped around his shins. Before him he could see several cabin cruisers and a few yachts out on the sea and behind them in the distance quite clearly the outline of the other side of the estuary and various islands in-between.

He stayed like that a long time, walking along the edge of the sea, enjoying the scenery as the colours changed and late afternoon turned to evening. It began to get chilly. Just as he was turning back towards the house, he spotted the sisters not far off, who had come to find him, their catching-up no doubt finished for now. He found himself linked both sides and chided roundly for staying out so long. It was nice to be told off by these two... kind of safe and sisterly. He suddenly felt that he had known them all his life. Dismissing their ministrations with a laugh, he set off at a run pulling them both by the hand until they arrived at the point where the beach met the road, laughing and out of breath.

On another beach, in another country, many miles away, Kieran and Beth were walking along hand in hand. It had been Beth's idea to go back to their old haunts, to blow the cobwebs away and take a break from studying. Kieran's idea of a break from studying did not involve going out on a cold June evening to a freezing beach where the wind whipped his hair and made his nose run but there were times when Beth could be surprisingly stubborn and this was one of them.

Still, it was a novelty to get out the new car and go for a drive. Paul had been true to his word and had come with him to choose a little Ford Fiesta that was second-hand but not that old really and helped him get it insured, lending him the money necessary till such times as Kieran's trust fund released the casket money. Kieran had been chuffed to get behind the wheel of his very own car and had been using every possible opportunity to drive it ever since.

"So any news of *your* driving test yet, Beth?" he asked, his mind still on the car.

"Soon. Very soon, but I'm not telling you the date. You'll only tell everyone else and I don't want anyone to know till I've passed," came the pert reply.

"Me? I wouldn't tell a soul. I'm discretion personified."

"No you're not. You're as bad as Eileen at times. You nearly blurted out the other evening that we... you know... sleep together."

"But we *do* and it's lovely and natural and really great!"

"To my *Mum,* Kieran?"

"Ah yes, that's was a bit unfortunate. Just as well she didn't catch on."

"Only because I jumped in to change the subject. You're an eejit, Kieran. She thinks I spend all my time at the flat revising for our A levels. Can you imagine what would happen if she found out the truth?"

"Well, she will, one day. One day we'll get married and have lots of children and we'll make her a grandmother. She'll have to know then."

"One day, we'll get our degrees and find good jobs and if we're still really serious about each other, we might get married. As for having lots of children, well, you can forget about that straight away. Two at the most."

"Only two?"

"At the most."

"I always wanted brothers and sisters. I think we should have about six or seven kids, the way they did in the old days. A great, big family where everyone sits round the kitchen table and the mother dishes up these wonderful meals."

"You're not serious!"

"Perfectly serious. I think you'd make a wonderful mother, Beth."

"Kieran Murphy, let's get a few things straight here: a) I do not intend to bring up a clatter of kids, with all the work involved, just so that you can make up for the fact you were an only child, b) I intend to go to Uni and have a career and make money and enjoy myself before... possibly... settling down to have a small family in a nice house, and c) I've spent most of my life looking after my kid sister Nina, and even though I do love her to bits, I know exactly how time-consuming kids are.

Believe me, these are some of the best years of our lives, when we're free to do as we want. Let's just enjoy them, okay?"

"Okay, spoilsport. Let's just keep to practicing then. We're getting good at that."

And he pulled her into his arms for a kiss and cuddle before suggesting a carry-out and back to the flat to 'practice'.

In another part of Kilmore, his mother and Paul were sitting side by side on the little wall that ran part of the way round the Oak Lodge lake. It wasn't a big lake, by any stretch of the imagination, but it was pretty and calm, bordered by trees and bushes and twinkling now in the evening light. Sharon had come back to the home specially, although Paul had been on duty all day. They had just finished the last of the interviews for appointing a new nurse and now it was time to take a decision.

The choice was down to three: a young nurse in her mid-twenties, wanting to get some experience in dementia, a forty-something lady who had put her career on hold to bring up her family and was now seeking to return to nursing, and a young man of about thirty-five who came from Poland.

"So, Sharon, any preferences?" began Paul. "I'm in a quandary, myself. They all seem qualified for the job, even the Polish guy."

"Mm... but he does have a strong accent when he speaks English and some of our old folk might have difficulties understanding him. I'm worried that his integration would be difficult."

"You just don't want another male nurse around the place, kill the competition. Come on, be honest," chuckled Paul.

"That's *so* not true! Of the three, his CV is probably the best, it really is. No, it's his accent that's worrying me, although he speaks fluently enough."

"Well, what about Mrs Corrigan, you know, the nurse who's coming back after a gap of eight years?"

"Yeah. I'm afraid she might need a refresher course before she's up to speed. I mean, Paul, this is a temporary job. Once the baby is born and my maternity leave is over, I'll be coming back to work full-time. We've made that clear to all the candidates. We're not really going to have the time nor the financial resources to propose refresher courses. We need someone operational right away."

"So you're thinking of the young nurse who wants to get dementia experience, then?"

"No. Or perhaps yes. She seems perfectly qualified and I suppose we all need to gain experience when we set out."

"This would be her first stint in an EMI unit, though. Hard to know how it would go. And she hasn't had much experience in nursing anywhere, really. She's only just got her degree. To me, she's no more operational than Mrs Corrigan. Both would need time to get up to speed, time which we can't really afford to give them."

"So who's your preference, then?" said Sharon, somewhat exasperated.

"The Pole. Definitely. He's trained in geriatric nursing and has worked in an old-people's home before now. Neither of the other two nurses have had any experience in dealing with old people. And, okay, his English is not faultless, and his accent is strong, but it's not that bad and a few weeks here would definitely see him progressing on that front. And let's face it, Sharon, some of our residents cannot even say what's wrong, themselves. So you have to rely solely on your medical diagnostic and nursing skills to treat them. This guy's perfectly qualified for that. And he's got himself registered here. He's a proper nurse."

"Paul, don't you remember the sensation you caused when you came to Oak Lodge?"

"No. Should I?"

"I mean, you were our very first male nurse. All the women were falling over themselves to be with you."

"All *I* remember is how they loved to take the Mickey. It was embarrassing."

"That's what you'll be inflicting on this poor guy, if we go for him."

"Well, my dear, if *I* can survive it, become deputy Manager and marry the boss, there's surely hope for Mr something Skolski, or whatever his name is."

"You eejit, Paul. Those things just happened. It certainly wasn't planned."

"Not complaining, sweetheart. I'm a very lucky man."

"So, shall we give Krzysztof Sokolsky a go, then? Take him on trial for a month and take it from there?"

"And you've been practicing that, haven't you? I know you, Sharon. You've been practicing his name!"

"Well, I thought all along he was the best candidate but I wanted to make sure you felt the same. After all, you're the one that's going to have to manage him, not me."

"Now who's the eejit, then, eh?" teased Paul. And despite her protestations that someone would see, he took her in his arms and kissed her roundly.

-oOo

Goûter = A children's snack usually eaten after school, about 4:30 pm

Chapter Twenty

Léa's secret

The week following the *Fest Noz*, Frank spent a lot of his free time battling with their Internet provider and France Telecom in order that they could move the office from the gatehouse gîte into the manor house within the next week or so. Owen, for his part, started packing up his things in order to vacate his gîte, and began a serious clean-up there as he did not want Solange coming in on the following Saturday to see the mess he'd made.

The *Fest Noz* had been fun, the beer had flowed and the galettes had been really good. Solange and Lea had made sure he got the hang of the dances, which were not unlike traditional Irish dances only simpler, but once he was up and running, so to speak, they had left him to fend for himself. He found himself once more sitting near Marina, the girl he had blown balloons up with at Antoine's party, and spent a pleasant, if somewhat heavy-going half-hour trying to communicate with her in French.

But he found he kept scanning the crowd regularly to try and spot the sisters. They were often deep in conversation, oblivious to all around them. Even Antoine had left them in peace.

But after another fifteen minutes had passed, he decided enough was enough. Freeing himself from Marina & Co, he headed to the twins with the intention of asking them both up to dance.

Traditional Breton dancing is done in lines. Everyone links hands and they move forwards and backwards with a kind of skipping step which is repeated over and over again to the accompaniment of the *biniou*, a smallish bagpipe instrument and the *bombarde*, a tinny-sounding flute, and other Breton instruments. The line gradually moves around the dance-floor and often forms a circle. A few of the dances are for couples who move forward procession-like, stopping and starting in time to the music. Owen, who by now had easily mastered the general rhythm, gave the girls no option but to follow him by simply grabbing their hands and making them stand up. Laughing, no doubt glad to be on the move, they accompanied him in a series of dances that had them all quite hot by the time the music stopped. He went over then to the bar to buy them a drink and seeing that Antoine had come back on the scene, bought him one too, Léa helping him carry the plastic goblets of beer and cider back to their table.

Then Antoine and Solange went off to order galettes for them all and Owen found himself, at last, alone with Léa, something he had been working towards all evening.

Looking back, that had been the best part. Léa was lovely, not only in looks but in her whole being too. He asked her about her work, her paintings, and listened, captivated, as she described what pleasure she had in creating something from nothing, the absolute joy of finishing a piece and getting it framed; she even made her frustrations and set-backs sound interesting. He could've listened to her all night.

Then Antoine and Solange returned and they all tucked into a hearty meal before someone suggested they make their own circle and he was back on the dance-floor again.

All in all, there were eight of them stopping that night in Léa's house. The festivities continued on there well into the night until one by one, people headed off to bed. One of the last to go, sitting happily in the company of Léa, Owen found himself at the end of the night having to share the sitting-room floor with Marina and another guy. As he tried to get comfortable in his sleeping-bag, he wondered dreamily where Léa slept, and whether she slept alone. He hadn't seen her with anyone all evening but perhaps she had a boyfriend stashed away somewhere else. He resolved to find out as soon as he could but for now he was very tired and quickly fell asleep.

The next day, he hardly saw her at all and certainly did not get an opportunity to be alone with her. She was up quite early and had made coffee while Solange made a trip to the nearest *boulangerie* for baguettes and croissants, the sisters providing all their sleepy guests with sustenance before they headed off. Solange was the last to leave but that meant Owen had to leave too and he had no way of getting Léa on her own to ask her out. He kissed her goodbye, though, which of course meant nothing, as everyone kissed everyone anyway, but on the way home in the car, with just himself and Solange, he was determined to know more about her sister.

"Solange, can I ask you a personal question?" he began.

"That depends on the question. You may ask but I may not reply," came Solange's response. "Tell me first, did you enjoy our *Fest Noz*, then?"

"I did. I'm not sure I like the music all that much. It's strident, although the rhythm's good and the dances are fun."

"Ah, the music will grow on you. And there are new versions of the old songs which are softer to listen to. I will give you a CD so that you can see for yourself. I am sure you will come to like it."

"About my question…"

"And the galettes. What did you think of the galettes? They are good, no?"

"They're really good. I like the ones with sausages; they're filling though."

"And the dances? You seemed to learn them very well, very quickly."

"Yes, they're easy to learn. The *Fest Noz* was good. I really enjoyed myself and thank you for taking me there."

"It is no problem. You are becoming popular with my friends. Marina, for example, she said to me…"

"Solange. Please! My question. It has nothing to do with Marina. I need to talk to you about Léa."

"Ah, Léa." Owen could sense Solange give a sigh.

"Yes, Léa. I like her very much. But I need to know. Perhaps she has a boyfriend? Do you think Léa would go out with me if I asked her?"

"Owen…"

"Please, Solange. I know she's your sister and you want to protect her. All I want to know is whether I can ask her out or whether she already has someone in her life."

Solange did not answer for some moments. Then she pulled the car into a convenient lay-by and switched off the engine. She was silent for so long that Owen began to worry.

"Solange, what's up? Is it Léa? Is it something I said?"

"Owen, you are a nice man. I would not have introduced you to Léa, if you were not a nice man. All my friends that you have met know Léa and keep her safe. They are good friends. They come to visit her and make her laugh. They bring her food because she sometimes forgets to eat."

Here Solange paused not knowing how to go on.

"She's not ill, is she?" asked Owen, sensing that there was something important about Léa that Solange was not telling him.

"No, physically she is not ill. Psychologically, it is another matter. You see, we are orphans. Our parents died suddenly when were about seventeen. It was a terrible time for us both."

"Yes, she told me about that. A car crash. I'm sorry."

"Thank you. Yes, we were very affected, and I suppose very lost too. We did not know what to do at first. Then a year later, Léa met this man. His name was Alex…"

Here Solange paused again and took a deep breath before going on.

"He was not a nice person, Owen. He was evil. At first he was charming and very understanding. He gave Léa the support to deal with our parents' deaths. He was much older than us, nearly thirty. I suppose he seemed like an older brother, someone she could rely on. Then after some months he betrayed her. Gradually, he began to take over her life. He tried to prevent me seeing my sister. He became domineering and violent. He made her give him money, money from our inheritance. He was horrible, Owen, and poor Léa, who was fragile, we were both fragile, was taken advantage of by this man. He was her first proper boyfriend, he abused her physically but also psychologically and financially, too."

"Oh God, Solange. I'm sorry. I didn't know. Poor Léa."

"It took me nearly a year to understand that something was very wrong and to get him away from my sister. Léa, she did not have the strength to stand up to him but I did. I waited one day till I saw him leave their flat and took Léa to the gendarmerie. They were very understanding. They let us talk to a lady gendarme. And Léa agreed to be examined by a doctor. And to make charges against this man. She was very frightened. And so was I. But when I saw the bruises on her body, I knew then that I was doing what was the right thing to do."

"Thank God you were there to help her, Solange. You probably saved her life."

"Yes, I wish I had acted earlier. But she always said she was fine. I knew something was wrong but I did not know just how terrified she was. I saved her life, Owen, but I did not save her mind. Léa spent nearly a year after that in a hospital for those who have mental problems. That is where she discovered how to paint. It has helped her to recover."

"And the man, this Alex, what happened to him?"

"He was given a prison sentence. But he was released after only five months. And made to pay back some of the money he took from Léa. It was horrible, all horrible. He is out of prison now but he is not allowed to approach her. But I still worry that one day he will try to see her again. Sometimes I get the feeling he is around, spying on us. And Léa, she is doing so well; you can see how happy she is. She has even been to art school and has taken a degree."

"Yes, she seems very happy now."

"But she is still in the process of building her life and she is still very fragile. That is why I talk to you about Marina and not Léa. Léa does not have a boyfriend and I am not sure she is ready for a boyfriend again. I hate that man, Alex, for what he did to her. I worry that she will never be able to have a proper relationship with someone again."

"I understand," said Owen softly.

"You are a nice man and I think Léa likes you very much. But I am so scared for her, my poor sister. She must not be treated badly ever again."

"And I have a reputation with the ladies, you mean?"

"You do have a reputation, Owen. I know how happy Clare was when you began to see Judith. She told me that you had had lots of girlfriends in the past. And now you and Judith, your relationship is over. And you are very popular with all my girlfriends. Some of them have said to me... Marina, she..."

"Marina's nice, Solange, but I'm not really interested in her that way. I don't know why; she's a very sweet girl."

"You may have to tell her that," said Solange, smiling, "because she is very interested in you."

"Can I be friends with her at least?"

"Who? Marina?"

"No, with Léa. Will you let me get to know her? I promise I won't rush into a relationship. I just want to be her friend, that's all."

"And more if affinities, as you say?" said Solange, sighing.

"Let's just cross that bridge when we come to it. But I won't hurt her, Solange, not after all she's been through. You can trust me there."

Solange looked hard at Owen and saw that he was in earnest. Once again she was silent, and this time he had the good sense to say nothing. Finally, she nodded, her decision taken.

"Owen, I would like you to be a good friend of my sister's, even her special friend, if you want. But if you want things to go further, please remember all I have told you. Do not betray her trust. She is fragile, Owen. Help her, do not hurt her."

-oOo-

Chapter Twenty-One

The New Nurse

Krzysztof Sokolsky arrived at Oak Lodge on Monday morning shortly before nine o'clock. Both Paul and Sharon were there to greet him and, after a quick cup of coffee together, Sharon took him on a tour of the building, introducing him to staff as they made their rounds.

Most of the care-workers were young and all were female. The arrival of *another* male nurse into the home soon had them all quietly buzzing with excitement. The older care-workers gave a collective sigh and rolled their eyes to heaven. They remembered the disruption caused by the arrival of Paul some three years ago and now it looked as if the same thing was going to happen all over again. Dear God, what was Sharon thinking of?

It wasn't as if this man was tall, dark and handsome. He was of medium height, quite stocky, thick light brown hair and had a very ordinary face. It was only when he smiled that everything changed. His smile was lovely, wide and heart-warming. Looks weren't everything but that smile could break a girl's heart. The older care-workers shook their heads and worried what ravages that smile might cause.

After Sharon had shown Krzysztof the outlay of the building, it was Paul's turn to take him on his rounds to check over the residents and prepare medication. He intended to let Krzysztof watch him on this first excursion together but he would then take a back seat the following time and see how Krzysztof coped.

Most of the residents were happy enough to have a new male nurse, although whether they registered that he was a nurse was not always clear. Krzysztof played along, what he lacked in fluency, he made up for in kindness and empathy, proof, if ever proof were needed, that he had worked in geriatrics. Paul was quietly impressed.

They came to Rita, sad, little crotchety Rita. She still had Sally's brooch, which she kept in its box in her pocket, and her hand permanently in her pocket as if the brooch would jump up and run away. She was sitting now in her armchair, staring into space.

"Morning, Rita," said Paul breezily. "How are you today, then?"

No answer from Rita. If anything, her scowl got worse.

"Just come to give you your medication and to let you meet Krzysztof. He's our new nurse," continued Paul.

Krzysztof came and sat down on the visitor's chair in front of Rita. Her gave her that lovely smile and took her free hand in his. For once, she didn't pull away.

"Hello, Rita," he said.

"Hello, doctor," she replied, her scowl fading as she looked into his eyes.

"I am not a doctor. I am like Paul, a nurse. But we are here to look after you. How are you, Rita? Tell me."

"I have a terrible drouth on me, doctor," said Rita.

Paul was surprised. Rita was not usually forthcoming about anything.

Krzysztof looked at Paul questioningly. "Drouth, Paul? That is a word I do not know."

"Ah, it's an old Irish word meaning thirsty. Funny, but Rita never complained about that before and I know she drinks all we give her. She shouldn't be thirsty."

"She is very thin and her breath smells of acetone."

"What are you thinking?"

"I am thinking diabetes. Has her blood sugar levels been tested?"

"No, I don't think so," asked Paul.

"Let us get her to give us a urine sample. And take a blood test. That is what I suggest," said Krzysztof.

"Okay, I agree. No time like the present. I'll get the blood-testing kit. Do you think you can get her to give you a urine sample? I'll send you one of the care-workers to give you a hand."

By the time Paul got back, Krzysztof had managed to get a small urine sample from Rita. She was cooperating quite well, which was a blessing in itself. But when Paul came to prick her finger, she reacted violently and would not let him touch her. Once again it was Krzysztof who coaxed her and the meter-reading showed indeed high blood-sugar levels. Paul decided that it would be best to contact her doctor and take it from there. He said as much to Krzysztof.

"I'll let you carry out the urine test when we finish our rounds, Krzysztof. But I think there's no mistaking she has developed diabetes. Good that you picked up on that. It must be in the early stages as there's no mention of diabetes in her medical history."

"Where I worked in Poland, we had a similar case. That is how I remember."

They worked their way round all the residents, giving medication, taking blood pressures, dressing wounds. Paul did most of the work, letting Krzysztof watch his methods, but by the time they were finished, Krzysztof was doing his share and it was clear to Paul that he knew what he was doing. He said as much to

Sharon when they found themselves alone in the office later that morning.

"Well, that's great, Paul," said Sharon happily, "but the real test will be this afternoon, when Catriona comes on duty. She hasn't met Krzysztof yet. I do hope they hit it off."

"Mm... yes. Our Catriona takes no prisoners. And she was on holiday last week, so she's not even aware that a new nurse has already started. I'll try and warn her before she actually meets him. Or *you* do, if you see her first, okay?"

"I certainly will," said his wife. "It's going to be an interesting afternoon."

Catriona had no idea indeed that the new nurse had actually been appointed, having spent the previous week taking a well-earned break, not only from the home, but from her parents too.

She had come to work at Oak Lodge some two years previously in order to be closer to her parents who were elderly although quite capable of living on their own. Since then, things had deteriorated somewhat with her father having had not one, but two hip replacement operations within a year of each other, which had left him weakened and diminished. Catriona spent a lot of time making him exercise, taking him for walks, encouraging him to get back into the garden, showing him the movements he was allowed to do and those that he had better avoid. She was quite confident he would fully recover, but it was a long and uphill process.

So when she got the opportunity to go for a weeks' holiday in Portugal with a friend from schooldays, she jumped at the chance, knowing that she needed the break, and set about badgering her younger sister into coming to stay with their parents on the grounds that one or two weeks a year would not hurt her when Catriona was there for them all year round.

Although not far from sixty herself, Catriona was still young and fit at heart. In the two years she had been working at Oak Lodge, she had become a fixture of the place, her ample frame, surgical stockings and comfortable shoes heralding efficiency and hard-work. She ran a tight ship and did not suffer fools gladly. Most of the care-workers were secretly scared of her and even Paul and Sharon were kept on their toes. And as for the Oak Lodge gossip Mrs O'Neill, Catriona was the bane of her life, always finding fault and preventing that good lady from enjoying a snoop-around or sneaking off work to have a well-earned cigarette.

But Catriona was a godsend, managing the staff with efficiency, unfailingly kind to the residents and their families, and Paul and Sharon blessed the day she had come to work for them. Now, as she let herself into the home, some twenty minutes early while everyone was busy with lunch, she was enjoying being back in the familiar surroundings, relaxed and happy from her holiday break. Because Catriona did indeed love her job and Oak Lodge meant much more to her than just a place to work.

Nodding hello to one or two people she met on the way, she headed upstairs to where the nurses had a little cloakroom and kitchenette of their own, determined to have a nice cup of tea to herself before her shift got underway. She was quite put out, therefore, to find that the room was already occupied by a man she didn't know, a man who was quite calmly drinking coffee, in her sanctuary, as if he belonged there.

"Excuse *me*," said Catriona, in her most matronly voice, "but what do you think you are you doing here? This is private."

The young man gave a start and got to his feet. He was smaller than Catriona, wide-shouldered and rather foreign-looking. He was dressed in a light tee-shirt and slacks. He didn't *look* like a workman, but these days you could never tell.

"I am sorry, Madam. I was told I could take my coffee here."

Definitely a workman, thought Catriona, as she noticed the thick mid-European accent.

"Well, I know you are entitled to coffee-breaks, young man, just like anyone else is, but really, this is not the place to take them. This room is out of bounds."

'Out of bounds' was obviously an expression that the young man did not understand. Catriona could see he was troubled. He seemed lost for words.

"I shall go get the Manager, yes? He will explain to you. He said I could come here, Madam."

"Paul said you could have your coffee-break here? Really! What a nuisance! I'm gone for just one week and the place starts falling apart. I'll have to have a word with Paul. He should not go around letting workmen use facilities that are reserved for the nursing staff."

"Ah, but Madam, you see…"

"Yes, I know you didn't mean any harm. This is not your fault, I quite see that now. Please don't apologize. I think we should go together and sort this out with Paul… with the Manager, don't you agree?"

"If that is your wish, Madam."

"It is. Now I'll just take my coat off and hang it here." She put her coat on a hook next to Paul's uniform. "Now, shall we go? The office is just across the corridor. No, no! Don't take that uniform. It's Paul's, it's not a workman's overall. It's for a nurse, see? A male nurse."

"But that is what I am trying to explain, Madam. You see…"

"Come along, come along. The quicker we get this sorted, the quicker I can have my tea. I'm due on duty in twelve minutes from now. I don't have all day!"

And she shuffled the unfortunate young man out into the corridor and rapped on the office door.

Sharon opened the door and saw Catriona and Krzysztof standing there with a huge invisible question mark on both their faces.

"Oh, hello Catriona. Welcome back," she began. "Did you have a nice holiday?"

"I did, thank you, Sharon, but I have come back to find this young workman having coffee in the nurses' restroom. He tells me that Paul said he could go there, which is obviously a gross misunderstanding. In fact, I do believe there has been..."

"Catriona, please, sorry to interrupt," said Sharon, "but there has indeed been a misunderstanding. While you were on holiday, we recruited the replacement nurse and he started this morning. Meet Krzysztof, Krzysztof Sokolsky. He's from Poland." She looked from one to the other.

"And he's our new nurse," she finished lamely.

"And what happened then, Eileen?" said Margaret, eyes wide in anticipation.

"Well," began Eileen, "our Sharon didn't know where to put herself, you know? There was Catriona, standing there like she'd just sucked a lemon, and that poor Polish man being treated like he was here to mend the cistern or something. Oh! I'd love to have been a fly on the wall!" She chuckled, imagining the scene all over again, when Sharon had related it to her the evening before.

"Then Paul, he comes along. He'd been downstairs helping to feed some of the residents and he takes in what's happening when Krzysztof and Catriona turned to look at him and Sharon's busy making SOS signs behind their backs."

"Go on. Go *on*. So what did Paul do then? Didn't Catriona tell him off?"

"Well, I don't think he gave her a chance. According to our Sharon, he summed up the situation at a glance, strode over to Catriona and lifted her up bodily, and God knows she's as heavy as me, and swung her round and kissed her on the cheek and said 'Welcome back' as if it were all perfectly normal. By the time he put her down, she was trying not to laugh and Sharon and Krzysztof, they were already laughing. And it made everything alright, you know?"

"Oh, what a wicked man! That's cheating, so it is. Using his charm to sweeten Catriona."

"It is, isn't it? But he's a terrible case, that Paul. Then he started pretending that Catriona had done his back in, and making her blush, until Sharon stepped in to suggest that Catriona give him a massage to make it better, when suddenly his back was fine! She said that even Krzysztof was playing along, so she asked them all in for tea and coffee in the office and everyone got to know each other properly."

"Oh! That's nice."

"Just as well, though, as Catriona will be deputy Manager when our Sharon goes on maternity leave. She'll be Krzysztof's boss. So it would've been awful to get off to a bad start; doesn't bear thinking about."

"And this Krzysztof?" said Margaret, eager to know all about this new male nurse. "What's he like? Is he nice?"

"You mean, is he good-looking?"

"Eileen Murphy, I'm a married lady!" said an outraged Margaret.

"And we're both far too old, I know," sighed her friend. "Well, it's like this. I haven't actually met him myself. But I've heard nothing but praise of him from both Sharon and Paul."

"Is he on duty today? Will we get to see him, do you think?"

"Oh! That must be him there now. Look, Margaret, with Paul."

"Oh my God, Eileen. They're heading our way..."

-oOo-

Chapter Twenty-Two

Aurore

So much was happening at the gîtes that Clare was almost dreading having to go all the way down to Rion des Landes to meet with the person who might be Meira's daughter, Aurore.

In the three weeks since her last visit, she had kept up a regular correspondence with Marcel and he had been able to confirm to her that none of the other ten Aurore's from the ledgers in Dax had been adopted, which only served to give weight to the idea that that Aurore Gaudin might indeed be George's heir.

Marcel had also been in contact with Catherine, Aurore's daughter, and a date for the middle of the third week in June had been arranged, Clare wanting to keep her week-ends free for the gîtes. According to Marcel, Madame Gaudin was just as anxious as Clare was to find out information about her real parents and was looking forward to talking to her.

So on that Tuesday in June, very early in the morning, Clare left the gîtes to start on the six-hour drive back to the Landes region where she had arranged to meet Marcel in a restaurant for a late lunch. She needed this little break to recover from the journey and catch up on all he had to relate to her concerning the quest. They took their time, lingering over the food and the coffee, their appointment with Madame Gaudin not until four pm.

Aurore Gaudin lived in one of the worker's cottages in a housing estate not far from the centre of the town. It was a two-bed, low, sloping roof cottage, surrounded by pine trees, similar to many Clare had seen on her last visit to the region. It was certainly no rich-man's mansion. Clare found herself having to quell the butterflies in her stomach as they made their way up to the front door and knocked.

The door was opened by a plump, middle-aged lady that Clare guessed was only several years younger than herself. She was smiling now and greeting them warmly. So this was Catherine. She bustled them in to the sitting-room to introduce them to her mother.

Aurore Gaudin was totally different from her daughter. Small, petite even, she had rich, auburn hair streaked with grey and beautiful large brown eyes. Elegantly dressed in that careless way that only the French can achieve, she greeted them now in a flutter of scarf and whiff of perfume, thanking them for coming all this way to see her. Clare could see that she was nervous, and trying to hide the fact, and she liked this woman immediately. They all sat down.

Speaking in French, Clare stating the reason for her visit, going back to the fact she had been the Manageress of an Old People's Home and how a solicitor in Ireland had asked her to find the family of one of the residents, how she had obtained proof that this man's lover, who had been French, had died just after the war and how their baby had been adopted by a family who did not want to see the child brought up in an orphanage.

"So, Madame Gaudin," said Marcel, when Clare stopped at this point in her story, "the reason for our visit is to determine whether you might be the Aurore we are looking for."

"Monsieur le Maire," began Aurore, hesitantly, "I know very little about my birth parents. The Delormeau family who raised me, were very kind but even they did not know who my father was. They talked to me about my mother. They said I had her eyes. They were sorry she did not live. Papa, that is Monsieur Delormeau, said that my real mother died from complications arising from my birth. She died a few days after I was born."

"How did Monsieur and Madame Delormeau meet your mother, Madame Gaudin? Do you know?" asked Clare.

"Please call me Aurore and I shall call you Clare, if that is alright?"

Clare smiled her agreement. "Of course."

"My mother told me that she was travelling from Paris back home to the Landes region after the war, to join Papa as it happened, and she met this Jewish girl called Meira."

Clare gasped and even Marcel sat up.

"Meira was pregnant and near her time but she was travelling to Saint Avit to find her parents and as Maman was going through Saint Avit to get to her own home, they stayed together. They came to the house in Saint Avit where Meira's parents' lived but it was all boarded up. Some of the neighbours, Jewish people, told Meira that her parents had been sent away to a concentration camp in Germany or Poland or somewhere. Maman said that she was very upset and cried and cried. Before leaving the house, they found a little box that Meira's father had meant for her to have and they found the key, which was hidden, and opened it. There was money, and some jewellery and precious stones and a letter."

Clare opened a bag she had brought with her and took out the old tin box. "Was this the box, Aurore?" she asked.

"That I do not know, Clare. But what I do know is that, when she read the letter, Meira was so upset she went into labour. Maman said she was frightened and did not know what to do. So she ran back to the neighbours for help and Meira gave birth in their house some hours later. That was my birth. That was where I was born six weeks before term." She paused.

"So what happened then, Aurore? Did your mother stay with Meira?"

"She did. They both stayed in this kind neighbour's house but my birth mother was very weak and ill. She knew she was dying. They brought the doctor but he could do nothing. There was no medicine you see and she needed antibiotics. The war was only just over."

"It must've been a very difficult time," said Marcel gently.

"It was. My mother, she often told me that story. She was very affected by what happened during that week. She had come to like Meira very much, even if she was Jewish and my mother was Catholic. And when she died, she could not let me go to an orphanage. She kept me as her own baby."

Aurore smiled, a little sadly. "I can tell you that when my mother arrived in her family with someone else's baby, she was not very welcome at first. But then they accepted me and the jewels and money Meria had given her before she died helped pay for food and clothes and my education."

"Did your mother tell you what your real father's name was?"

"Yes. It was Amilta. So she put that name on my birth registration. It is the only link I have had to him. My birth mother was so ill and died before she could tell

Maman where to find this man. I only have a small photo of him, and Meira, in a locket."

Clare looked at Marcel. "Do you still have this locket, Aurore?" he asked softly.

"Yes, I have it here. It is all I have from them. Meira was wearing this when she died. Please be careful, it is very old." And she handed over the locket for Clare to see.

Clare could feel the tears pricking at her eyes as she looked down and recognized the tiny faded photographs. For here indeed was Meira and George, the same photo of them together that Paul had sent to her by email, smiling reminders of a time when they were together, and happy. She handed the locket gently to Marcel who examined it in his turn. She was silent for so long, Aurore signalled to her daughter to go to the kitchen, where she had prepared a tray with coffee and biscuits.

"Aurore," began Clare, when she was composed once more. "You are the Aurore we are looking for. And I have important information to give to you about George, your father."

"*Oh mon Dieu*! Is my father still *alive*? Clare, are you telling me my father is still alive after all these years?"

"He is, Aurore. And he lives in that Old People's home I mentioned, in Ireland."

This brought tears to Aurore's eyes and for some minutes she was silent, fighting for control. Catherine quietly served them all coffee, then went over to put her arms around her mother's thin shoulders. Mother and daughter sat like that for some time in silence.

Finally Aurore said : "Clare, Monsieur le Maire, forgive me. This has been a shock. I am not even a good hostess. Please have some more coffee, help yourselves to biscuits."

She got up and went out of the room. Catherine watched her go, a worried frown darkening her face. She turned to Clare and Marcel.

"My mother, she has not been well. A cancer but she is over it now. The treatment, though, has left her very weak. I worry that she does not eat much, you know?"

"Yes of course, Catherine. I am a nurse. I understand," said Clare.

"This has come as a great shock to your mother," added Marcel kindly.

They sipped their coffee in silence, broken, from time to time, with pleasantries about the weather and how nice a town Rion des Landes was. Clare asked Catherine if she had any children of her own.

"Yes I do. I have two boys and one daughter. They are nearly grown up now. My daughter, she is at university. She is currently taking her final exams."

"And what does she study then?" asked Clare, more to say something than anything else.

"Languages. English and German. She speaks very good English and German."

"Oh, *really*?" said Clare, a hundred thoughts chasing themselves round in her head on learning this information. "Catherine, we must organize a meeting between Aurore and her father. It will have to be in Ireland because George is too old to travel now. He is ninety-two."

"Yes, I understand. Maman is weak but she will make this journey. I know she will. She has wanted to know about her father all her life. I will go with her to Ireland and... and... I shall get my daughter to come too. She will translate for us, yes she will speak English for us all!"

"And of course I shall come too, Catherine. I want to see this through to the end," said Clare.

At that point, Aurore came back in, her make-up re-done. Only a certain brightness about her eyes betrayed the emotion she was experiencing.

"Maman," said Catherine excitedly. "We are saying that you must go to Ireland and meet your father. He is very old now, ninety-two! I shall go with you and so shall Angélique. She will translate for us. And Clare, she will come too."

Aurore looked from one face to the other, hesitating. Then she nodded in agreement. "Yes, I will make this journey to Ireland. We shall go by plane. I will meet my father at last."

Clare beamed at her. "No time like the present, Aurore. Let me phone the home where George lives so that they can tell him we have found you. The managers there know that I was coming to see you today." And she took out her mobile, banishing the thought of the cost, as this was one phone-call that could just not wait. The others listened in silence, and not a little awe, as she spoke quickly in English.

"Oak Lodge? Hi, it's me, Clare. Is that you Geraldine? How are you?... Good, good. Can you put me through to Sharon, or Paul?... Sharon's at the hospital but you can put me through to Paul. Okay, thanks Geraldine."

They all waited while Paul came to the phone.

"Clare, how's it going? Any luck with the search for George's daughter?" he began in a terse voice.

"I have, Paul, I have. I'm sitting here in Aurore's house, Meira's daughter's house. And she has given us proof that George was her father. She has a little locket with a photo of both her parents and it's the exact same photo you sent to me by email that time!" Clare could hardly contain herself with excitement.

"I'm really glad that you've found Aurore, Clare," said Paul, relieved. "That's the best bit of news I've had all day. I was going to email you tonight but I think Aurore should come as quickly as possible. George took another TIA this morning. He's at the hospital now; Sharon's with him. It was a bad one, Clare, and I'm worried he'll not pull through."

-oOo-

Chapter Twenty-Three

Plans for Ireland

When Clare had finished speaking to Paul, she sat numbed by the awful news he had just given her. It would be just too terrible if father and daughter never got to meet when they were so close to doing so. She raised her eyes to see three expectant and now worried faces looking at her, having got the gist that something was wrong but not knowing what. Clare hastened to tell them what had happened.

"You must go, immediately, this week, Clare," said Marcel. "This cannot wait any longer. This old man might die."

Clare took a deep breath, put herself into organization mode.

"Right. First things first. Aurore, are you free to come to Ireland for the next few days? And what about you, Catherine? And Angélique?"

"I am free to come, Clare," said Aurore, looking at her daughter, "but Catherine, at the gallery, they are depending on you." She turned back to Clare and Marcel. "Catherine runs an art gallery in Dax and there is a big exposition opening on Friday."

"Oh, Maman! I did so want to come. I will join you next week, just as soon as I can, but for now I must be present at the gallery. My presence is imperative. There are so many people coming from far away. I cannot disappoint them." Catherine was clearly upset.

"What about Angélique? When does she finish her exams?" said Clare.

"Tomorrow. She will finish tomorrow at lunchtime," said Catherine.

"And where is she studying?"

"At Bordeaux. She is at the university of Bordeaux."

"Good, then we shall go on the Internet and book tickets from Bordeaux. Catherine, can you phone Angélique and check whether she is available tomorrow afternoon to come to Ireland and if so, get her identity card details? Aurore, you must bring that little locket you showed us. That will mean so much to your father. Now I must phone the gîtes. If we leave tomorrow, Wednesday, I should be able to get back by Friday. I need to be at the gîtes for Saturday, you see. It's our busy day."

"Ah, with guests leaving and others arriving, I suppose?" suggested Marcel.

"Exactly. Marcel, do you wish to come with us? After all, this had been your quest too."

"If George were not so ill, I would say yes Clare, with pleasure. But given the circumstances… no, I will not come this time to see your beautiful Ireland."

"Well, I hope you will come to our gîtes in Brittany one day. Come in the off season. It would be our pleasure to spend time with you and your wife. At the moment though, everything is booked up for the next three or four months."

"That is excellent for business, Clare. I am happy for you. And we will take you up on your offer one day."

This settled, Clare asked Aurore if she had a computer with access to the Internet.

"Yes, I do. Here, it is through here," she said, leading Clare to the back of the house where what was normally a small dining-room had been turned into a study.

Clare went on the Aer Lingus website to book two one-way flights from Bordeaux to Dublin, Catherine having confirmed that Angélique would be going too, and hired a car at Dublin airport. She then booked a return flight for herself, blessing her good sense that made her carry her passport with her at all times. When Aurore wanted to pay, Clare told her politely but firmly that the costs of their flights and their stay in Ireland, were all taken care of. At this stage, she did not want to go into details about George's estate. The priority for now was that he got to meet his daughter.

With tickets bought and boarding passes printed out, she put a call through to Paul once more to let him know they were on their way and to ask him to arrange accommodation near Oak Lodge for them all and forward the invoice to Damien Murray, the solicitor.

By the time everything was arranged, it was nearly seven pm. Declining the offer of aperitifs at Aurore's house, Clare and Marcel took their leave, but not before Clare had handed Aurore photocopies of the two letters that the little tin box had contained, assuring her she would receive the originals in due course.

She left Aurore to peruse the letters in peace, the one from the Jewish grandfather she had never known, as he waited for capture and deportation, and the other from her adoptive mother who, as a young girl, had been present at her birth and given her a home and all the love she could.

Back at Oak Lodge, the atmosphere was clearly much more sombre than it had been the previous day when Krzysztof had begun his new job. Paul was particularly distressed at seeing George so ill, frustrated that he might not get to see his daughter before he died. After all he'd been through, after all Clare's searching, they were so close; things could just not end like this.

Sharon had phoned him around 8pm to tell him that George was stable, although very weak. They couldn't tell exactly what damage had been done but it boded no good to see him limp and lifeless. Paul took a decision. Leaving Catriona in charge until Carmel came on duty at 10pm, he left the home and headed to the hospital where George had been taken earlier in the day. There he took Sharon's place at George's bedside, shooing her off for a cup of tea, telling her to bring him one too.

Then he sat down in the visitor's chair and took the old man's hand in his. George lay with his eyes closed, breathing gently, sleeping quite peacefully. Paul wondered sadly if he would ever wake up again, and if he did, what part of George would've been damaged this time.

He had been with Krzysztof doing the morning rounds when they had entered George's room. This time it was Krzysztof doing the work and Paul doing the observing. George had already been washed and dressed by the care-workers and was sitting in his armchair. Paul's cheery greeting was met with silence, which did not immediately bother him until Krzysztof dashed over to the old man to flash a light in his eyes and feel the pulse at his neck.

"Paul, this man, this George, is ill. Look, look at him. We must get him to hospital immediately," he cried.

Paul's heart began to thud. George did indeed look ill. He was slouching in his armchair, his eyes closed, not moving a muscle, quite unconscious. Paul whipped out his mobile to call an ambulance.

And now here he was, in hospital, and they didn't know if he'd survive the night. Poor old George! A lifetime of waiting only to have happiness snatched from him at the last possible moment. It was so bloody unfair...

When Sharon came back with two foam beakers of tea, she brought him up to speed with all that had happened that day. George had regained consciousness sometime during the afternoon but he hadn't recognized her, which was upsetting, and now he was sleeping and possibly would sleep all night.

Paul told her all about Clare, and her finding of Aurore. He was determined to spend the night with George, just in case he woke up, and tell him, over and over again if needs be, that his daughter was on her way to see him. Then he made Sharon leave, in spite of her protestations, as he could see that she was very tired.

And so began a long vigil for Paul, sitting, watching George sleep. He thought of all those quiet evenings when they had sat in his room, sipping that fabulous whiskey, talking about the days gone past. George had a way of bringing the past to life, his mind flitting from one little detail to another in a patchwork of memories, each fragment a photo to be pored over and commented.

And when everyone else on the ward was sleeping soundly, Paul began to talk softly, a simple monologue telling George all that had happened that day, why it was so important this time to fight back. He spoke the names of Meira and Aurore and Saint Avit over and over again well into the night, hoping against hope for a miracle he feared would never come.

He was woken by a nurse sometime around six, stiff and sore from having fallen asleep in the chair. For a second or two, he didn't know where he was; then it all came back to him in a rush. He hastened over to George.

George was awake and looking at him strangely.

"You need a shave, young man," he said quite clearly.

"I probably do," chuckled Paul, putting his hand on his cheek and chin to feel the stubble. "Tell me, how are you feeling, George?"

"Could do with a wee dram."

"George, it's six in the morning. That's far too early to be thinking about whiskey," chided Paul.

"No time like the present. Not long to go now," whispered the old man.

"Don't be daft, George. You'll pull through this. You've done it before. There are people coming to see you tonight. People from France."

George pondered on this information for a while.

"Meira went to France. She didn't come back," he said sadly.

Paul was pleased. George still remembered Meira. He remembered the whiskey. All was not lost. He was too long in the tooth to know that things were far from over, though. The TIA would continue to wield its ravages over the next few weeks and what George remembered now might be taken from him later on. But one day at a time. And this day was going to be a very special one for George, he was certain of that.

"George, Meira died. Just after the war. It was a long time ago. She died giving birth to your daughter, to Aurore."

"My baby daughter," said George slowly, the effort of remembering visible as he closed his eyes to concentrate.

"Yes, George, Aurore is no longer a baby. She's seventy now and she's coming to see you. She's on her way, George. Clare found her for you. Aurore is on her way."

"On her way," repeated George. But the effort of concentration was getting too much. Paul decided that he'd said enough for now. He held the old man's hand, rubbing the crinkled skin gently as George slid back into sleep.

By the time Paul got home, it was nearly eight am, having called into Oak Lodge to see Carmel before she came off duty. Beatrice was on the early shift and

Krzysztof was due in at nine, so he decided to go home and grab a few hours' sleep. Sharon was already in her nurse's uniform when he let himself into the kitchen.

"How is he, then?" she said anxiously, as Paul came over to kiss her hello.

"Much better than I thought he would be. He's very weak and tired but he was able to say a few words to me this morning and most of all, he still remembers Meira, and Aurore. I think he took on board the fact that Aurore will be coming today, but it was difficult to tell."

"You must be exhausted. I'll make you a bite of breakfast, then why don't you get some sleep? I'll go on duty today, I'm feeling well enough. I'll replace you till such times as you're feeling up to it."

"Thanks, Sharon. I'll not say no. I stayed awake most of the night but must've fallen asleep around five. I'm all stiff and sore."

"Old age," said Sharon emphatically. "Now have some cereal and toast and off you go to bed."

"I will. But tell me, any news of how Kieran got on? Yesterday was the first of his exams, wasn't it? I'm losing track of time."

"It was and he says it was harder than he thought."

"When's the next one?"

"Friday. Then four more papers next week and it's over." She sighed. "I just hope he gets them Paul. He *assures* me he's studying hard but with Kieran you never can tell."

"Mm... well, he knows what's at stake. And he did well last year in the AS credits. Let's give him the benefit of the doubt, shall we? And Beth, she's a hard worker. She'll keep his nose to the grindstone better than we could."

"True enough." Sharon sighed. "But I'll be glad when it's all over."

Over at Paul's old flat, Kieran was still trying to come to terms with the fact that he'd made a total hash of his first Physics paper and panicking at the thought he might not get into Uni after all.

-oOo-

Chapter Twenty-Four

Céline gets a posting

It was in the afternoon of the second day that Céline received the news. She had got back from work early, as she had some free periods on Tuesday afternoons. Thoughts of her posting still uppermost in her mind, she went on to the academy website to see if her name had come up, quite convinced that she didn't stand a chance but unable to stop herself.

But there it was! Guéri, Céline, *épouse* Maher. No doubt about it. She had got her permanent posting. With trembling fingers, she clicked on the mouse to read on. Thoughts raced around in her head. If it were a permanent posting so soon, it was probably to an area where no-one else wanted to go. Oh Lord!

Saint Aubert des Loges. Céline had never heard of it. But by the postal code it was in the Ille et Vilaine *département**. The Rennes area!! Near where Ian worked. Not far from the gîtes and not far from her own family in Le Méaugon. Her heart pounding, she brought up the Mappy website and typed the code to see where she had landed.

It was to the north of the *département*, not far from Saint Malo, or Dinan, or even Fougères. Oh Lord! This was great! It did not seem very big, a small town really, or a big village. She Googled it. It looked lovely. Oh! Céline stopped. *Calm down*, she told herself. First, is it a *collège* or a *lycée*? She much preferred a *collège*, the 11 to 15 year olds were easier to deal with although the 15 to 18 year olds would be rewarding too, especially when they realized the usefulness of learning English. It was a *collège*. Okay, perfect. She went on the school's website and was really pleased to see that they had adhered to the PELVE* programme for the teaching of foreign languages. This was a new way to teach languages with pupils being taught a second foreign language as of their second year and reinforced teaching of their first foreign language, which was usually English, using all media forms and even, in some cases, teaching other subjects in English as well. Céline hugged herself. This was going to be *so* good. She couldn't wait to visit her new school and meet the staff and the pupils. She couldn't wait to tell Ian.

She then went back on Mappy to see just how far Saint Aubert des Loges was from Rennes (about 45 minutes), from Le Méaugon (1 hour and 15 minutes) and from the gîtes (about 2 hours). Just right. Not too near to anyone, so as to keep their independence, and not too far either. Bliss! Absolute bliss! Céline was drunk on happiness.

It was hard to settle to do school-work but she made herself do it. Ian was due back around seven pm and she wanted to have the rest of the evening free to celebrate. Around five she slipped out to the local shops to buy bread, and wine, and smoked salmon, which she intended putting into a pasta dish, knowing that it was one of Ian's favourite foods. Two hours later, all was ready, the table set and Céline was counting the minutes.

Meanwhile Ian sat in his office in Rennes, going over, for the umpteenth time, the problem that had been worrying him all afternoon. He mentally kicked himself for not being more on the ball but the bottom line was that he had totally messed things up. He hadn't seen this coming, when he should have done, and the client was furious and counting on him to put things right. But to put things right, it was going to take him *at least* three whole days' work, days that the customer was perfectly entitled not to pay him for, since it was Ian's fault that things had gone so wrong in the first place.

He had battled all afternoon to avoid having to go back and re-do this particular configuration, trying to find a quick way out. But he had finally come to the conclusion that it was just impossible and now everything was running late. And all due to the fact he had missed one little thing and the whole programme had to be gone through, line by line, to find out where the problem lay and be rewritten. Finally, with a sinking heart, he knew he had to inform his boss and admit his error. He needed help to solve the problem and also for the sales rep to intervene to negotiate payment of at least some of the extra man-hours needed. He got wearily to his feet.

On the drive home later that evening, he was still cringing from the interview. If only they'd shouted at him, called him useless, or done something where he could retaliate, defend himself. But watching their anxious faces, their rapid grasping of the problem and its implications, their refusal to let Ian work for nothing to solve it, made him kick himself all the more. Eating humble pie was one thing, but everyone being so nice about it was quite another. He was very embarrassed, upset and angry. Try as he might, this was one evening when he just could not disconnect.

It was nearly half past eight when he got in by which time Céline had been fighting visions of him in a car accident or a breakdown or, more realistically, a meeting that went on far too long. She had been struggling with herself not to phone him as she knew he'd be driving, and her excitement at her posting had melted to worry as the minutes passed. She flung herself on him as he came through the door.

"Oh! J'étais inquiète! T'étais où?" she cried.

It was not often that Céline spoke French to Ian. Now that he spoke the lingo fairly well, she complied to his request of speaking English at home. He needed that break to clear his head from work. But just now, in his angry state, and feeling guilty because he should've phoned her to say he'd be late, he rounded on Céline in a way that she'd never seen him do before.

"Céline, talk English! I'm up to here speaking French. And it's not because I'm a bit late that you have to kick up a fuss. I'm home, alright?"

"But I was worried, Ian. I thought you had had a car crash. It is half past eight!"

"I know perfectly well what time it is. I was held up at work. I've had a God-awful day, Céline. Now I'm really knackered. Just leave it, okay?" He looked round the sitting-room, all tidy and the table laid for two. "Look, I've got a lot of work on, so I'll just head on up to my study. I'll grab a sandwich later."

And he made to go up the stairs. He hadn't even kissed her hello. Céline was puzzled and hurt.

"I have something nice to tell you, Ian," she called after him as he went up the stairs.

"Can't it wait, Céline? I've got to get on here. I'll see you later." And he was gone.

When the sound of his footsteps had stopped, Céline sat down heavily at the pretty table she had taken care to prepare. She wasn't quite sure what had happened. Her stomach felt like lead. Their first argument, their very first real argument, and she didn't even know what it was about. She'd been looking forward to this moment all day, ever since she'd got the news of her posting. They'd talked about it so often. It was the rock upon which all their plans for the future depended. And now, the very moment they should be jumping for joy, here they both were, angry and upset. Tears of self-pity welled up inside her and spilled down onto the table-cloth. Try as she might, she could not stem their flow.

One good cry later, she blew her nose and tried to analyse what she had done wrong. Once again she came to the conclusion that it was not her fault, whatever it was that had Ian in such a bad mood. She guessed rightly that it must be to do with work. Ian took his work so seriously, he always went that extra mile. And she knew he was liked and respected in his job.

So what had gone wrong?

All evening Ian stayed in his study with the door shut. At one point, Céline had tip-toed up the stairs to see if she could coax him to come down but that shut door spoke volumes. She decided to leave him alone.

Not feeling up to eating a solitary celebration meal, she made herself a sandwich around ten pm and one for Ian, which she left outside his study door. Then she lay down on the sofa to watch the evening news, exhausted with worry, and soon after fell asleep with the telly still on.

Sometime after midnight, Ian came out of his office and nearly trampled on the sandwich left for him by Céline. He was immediately stricken with remorse. He'd been angry at himself and he'd been horrible to her. She didn't deserve this and he didn't deserve *her*. Noting that she wasn't in bed, he went downstairs to find her and apologise.

Seeing his little wife curled up on the sofa, her cheeks streaked with mascara where she'd obviously been crying, made his heart melt. She's had something nice to tell him and he'd gone and spoiled it all for her. Bending down he kissed her forehead gently so as not to wake her. Then he switched the television off and hunted out a spare blanket which he draped over her sleeping form.

For a minute or two, he stood fondly watching her sleep. Then he turned and went quietly up the stairs and back into his office.

Céline woke sometime after four in the morning surprised to find herself on the settee. Then the previous night's fiasco came back to her in a rush and with it that dreaded sinking feeling of things all gone wrong. She got up to go to the loo. When she had finished, she decided that Ian or no Ian, she was going up the stairs to spend the rest of the night in her bed. Settees were perfectly alright for a nap but she had a job to do on the morrow and needed her sleep.

This time his office door was open and Ian was still at his computer. She went to chide him for working so late, make him come to bed, but remembering his attitude of earlier in the evening, she stopped herself. Tip-toeing past, she went on into their bedroom, undressed, and lay down on the empty bed. Ian had not even heard her come up.

The next morning Céline was due in school for half pas eight. That meant leaving home at a quarter to. When her alarm sang out gently at seven am, she got up quickly, noticing sadly that Ian had not come to bed, and showered and dressed with a heavy heart. On her way past his office, she looked quietly in, only to see his desk abandoned and Ian stretched out fully-clothed, fast asleep on the sofa-bed they kept there.

So he hadn't even come to bed. This was the first time he had deliberately not spent the night with her. More hurt to add to all the other hurt she had already stored up since the previous night. And she still didn't know why.

Later that morning, during a free period, she went to see the principal of her school to let him know that she would not be teaching there the following school year and to share the news of her permanent posting. The principal was nearing the end of his career, the year to come would be his last. He was a tough old nut, but kind and just. He liked Céline, not only for her skill in dealing with the pupils, and her excellent command of English, he really liked the person she was and was sorry to hear that she was moving on. They talked about her new posting and the PELVE system that meant so much to Céline and Saint Aubert des Loges which the principal knew personally, having holidayed in Saint Malo the previous year.

When she left to go back to class, he could not help but wonder, with all the good things that were happening to her, when all her dreams were finally coming true, why she was so sad. It wasn't like Céline at all.

Céline didn't know just exactly how it happened but, if anything, things got worse over the next few days. Ian was either permanently in his study or away in Rennes. He got home late every night and although he had found a few minutes to apologise to her at some point, he still was not forthcoming about what the problem was and she felt totally excluded from his life. Meals were not taken together, he came to bed only when she was already asleep, all attempts on her part to find out more were met with 'it's too complicated to explain' noises. In this fraught atmosphere, she was certainly not going to talk about her new posting. She was determined that she would not have her good news all scrunched up and rejected by a husband who couldn't even confide in her anymore. By the end of the week, anger had become a buffer for the hurt and she found herself on the Friday afternoon packing a suitcase. Visions of Pierre, her first real boyfriend, who had turned his back on her on learning of her year out in Ireland, came flooding back to taunt her. She had been so hurt at the time, she thought she would never get over it. Now those feelings of rejection, long buried and forgotten, had resurfaced, and with them the worry that she was somehow responsible but not knowing why.

As she zipped her case shut and gathered her coat and handbag, Céline wondered fearfully how on earth she came to find herself in this position at all.

-oOo-

PELVE = Projet d'établissement pour les langues vivantes étrangères : a project for the teaching of foreign languages

Département= County

Chapter Twenty-Five

Refuge

Céline sat in her car, in a lay-by not far from the roundabout, her hands shaking, not knowing what to do. The note she had left him just stated that she had gone away for the weekend to 'think things through' and that she would be back on the Sunday evening. Fortunately, or perhaps unfortunately, she was due back at school on Monday.

It was all very well, thought Céline, to make this huge statement, leave Ian to stew in his own juices and (hopefully) come to his senses. It was quite another when you'd actually gone and done it.

Where should she go? There was no question of spending time at one of her colleague's places. It would be just too embarrassing for words. Her parents? No, this was the week-end they were away visiting her grandmother. Her brother didn't count. Brothers don't count in these situations, especially younger brothers, but what about Julie in Paris? A sisterly week-end doing a bit of retail therapy, downing a bottle or two of wine, raking men in general and having a good cry would certainly go a long way to cheering her up. She went into her contacts and brought up the number.

Julie was delighted to hear from her sister and rushed to bring her up-to-date. She was actually at Montparnasse train station, meeting René's train. He had taken the Friday afternoon off to travel up from Brest and spend the week-end with her. As this only happened about once a month, she was happy and excited. Céline could hear it in her voice. So when she asked, in her turn, how they were both keeping, Céline did not have the heart to burden Julie with her problems. It was just something she could not bring herself to do, knowing, as she did, that it would spoil the lovely week-end Julie was looking forward to. As luck would have it, René's train was pulling into the station as they spoke so she didn't have time to say much and did not have to keep up the pretence of happy married life for longer than it was humanly possible to do so. She wished them both a lovely time.

Sitting in the car, watching the evening traffic as rush-hour began, Céline knew that there was one place she could go where she would always be welcome. It might be the one place Ian would not think to look for her but she knew she needed to be with friends at the moment. She turned the car and drove off decidedly in the direction of the gîtes.

It was still quite light when she got there, the long June evening a welcome ally to lift her spirits. She had stopped to phone the gîtes at one point but as no-one answered, she left a message hoping that her unexpected visit would not cause problems.

Céline and Ian had lived a year with Clare and Frank when they first took over the gîtes, Céline studying for her CAPES* teaching exam and Ian running the IT courses, and studying French, and both helping out with the 101 jobs that went with running the business. They had moved to Laval some ten months ago when Céline got her first teaching post as a probationary teacher. But deep down, the gîtes would always seem like home from home. Céline was looking forward to a motherly hug from Clare, trying to persuade herself, over and over again, that she would not break down, blurt out the whole sorry story, and cry.

But as she drove into the complex, she could see no sign of Clare or Frank. She stopped at the swimming-pool cum games-room but could only make out the unknown faces of quite a few guests. All the gîtes seemed to be rented out, or nearly, which meant that it was highly unlikely that Clare and Frank had left the place unmanned. She got back into her car and drove on to the gatehouse gîte.

Here again, all was in darkness, which was a very unusual state of affairs. She parked the car, got slowly out and went over to try the office door. It was locked.

Céline stood there waiting, convinced that Clare would appear out of nowhere any minute now. After ten minutes or so, she walked round to where they usually parked to see if Clare or Franks' cars were there. No sign of either of them. It was all very out of character and not a little worrying. She walked slowly back to the office. Suddenly the quiet of the evening was shattered by the sound of the telephone ringing within. Hesitating for just a second, Céline went quickly over to fish out the spare key from its usual haunt and opened the door, dashing over to the phone to catch it before the ringing stopped.

"Allo?" she cried, rather desperately.

"Who's that?" came a voice she was relieved to hear.

"Clare, it is I, Céline. There was no-one in the office so I opened the door to answer the phone."

"*Céline?* You're at the *gîtes*?" came Clare's astonished voice.

"Yes, I have come to ask you could I spend the week-end with you? Do you mind, Clare? I phoned on the way but no-one answered."

"Of course I don't mind, darling. But you'll have to use one of the bedrooms upstairs in the gatehouse gîte. Owen's using the other. All the gîtes are booked out at the moment and the manor house isn't quite ready for sleeping in."

"Thank you Clare. You are so very kind, as always."

"On the contrary! I'm delighted you've come. This is a lovely surprise. But I'll be roping you and Ian into helping out with the changeover tomorrow though. We're really quite busy. You don't mind?"

"No, of course not! I would be happy to. But I am on my own, Clare. Ian is not with me this time."

"Oh! Really? Too much work on, I suppose."

"Yes. Too much work," said Céline sadly.

"Well," said Clare, briskly, sensing that there was more to this than met the eye, "I'm glad we'll get to spend time with you, dear. I'm on my way back from Bordeaux airport. I had to go to Ireland on Wednesday. It was all very sudden. I'll let you know all about it when I get home. Now, tell me, is Frank back from the language school yet?"

"No. All was in darkness when I got here."

"And where's Owen?"

"I have no idea."

"I *told* him not to leave the gîtes unless it was absolutely necessary." Clare was vexed. "But when I think about it, he's probably had to go over to the manor house for some reason or other. The foreman there likes to talk to him before leaving for the week-end." She was relieved. "Yes, that's where he is, most likely."

"Do not worry, Clare. I shall stay at the office till either Owen or Frank get home. What time do you think you will arrive?"

"Another hour and a half, unfortunately. I've just by-passed Nantes. I should be there about half-past nine."

"That is fine, Clare. I shall prepare us something to eat."

"Oh Céline! You're an *angel*! There's plenty of foodstuffs in the freezer. Just help yourself. See you very soon."

"Bye, Clare. *Sois prudente*!"

Now that she had a purpose to fulfil and confident that Clare was sincerely pleased to have her around, Céline got to work, happier than she had been since Tuesday night. She first carried her small case upstairs and put it in the bedroom that looked unoccupied, the other, with its unmade bed and clothes strewn all over the place, left her in no doubt as to where Owen was sleeping.

Then she went downstairs into the kitchen to work out a menu for four that would please them all, a little challenge that was just what she needed right now. Glancing at her mobile phone, Ian hadn't rung which meant that he still hadn't got home from work yet, she put it resolutely back into her handbag, found an apron and got to work.

Nearly an hour later, the door opened and in came Frank. He stopped in his tracks when he saw Céline in the kitchen, then came quickly over to kiss her hello. He looked tired, but happy to see her.

"Céline! Wasn't expecting you. Clare never said. This is great! Are you here for the week-end? Where's Ian?" he began.

"I am here on my own, Frank. Ian is working all the time. Problems at his job."

"Know how he feels. There are times when it just takes over your life. I could do with a nice lazy week-end but the gîtes are fully booked up as of next week and the manor house, and the gardens, all swallow up any chance I get of a free hour or two. It's all go. Beginning to feel my age, I suppose."

"Well, I shall help you out with the changeover tomorrow. And Solange, she will be here too?"

"She will, thank God. She's great, that girl. Has even got our Owen helping out. Never actually thought it could be done, that."

"Do I hear my name taken in vain?" came Owen's cheery voice from the doorway.

"Just saying what a good influence Solange has been on you, Son. Come in. Look who's here!"

"Hi, Owen," said Céline, a little shyly. This was Ian's best friend.

"Céline! Happy days! You come for the week-end?"

"I did phone, but no-one was here," said Céline, trying to explain something that was actually explainable. It would be harder to explain why Ian was not with her.

"Been helping Jean-Christophe in the garden most of the afternoon. We're very busy. And then I had to go over to the manor house before they left off work. But, listen, great to see you. Where's Ian?"

"I was just telling Frank. Ian is not with me this time. He has too much work."

"Aw! That's a pity. Still, I see you've been busy. Something smells good."

"I talked to Clare on the phone. She will be here in about half an hour from now."

"Time for a well-deserved aperitif, then," said Frank, happily. "What'll it be, Céline?"

"Could I have a glass of white wine, Frank? There is some opened in the fridge."

"Perfect. I'll see to it. Owen, the usual, okay?"

Just then Céline's phone rang. She stopped, looked worriedly at her handbag, hesitated, then took the phone out, put it to her ear and went outside. Father and son looked at each other.

"Everything okay with Ian and Céline?" said Owen, voicing what they both felt instinctively. It was so very unusual to see Céline by herself.

"No idea," said Frank, clearly tired. He sighed. "They say that the course of true love never runs smooth. Let's give her some space. She'll confide if she wants to, although it'll probably be to Clare, not to you or I."

He busied himself pouring out the pre-dinner drinks while Owen nipped upstairs to have a quick shower and surreptitiously tidy up the bathroom he would be sharing with Céline.

He was surprised, on coming down some fifteen minutes later, to see that Céline was still outside, hands gesticulating, clearly in a heated discussion with Ian.

"God, she's still on the phone!" he said to Frank. "Must be one helluva bust-up. Our Ian's ear is getting a bending by the looks of things. Do him good. Probably deserves it. Wish I could hear what she's saying."

"Owen! Leave them alone. Come into the kitchen and give me a hand to lay the table. Here's your drink. Bring out some nibbles. I'm starving," said Frank, paying lip-service to decorum but inwardly just as curious as his son was to know what was going on.

It was some ten minutes later that Céline eventually came back into the kitchen, eyes bright, head held high.

"That was Ian," she said.

"Um… so we guessed," said Owen, as his father remained discretely silent. "Everything alright?"

"We had some explanations to make. It… It has been a difficult week… for us both," she added, with an effort at being fair.

"These things happen, Céline," said Frank gently. "Anyway, we're happy you're here with us tonight. That casserole smells good. I turned in down to low. And I've mixed the soup. It was ready."

"Thank you, Frank," said Céline. "And thank you for not asking."

He came over to give her a hug. This was almost too much for Céline. Owen could see she was about to cry. He jumped in both feet first.

"Well, if my Dad doesn't want to know why you and Ian are fighting, I do," he announced happily. "Go on, Céline. Tell us all. What's my stroppy uncle gone and done on you now? Just give me the word and I'll bash him over the head."

"Oh, Owen!" said Céline laughing in spite of herself. "There is no need for violence. And I do not think Ian would let you attack him. He is taller than you are."

"Ah, but only just and I'm a lot younger than he is. By about twelve years. And I'm very fit. Look, Céline, just look at those arm muscles! I've been doing so much gardening and cleaning since I came to the gîtes, my body is now quite perfect!"

"Owen, you are a perfect *eejit*," countered Céline. "You always have been. But I think I love you, just a little, for that."

Just then, they heard a car arriving and turned to watch as Clare pulled into the car-park. They all trooped outside to help her with her case and various bags of duty free she inevitably brought back with her each time she went to Ireland.

"Céline, this is lovely! So please to see you! But... are you okay?" began Clare, as she struggled to get out of the car and stretch her limbs, stiff and cramped from the drive.

"I am fine now. Thank you Clare," came Céline's sincere reply.

"Great! I'm so glad. Frank, take this soda bread, will you? We'll have it for breakfast tomorrow. Owen, get that case for me. It's in the boot, there's a love. I can manage the rest, thanks."

"Hey, ho! She's back. It's been a quiet few days without orders from Mum, hasn't it, Dad?"

"Brace yourself, Son. She'll be wanting to make up for lost time."

"Pay no attention, Céline," said Clare as she linked her arm though the young girl's. "Now, I can smell something nice cooking in there. You've made a casserole, haven't you? Oh, you lovely person, you! Now hurry up with that case, Owen. Just dump it in the bedroom. God, I've so much to tell you all, you wouldn't believe it!"

-oOo-

CAPES* = Le Certificat d'Aptitude au Professorat de l'Enseignement du Second Degré : The French official teaching diploma.

Chapter Twenty-Six

Clare's story

Over the soup, Clare began her tale. She first brought Céline up to speed with all she had undertaken on behalf of George, all the searching and finally the finding, of George's heirs. Céline was quietly impressed. Seventy years on and Clare had managed to do what even George himself had not been able to do all those years ago.

"Well, as I was saying, we got to Dublin airport and I had the hired car waiting and we raced up the M1 to the hospital, 'cos Paul had told me the day before how ill George was. He'd had another TIA stroke, a bad one apparently. I was with Aurore, George's daughter, and Angélique, Aurore's granddaughter, who actually speaks very good English. She'd just finished her final exams at university in Bordeaux that self-same morning. Imagine!

Anyway, there we were, breaking our necks to get to George in time and when we got to the hospital, he was sitting up in bed, drinking tea and reading the paper, as if nothing had happened!"

"So he didn't have an attack after all, then," said Frank.

"Actually, he did, but it wasn't such a bad one as the doctors originally thought. He didn't know who any of us where, obviously. He'd forgotten about me a long time ago which is only natural with Alzheimer's disease, but when Angélique came in, he put down the paper and his hand began to tremble. I had to take the tea-cup from him he was shaking so much. And then he looked at her, and looked at her, and put out his hand to her. And he just said 'Meira'."

"He thought Angélique was Meira?" said Owen, trying to fathom this one out.

"He did, he really did. And it's not surprising, in a way. She's very like her great-grandmother in many respects. She has long dark hair and she's about twenty-two and you can see Meira's traits in both Angélique and Aurore, even though the photos I have of Meira are small black and white ones, not easy to make out."

"So did you tell him this was not Meira, then, but Angélique?" asked Céline. "Was he not confused?"

"He was. He was confused and quite tearful. We had to take it step by step. The poor man's life was being turned upside-down; I was getting worried that it would all be too much for him. Then Paul arrived, as it happened. He'd been calling in to see George regularly and the nurses told me he'd spent the previous night by George's bedside, all night long. It was lovely to see him and he had a wonderfully calming effect on George. He helped me introduce Aurore to her father and even George could see how very moved she was. It's not every day you get to meet your dad for the first time at the age of seventy."

"Yes, and how many men get to meet their daughter for the first time at the age of ninety-two? It must have been an emotional time all round," added Frank.

"It was, Frank. It was. And when Aurore brought out the little locket, with photos of Meira and George, it brought tears to his eyes. He remembered it, he did! I think that's when he realized that Meira was really dead. Poor man, the tears were rolling down his cheeks. And then Paul suggested we call it a day and let him rest. It was a lot for anyone to take on board. And Aurore was upset too, and tired after the journey, so we headed to the hotel Paul had arranged for the three of us and he stayed behind with George to make sure he was alright. He joined us later and we all had dinner together. He told us that George had eventually fallen asleep with the locket still clasped in his hand."

"What a wonderful story, Clare! You have been so good. And so clever to find this Aurore and her granddaughter," said Céline, impressed.

"So what happened then, Mum? Did you spend all day yesterday with George at the hospital?" asked Owen.

"Actually, George was released from hospital Thursday morning after the doctor had made his rounds; they don't keep people in very long these days, especially when they know he's in specialized care. So we all met up at Oak Lodge and were there when the ambulance brought him to the home. He was carrying the little locket in his hand still and even remembered who Aurore was. We still had to talk him through the presence of Angélique. She looks so like Meira, apparently, that George is thrown every time he sees her. Meantime I'd been on the phone to Damien. Damien Murray, the solicitor, remember him, Owen? You were at school with his younger son Declan."

"Oh yeah! I'd heard he'd gone in for law. Haven't seen him in ages."

"Well, I had a meeting arranged with Damien at his offices for five thirty Thursday afternoon. Yesterday afternoon as it was. God, I'm getting mixed up. There's been so much happening this week. Anyway, I took Aurore and Angélique there and between us, Angélique and I, we translated to Aurore the fact that she was George's heir, that she would be quite rich on his death and that she would be entitled to a seat on the Board of Governors of Oak Lodge itself."

"She was happy then, when she learned of all this good fortune?" asked Céline.

"Actually, not really, Céline. It's all been a huge shock for her. Aurore had cancer not so long ago and she's still recovering from it and is not very strong. In the space of a few days, she's learnt the existence of a father she did not know she had, took a plane journey to a country she's never been to before, and met this old man who thinks her granddaughter is her mother. Then I come along with more surprises about a big inheritance and shares in Oak Lodge. She was actually quite upset. It made her cry. She was much happier back in Oak Lodge just sitting by George's side and holding his hand." Clare took a deep breath. "Anyway, to cut a long story short, she agreed to the DNA test that Damien needed in order to prove who she was but, really, it's only a formality. Anyone can see that Aurore is George's daughter and the fact that she had her mother's locket with the photos in it, is proof enough for me, at any rate."

"Quite a story, love, isn't it?" said Frank, taking Clare's hand. Even though it had meant extra work for him and Owen at the gîtes, he couldn't help but admire all that she had done to bring this about. All the Internet researching, the phone calls, the to-ing and fro-ing down to Saint Avit. And now the big trip to Ireland and all the emotional upheaval involved. And tomorrow she would be cleaning kitchens and making beds in the weekly gîte changeover just as if nothing had happened, while over in Ireland, thanks to Clare, Aurore now had a father, and George, a ready-made family he thought he'd never see.

"Did Aurore and Angélique come back with you then, Mum?" asked Owen, as he tucked into the casserole that Céline had been serving out. "God, this is good, Céline. Our Ian doesn't know what he's missing." Then he stopped, momentarily stuck for words.

"No, actually," said Clare, choosing not to continue on the subject of Ian for now. "Aurore and Angélique have decided to stay for at least a week in Ireland. Angélique's mother, that's Aurore's daughter you understand, will be joining them next Tuesday and all three will probably come back to France at the end of that week. It's not sure yet. But I know they'll be going back to Ireland very soon to stay much longer with George, and Damien is arranging for them to stay in George's own house the next time, not in a hotel. After all, it will be Aurore's when he dies. Poor Aurore can't really take on board things like that just now but I know Angélique is giving up the summer job she had lined up in order to chaperone her grandmother over the next few months. I got a hired car sorted out for her before I left, so they're quite independent now. And, of course, Paul is being a big help, making sure everyone is okay and keeping a very close watch on George to check that it's not all too much for him. But really, when you see how quiet and content he is, just sitting with his daughter, holding her hand, and remembering the girl he loved every time he looks at Angélique, it makes me feel that he's found peace at last. It's quite moving, actually," she faltered.

"Sweetheart, there now, don't cry. It's a happy ending. Come here," coaxed Frank, giving his wife a hug. "Here's a tissue. Now why don't you have some of that lovely meal Céline has cooked? You're going to need all your strength for tomorrow. There's seven gîtes to clean this week-end, not to mention the games-room and the pool."

"Talk about coming down to earth with a bump," laughed Clare, her eyes bright. "But it *is* nice to be home. And Céline, you haven't even seen the Manor House yet! I'll take you there after breakfast and you can see all the work that has been done on it, thanks to Owen, here. We'll be moving into it in next week most likely. Oh! I can't wait!"

The rest of the meal passed off in happy reminisces of Oak Lodge, Clare bringing them up-to-date with the latest goings on. She'd found the time, no-one could fathom how, to talk to staff and residents, old faces and new, even to the new Polish nurse. Sharon had come back on duty specially to see her and Clare was pleased to report that the morning sickness Sharon had been plagued with for the past few weeks was gradually receding.

By half past eleven, everyone was stifling yawns and needed no encouragement to head to bed. By half past twelve they were all fast asleep.

Owen was by no means a light sleeper. Once he got over to sleep, it usually took a mild degree of physical violence, at least, to wake him up. So when his phone began buzzing insistently at half-past four, he paid absolutely no attention to it at the start, integrating the noise into some dream or other which might, or might not, have been about bees.

But the noise persisted, so he eventually surfaced, basically with the intention of hurling the offending phone to kingdom come. Then he saw who it was.

"Ian, bloody hell, do you know what *time* it is?"

"Sorry mate, emergency, do you know where she is? She wouldn't tell me."

"Céline, you mean?"

"Of course I mean Céline. Who the hell do you think I mean?"

"Actually, I can hear her. I think she's in our bathroom."

"What the fuck is she doing with *you*, Owen?"

"*What?*"

"You heard!" said Ian, shouting now.

"Hey, Ian, calm down! We share the same bathroom, okay? That's *ALL* we share. What's got into you? We're in the gatehouse gîte, in the new bedrooms upstairs. It's a Jack and Jill bathroom which we both share. And I've just heard Céline use it. She must've woken up when she heard my phone ringing."

He sighed, his voice coming down an octave. "You *eejit,* Ian, what the hell's got into you? You've obviously had a barney with Céline otherwise she wouldn't be running to the gîtes for comfort. And now you're phoning me at half-past four in the morning to accuse me of God-knows-what with your *wife*! Catch yourself on, mate. Either you stop this nonsense right now, or I'll... I'll... disown you, you daft oaf."

"Oh! Oh God, Owen."

"Yeah? I'm listening..."

"Christ, I'm sorry Owen. I'm not thinking straight. Céline has turned her phone off. I've been trying to get hold of her all night. I've been such an idiot. I... I don't want to lose her. You know I don't want to lose her, don't you? God, why is life so complicated? I didn't want this to happen." Owen had never heard Ian so upset.

"Listen, Ian. Listen... *Listen* to me! I don't know what caused this row between you two but I *do* know Céline is still nuts about you. Why she still loves you is actually beyond me at this point in time but facts are facts. Now, take a bit of friendly advice at get yourself to bed. Céline'll still be here in the morning and Mum already has her roped into helping out with the changeover tomorrow afternoon. It's Saturday, remember?" He softened his voice. "Ian, get some sleep. It'll all seem less fraught in the morning. Céline has no intention of leaving you. Take it from me, and God knows I'm something of an expert on the subject... as you bloody well know!"

There was silence on the other end. To Owen, it seemed to go on forever. Then he heard Ian sigh heavily, obviously dog-tired. "Okay Owen. I'll take your word for it. I'll be along during the day sometime. Don't say anything to Céline, though. Please."

"So long as you head to bed right now. You sound really knackered, Ian."

"I am… and I will."

"Promise?"

"Promise."

"Then that's okay then, isn't it?"

"Nite, Owen."

"Yeah. Get to bed."

-oOo-

Chapter Twenty-Seven

New Directions

The following morning saw everyone tucking into an Ulster Fry for breakfast, to use up the Soda Bread Clare had brought back with her together with some Denny's pork sausages that she had bought at Dublin airport and slipped into her case. After Ian's phone call during the night, Owen had gone back to sleep almost immediately but Céline was looking wane, proof that once awake, she hadn't had much sleep since half-past four.

But she set off cheerily enough with Clare to visit the manor house once Solange had arrived to man the office.

By now the manor house was fully insulated and all the windows double-glazed. The firm looking after this job had also managed to place a second layer of glass over the two windows that had stained glass in them, the one in the stairwell and the other in the dining-room. Both windows had had to be removed for this operation to be carried out. It was one item that was particularly expensive in all the renovation costs.

Now that a new boiler had been installed, the radiators checked out, the insulation done and the windows changed, the house was beginning to look less like a building site and more like a home. This week, the chimney sweep would be coming and Owen had engaged a plasterer to skim those walls that needed doing most. He'd already examined the cracks that were showing over the chimney breast in the sitting-room and in one of the ceilings, pronouncing them surface cracks, not structural ones. Once those particular jobs completed, they would just need to hire machines to sand and polish the wooden floors. If they all worked at it, he told them, it could be done in two days.

"It's lovely, Clare, really, really lovely," cried Céline, looking round the garden and back up at the house itself.

"Isn't it just?" came Clare's proud reply. "Frank has worked very hard in that garden, after Jean-Christophe and Owen cut back all the trees. He's cut the branches into logs and stacked them up in that small outbuilding there. We'll have enough wood now to keep us going all winter."

"It is not surprising that he looks so tired. He has been working very hard."

"I know what you mean. We've both been working flat out. And I must say Owen has done his share. It's been great having him around these last weeks."

"Was he very upset when Judith went to America?"

"Actually, much more upset that he would ever let on to *me*. But he was cut up about it, yes indeed. That was until Solange came along and took him to a few parties and introduced him to new friends."

"Oh, that was kind of her."

"Absolutely! And he broke it off with Judith. It was over anyway, or so he says, and now he seems quite happy without her. And from what I gather, she's quite happy without *him.* She has a new life in San Francisco and really enjoying her job out there and making friends too."

By now they were going up the stone steps and Clare let them into the house.

"Oh Clare, doesn't this look so very grand? That's a wonderful staircase, is it oak wood?"

"No, I don't think so. Oak would be much darker, I believe. I'll have to ask Owen that one, though. I've no idea, myself. But look, come into the sitting-room, or drawing-room as I suppose you would call this and there, behind it, is the dining-room, next to the kitchen. The kitchen is quite old and grotty but we'll give it a good clean out when we move in. We can't afford to rip it out just yet."

"All is light. Light and bright. It looks wonderful!"

"And you haven't seen the half of it. Let me show you in here, the study. Then that's a snug and there you have the conservatory. That's another room that'll have to be cleaned thoroughly but all in good time."

She rattled on about her beloved manor house, taking Céline upstairs to admire the huge bedrooms and down to the cellar to see the multitude of little rooms that were housed there. Céline was very impressed. It was a fantastic house.

"So when will you move in, Clare?" she asked as they strolled round the garden once more before heading back to the gîtes.

"In about 10 days or so. We'll do it mid-week, which is when we have the most time to ourselves. And then I estimate it'll take me another two weeks after that before I'll have the place cleaned and to my satisfaction. All those kitchen cupboards, for a start."

"I wish I could help you Clare but I cannot leave school until the *Brevet** is over."

"That doesn't matter, Céline. I'll rope Solange into helping, if she has the time, and Frank and Owen too, of course. And perhaps some of Solange's friends for the actual move. But tell me, when's the *Brevet* exams then?"

"End of June, Thursday 25th and Friday the 26th. But the school year does not officially finish until the 3rd of July. I could come then and help you out. I'd like to. Really," she added to emphasize her point.

"And what about Ian?" said Clare gently, knowing she was treading on eggshells here.

"I... I don't know about Ian, Clare," faltered Céline, suddenly sad.

"Want to talk about it? Or perhaps I'm not the best-placed person to be discussing him with you?"

"Oh, Clare!" said Céline, tears starting in her eyes. Clare put her arm around her.

"Céline, he's made me cry too, you know. He used to get up to all sorts of mischief as a child and I couldn't bear to see him get into trouble and I took the blame for him more than once..."

"I love him, Clare, I really do. But these last few days, I've seen another side to him. Where he puts his work first and excludes me totally. I have been hurt at his attitude. That is why I had to get away."

And she proceeded to tell Clare the whole sorry story.

"Oh, sweetheart! And you were so happy with your wonderful news. I'm so pleased you've got that permanent posting. Now you'll be able to buy a house, or whatever, just like you've both always wanted. What did he say about that? Wasn't he pleased at all?"

"He doesn't know, Clare. He never even gave me time to tell him. And I had organized a nice meal and wine and set the table and... he noticed nothing. Nothing at all!"

"Oh, dear! Typical bloody man! A one-track mind. He's obviously got this huge problem at work and it's blotted out everything else, even you, Céline. Oh, I could shake him, making you so unhappy!"

"We talked last night... on the phone. We talked a long time. He tried to make me understand what had happened at work," said Céline. "But I did no longer want to know what had happened at his work. I had begged him to tell me about it on Tuesday, and on Wednesday, and on Thursday. To understand, you know? Three times he refused to discuss it, Clare. Three times! And now he thinks he can make everything right by technical explanations!! I was very angry last night. And now I am ashamed. I fear that Ian has also seen a side to me that he did not know about." She sighed. "Oh, Clare, how am I going to put this right?"

They were nearing the gîte complex by now. Clare could see in the distance families getting ready to leave. Very soon now they would all be swamped by the work involved in the changeover. She again put her arm round the young girl.

"Céline. It *will* work out. I'm sure it will work out. Ian's not a bad person. You and I both know that. He's a stupid, pig-headed, unfeeling person right now. And I bet you my bottom dollar he's regretting his attitude of this past week. This problem at work has made him go off the rails. It's the only logical explanation I can see right now." She gave the girl a hug. "Darling, I'm sorry. I'm going to have to leave you to start the changeover. If you prefer to stay quietly on your own, perhaps give Ian a ring, I'll understand."

"No Clare. Ian can wait. After all, I have waited four days. But I will ring him at four, when we have finished. And I will try to make things right."

"That's my girl. Now, how shall we do? Will you partner me and Solange will partner Owen? They make a good team. We'll leave Frank to man the office, see the families off and things like that. It's a cushy job and I know he'll not say no. Right, we're home." She pushed open the door to the office. "Hi everyone. All set?"

As two of the families were finished vacating their gîtes, the two teams of cleaners swooped in to begin their jobs. By the time this was done, another two of the gîtes had been freed. Solange and Owen had previously made a start on the games-room and swimming-pool but Clare decided to finish that area off before starting on a third gîte. By the time this was completed, the others had done two more gîtes which left only the biggest gîte to clean. They tackled it all four of them together and in no time at all, everything was done and they all trooped back to the gatehouse gîte where Frank had prepared soup and sandwiches as a late lunch.

They had hardly finished this when the first of the new guests began to arrive, with all that that involved. Each family was shown to their accommodation, and all the electrical appliances explained, although written instructions in English and French were to be found in each gîte. Then they were shown the grounds, the games-room and the swimming-pool, told that fresh bread and emergency food supplies could be bought there each morning. Finally they were invited to come to the gatehouse gîte should they need anything or if any problems occurred.

Céline was doing her share as naturally as if she had never left the gîtes and was just seeing a family safely into their abode when she turned and gave a start. Before her, barring her way, stood Ian.

He looked awful, wild-eyed and unshaven and her heart leapt at the sight of him.

"Céline... oh Céline," he said and held out his arms. He didn't get any further as the breath was knocked out of him and Céline was hugging him as if she would never let him go.

"Please, don't... don't ever do that to me again," he murmured, kissing her passionately, right there, in the middle of the gîtes. "I thought I'd lost you, Céline. I thought you weren't coming back."

"Come, let us walk in the grounds. Let us talk this problem away and then we will forget it once and for all," said Céline softly, aware that it was necessary for both of them to explain their actions before the wounds could heal.

Half an hour later, Frank suddenly remembered the presence of Céline and wondered out loud where she had got to. It was Solange who answered. She'd seen Ian arrive in his car and spot Céline as she came out of a gîte, saw them kiss and hug and go off together.

"Oh, I *am* glad," said Clare, on hearing this. "Here's hoping it's a case of all's well that ends well."

It was another half hour or so before they came back to the gatehouse gîte. Clare was the only person present as the others were all showing guests around. She immediately suggested tea and soda bread and perhaps a shower and a shave for Ian?

"Okay, big Sis. I'll have to check out this Jack & Jill bathroom you've got up there. Been hearing all about it during the night."

"So it was *you* that phoned Owen at half-past four this morning, Ian?" said Céline. "I heard his phone ring and I could not sleep after that."

"Guilty as charged, love. I think I was half out of my mind. You'd turned your phone off. I was looking for you. I was worried..."

"Well just go on up and have that shower," said Clare, not wanting them to waste time on more explanations. "You'll find extra towels in the cupboard under the wash-hand basin."

By the time he had finished, he was looking more like his old self. Lines of fatigue were still showing round his eyes but the old Ian was definitely back.

"Now I don't want to hear any explanations but just tell me, did you get your problem sorted out at work?" began Clare in her most matronly manner.

"I did, ma'am."

"Good. Now Céline, did you explain… umm… what you wanted to explain to Ian right from the very start?"

"No," said Céline. "I have decided I will not explain."

"Oh, why not?"

"Because I am going to show him. That is why."

"Show me what? What's going on here? Oh, I get it. Is this the 'something nice' you wanted to tell me about that first evening and I refused to listen? I'm so sorry about that, love."

"Yes, well. We will not speak of that anymore."

"So what's the big news, then? Are you going to show me your tummy and tell me that in seven or eight months from now there'll be a little Ian or a little Céline around?" He laughed at his own joke. Then nearly choked as this idea hit him seriously.

"Céline, are you expecting a baby? Is that it? Is that it?"

Watching his anxious face, his happy anticipation at this possible outcome, Céline could not help but laugh.

"No, you silly man. I am not pregnant. Not this time. One day, perhaps not too far away." And she looked over at Clare and smiled.

"So you'll not be staying the night, then?" said Clare wistfully.

"No, forgive us, Clare. First we shall go to Rennes, it is on our way, and leave Ian's car at his work. Then I shall show Ian what I have to show him."

"This is all very mysterious, Céline. What is it you have to show me, then?"

"Patience, patience," said Céline, smiling.

And Clare chanted, much to Ian's disgust, "Patience is a virtue, possess it if you can, rarely found in women, but never in a man!"

-oOo-

Chapter Twenty-Eight

Saint Aubert des Loges

They said a quick good-bye to Owen, Solange and Frank, catching them as they shepherded guests around the gîte complex, Owen telling them, for good measure, to get their act together and not be ringing him at four in the morning anymore. Then he gave Céline a hug and encouraged them both to come back to the gîtes very soon as no doubt Clare would be having a housewarming party one of these days when the move to the manor house was completed.

They followed each other to Rennes so that Ian could leave his car in the office car-park. It took them slightly out of their way but Céline wanted them to be together when they drove into Saint Aubert des Loges. She was, by now, quite excited about her big surprise, giving herself up fully to the anticipation of seeing Ian's face when he realized she'd got her permanent posting so soon.

Another 40 minutes north of Rennes, with the sun sending out red shards over the sky to their left, they entered the little town of Saint Aubert des Loges. Céline, who had scoured the Internet looking at pictures and maps of the place, drove quite confidently up to the school complex which housed three schools in all: kindergarten, primary and secondary. Although each school was relatively small, the grounds on which they stood were actually quite big, with sports facilities and even the municipal swimming-pool nearby.

"*Et voilà!*" she said. "*C'est ma nouvelle école!*"

"All this?" said Ian, taking it in.

"No, just this school here. Look, this is the *collège* I will be teaching at next year."

"It looks grand. And it's not too far from Rennes, which is a bonus for me. I'm pleased for you Céline. It'll be better than Laval, at any rate, won't it? We'll find somewhere nice to rent that's not far away."

"Ian, you have not understood! This is my *collège*. It is a permanent posting. This is where I can stay teaching for as long as I want to."

"Holy smoke! You've got your permanent posting? Céline, this is wonderful! Why didn't you say?"

"*Ian*! I tried. It is you who would not listen to me!"

Both their voices had risen in their excitement and frustration.

"Oh Céline!" said Ian, immediately contrite. "I am so sorry. That must've been awful for you."

"Yes but that is over now. And forgotten. Now we can make plans for the future, buy a house, put down roots... oh, Ian! It will be so good!" And she flung her arms around him there and then, hampered somewhat by her seat-belt but too happy to care.

Then they got out of the car to have a wander around.

On this Saturday evening, all was quiet at the schools, the kindergarten and primary school windows almost obliterated with drawings and posters and projects that the children had undertaken throughout the school year. The collège windows were much less cluttered and this let them see better into the school and the classrooms. It was all quite new and modern, a two-story glass-fronted building which let in lots of light. On each side of the central staircase, large green potted plants stretched upwards towards the well of light which flooded in from the roof. The décor was in blues and greens and greys, quiet, studious colours with a touch of white here and there to brighten everything up. Céline loved it all immediately. She felt she would be very happy here. How could she not be?

On leaving the schools, they got back into the car to have a quick drive around the town which was built up on both sides of the river La Mollée. It was obviously a historic town with wooden-fronted buildings dating back to the Middle Ages, narrow streets in the town centre now designated as pedestrian zones and an abbatial with its tiny church, sprawling lawns and view over quite a large lake.

The town centre also sported a second church, much larger than the last, and behind it a pretty park dotted with swings, a few tennis-courts and areas dedicated to one of the national sports of France... *boules**. Just off this was to be found a generous-sized hotel and restaurant, the Jardin de l'Abbaye, with its reappointed stonework and baskets of geraniums rocking gently in the evening breeze. Away from the town centre the streets became wider, flanked by houses and flats, a mixture of privately-owned properties and council flats, the HLM's. Further out were one or two quite generous properties overlooking the lake and the woodlands surrounding it. It looked quite perfect, a lovely place to live.

"And we're not far from Dinan and Saint-Malo," enthused Céline, anxious to tell Ian all she had learned about the place since knowing where she was posted to.

"It looks really good, love. But don't you think we'd better be getting back? It's getting late," said Ian, stifling a yawn.

"Oh, do we have to? Let us stay tonight in the hotel and visit the area tomorrow. Please, Ian?"

He laughed, seeing how serious she was.

"But what'll I wear? I came away without any clothes, not even a toothbrush," he protested, to tease her.

"There is a big supermarket where you can buy anything you want. I saw it when we were driving round the outskirts of the town. Oh, please, Ian? I want to continue exploring with you. We *need* this!"

She was so sincere, he could not refuse. So back they went to the supermarket before it shut and Ian purchased a few necessary items to carry him over for the night. Then they returned to the town centre to the hotel where they were lucky enough to secure a room.

By now, Ian was fighting sleep as the events of the past week began to catch up with him. But he enjoyed the meal that the restaurant provided and happily celebrated with Céline over an aperitif and a shared bottle of wine. He began to relax, really relax, enjoying the happy chatter of his little wife as she made all sorts of plans for their life together in Saint Aubert des Loges.

She was still on a high when they got back to their room. So he used the bathroom quickly to let her take a shower. He lay back in the wide, comfortable bed enjoying the thought of taking her into his arms, of the kissing and caressing and love-making that would follow, of revelling in the feel and the smell of her...

Some fifteen minutes later, Céline emerged from a lovely, hot shower, all fresh and tingling and ready for sex, only to find Ian fast asleep, arms outstretched, and she was quite put out to find that no amount of persuasion could wake him.

Back in Ireland, Paul was coming to the end of what had been one very busy week. It had been great seeing Clare again, meeting Aurore and Angélique, and seeing George so happy. The fact that George was well enough to understand what was happening, most of the time, was a wonderful bonus and Paul felt a quiet glow of satisfaction that they had all got this far.

Each day, Aurore and Angélique came to Oak Lodge and spent most of the afternoon with George in his room. He was still quite frail and shaky and often prone to tears. But they were tears of happiness, not agitation, and the little room, with its big sash windows overlooking the grounds, was very often witness to quiet joy and scenes of laughter.

They never stayed too long and always left immediately they felt that George was tired. From time to time, with Paul's encouragement, they had wheeled him, well wrapped up, out into the grounds to sit under the oak trees or down by the lake. Angélique, in spite of her smallish frame, was athletic and strong, which was just as well as Aurore could not have pushed the wheelchair back up to the house on her own. Ireland was enjoying a short period of exceptionally good weather, which meant that many of the residents were being brought outside where possible, but George's contentment, as the sun warmed his skin and the gentle breeze ruffled his hair, was a treat to see.

Krzysztof had settled in well and had taken over a large share of Paul's work in order to leave him free to be with Clare and George. With his ready smile and easy-going nature, he had won over most of the residents and was popular with the care-workers, who teased him mercilessly, jokes that often went over his head but that he joined in whenever he could, never taking offense where no offense was meant. Even Catriona had warmed to him, no doubt a teeny bit embarrassed at having taken him for a workman, and Krzysztof was always careful in deferring to her when the need arose. He was kind, and affable, and good at his job.

There were times when he was tired and that was when his English became stilted and his accent hard to understand but most of the time he was proving himself an asset to Oak Lodge and Sharon, freed from morning sickness and back running the home, had to agree with Paul that his presence was a bonus.

As usual most evenings, especially when the weather was so nice and the days so long, Paul and Sharon would walk up to the building site behind Eileen's cottage, where half a dozen new houses were in the final stages of completion. There they would take a walk around their house-to-be, noting with satisfaction every little progress made. Sharon's pregnancy was beginning to show but she was feeling well and extremely happy. Some evenings, when they had the time, they would call into Eileen's for a cup of tea or a glass of something to drink and she would regale them with tales of Kilmore gossip that only someone like Eileen, or her nasty counterpart Mrs O'Neill, could possibly know about.

So on this Saturday evening, after a very satisfactory inventory of all that was happening at the new-build, they knocked on Eileen's door to be greeted with a flurry of happiness and a cacophony of barking from Whisky.

"Hello, you two! Just finished baking apple-tart. I know our Kieran loves apple-tart. He said he might call in."

"Smells good, Eileen," said Paul. "Mind if I beg a slice?"

"Paul!" said Sharon, reproving.

"Well, we didn't have dessert and I'm still hungry!" protested her husband.

"No problem. I've made two. They do get eaten up quickly, I must admit. Sharon, would you like a slice too? I've got vanilla ice-cream to go with it."

"Oh, go on, Eileen. I'd love a bit, actually. Your apple-tarts are amazing."

"*See*?" said Paul.

"So you said Kieran might call in?" said Sharon, changing the subject.

"Yes. Now that his exams are over, he's got more time on his hands and he doesn't start back in Tesco's until Monday."

"You know more about his life than I do these days, Eileen," said Sharon wistfully.

"That's because you're back at work full time, love. You can't be everywhere."

"So, did he tell you how he got on then? To me, he's not very forthcoming."

"That's 'cos you worry about him all the time, Sharon. Give him space," said Paul. "When he sees you fussing, he doesn't like it. He doesn't want to upset you during your pregnancy and he was concerned that you were so sick at the start."

"Why? Is there something I *should* be worrying about, Paul? Do you think he's done badly in his exams, then?"

"See what I mean, Eileen, see what I mean? Worrying and fussing. Leave the boy alone, love. Let him take responsibility for his own life now. He'll be eighteen soon."

"Now, now, you two. No squabbling. Here's the apple tart and help yourselves to ice-cream. No, Whisky, you're not allowed apple-tart and ice-cream so stop begging!"

Just then there was a knock on the door and Whisky began barking and jumping up and down. Next moment Kieran himself came in and Eileen's little sitting room suddenly seemed very crowded indeed. It occurred to Sharon, as she stood up to give her son a kiss, how Eileen could see Matt in this boy every time she looked at him. He'd grown so tall, nearly as tall as Paul now, he needed a shave and that was something new to witness, and sometimes when he looked at you, it was so uncanny, just like Matt had never left them.

"Gran, apple-tart! And ice-cream! Happy days!" he exclaimed.

"The way to a man's heart is through the stomach, is what I always say," said Eileen, as she happily helped her grandson to a generous portion of tart.

"Been up at the house, then?" he asked Sharon and Paul. "How's it coming along?"

"Grand, just grand," said Paul. "Might even be ready before the end of July."

"Hey, that's great. And what about our house, Mum. Any offers?"

"There's been several visits. Only one person has put in an offer so far but it's far too low. I'm holding out for a better one. The estate agent is fairly optimistic."

"Actually, the irony of it is that you're in competition with the new-builds. There's five other houses up for sale a part from ours," said Paul philosophically.

"Oh, no, Paul. At least three of those houses are already sold," said Eileen emphatically. "Heard all about it when I was working in the charity shop the other day. Mrs Colter, you know, Sharon? She's one of the canteen ladies at St. Brendan's. Well, Mrs Colter brought in some clothes, good clothes actually, and she stayed to look around the place and was particularly interested in the section I've built up for bigger sizes." She paused to get her breath, then went on *sotto voce* to Paul. "Mrs Colter is a wee bit overweight, you see."

"A *wee* bit overweight, Gran? Why in the canteen she's known as…"

"Kieran, that's enough!" said Sharon sharply.

"Well, as I was *saying*," said Eileen emphatically, "Mrs Colter's sister-in-law's son and his wife are buying one of them. And *she* heard that two others, apart from yours, were definitely sold. That leaves only two houses left. And they're quite big houses…"

"And quite expensive," put in Paul.

"And quite expensive," agreed Eileen, "which means that someone wanting a smaller, more affordable property wouldn't be interested in them. It's all to do with the market, you see," she announced confidentially. "*Supply* and *demand*, it's called. Saw a documentary about it the other day. Very instructive, so it was."

"Well, Eileen, that's good to know," said Sharon, amazed, as always, at the things Eileen knew. "I hope we get it sold before the baby arrives. If not, I could always consider renting it out. The mortgage is paid out. Any money I'd make would all be profit." She smiled. "And it would always come in handy."

"If I don't get into Uni, Mum, I'll rent it out from you," said Kieran before he could stop himself.

"What are you talking about, not getting into Uni?" said Sharon, her voice rising.

"Umm… just a joke, Mum. Don't go worrying. Everything will be alright. I promise."

"Is there something I should know, Kieran?" said Sharon softly, knowing that she would probably learn much more this way than through a head-on clash with her son.

Kieran looked from his gran, to Paul, and back to his mother. He looked like a rabbit trapped in the lights of an on-coming car. And for once, he had no yarn all ready-made to spin to them. He was genuinely worried sick about his exam performance, and not only in the first physics paper, either. He decided to come clean. The truth would out sooner or later... inevitably.

"Don't think I did too well in the exams, Mum. I've been kicking myself ever since."

Sharon digested this news in silence. So *that*'s why she hadn't seen Kieran these last few days. He'd been avoiding her.

"Think you've failed then?" she asked gently.

"Don't really know. Perhaps my AS results will help me scrape through but I know I've mucked up in physics and I think I've got at *least* one maths question all wrong, if not two. Worst thing is, I *knew* the answers. I just didn't have time to finish the papers properly and absolutely no time to look over what I'd written."

"How did the rest of the class feel about it?" asked Paul.

"One or two of them felt it was okay but most of them felt the same way as me, actually."

"There you are then."

"Doesn't stop me worrying about it, Paul."

"And how did Beth do?" asked Sharon.

"Beth? Oh, fine. Sailed through it. No sweat there."

"Well, that's good news, at least, isn't it?"

"But what if she gets in and I don't, Mum? That's what I'm really pissed off about."

"And when do you get the results, Son?" asked Eileen.

"August 13th, Gran. I only have a conditional offer from Queen's which means I need to get the grades to get on the course I've chosen."

"I'm sure you'll do alright, Kieran. Try not to let it spoil your summer," said Sharon, putting her hand on his arm. "And if the worst comes to the worst, you might get on another course or into another Uni. Or even go back and do the year again. It's not the end of the world."

"Thanks, Mum. I'm glad you're not cross."

"If you did your best," said Sharon righteously, "then that's all I ask."

"So, you told them then?" asked Beth, later that evening, as they sat eating chips in Kieran's car outside her house. "They weren't upset or anything?"

"Actually, it all went quite well, really. Instead of shouting at me, which Mum would've done if we'd been on our own, she was quite understanding and told me it wasn't the end of the world and such."

"And what about Paul? Did he say anything?"

"Umm... no. But he gave me a look as much as to say, *I know what you're up to Kieran Murphy but I'll not give you away.*"

"Giving you the benefit of the doubt, I suppose."

"No. Not really. I think Paul knew there wasn't much he could say to change the situation now and that Mum would only be upset if he bawled me out. He'll probably collar me some day and read the riot act about not studying hard enough, though."

"He's probably right."

"*Beth!*"

"Kieran. You *didn't* study hard enough. We both know it. So stop pretending. I'm just as upset about this situation as you are. I don't want to go to Queen's without you."

"Well, if I get into Queen's, I'll work harder. I promise. There! That okay?"

"It's a start."

"Deserves a kiss that, at the very least."

"Oh Kieran. You eejit! But I'll only kiss you when we've finished those chips. We're both sticky and greasy. I'm not kissing you like that."

One finger-licking, mouth-wiping and satisfying kiss later, Beth got out of the car.

"Bye Kieran, see you Monday in Tesco's, okay?"

"What time do you start?"

"Nine."

"Me too, I'll pick you up."

"Great. See you at half past eight, then."

"Quarter to nine."

"Half past eight or I'm taking the bus, Kieran."

"Okay, half past eight, then. Night, night."

-oOo-

Brevet = The French equivalent of GCSE's

Boules = The French version of bowls.

Chapter Twenty-Nine

Alex

By the time Céline and Ian had left the gîtes, most of the guests for the week ahead had already arrived. Two of the families were staying for a fortnight, those with young children that were pre-school age, taking advantage of the lower rates in June.

Owen was walking back to the gatehouse gîte with Solange, his thoughts still on Ian and how very distraught he had been over the whole bust-up with Céline. He tried to cast his mind back to when Judith had left him, to recapture that sensation of loneliness and despair, but the feelings were gone, buried forever under all the new and exciting things that were happening to him now.

Just being with Solange was pleasurable; partnering her for cleaning the gîtes something he now enjoyed doing. But his deepest thoughts were with Léa, had been ever since the Fest Noz. For the last fortnight he had been wondering how she was, what she was doing, how her latest painting was coming on.

Several times during their cleaning sessions that day, Owen had tried to bring up the subject of Lea, but Solange had not been very forthcoming. In fact, she wasn't her usual, confident self. Owen could see that she was preoccupied, often silent, even morose. He decided to tackle her now about it head on.

"So what's up, Solange? You've been very quiet today. Is something wrong?"

"I don't know, Owen." She sighed. "I'm just worried, that's all."

"About Léa?"

"About Léa."

"Why? Isn't she well? She seemed to be in top form at the Fest Noz."

"It's not Léa, Owen. It's Alex. I think he's following her... us."

"What the *hell*? He's not allowed near her... a restraining order or something. Isn't that what you told me?"

"Yes. He is not allowed near her. But do you remember what I said when we talked about this? Once or twice I have had a feeling that he is watching us. I have never been sure before. But I went to see Léa on Wednesday last." She smiled wanly. "Even at University we do not have classes on Wednesday afternoons."

"And what happened on Wednesday?"

"I saw him, Owen. I am sure it was him. He has changed, grown a beard, but it was him."

"So what did you do?"

"I made a pretext to stay that night at our parent's house. To be with Léa, you know? She was delighted. But all the time I was watching out of the window. When Léa was out of the room, I would watch. And several times I saw him. Until quite late in the evening."

"Christ! This is serious, Solange. Has Léa seen him too?"

"No. She is totally unaware of my feelings. And I do not want to upset her. Perhaps I am mistaken after all."

"So you're not sure then?"

"No. But today I had a text message from Léa. Several times the phone has rung and when she answers, the line goes dead. She wanted to know if she should contact France Telecom."

"So it's the land line this is happening on. Not her mobile, thank God."

"No; not her mobile. Obviously she changed her mobile phone number when... when she left him."

"Solange, let's go to Léa's house. Now! Get Antoine to meet us there. And we'll tackle this man if he's still around. Then at least we'll know who he is, okay?" said Owen, angry that Alex might have the gall to show his face after all he'd done to Léa in the past.

"Antoine is away this week-end," said Solange with a worried frown. "He will return only on Sunday evening. And I do not finish work till six, Owen. We must wait till then."

"No way! Let's go and find Mum. Most of the guests have arrived by now. There's not much more that needs doing today. She'll let us off early, if we ask her. Come on!"

Clare was clearly puzzled but agreed quite willingly to let them off work early. She was even more puzzled when she realized that Owen had packed an overnight bag but she wisely said nothing. After all, it could just be another party that Solange was bringing him to, like the Fest Noz two weeks ago or the birthday party the week-end before that. But some instinct told her it wasn't. She knew her son and could see that he was angry. And even Solange was not her usual chirpy self. Come to think of it, she had not been her usual self all day. She watched them drive off, intending to talk to Frank about it later that evening. He might know what was happening…

Or perhaps it was nothing at all.

Léa was delighted to see them, kissing them both hello. If she was surprised to see Owen, she didn't show it, taking him by the hand to show him her latest work, while Solange made them all a coffee.

Léa's paintings, Owen realized, would never be sold at Sotherby's. They were pretty watercolours for the most part, of local scenes, or copied from photos or postcards. Bright skies with billowy clouds, choppy seas licking country landscapes, all very chocolate-boxy but quite expertly done. As he admired her latest work, he thought privately that a painting like that of the manor house would make a nice Christmas present for his parents. He said as much to Léa.

"Owen! Do you think so? Am I good enough to paint this house of your parents?"

"Absolutely, Léa. I love the way you capture things on canvass. Those skies, and the seas, they're really good."

"But skies and seas are what I paint mostly. I have not done many houses close up, in detail."

"Have you any paintings of houses, then?"

"Oh, yes. There is one that I work on from time to time. It is still not finished. I am doing it in oils. That takes me longer, you see."

"Will you show it to me?"

"Yes, it is here. Look." And she unveiled a painting that was standing apart on its own easel. It was of her own house, as seen from the road. It was cleverly done. Léa had captured the colours of Autumn as they turned the few non-coniferous trees to burnished gold. The house stood out proudly against this background; grey, granite-stone walls contrasting with the off-white pebbles that served as a courtyard to the front of the house and the wooden shutters painted dark blue that flanked the windows.

"Hey! That's really good, Léa. Something like that would be just perfect for my parents. It's really, really, beautiful," he finished softly, admiring the painting.

"It will cost you one hundred and fifty euros and you must take me to this house so that I can see it with my own eyes and take some photographs," came the pert reply.

"Done... and done!" he laughed. "I'll take you there very soon."

He continued looking round the little art studio she had made for herself, and, as always, gravitated towards the big bow window-seat which overlooked the sea. He sat there, admiring the view, while Léa continued painting, until suddenly he became aware that someone was watching *him*.

A heavily-built man was sitting astride a motorbike, dressed in black leather. He had taken his helmet off but was still wearing sun-glasses. As Owen watched, he fished out a mobile phone from his jacket and brought up a number. Several seconds later, Léa's house phone began to ring. She went over to answer it.

"Léa. No! Let me," said Owen.

"Owen? Why?"

"Solange told me about someone hanging up on you several times. Quick. Pass me the phone!"

He took the phone from a puzzled Léa and hit the speak button, walking back over to the window as he did so.

"'*Allo*," he said in French.

There was silence on the other end.

"'*Allo*," said Owen, louder this time. "*Qui c'est?*"

Then, eerily, as he stood watching, the man on the motorbike hung up and just at that moment the line went dead.

"That has happened three times today now," said Léa. "It is very strange. I do not understand."

"Umm... yes. Very strange," said Owen. "Er... I'll just go and see if Solange needs a hand, okay?"

And off he went before Léa could say anymore.

Solange, when she heard, became serious and thoughtful.

"You say he was on a motorbike, Owen?" she asked, anxiously. "Alex always had a motorbike."

"He was. Tall guy, quite strong-looking. Didn't see him closely and he was wearing sun-glasses, but he did have a beard."

"I... I really think it is Alex, Owen. Is he still there outside?"

"No, when he saw me watching him, he drove off."

"Do you think it is best if we take Léa away from here?"

"Do you want to?"

"No, I do not. If we start running now, we will be running all our lives. This is our parents' house. Léa is happy here. But I do not want her to be alone and unprotected. Not if that... that horrible person is around."

"I've got an idea."

"Okay. What do you suggest?"

"First you go to the gendarmerie and tell them your fears. They will surely have a report of what happened to Léa, especially if this guy did time. I'll stay with Léa. And tonight, I suggest we both keep watch on Léa, at least till Antoine gets back tomorrow evening. If this guy comes back, then we'll make ourselves known, show him that we know he's breaking the law."

"And what if he attacks you, Owen? What will we do then? He has been violent in the past."

"I hope he doesn't, actually," said Owen, with an attempt at humour, "he looks a bit heavy for me to tackle on my own. I'll be much braver once Antoine gets back."

This made Solange smile.

They had their coffee companionably, chatting to Léa about the gîtes and the various families that came and went. In the space of a week, it was often quite easy to get to know the guests and Owen, who had hitherto been consigned to the Dutch and English, was now bravely insisting on meeting and dealing with the French guests too.

Solange said she would nip out to the supermarket to get them all some food for the week-end, Léa's fridge, as usual, being quite bereft of substantial nourishment. Owen knew that she was also calling in at the gendarmerie and had his phone ready just in case he was needed. Meantime, he asked Léa would she mind showing him round the house. He was interested in its layout and architectural features. It had so much more character than more modern houses. In fact, it was similar to the manor house in that respect.

They talked a lot as she showed him round, comparing the two, and Owen showed Léa some photos he had taken of the manor house using his phone. Then, to tease her, he took a few photos of Léa while she continued working and swung her round to steal a selfie of them both.

Absorbed as she was in her painting, Léa was thus totally unaware that the man on the motorbike had now come back.

Owen saw him almost immediately, drawn to the window by the noise. He watched with consternation as the man slowly got off the bike, put his helmet into a large storage area at the back and locked it carefully. Then he stood, looking up at the house for what seemed like ages, before deciding to walk up the path.

Hearing his footsteps scrunch on the gravel, Léa said:

"There is someone coming to the front door. I know it is not Solange. She will be using the back door. To the kitchen, you know?" She wiped her hands on an old rag and made to go down the stairs.

"I'll go, Léa," said Owen.

"You are silly, Owen," said Léa, smiling. "It is my house. It is I who must answer the door." And she tripped lightly down the stairs, just as the doorbell rang out loudly.

Owen was hot on her heels and almost bumped into her as she stepped back to open the door. He felt her whole body stiffen with fear as she looked into the stranger's eyes and realized who it was.

"Alex!" she whispered, catching her breath.

Ignoring her totally, Alex turned on Owen. "*T'es qui, toi*?" he said in a threatening voice.

"*Son ami*," said Owen, standing his ground, anger dominating any other feelings he might have had. So this was Alex. And nope, he didn't look any friendlier close up. Owen's heart began to thud.

"*Son ami?*" growled Alex, turning an accusatory look at Léa. "*C'est ton ami?*"

"What are you doing here, Alex?" went on Léa in French, her voice betraying her shock at seeing him after all these years. "You know you are not allowed to approach me. I do not want to see you anymore. You *know* that."

"That is all in the past, Léa. I have missed you. I want you back." The voice was softer, tender almost.

"I do not want *you*. Go away, Alex. Go away for good and do not bother me again!"

Owen, struggling to understand this exchange, judged it the right moment to put his arm around Lea's shoulders. She did not resist. They stood there in silence and Owen could feel Léa's body trembling under his hold.

Giving Owen a scathing look, Alex turned his attention back to Léa.

"Please, Lea, give me a chance. I have changed. I can give you more than this... this *person*." He made it sound derogatory. "We were made for each other."

"Léa is with me. She does not want you. Leave her alone," said Owen in stilted French, his arm tightening around Léa as he spoke.

"Oh, it's like that, then, is it?" said Alex, imitating Owen's accent. "And just what are you going to do to stop me, then, Briteesh? Drown me in five o'clock tea?" He seemed to think this very funny. He was still smirking as he reached out for Léa's hand.

Owen knew a bully when he saw one. There was no backing down now. He pushed Léa gently behind him and took a step forward, effectively barring Alex from touching her.

"Just go," he said. "Now. Don't come back."

"And who's going to make me, then? You?" sneered Alex.

"No, Alex. The gendarmes will. They are on their way," came Solange's measured voice from behind them in the hall. "I have just been telling them that you have come back to bother us. They should not be long now. Do you wish to wait for them?" she added sweetly.

"I'll be *back*," said Alex, shaking his fist in Owen's face, the bad temper that he had held in check up till now finally breaking through. "Lea! I want you back. Don't you forget it!"

And he stomped off. Within seconds he was on his bike and roaring off. The silence, once he'd gone, was deafening, and Owen, closing the door, turned round just in time to catch Léa as she fell.

-oOo-

Chapter Thirty

Trouble brewing

He picked her up and carried her into the sitting-room, laying her gently down on the couch. Visions of medieval ladies swooning and knights in shining armour flitted briefly in his mind but it was a little different in real life, he realized. His own knees had nearly buckled as he stood looking up into Alex's twisted, angry face. The guy was huge! He'd have made mince-meat out of me, he thought wryly. Thank God Solange had arrived when she did.

He was kneeling by the couch, brushing strands of Léa's hair out of her face. Solange had disappeared somewhere; he could hear her in the downstairs bathroom. Léa was coming round, a 'what-am-I-doing-here?' look on her face. Owen took her hand.

"Shush, it's okay, Léa," he said tenderly, "you're safe. He's gone."

It all came back with a rush. Léa tried to sit up, her eyes wide with fear, beads of perspiration broke out on her forehead.

"Alex! It was Alex!" she said, beginning to cry.

Owen pushed her gently back down on the couch, his free hand caressing her face, wiping the tears that were starting there.

"Léa. Listen to me. It's alright. I won't let him hurt you. And look, Solange is here. We'll stay with you tonight. You'll be safe," he said.

Solange had brought a warm, wet face-cloth and was now wiping Léa's face. Between them they managed to calm her, to get her to understand that they would not leave her alone. Solange put a rug over her and in the dim light of the setting sun, with them both watching over her, Léa finally fell asleep.

They left her then and went to sit in the kitchen. Solange poured them both a beer.

"When did the Gendarmerie say they'd be here, then?" asked Owen.

"Oh, they will not be coming. I only said that to frighten Alex into going away." She smiled.

"Solange, you are *good*. You had me believing they'd be arriving any minute!"

"I did go to the Gendarmerie and filed a complaint but as I could not be 100% certain that it was Alex who was watching, they could do nothing for the present time. Now, of course, they will come and take a statement. Perhaps we can get them to patrol more often in this area. We will see. I will call them now."

She was gone about ten minutes, and Owen stole into the sitting-room to check on Léa. She was sleeping peacefully enough; she'd obviously been suffering from delayed shock. He stood looking down at her, anger, admiration and tenderness clouding his thoughts. It had been nice holding her tight, though. And she hadn't resisted it either...

Just then he heard Solange coming back down the stairs and they met up in the kitchen.

"How is she?" she asked softly.

"She's still sleeping. It's been a big shock to her, seeing Alex standing there at the door."

"Mm... I heard what he said. He did not like it one bit when you said you were her '*ami*'."

"Yeah. I was wondering about that. He seemed to take it we were an item when I said '*ami*'. I mean, it was good that he thought that but I thought '*ami*' meant friends, just platonic friends, if you know what I mean."

"It was the context, Owen. You put your arm round her shoulders. In the context, '*ami*' meant a lot more than a platonic friendship. It can mean lover, partner or boyfriend."

"She must've been terrified of him, Solange. All that time. She must have been really scared."

"I know." Solange sighed. "I'll never forgive myself for having waited so long to intervene."

"Solange, you saved your sister. You did what you had to do. As soon as you were sure, you got her away from him. Anyone can see that she'll always be grateful to you for that," said Owen gently. "And things have changed. You don't have to deal with this all by yourself. I'm here. Antoine is here. And there's a whole host of good friends out there that will help us protect Léa."

"Thank you." she said softly.

"Are the Gendarmes coming then?"

"No. I asked them to wait until tomorrow. Léa is not fit to make a statement at the present time. But they will patrol near the house on their rounds tonight. That is reassuring."

While Solange busied herself making a simple meal of pasta, mushrooms and lardons, Owen decided to make sure that all the doors and windows were locked. He spent some time upstairs in the art studio as that room afforded the best view of the front of the house and the road.

All was calm. In the darkness he could see the moonlight reflecting on the sea, a reality so very like the scenes Léa was wont to paint. He smiled as he thought of her, brave little Léa, fighting to regain possession of her life after all that that bastard had done to her. The year spent in mental care, the artwork, obtaining her degree, so many achievements, so many little victories. No wonder she was scared stiff to see him again. Owen prayed this would not set her back.

But how were they going to protect her from this monster? They might manage it this week-end or for the coming week, but he could always find a way to get to her if he wanted to. Léa spent a lot of time at the house, in her studio, but that didn't mean she never went out. What would happen then? And both sisters were frightened of him, each in their own way; that much was clear to Owen now.

He hoped fervently that the reinforced presence of the Gendarmerie would dissuade Alex from coming back.

But what on earth did the guy want? Was he really that interested in Léa for herself? He didn't look the love-sick type by any stretch of the imagination. Perhaps it was Léa's money he was after. From what Owen could gather, their parents had left the girls fairly well off. Léa painted for pleasure, not to earn a living, and Solange, well, he could not imagine Solange *not* having a career. She was too energetic and competent for that. That didn't prevent her from being well off. Perhaps it was a question of money after all. And Alex had got money out of Léa in the past. Owen was determined to ask Solange about the subject outright.

But when he went back down into the kitchen, Léa was seated at the table, a mug of hot tea in her hands. She looked better, the colour had come back into her cheeks and she had been smiling at something silly that Solange had just said. She looked up now at Owen and actually blushed.

"I was stupid, Owen, to faint like that. I am embarrassed now," she said, avoiding his eye.

"Nonsense, Léa. Between you and me, I nearly fainted too."

This made everyone laugh. Solange put the dish of pasta on the table and they all tucked in. Even Léa made a good attempt at finishing her plate and looked much better for it.

That night Solange slept in her room next to Léa's and Owen in the guest bedroom just along the corridor past the art studio. His good intentions to remain alert and vigilant all night long remained just that, good intentions. He slept like a log in an antique brass bedstead with a duck-down filled mattress that dated from way-back-when and oh so comfortable...

But the night was quiet enough with no Alex in sight.

The next morning, shortly after ten, the gendarmes arrived and took Léa's statement confirming the return of Alex. They asked her did she wish to press charges and looking from Solange to Owen, she bravely said that she did.

That meant that he was now wanted for questioning. He had broken the law inasmuch as he had contacted Léa when he was not allowed to. It was not considered a dreadful offense as such but, given his past history of violence, the gendarmes were aware that she could actually be in danger from this man.

After a light lunch, Solange suggested a walk on the beach. It was a lovely, sunny June day, quite warm, and Lea and Solange decided to go for a swim. Owen realized that this was something that they often did as both girls already had their bathing costumes on and had stripped off and were in the water within a matter of minutes. They were obviously good swimmers and Owen sorely regretted not bringing his own gear when he could see they were having such a good time. In the end the temptation was too great and, while they looked on and laughed, he stripped down to his underpants and dived in.

The cold water was invigorating and the temperature prevented any of them from staying still. After several races across the bay, which he won quite easily, he was attacked by the sisters who cheerfully tried to drown him, causing him to retaliate amid squeals and giggles. In this two-against-one free-for-all he found it increasingly hard to keep the upper hand until finally he had to surrender and they all waded out of the water exhausted and out of breath. Towels were fished out of backpacks and they lay down on the beach to dry out. In the absence of clouds, it was really quite hot and all thoughts of Alex were banished as they settled down to sunbathe.

It would've been a perfect afternoon. It certainly started out that way. But half an hour later, as Owen turned over on his stomach and looked back up the beach to the house, he could just make out a familiar form on a motorbike and the glint of the sun on a pair of binoculars.

Back at the gîtes, Clare had been wondering what had caused her son to leave hurriedly and in such a bad temper. It was obviously something to do with Solange, who had been on edge all day Saturday. Her ever-reticent source of information, Frank, had had nothing to contribute and the not-knowing had been nagging at Clare all weekend.

Once he knew that Alex was spying on them, it was difficult for Owen to continue sunbathing as if nothing was wrong. He was lying between the girls so it was relatively easy for him to indicate to Solange that something was up without Léa noticing. Together they watched with growing apprehension as a second motorbike drew up and its rider, smaller and thinner than Alex, came over and took the binoculars off him to scan the beach in turn for what seemed like ages, before both riders mounted their bikes and eventually sped off.

Solange looked at Owen who nodded. It was time to go back to the house. They gently shook Léa awake and put on a minimum of clothing for the walk back up the beach. Once in the house, Owen let the girls shower first while he checked the doors and windows again. The more he thought about it, the more he wondered if Alex's declaration of undying love rang true. If that were so, why wait all these years to come back? It didn't make sense. The money aspect seemed a much likelier enticement. He resolved to ask Solange whether there was anything of value in the house.

His own shower completed in a quarter of the time it took the sisters, he managed to get Solange on her own while Léa made coffee. He asked her about valuables and whether Alex had ever been inside their parents' house.

"He only came to this house once or twice," said Solange, thinking hard. "I was living here at that time, it was before I met Antoine, and when he began preventing Léa and I from seeing each other, he refused to let her come back here to see me. And as for valuables, we have some nice furniture from when my parents lived here and one or two vases or paintings that might be worth something. But nothing of immense value. Anything like that, such as my mother's jewels, papers to prove ownership of shares etc. and the deeds of the house, the apartment in Paris, and the cottage on Groix, they are all in a safe in the bank, you know? We have not taken them out in many years. Do you think that is what Alex is after?"

"I just find it hard to believe he is still head-over-heels in love with Léa, that's all. Don't get me wrong, Léa is lovely. Anyone would fall in love with her. But if Alex still is, why has he waited till now to come back and declare it? He came out of prison years ago. I... I don't understand his *timing*."

They were both thoughtful as they made their way downstairs to join Léa in the kitchen.

Afterwards Léa went back to her painting. She was so wrapped up in her art, it was hard for her *not* to paint, she explained. Painting took her mind off Alex, for one thing, and it helped her to stay focused and sane. Owen joined her after a while, just happy to stay quietly in the same room as her. As usual he settled himself in the window-seat where he could look out over the bay. His mind whirled with thoughts all trying to decide what should be done. At one point he watched as the dark blue Gendarmerie car drove slowly past. The fact that they were keeping an eye on the house was reassuring, at least.

The afternoon wore on. Léa had by now settled herself in an armchair, her sketch-pad on her knees. Solange was in the study downstairs, working on her laptop. Owen was looking out of the window, his face turned towards the sun, enjoying its rays as it warmed his face. His eyes were half closed.

They were suddenly yanked from this Sunday afternoon torpor by a strangled scream coming from below. Owen was on his feet instantly, signalling to Léa not to make a sound.

"Léa, is there somewhere you can hide?" he whispered feverishly.

"But Solange. That is Solange who screamed, Owen. We must help her. Something bad is happening. Something bad is happening to my sister. It's Alex. I know it's Alex. Oh my God," she finished in a high state of panic.

Owen grabbed her by the shoulders. Pulled her round to face him.

"Léa, when you were a child, did you play hide and seek in this house?"

She looked wildly at him but did not reply.

"Léa! Hide and seek?" he insisted.

"Cache-cache, yes we did."

"So you know a good place to hide?"

"Yes. I do."

"Go there, go there now. Please! And don't come out till I come for you, okay? I'll go and help Solange. But you, you must hide. Right now."

She nodded, not trusting herself to speak. Owen could see she was on the verge of tears. But she slipped quickly out of the art studio and the last he saw of her was that she was running soundlessly towards the bedroom where he had slept the night before.

-oOo-

Chapter Thirty-One

Alex makes a move

In the few seconds it took Léa to hide, Owen had dashed back into the art studio and grabbed the phone. He knew that the version of 999 in France was 18, or was it 17? He was about to dial 17 when he realized that the line was dead. Oh shit! He whipped out his mobile phone.

"Not even in your dreams!" drawled a female voice in French from the doorway. And Owen, surprised, turned round to find himself staring at the barrel of a gun. He put his mobile down, his heart thudding in his chest, his mouth suddenly dry.

"Give me your phone," she said, the gun never wavering. "No. Not like that. On the floor. Kick it over."

He did as he was told, taking his time, wondering who the hell *this* was. She was of medium height, mid-thirties, long dark hair, too much make-up on and dressed in black leather. In a flash he understood that this was the second biker he had seen from the beach earlier that afternoon.

"What do you want? Where is Solange?" he asked, fear gripping him like a vice.

"Alex! I have found the boy," she called from the doorway. "He is up here."

A mingled sound of footsteps could be heard on the stairs, then in the corridor, and Alex propelled Solange into the room. He was using one hand to hold her right arm painfully high behind her back and had clamped the other over her mouth to stop her giving the alert. He pushed her roughly towards Owen, who caught her as she stumbled.

"So," said Alex, slowly. "Where is Léa, Briteesh?"

"Solange. Are you alright?" said Owen, ignoring him.

"Yes, I am alright now. They took me by surprise. I did not hear them come in." Solange was rubbing her arm to get the circulation back.

"I *said*," growled Alex. "Where is Léa?"

"Gone to stay with some friends in Paris," said Owen with attempted cheerfulness. "We took her to the train when we came back from the beach. She did not want to stay here any longer." He was surprised to see that he could speak French reasonably well when he had to.

"*Chérie*, go check the other rooms. Find her. I bet she is still here."

Owen looked at Alex, too stunned to be afraid.

"*Chérie*?" he said. "That was quick."

"Shut your face, Briteesh," said Alex, momentarily put off by the fact that he had let this slip. He took the gun out of the woman's hands as she passed him in the doorway.

"What do you want, Alex?" said Solange. "You don't want Léa. What is it you're after?"

For an answer, Alex motioned them both to the sofa that ran the length of one wall.

"Sit!"

They sat.

Owen's brain was in turmoil, trying to decide the best way to get out of this situation. Beside him, he could sense that Solange was shaken by this turn of events but he didn't dare take her hand in case Alex thought he was not Léa's boyfriend. After what seemed like an age, the woman came back.

"She is not here."

"What?" growled Alex, very put out.

"I tell you. She is not here. But I found this," and she held up Léa's handbag.

"So, Briteesh, if she left for Paris, why did she not take her handbag, then? All women take their handbags."

"She was so upset she forgot it," said Solange, her voice shaky. "I bought her ticket with my own money and lent her more for her stay. That is what sisters do. She will pay me back," she added unnecessarily.

"I do not believe you," said Alex, taking out the mobile phone he'd confiscated earlier from Solange. He scrolled down the contacts till he came to Léa and hit the button. Owen, trying to act as if nothing were amiss, was nonetheless praying that Léa hadn't taken her mobile phone with her into hiding, or that if she'd had, it was now switched off. They waited.

Suddenly Léa's phone rang out, sounding quite near. In fact it was in the studio-room with them, near her easel.

"See?" said Alex angrily. "I told you she had not left. That is her phone!"

"But she *has*, Alex," said Solange, desperately trying to protect her sister from this man. "We left her at the station. She was very upset. She never thought about her handbag, or her phone or things. She just wanted to get away from here. Without delay!"

This immediately put Alex into a rage. The suddenness and intensity of his anger surprised even Owen. He stalked about the room, cursing and swearing, swiping the painting Léa had been working on from its easel so that it flew across the room, thumping the walls in his temper. Solange was shaking and even the woman in black leather seemed to cower. When Alex headed towards the sofa intending to grab Solange, Owen leant over and blocked his way. He found himself yanked roughly to his feet.

It was difficult to try and defend himself as Alex was still wielding the gun. This he now took by the barrel and directed a blow to Owen's head. Solange screamed in fright. Owen just had time to move his head slightly but the gun connected with his upper arm, causing him to stumble and fall to his knees. Pain from the blow spread out from Owen's arm, down to his fingers and up towards his neck. He gasped in agony. But before he could recover, he was hauled to his feet once more and flung back on the couch. His left arm felt numb. He hoped to God nothing was broken.

This excess of physical violence seemed to calm Alex somewhat although he still paced the room, thinking hard and muttering to himself. His girlfriend, sensing the crisis was over, took out a packet of cigarettes and with shaking hands, lit one. To Owen, it did not seem the right time to ask her to smoke outside, but thoughts like this helped him take his mind off the pain.

He wondered how on earth they had got into the house. He'd checked all the doors and windows himself and hadn't heard the sound of breaking glass. Throwing caution to the winds for the sake of curiosity, he said to the woman:

"I locked all the doors and all the windows. How did you get into the house?"

"That was simple. Alex has a key."

A *key?*

"Léa had a key to this house," she went on. "He took it one day when she was not looking and made a copy. Stupid cow, she never even realized."

So much for locking doors and windows then. The Gendarmerie would not be alerted by broken glass... *Great*!

"And what is it you both want with Léa? Why come back after all this time?" Owen knew he was pushing things but the pain in his arm was subsiding ever so slightly and discrete checks on his capacity to move it were proving that things might not be as bad as at first feared. In fact, when Owen thought of it, that blow from Alex should've hurt even more. It was the force of the blow that had hurt. The gun itself was lightweight. Odd.

Alex rounded on Owen. "We need money. And Léa gave me money in the past. She is rich. Very rich. She does not need all that money for herself."

Money, thought Owen to himself, just as he'd thought.

"Ah, but Léa is gone. And we do not know when she will be back," he pointed out. Solange put a hand on his arm, signalling that he should not antagonize Alex further.

But Owen was looking hard at the gun. And the more he looked, the more he could see that it was certainly a fake. If the gun were a fake, then it was just a question of getting the upper hand of Alex. A technicality, really.

Just then, Solange's phone rang out. Everyone stopped in their tracks and looked at it. It eventually stopped ringing and a 'ping' some seconds later indicated that there was a voice message. Alex strode over and picked it up. He listened carefully and what passed as a smile, more of a sneer, spread over his face.

He replayed the message and put the phone on loudspeaker. It was Antoine speaking in French.

"Solange," it said, "I am sorry, my love, but I cannot make it back tonight. In fact, I will not be home before tomorrow night. If you are free, we will go and have dinner together, that nice restaurant on the coast, remember? The Bailout. I will make it up to you. Bye, darling."

"Ah ha!" sneered Alex. "So this Antoine was to come tonight. And now he will not. What a pity! Such a pity for Solange."

Owen felt Solange's hand touch his. So she'd heard it too. That word 'Bailout', could it really mean a restaurant or was it a code to let them know that Antoine knew what was happening? Had Antoine deliberately slipped that English word into the message?

But Alex, fuelled by this good news, was back on the rampage. He grabbed Solange and pulled her to her feet.

"If Léa cannot get me money, it will just have to be you, sweetheart. You will come to the bank with me now and empty your account. And tomorrow we will go together and take your mother's jewellery out of the bank. Léa told me that was where it was kept."

Tomorrow?

"I... I do not have much money in my account, Alex. Less than 800 euros, I think. My money gets transferred every month. We are only half-way through the month and I have just paid all my bills."

"But you forget, we have Léa's bank card too," said Alex calmly.

"I do not know her code, Alex!" insisted Solange.

"Well, we have Briteesh here. He will have money in the bank."

"Less than Solange," said Owen. "But I will go with you to the bank. Just leave her alone, okay?"

Alex seemed to consider this for a moment. Then he announced :

"You," pointing to Solange, "will come with me to the bank. Now. And you," indicating Owen, "will wait here with my lady friend."

He pulled Solange roughly round to face him. "If you try to escape me, Solange, she will shoot him, simple as that."

Owen, who was by now getting back some use in his arm, saw a glimmer of hope. If he were left alone with the woman, he knew he could overpower her. Especially if the gun were a fake. He hoped to God that it was.

But Alex was taking no chances. A rapid exchange between him and the woman, most of which escaped Owen, had her nodding and even smiling. She disappeared downstairs for several minutes and came back triumphantly carrying a rope. Alex then took Solange firmly by the elbow and pushed her into the small en-suite that adjoined the room, which had once been her parent's bedroom; he took the key from inside the lock and locked the door from the outside.

Now it was Owen who was pulled to his feet. Passing the gun to the woman, Alex propelled him roughly towards the door of the studio. Owen, realizing that the rope was meant for him, cooperated for a yard or two giving the impression that he would not resist, then taking him by surprise, he wriggled from Alex's grip and turned to face him, putting all his force into bringing Alex down.

It worked. Alex fell heavily onto his back and Owen was on him in a second. With his good arm he managed to land several punches before Alex could react. But he wasn't counting on the woman who jumped on his back, pulling his hair painfully and hampering his movements. While Owen struggled to stand up in an effort to shake her off, Alex scrambled to his feet and landed him a blow to the jaw that had him staggering. He fell back against the door-frame, his head spinning.

The next thing he knew he was being pushed back onto the bed that he had slept in the night before and his hands were being tied together above his head to the brass bedstead. Blood was trickling from the corner of his mouth. His left arm was protesting vehemently at being attached. He was struggling wildly but it was a losing battle. He hoped fervently that Léa would not come out of her hiding-place to help him.

Panting from their exertions, Alex and the woman climbed down off the bed and stood there openly laughing at him. Owen noted with grim satisfaction that Alex was also bleeding from his mouth. The woman then slid her hand under his backside and pulled out his wallet.

Pocketing the cash there, she then took out his debit card.

"The PIN code, Briteesh" said Alex, looking at him.

Owen remained silent.

"The *code*," repeated Alex, grabbing Owen's left shoulder, making him cry out in pain.

Owen gave him the code.

They left him then, going into the studio next door. They released Solange from the en-suite and Owen could hear them kitting her out with a crash helmet and jacket and forcing her down the stairs and out the back door.

All was silent for a few minutes. Owen continued struggling to free himself from his bonds but they were tightly done and his struggles had little effect. He heard footsteps coming back up the stairs and along the corridor and then the woman was standing by the bed, looking down at him, laughing quietly.

"So, you Briteesh boy, you have learned that you cannot beat Alex, no? He is big and strong and now you are put to bed, like a naughty child. Poor Briteesh boy."

And she leaned over, cupping his face in her hands, and kissed him on the lips.

If Owen had ever fantasized over been tied to a bed and kissed by a woman clad in black leather, those fantasies disintegrated rapidly now. The more he struggled to get away from her, the more she seemed to enjoy it. She released him at last, laughing and panting, and going to the door, retrieved the key and locked it from the outside.

-oOo-

Chapter Thirty-Two

Help!

Owen lay getting his breath back, choking with anger at letting himself be put into such an embarrassing situation. So much for the knight in shining armour! Alex's last punch had almost knocked him out there. And as for that bitch of an accomplice, visions of getting his own back on her kept his mind satisfyingly occupied for quite some minutes.

What a mess! What an unholy mess they'd got themselves into. Why hadn't they just left Léa's house when they all had the chance? Now Solange was being driven into town to empty their bank accounts and Alex was fully intending to keep them all prisoners here until the bank opened the following day. Owen didn't think that banks opened on Mondays in France. Trust their luck to have one of the rare banks that did. Or perhaps

Alex had forgotten that fact and was going to keep them prisoner till *Tuesday*? Christ! Owen was already dreading the night to come as it was.

But what did Antoine's message mean? If only he'd been able to talk to Solange. She had touched his hand at the word 'Bailout'. He hadn't imagined it, of that he was fairly sure. Did that mean rescue was on the way?

Better not get his hopes up. He lay there, his mind going round in circles, trying to ignore the pain that threatened to invade his whole body, when suddenly in the quiet of the room he heard a small noise coming from a cupboard that was situated to the left of the chimney breast. He watched, fascinated, as Léa crept out.

"Léa, are you alright?" he whispered.

"I am fine, Owen. Much better than you, I see," she whispered back.

"I thought you would be found when that woman searched the house for you."

"This cupboard has a double wall at the back of it. It leads on to a small dressing-room. I had almost forgotten about that room. Solange and I, when we were children, we called it Narnia, like in the story, you know? I have been hiding in there, among the spiders."

"Spiders? Aren't you afraid of spiders? All girls are afraid of spiders."

"Not I. I am only afraid of big horrible men that pretend they are in love with me when they are not."

"Yeah. I'm afraid it looks like he's gotten over you after all," agreed Owen wryly.

Léa giggled nervously. It was so good to hear her laugh. In spite of his aching body, Owen laughed quietly too.

"I shall take these bonds from your hands, Owen. I will free you."

"Great. But let's hurry before her ladyship decides to come back for more."

"For more what?"

"Umm... nothing much, believe me. Help me, will you? Yes like that. Good girl! You're getting there."

Suddenly the unmistakable sound of footsteps echoed in the landing. Owen and Léa both froze. Then Léa quickly put back the rope to make it look like she had not touched it and slipped rapidly back into the cupboard, closing the door over, leaving a small crack to see through.

She was just in time. The key turned in the lock and the woman stood framed in the doorway, Owen's phone in her hand.

"You have a text message."

Great! Tell them to call the police, send for the fire-brigade, oh, a few paracetamols if that's not too much trouble?

"Oh?"

"In English."

"Oh."

"What does it say?"

She sashayed over to him and let him read the text. It was, inevitably, from Clare, wondering where he was and was he coming home that night? He had a meeting with the foreman at the manor house the following day at nine.

"It says that Father Christmas will be early this year."

"You are so funny, Briteesh boy. So very cute," she added, taking his jaw in her free hand, making him wince with pain, and planting yet another kiss on him, not quite so lingering this time. "You will answer this text. You will say what we tell you to say. Solange will tell us what it means. Then we will turn your phone off. See? No problem."

And she sauntered out locking the door behind her.

She was no sooner gone than Léa crept out from her hiding place.

"Did she really *kiss* you?" she whispered, as she got to work on Owen's bonds once more.

"Only 'cos I couldn't stop her. I wasn't exactly enjoying it, Léa."

"Umm... I shall have to check that for myself one day."

Owen looked at her and smiled. Now that she knew that Alex was only interested in her money, Léa seemed to have shed that frightened, little-girl-lost look she'd had before and was showing more courage than he had dared to hope for. It was a good sign.

She finally got the rope untangled and freed his hands. The relief was overwhelming although the blood rushing back into his left arm hurt like mad. He massaged it gently for a few seconds before scrambling off the bed.

He looked round the room for a means of escape. Trying the door gently, so as not to make a sound, he realized that it would be impossible to open it from the inside. And looking through the keyhole, he could see she had taken the key away with her also.

Next he tried the window. But it was a sheer drop to the concrete paving at the side of the house and he doubted if the Virginia creeper would take his weight. He left the window open, though, an idea forming itself in his mind.

"Léa, show me your hiding place, will you?" he whispered.

She obeyed silently, bending down to squeeze into the cupboard and remove the panelling at the back. Owen followed more slowly, the lack of space and his weakened arm making his progress slow. Once in the dressing-room he stood up stiffly and realized that it was a lot larger than he had thought. It even had a small window, grimy from years of not being cleaned, which let in streams of light through the slats of the shutters. The room itself was about two metres in depth and one and a half metres wide. Old wallpaper peeled from the walls and traces of damp could be seen, coming no doubt, from the bathroom next door.

Léa, meantime, had crawled back into the cupboard to close the outer door and put the second panelling back into place. Owen had no doubts that the woman would be back before long to check on him again. She had enjoyed taking advantage of him when he lay there helpless. Now, when she unlocked the door and saw him gone, it would be his turn to gloat.

But before that, he had to see if there was a way out of their hiding place, preferably indeed out of the house. He went over to the window.

It was small, actually quite small indeed, but he thought he could just squeeze through. Listening carefully for the least little noise coming from the room next door, he turned the handle and tugged gingerly at the catch till he could feel it moving. Easing it inch by inch he eventually got the window open. Now for the shutters. These, if anything, proved to be stiffer than the windows but he was rewarded when he could make out that just below them was a low wood-shed with a sloping roof. It would not be too difficult to ease himself down onto that roof and fetch help. He told Léa briefly what he intended to do.

Léa looked at Owen, saw his blood-splattered shirt, saw how he involuntarily kept trying to protect his left arm and realized that even if he *did* manage to get through the window, he would never be able to take his own weight on that arm.

"I will go, Owen," she said.

"What?"

"I will climb through the window and get help. Your left arm may be broken. It will be useless to you. Besides, I know my neighbours. They will let me in to phone for help. If they see you, with that blood on your clothes, they may not want to let you into their house."

Owen went to argue but he knew the truth of what she was saying. His left arm hurt worse than ever. He would not be able to lower himself down using it. He sighed.

"Léa, promise me you will take care? If you hear Alex's motorbike, lie down flat on the roof till he goes into the house. He will be coming in the back way, he could see you."

"I will take care, Owen. But we must hurry now. He will be back soon."

She clambered neatly over the window ledge and hesitated, trying to find the safest way down. She turned back to face Owen.

"If only we had a rope," he said.

"We *do*. It is in the bedroom," she cried, climbing quickly back into the room and going over to the cupboard to remove the panelling again. She had crawled through and was back almost immediately. The whole operation had taken less than a minute. She put the panelling back into place.

Owen helped her tie the rope around her waist and this time was able to help lower her to the roof below with his good arm. But before she could get down onto the ground, they both heard the noise of Alex's motorbike as it roared up the road. Léa flattened herself on the roof and Owen closed the shutters over leaving only a crack to let him see through.

They watched as Solange got off the bike and was shepherded into the kitchen by Alex. Owen could hear him calling out as they arrived in the hallway.

Through the crack in the shutters, he saw Léa jump down from the woodshed and scarper off through the garden to the back of the house and then he lost sight of her. He hoped fervently that she would get to safety and be able to bring help.

From inside the house, he could hear Alex pushing Solange up the stairs ahead of him and the woman unlocking the bedroom door. Her cry of stupefaction at seeing Owen gone was drowned by the curses and swearing that Alex was screaming at her. They clearly thought he had escaped via the window. Owen could not help chuckling to himself as he imagined the scene next door.

Suddenly he realized that Alex was shouting about something else. Solange, taking advantage of the commotion, had clearly decided to make a run for it. Owen watched her as she ran out of the kitchen door, across the yard where the motorbikes stood… and straight into the arms of Antoine.

Owen gave a whoop of joy. Antoine had not come alone; with him were about half a dozen Gendarmes, the flashing blue lights of their cars coming into view. Within minutes they had invested the house and cornered Alex, but not before he had threatened them with the gun, even going as far as to aim to shoot. His girlfriend was quickly apprehended, as she cowered in the bedroom next to Owen. He could hear her protesting wildly that none of this was her fault.

Shortly after, Owen crawled stiffly out of his hiding place and was apprehended by the Gendarmes too. But he was rapidly released once Solange and Léa explained his part in the proceedings and when the girls were allowed to see him, they flung themselves on him in joy. Owen's poor arm took another battering as he tried to hug them both. Then, among all the fussing and celebrating, his legs just seemed to give way and he sank to his knees with the pain.

Next thing he knew, he was being carried out of the house on a stretcher. His arm was strapped up and Léa was by his side, an over-anxious look on her face. He was gently lifted into the waiting ambulance and she climbed in beside him.

"Sorry 'bout that, Léa. Didn't mean to cause a fuss," he said in a tired voice.

"Your arm is broken, Owen. Near the shoulder where Alex hit you with the gun. Solange told me."

"He's a big lad."

"He's a stupid person who thinks he can come and steal from other people and tell lies and blackmail and use violence and threaten. He even threatened the Gendarmes!"

"I'm sure they loved that," said Owen, his eyes closing.

"You are tired. They have given you morphine for the pain," said Léa taking his hand.

"Morphine's nice..."

"*You* are nice, Owen".

Owen heard her words and felt really good inside. He wanted to tell her that he was very proud of her, that he thought she was wonderful, that he wanted to spend lots of time with her, be her friend, be *more* than her friend, that she was lovely and funny and brave.

But talking was far too big an effort. So he just squeezed her hand and drifted off to sleep as the ambulance carried them swiftly in the direction of Lorient hospital.

-oOo-

Chapter Thirty-Three

Afters

It was early Monday afternoon and Owen was awake and feeling much better. He had had an operation on the Sunday night to set the bones of his upper arm and the morphine he was still taking deadened the pain to a very manageable level indeed. If it wasn't for the inconvenience of having his arm strapped up, no plaster-cast thank God, he felt like a new man indeed.

Léa and Solange had come to see him as soon as visiting hours began at mid-day. They fussed over him like two mother hens, their gratitude at his part in the previous days' events all too apparent. Alex, they told him, was back in prison for everything the law could throw at him, not the least being GBH. His girlfriend was still being held for questioning by the Gendarmes.

Solange and Léa had spent a long time with the Gendarmes themselves, giving statements and pressing charges. It was late when they were free to go but Solange had rung his parents to give an edited version of what had happened and why Owen was now in hospital. She had persuaded them that it wasn't worth their while coming to Lorient that night but Owen had already learnt from the nursing staff that Clare had rung several times and was coming to visit later that afternoon.

"Solange, there's one thing that's been puzzling me since yesterday. About Antoine. His message, remember? He said he was going to take you to a restaurant called the 'Bailout'. Was that a code between you?"

"Ah, so you *did* catch that, then. I tried to make you understand but Alex was watching me closely. Yes. It was a coded message. You see, I had informed Antoine of our situation Sunday afternoon when you were upstairs with Léa. We had agreed that I would text him every half hour until he got to the house. He was worried for us and he was glad you were here, Owen. But when I didn't text he knew something was very wrong. So he sent that message to say he knew we were in danger, to give us hope, you see."

"I wanted to hope but I was afraid I might be wrong." He smiled. "Anyway, good old Antoine. He brought the cavalry."

"And good old Owen, you saved us too," said Léa taking his hand.

"I was so proud of you Léa. You put all your fears to the one side and you helped me enormously. Wasn't she just great, Solange?"

"She was wonderful. I am so pleased. I feel that Léa has met her old demons and this time she has mastered them!"

Léa blushed and smiled. She went over to the art folder that she had brought with her and shyly took out a picture which she carried over to Owen's bed. He looked in wonder on seeing a pencil drawing of himself, as he sat in the window seat, his arms resting on one drawn-up knee, the other leg dangling, his head back against the wood and his gaze directed towards the sea. It was so perfectly done, so very lifelike. She must have been putting the finishing touches to it when all the commotion of Alex's interruption had begun.

"Wow, Léa, that's really good, isn't it Solange?" said Owen in wonderment.

"Yes, it is. But I am always subjective when I see my sister's work. I think she is very talented."

Just then there was a knock on the door and Clare and Frank entered. While Frank took the time to greet Solange and Léa, Clare went quickly over to Owen's bedside and gave him a crushing hug. She wasn't letting go, either.

"Mum," came Owen's muffled voice. "I'm grand. I'm fine." Then, "Really!" as Clare released him at last.

"Owen, I was so worried when I heard from Solange that you were in hospital."

"Mum, I needed a small operation to set the bones, that's all. I'm right as rain! Here, I want you to meet Léa, Solange's twin sister. Léa, meet my Mum."

"Léa! This is nice. You were the girl from the Fest Noz, weren't you? And Solange's twin. I would never have known you two were sisters."

And she went over to kiss them both hello.

"Well, Owen," said Frank, as Clare left the bedside to quiz the girls all about the events of the day before, "heard you've been in the wars. You okay?"

"I'm fine, Dad. He was bigger than me, that's all." Owen smiled. "But I did my best."

"From Solange's glowing accounts last night, you saved the day. Proud of you, Son."

And he squeezed Owen's hand.

Just then Clare let out a squeak of joy at seeing the drawing Léa had done of Owen.

"Oh, Léa. That's really good. So very lifelike. When did you do that?"

"Yesterday afternoon. After we had been swimming in the sea, Madame."

"So it *wasn't* all fighting and risking your life then," laughed Frank turning back to Owen. "Swimming with these two lovely ladies and posing for Léa to draw you. Ah *ha*!"

"I didn't know Léa was drawing me, Dad. But I'm glad she did. It's good, isn't it?"

Clare said softly. "It's lovely."

"Would you like to keep it, Madame Hunter?" said Léa. "I was going to give it to Owen but I will draw him something else. Something very nice to say thank you for saving us."

"Oh, Léa. I'd love to have it. Thank you so very much. I'll get it framed."

"Oh *Mu-um*!"

"And I'll put it in my bedroom at the manor house. Where I can see it whenever I want," she added, to antagonize her son. "And please, call me Clare."

"And I'm Frank," said her husband. "You draw wonderfully well. And your English is as good as Solange's too."

Just then there was a heavy knock on the door and two Gendarmes entered. They had come, they explained, to take Owen's statement and they asked everyone, except Solange, to leave the room. Solange was to stay in case Owen needed help in understanding the questions or giving his replies.

Frank suggested taking Clare and Léa for refreshments at the hospital canteen and when Solange was free, they would all go for a late lunch in town. As it was the beginning of the tourist season, there were surely restaurants that were open all day long. This met with everyone's approval and Owen could see that it was going to be forty-questions time for poor Léa at the hands of his mother. Still, she was a big girl now and could stand up for herself. And there was always Frank around to temper his wife's curiosity and her propensity for match-making.

And now Owen had forty questions of his own to answer...

He was released from hospital on the Wednesday afternoon, given prescriptions for a nurse to attend him regularly to change his dressing (he seriously doubted whether his mother would let anyone else near him) and take the stitches out after a further seven days. And he was then to attend fifteen physiotherapy sessions to get back the full use of his arm.

Plus, *ugh*, a trip to the dentist to sort out a chipped tooth. Owen cursed Alex much more over this than over the broken arm.

Frank collected him on the Wednesday lunchtime and Owen gratefully left the boredom and bland food of the hospital to reintegrate the gîtes. He was still quite tired from the events of the previous week-end, plus the anaesthetic and the morphine, which he had since stopped taking. He didn't protest when Clare made him go upstairs to bed.

But he came down for dinner and spent a pleasant evening with his parents, secretly enjoying being cossetted by his mother. The next two days passed smoothly enough with Owen alternating time spent in bed resting and time spent in the office. He didn't go out much and was still taking pain-killers when necessary.

The following day being Saturday, he was still in bed when there was a knock on his door. Grateful that he hadn't yet had the time to un-do Clare's tidying up of his room, he said 'come in' and there stood Solange (whom he was expecting) and Léa (whom he wasn't). He grinned in pleasure at seeing them both.

"Léa has come with me today to help with the changeover," said Solange, smiling.

"It is the least I can do," added her sister. "And now I am seeing these gîtes for myself. I have heard Solange talking about them so much."

"Wow! That's great! Now I won't be bored," said Owen happily.

"We are here to *work*," Solange pointed out sternly.

"Yeah, sure. I'll help you too. I've still got one good arm left."

"You will man the office, then. That is all Clare is allowing you to do. And she is the nurse. And the *boss*," she added for good measure.

They left then to begin work on the games-room and swimming-pool and shortly after Clare came in armed with sterile compresses and antiseptic to carry out the job of changing his dressing. She was quick and efficient and Owen couldn't help asking her if she didn't miss the nursing career she had left in order to manage the gîtes.

"Only sometimes, I suppose," she said wistfully. "But I'm really enjoying the gîtes so much. I wouldn't give this up now for anything."

"Were you always in geriatrics, Mum?" said Owen, suddenly seeing a side to his mother that he had never been interested in before.

"I was in nursing for over thirty years," she answered, smiling. "And not always in geriatrics and senile dementia. My first two years were spent at the Royal, in Belfast, in the A & E department. That's where I met your dad."

"Really? I didn't know. What was wrong with dad, then?"

"Burst appendix. He nearly died."

"He never said anything about that to me."

"Doesn't surprise me. It was his own fault for carrying on when the pain was so bad. He thought pig-headedly that if he ignored it, the pain would eventually go away."

"God, that must've really hurt, though."

"Not according to your father. But in the end, he collapsed, right there in front of his class. You can imagine the scene. He was only about your age then, and he was teaching an A level class. Half the girls were screaming and the other half were suggesting anything from the kiss of life to amputation. Happily someone had the bright idea of informing the Head. And he was rushed into emergency."

"Where he met you."

"Where I gave him a good telling off."

"Things haven't changed much since those days, have they?" said Owen laughing.

"Cheeky article! Right. I'll wipe that smile off your face. Time to make that appointment to see the dentist."

"Oh no, Mum. Not that!... God, you're enjoying this, aren't you?"

"Takes me back to when I worked in A & E," she said happily and closed the door.

For Owen, lunch, that Saturday, was enhanced by the presence of Léa. But as usual on a changeover day they were regularly interrupted by guests leaving and calling into the office to say good-bye and sandwiches were eaten hastily as the gîtes were vacated and the teams of cleaners swooped in to begin their work, Léa partnering her sister and Frank his wife.

Owen was kept busy in the office with the phone ringing and emails needing answered (a slow process with only one hand). The gatehouse gîte was already fully booked up all summer from the 4th July onwards, after only being on the website for a couple of weeks. This had Clare vacillating between satisfaction that she was right all along and worry over how they were going to manage the move to the manor house without the help of Owen. She resolved to talk to Solange about it.

Solange was always willing to help Clare out but even she knew that cleaning the manor house and moving the relatively modest amount of furniture and personal items from the gatehouse gîte to it and getting the gatehouse gîte ready for rental would be quite a job, several jobs in fact. And time was running out. She asked Clare to leave the problem with her and she would see if she could come up with a solution. Clare had suggested paying any help obtained at the going rate with lunch thrown in and Solange knew that several of her student friends had just finished exams and had not yet been swallowed up by holiday jobs. She sent off a text there and then.

Meantime, the changeover came to an end with Léa doing her share. Frank and Clare were the first to return to the office and Clare made coffee while Frank took over from Owen. The girls arrived soon after and all sat down gratefully to have a breather, Solange stating that she had already had a few positive replies to the round-robin text message she had sent out earlier on.

While she discussed a time-frame for the move and details with Clare, Owen suggested taking Léa to visit the manor house. This was met with inevitable reticence from his mother until Léa suggested shyly that she would drive him there and bring him back immediately she felt he was getting tired.

So off they went, Owen's camera to hand and the big iron key in his pocket.

Léa loved it, as he knew she would. She followed him round the empty rooms their footsteps echoing together on the parquet flooring. They went upstairs and Owen showed her the room his mother had chosen as his parents' bedroom and Léa, after inspecting the other three, promptly chose the room she thought would be good for him, which happened to be as far away from his parents' room as it was possible to get. As this was his own sentiment exactly, he laughingly agreed.

She particularly liked the conservatory which was bathed in light as the long June evening began and decreed that it would make a wonderful place from where to paint. Her enthusiasm was contagious and Owen found himself revelling in her presence, never wanting her to leave. They went outside to the garden to take the photos that she would then use as a basis for her painting, agreeing with Owen to keep the whole thing secret from Clare until Christmas day.

Christmas day... As Léa took photo after photo, Owen wondered how he could be making plans so far ahead. After all, he was only here to see his parents through the season, wasn't he? His work overseeing the refurbishment of the manor house was all but over. Come September he would be (hopefully) qualified and applying for jobs. He could end up anywhere.

And why didn't that thought make him happy anymore?

-oOo-

Chapter Thirty-Four

Mrs O'Neill

As Owen was wondering about his future in France, back in Ireland Aurore, her daughter Catherine and her granddaughter Angélique were saying goodbye to George. It was only an *au revoir*, really, as the idea was to go back to France, pack a bigger suitcase and come to Ireland for a much longer stay. Angélique had by now officially given up the summer job she had had lined up in order to be chaperone to her grandmother. And Catherine, now that she had made the acquaintance of George, had promised to come back to Ireland in a few weeks as soon as her professional commitments at the art gallery in Dax would permit it.

Damien Murray, George's solicitor and good friend, had organized for Aurore and Angélique to stay at George's house when they returned, and his housekeeper had welcomed them warmly, glad to see that the place was going to be lived in once more. Mrs Curran was a widow, with one daughter, Rosie. She lived on the top floor of George's house and had missed him terribly when he'd gone into Oak Lodge. Although she visited him regularly, and Rosie too, it was not the same as having a presence in the house. Now these two nice French ladies were coming to stay and the younger one spoke English just beautifully. Mrs Curran was certain that they would all get along splendidly. She happily set about giving the place a proper spring-clean.

Paul was there to see George's family off and to make sure George understood what was happening and that they all would be back again very soon. He had wheeled him out to the car-park and stood there waving as Angélique drove away. It had been heart-warming to see George on such a roll of good health. Who would have thought it, Paul said to himself, as he wheeled the old man back to his room. Mind over matter; something to be said for it. Though poor George's mind was getting quite selective these days. But still. He was back in the 1940's and who would blame him? Paul hoped it would last for a long time to come.

As he was coming out of George's room, having got him settled and watching TV, he almost bumped into the ubiquitous Mrs O'Neill who was dusting the old-time prints that lined the corridors of Oak Lodge.

"Them Frenchie's all gone, then, Mr Harrison?" she asked.

"George's family have left for now, yes."

"Never trusted Frenchie's myself. All foreigners, if you ask me."

There didn't seem to be anything to say to that one, so Paul didn't, and made to go back in the direction of the office. But that was without counting on the tenacity of Mrs O'Neill.

"If you ask *me*," she added, in such a tone as to make him stop and turn around, "those women are just after his money. I know George Hamilton is rich and I know he has no heirs. You mark my words, Mr Harrison, those Frenchie's are just after his money."

"Well, Mrs O'Neill," said Paul, seriously exasperated, "I did *not* ask your opinion. And I'd be grateful if you kept your opinions to yourself. You know nothing of the situation and you are only making conjectures. And if I hear you spreading false rumours about George or his family, I shall personally go down to Kilmore Police station and file a complaint against you for defamation."

And he stalked off leaving Mrs O'Neill's mouth in the shape of a large 'O'.

And her mind working overtime to find a way of getting her own back. That Paul Harrison was getting too big for his boots. He should be ashamed of himself, treating her like that. After all, they were almost family now with his Kieran walking out with her niece Beth.

The more Mrs O'Neill thought about it, the more she felt justified in taking action. There was George Hamilton, old and ill, no proper relatives to speak of and stinking rich. And here were a so-called-family, foreigners indeed, trumped up out of no-where, ready to swoop in and take his money once old George snuffed it. Wasn't right, so it was. Something should be done.

Mrs O'Neill began to dream about what she would do with some of George's money. Nice new telly for a start, one of those flat-screened ones that everyone but her seemed to have these days. And her husband needed a new car. That might be going a bit far but Joe would be all chuffed up if he got a new car. Well, why shouldn't they have a tiny share in all that spare cash? George would never miss it, she was sure of that.

She decided to slip into his room and see what she could do.

"Morning, Mr Hamilton," she said brightly.

"Oh... Good morning," said George neutrally. He went back to watching TV.

"Just doing a bit of dusting, don't mind me," said Mrs O'Neill.

"Alright... carry on," said George, his mind elsewhere.

Mrs O'Neill gave George's room a perfunctory dusting while surreptitiously opening drawers and cupboards looking for cash. Of cash she found very little but at the bottom of his sock drawer, she came across his cheque-book. Bingo! Looking around her to make sure George wasn't watching, she pocketed the chequebook and turned to leave.

Then she turned back, having realized that she would need George's signature. Damn! She went around the room again looking for any document that might contain it but she found nothing that George had signed.

Then in a flash, she knew where she would find it. In the office! In George's file. There was bound to be a document somewhere with his signature on it. Now it was just a question of getting into the office without the bosses knowing. She would have to watch and wait. Mrs O'Neill smiled to herself. She was good at watching and waiting.

It was later that day that Paul realized that something was different. It was one of those days where he was needed all over the place for a hundred different reasons, none of them earth-shatteringly important but it all ate into his time. Around 5pm he at last made his way to the office to catch up on some long overdue paperwork. Sharon was coming on duty in an hour and he didn't want to leave it all for her.

He went to unlock the office door and found it already unlocked. Strange. Only four people had a key to the office, himself, Catriona, Sharon and Carmel. Sharon hadn't been here and it was difficult to imagine Catriona forgetting to lock the office door behind her. It had been locked when Paul came on duty that morning, so it wasn't Carmel either. Could he have forgotten to lock the door himself?

For conscience sake, he had a look around the room to see if all was as it should be. Everything *looked* quite normal. In the end he put it down to carelessness on his own part and resolved to be more vigilant in the future. He settled down to work.

Sometime later he got up to make a photocopy of a document, his mind on the business in hand. But when he raised the lid of the photocopier, he found that there was a document that had already been left there face down on the glass, obviously forgotten. He picked it up. It was a letter, belonging to George's file, and signed by him, attesting to the fact he was not putting in a claim for subsidies for his care at Oak Lodge. It was not a document that had been taken out or needed for years. How very odd!

Paul went to put the letter back into George's file, only to find that the file was missing. He eventually found it where it had been shoved at the back of the filing cabinet with its contents stuffed in willy-nilly. Paul was on the alert now. This was the work of someone who had been rifling in the file and didn't know the filing system they used in order to put it back in its proper place. Someone who had, somehow, managed to get a key to the office and photocopied that letter from George's file. Buy why? What was so important about that letter? It was only a formality, part of his registration forms when he came to live in the home.

Paul crossed the landing to call into the nurses' rest-room. There he found Krzysztof and Catriona sharing a coffee before Catriona left for home. He asked them if they had needed George's file and was not surprised to learn that neither of them had consulted that file recently at all.

It was obvious to Paul that someone had managed to get a key to the office and had been snooping in George's file. Well, first things first. He went back to his desk and phoned the local locksmith, asking him to come round as soon as possible to change the lock and provide four keys to the new lock. He was told it would be done the following day.

Next he went to see George and questioned the old man to see if he knew any reason someone would want to consult his file. But no joy there. George had no idea what Paul was talking about.

Paul knew it could not have been any of George's French family as he was sure they didn't even know where the office was. Only someone like Mrs O'Neill could seriously think that these nice, unassuming women were out to collar George for his money. You only had to see them together to understand how they loved him and he returned that love, unconditionally.

Mrs O'Neill... Mrs O'Neill... did the pass-key *she* have open the office door too? Had no-one ever bothered to check? She wasn't permitted near the office, nor even on that floor but she used to clean up there until she was caught listening at the door once too often by Catriona, who had made sure she never was allowed near the office again.

Buy why consult and photocopy that letter from George's file? What did she want? Paul shook his head in exasperation. He promised himself that he would collar her the following day but doubted if he'd get a straight answer. And thankfully, the lock would be changed by then too. There wasn't much more he could do in the circumstances apart from keeping an ever-watchful eye.

Then again, he said to himself, trying to be fair, I'm always finding fault with Mrs O'Neill. Perhaps this has nothing to do with her whatsoever.

Paul thought about this for all of two minutes.

Nah! He concluded. There's something fishy going on and when that happens, you can bet your bottom dollar Mrs O'Neill is involved...

It looked really class, so it did, on its stand in the corner where the old television used to live. Now that telly was in the bedroom. Such a luxury! And this new telly was miles better than the old one; bigger for a start and the picture was clearer, like being at the cinema, only the cinema was in her own sitting-room!

Mrs O'Neill didn't know why she hadn't thought of doing this before. It went a small way to making up for how badly she was treated at Oak Lodge. George Hamilton didn't miss the money and with his Alzheimer's he probably didn't even know what money he had. And as for those Frenchie's, they were due back any day now, so she'd heard. Pretending to be his family. Did you ever hear anything like it? Sure they couldn't even speak the lingo! Just waiting for the old man to die to get their hands on his money. Well, said Mrs O'Neill to herself, *I'm going to have my share before they grab it all.*

And no-one will ever know.

Kieran, still on a high from having his own car, called for Beth one evening after work. Beth had been on the early shift all that week and their paths had only crossed briefly, much to his frustration. But tonight was Saturday night, neither of them were working on the Sunday and it was make-up-for-lost-time time. He went up the path to Beth's house with a jaunty step.

It was Beth who answered the door, delighted to see him. She asked him to come in for a second till she would get her coat. Her mother was there and so was her aunt Agnes. Kieran thought privately no wonder Beth was happy to see him. Her aunt Agnes was not someone he liked to meet either.

"Hello, Mrs O'Neill," he said to Beth's mother. "And Mrs O'Neill," he added turning to her aunt. "How are you both?"

"Oh, hi there Kieran," said Beth's mother. "How's it been going after your first week back in Tesco's?"

"Oh, alright, I suppose. Just a pity my shift doesn't coincide with Beth's. But next week we're both on the ten-till-six one. We'll be able to travel in together."

"How's your mum keeping these days? I heard she was pretty ill at the start of her pregnancy."

"Oh, Mrs Harrison's feeling a lot better now," butted in her sister-in-law. "I could see that for myself at Oak Lodge. She's back working full-time now, right as rain."

"Um… yes. Mum's a lot better now," added Kieran.

"I suppose she'll be getting rid of that Polish nurse, then, won't she?" came the smarmy rejoinder from Agnes. "No need for him now she's back. Oak Lodge doesn't need foreigners like that, taking jobs from good local people that need them."

"I wouldn't know about that, Mrs O'Neill," said Kieran, angry at this remark, "all I know is that Mum's pleased with his work. And so is Paul. They say he's an asset to the home. You ready Beth?"

And he shepherded Beth in the direction of the door.

"Bye you two. Have a nice evening," said Beth's mum as they left. Even to Kieran she sounded wistful.

"God, I can't stand that woman," said Kieran. "How do you put up with her?"

"With difficulty, believe me. Thankfully she doesn't come to visit us often."

"And that husband of hers, Joe, isn't it? Waste of space, he is."

"I know. And poor Nina can't stand him either. Dad took her over to her friend's house for a sleep-over 'cos we thought he'd be coming too. Dad'll be back any minute and he'll give mum a breather."

"What does she want with coming over anyhow?"

"To brag, basically. They've just bought a flat-screen telly, and a new washing-machine and one of those coffee machines where you put capsules in. They're off their heads. I mean, they don't even *drink* coffee. It's all for show. And Agnes just had to come over and tell my mum all she's bought. Busy saying she's had a windfall. She's even talking about a new car for Uncle Joe."

"Wow! Some windfall."

"I know. Anyway, 'nuff about Aunt Agnes and Uncle Joe. What are we doing tonight, then?"

"You mean before or after? We haven't seen each other all week. That's a lot of catching up to do, Beth. And we only have a few hours."

"Well, Kieran Murphy, I'm starving. So there'll be no shenanigans before we have something to eat. How about a pizza? I fancy a pizza."

"And I fancy you... no?" He put the car into gear and pulled out onto the road. "Well, okay, one pizza coming up. But I know what we're having for dessert."

-oOo-

Chapter Thirty-Five

Revelations

It was Sunday evening and Kieran had just left Beth home so he decided to call round to his gran's house to see how she was. He thought he might catch his mum and Paul there too and kill a few birds with the one stone. Life was very full at the moment for Kieran.

He was in luck. Paul and Sharon were on their way out but sat down again while Eileen happily made a fresh pot of tea.

"Hello, stranger," said Sharon to her son. "How's it going in Tesco's then?"

"Fine, Mum. The usual, you know."

"And Beth, she doing okay?"

"Yeah. Fine too. I've just left her home. Couldn't get away quick enough. That old bat Agnes O'Neill was there again. Can't stand the woman. I mean, she was there last night when I picked Beth up, and there she was back again today when I left Beth home. Bragging about some car or other her and Joe had been to see and were thinking of buying."

"Good for her," said Paul. "Only we'll probably be hearing all about it *ad nauseam* at the home for the next week or two, I suppose. Still, if it keeps her nose out of other people's business for a day or two, I'll not complain."

"I know what you mean. Beth was saying, apparently, that yesterday she was busy bragging about a new flat-screened telly, and a new washing-machine or dish-washer or something. Oh yes! And a new coffee machine with capsules. And they don't even drink coffee. All for show."

"So where did she get all this money, then?" said Sharon, knowing full well Mrs O'Neill was always short of cash. Her husband didn't earn much and they both smoked heavily. They spent a fortune on cigarettes every month.

"A windfall, apparently."

"Really? That's interesting."

"Have some Victoria Sponge, love?" said Eileen, coming back into the sitting-room with a laden tray.

"You bet, Gran. Thanks."

"Sharon, Paul, room for more?"

"Oh no, Eileen, I'll be the size of a house soon without taking second helpings. It was lovely though."

"Paul?"

"Well, just a little, then. Have to watch my figure too, you know. Not getting any younger."

"What age *are* you, Paul?" said Kieran innocently. "Forty-something, isn't it?"

"Not yet, as you well know," came Paul's curt reply, making Kieran laugh.

"Remember when we used to go for those runs?"

"I do. And I miss them. Fancy going for one later on tonight? I'll show you who's over forty, if you're up for it."

"You're on. An hour from now, on the promenade by the beach, okay?"

They spent another half hour together in Eileen's catching up on each other's lives over the week gone past. Then Paul and Sharon left to walk back home and Kieran soon after to change and head out again for the run.

It was good to spend a warm June evening running along the sea-front with the black granite Mourne Mountains in the distance and the sea lapping the pebble-strewn beach to their left. They weren't alone. A lot of other people were out running or walking and quite a few families were strolling along pushing buggies, enjoying the summery weather.

They stopped eventually to catch their breath and stretch their limbs. Both knew they would probably have some stiffness to cope with on the morrow. But it was so good to be back jogging. They made a date for later in the week to do it again.

"So," said Paul, when they were seated on the stone wall that ran the length of the beach. "Tell me about those exams of yours. I get the impression you feel you could've done better. Worked harder perhaps?"

Kieran went to deny this but thought the better of it. He sighed.

"Yeah. I should've worked harder. I know that now. I've promised Beth that if I do get into Queen's, I'll not take exams so lightly again."

"Well, that's a lesson learnt, I suppose. Just hope it's not too late."

"Me too."

"And what were you doing when you should've been studying then?"

Kieran gave him a look.

"Seriously? Okay, stupid question. But you'll have to get your act together, Kieran. No use getting into Uni if you're going to spend your time having sex. It's a question of balance. And if Beth can cope, and find time to study, so can you."

"I know."

"Okay. Lecture over. Fancy the chippy? We always ended up at the chippy, remember?"

"Yeah, great. I'm starving."

"It's not a stomach you've got, Kieran. It's a bottomless pit!"

The following day Paul was just finishing his rounds when Krzysztof came along to see him.

"Can I see you for one moment, Paul?" he asked.

"Sure. Anytime. What's up?" replied Paul.

"In private, please?"

Intrigued, Paul led Krzysztof into the library, which was vacant, and they both sat down.

"Fire away," he said.

"A fire? Where?" began Krzysztof getting up again.

"Sorry, no," said Paul, smiling. "It's just an expression. What's the problem then?"

"It is about George."

"He's okay, isn't he? I saw him myself only this morning."

"He is fine. No it is about a missing cheque-book."

"Really?" said Paul, alarm bells beginning to sound in his head.

"Yes. Mrs Curran, his housekeeper, you know? She told me his cheque-book was missing. She is worried."

"What? You mean from his house?"

"No. From his room, here at Oak Lodge."

"What on earth is George doing with a cheque-book in his room? Things like that are kept in the office, in the safe."

"That is what I had understood, too. So I said I would tell you. And of course, I have searched for the cheque-book myself but without success."

"Is she still here, Mrs Curran?"

"I think so."

"I'll speak to her myself. Thanks for letting me know, Krzysztof. I'll take it from here."

And Paul went quickly out of the library and into George's room. Mrs Curran was just putting on her coat to leave. She looked flustered and unhappy.

"Mrs Curran, what's this about a missing cheque-book, then?"

"Oh, Paul. I'm sorry to be a bother but I can't find it anywhere. I'm sure I put it in his sock drawer. I always do that."

"Mrs Curran, it's against our regulations to keep means of payment in the resident's rooms. I wish you'd told me. I could've kept the cheque-book in the safe."

"Oh dear! It's just that it was handy to keep it here. I need Mr Hamilton to sign a cheque from time to time, for the house bills, you know, and there's never been a problem before. I... I never thought..."

"You've looked everywhere, I suppose?"

"Oh, absolutely. And that nice Polish man has helped me too."

"Well, Mrs Curran, you're going to have to call into George's bank and get them to cancel that cheque-book and see if it has been used fraudulently. That's very important. Could you do it today?"

"Oh, Paul!"

"I know. But we can't take any chances. And, please, let me know the outcome, will you?"

"Yes, I'll do that."

"Secondly, I suggest you have a chat to Damien Murray. He could perhaps set up a system, open a separate bank account or something, where you would have access to a set amount of money each month for paying the bills." He lowered his voice. "George will soon be getting to the stage where he won't be able to sign a cheque, or where he won't understand why a cheque needs signing. It would be all for the best, you know?"

"Alright, Paul. I'll get on to that right away. Oh, who would've thought this would happen? And poor Mr Hamilton so happy to have found his family at last. And I just *know* it could not have been any of them, Paul. They are all so very *genuine*."

"Mrs Curran, don't distress yourself. I'm certain myself that George's family had nothing to do with this. But I *would* suggest that you go to his bank right now. Just in case someone else has taken that cheque-book and are using it to bad ends."

Mrs Curran hurried off to do as bid and Paul went slowly back down the corridor, the corridor whose walls were lined with old prints of days gone by, his mind working furiously. Something wasn't right, he felt it in his bones, the missing cheque-book, the office door left open, George's file stuffed at the back of the filing cabinet, the letter from George left on the photocopier.

What was so special about that letter? Nothing, really, except... except that it had George's signature. That meant... that meant that the person who stole the cheque-book was the same person who broke into the office and photocopied George's signature.

And who was going round accusing George's family of wanting to steal his money? And who was going round bragging about new televisions and coffee machines and looking to buy a car? Paul's fists clenched involuntarily with anger. Well, this time he had her. And by God, he was going to make sure she didn't get away with it either.

But there was nothing he could do till he received that call from Mrs Curran. Nothing to do but wait. In the distance he could see Sharon arriving to take up duty. He decided to go with her to the office. And this was one occasion when they would sit down, have a long coffee-break and chat.

It was Thursday and Margaret and Eileen and Whisky the dog were at Oak Lodge for their weekly visiting session together. They were in the common-room and as always, Whisky was the life and soul of the party. All the residents present and most of the staff had their eyes riveted on his antics but Eileen, who missed nothing, saw the police car arrive and Paul come to greet them in person. Then they all went upstairs in the direction of the office.

"Did you see that, Margaret?" she said, as soon as she had a chance to get her friend alone.

"See what?"

"The police! Look, that's their car outside. They're with our Paul upstairs, right now!"

"Is anything wrong?"

"I've no idea. He hasn't said anything to me at any rate."

"It can't be any of the family. He would have told you straight away."

"Yes, Margaret. You're right. No, it must be something to do with the home, or someone in the home."

"It might be nothing at all. Just a friendly chat, you know..."

"Margaret, did you ever in your life see the police calling in just for a friendly chat? There's something up, mark my words."

It took a few days for people to notice that Mrs O'Neill was no longer working at Oak Lodge. In spite of her questioning, Eileen could get nothing out of Paul or Sharon. She was lamenting the fact to Kieran one evening when he called round after work hoping to scrounge a proper dinner instead of the hamburgers and chips he was wont to eat. After defrosting a generous helping of shepherd's pie, rustling up a side salad and watching with pleasure as Kieran ate ravenously, she had brought the subject up.

"Mrs O'Neill? Yeah. Heard from Beth that she's no longer working at Oak Lodge. Got the sack apparently. Bet Mum and Paul were glad to see the back of her, to be honest."

"But why did she get fired? Oh I know she's a terrible gossip and always poking her nose into other people's business but I didn't think they'd go and fire her for that."

"Well, I don't know why she got fired but according to Beth, that's not the only problem she's got. She overheard her parents saying that the police had been round to her aunt's house the other day. Don't know why though."

"The police! And the police were at Oak Lodge the other day too. Really! Spent ever so long up in the office with Paul. Do you think the two are connected?"

"No idea, gran."

"Umm… perhaps it's got something to do with that windfall you were mentioning the other day. Remember? The evening you went out for a run with Paul."

"Yeah. You're right. She was busy bragging about this stuff they'd bought, though I don't think they ever got the car she was after. But still, makes you wonder, doesn't it?"

"It does indeed," agreed Eileen. "It does indeed."

-oOo-

Chapter Thirty-Six

Moving House

When the dentist announced to Owen that he would have to have his tooth crowned, which meant having the nerve removed beforehand, he inwardly cursed Alex to hell and back. This would be his first. All those years of careful dental hygiene only to have some thug come along and chip his tooth. Not wanting the patient to change his mind, the dentist set about taking the nerve out immediately. Owen shut his eyes, suffered the anaesthetic injection, cringed at the different sounds coming from his mouth and was back on his feet in the space of fifteen minutes, one tooth nerve-less and a temporary filling in place. It hadn't been particularly pleasant but only because of his own fear, not from any sense of pain or discomfort. An appointment was made for the following week to have the tooth ground to the required shape, which sounded equally nasty but apparently wasn't, and an imprint taken.

Clare was waiting to drive him home. It was good of her to take the time. He knew she was up to her eyes packing cases, even his own, but at least Frank had taken a few days off work to help and Solange's army was arriving the following morning.

Everyone was due at the gîtes for coffee at 9:30 am and Frank would explain what had to be done and make teams.

All in all there were ten students who turned up, including Marina, Logan and Audrey. Plus Alain and Françoise, Jean-Claude and Yolen, two other girls and one lad. And Solange and Léa of course. Antoine, who was not a student and had to work that day, was absent. Owen, in spite of an arm strapped across his ribs, was determined to do his share too.

While Clare poured out coffee and tea, Frank gave his speech. The first job to be tackled was a serious cleaning of the manor house while it stood practically empty, to get rid of the residual dust, on the walls, floors and windows. Second, while the men did the actual move from the gatehouse gîte, to the manor house, the girls would finish cleaning the cupboards in the kitchen, the bathroom and any furniture that had come with the house such as the armoires and the dining table.

Alain and Jean-Claude had volunteered to be chefs for the barbeque lunch and Clare showed them were all the food was stocked in the games-room freezers and fridge and where to find the barbeque. She had concocted a simple menu of salads and crudités, all made in advance, and was counting on the lads to cope with grilling chicken drumsticks, pork chops, beef-burgers, salmon and sausages. Dessert was to be fruit and patisserie, the latter having been chosen that morning when Frank was buying the bread. They reassured her that everything would be perfect, what could go wrong? Alain's mother was a chef in the local school canteen and cooking was (by force) in his blood. And if Clare had heard properly, it was in Jean-Claude's too by association with Alain.

She secretly decided she would keep an eye on those two pranksters; she didn't trust them one inch.

And so it began. Everyone set to in the manor house to clean. Frank divided them up into groups of two and gave them the responsibility of doing a room each. Clare made sure each group had the necessary equipment and cleaning agents and started work herself on the downstairs cloak-room. Forty minutes later she went to check on the others.

Everyone was working away, rooms that had before been a haven for dust motes were now beginning to look fresh and new. Windows, skirting boards, wood-panelling and fireplaces were all getting a good clean out. Clare was pleased, that is, until she entered the bedroom that Alain and Jean-Claude were supposed to be doing to find them sitting on upturned plastic buckets smoking cigarettes.

"You can't smoke in here!" she cried, aghast. "That's the whole point of cleaning. It's to make the house look nice and *smell* nice!"

"But we opened the window," protested Jean-Claude.

"That's not the point. Smoking is forbidden inside the house. Go out into the garden if you want to smoke."

"Yes, Madame," came the sober reply.

"And you obviously could do with some help. Shall I join you here?"

"Oh no, Madame, we can cope very well on our own, can't we Alain?"

"Perfectly well. We're nearly finished."

Clare looked around the room and could see very little evidence that the room had seen a duster. Even less evidence of skirting-boards or windows being washed. Cleaning was obviously not one of these guys' better life skills. But Clare had not run an old people's home and a large staff for over twenty years for nothing. She looked at them both hard and long. Both boys got to their feet and shuffled.

"I shall give you half an hour. In half an hour I shall come back and check what you've done, walls, skirting-boards, door, windows, all cleaned, okay? And when you are finished come and get the hoover for the floor. Understood?"

"Understood, Madame."

Clare went to find Solange who was working in another bedroom with Marina.

"Solange, I get the feeling your friends Alain and Jean-Claude are not very good at cleaning."

"Oh, did you put them together, Clare? *Oh là là.* That was a mistake. Separately you might have got some work out of them. Together, a disaster. I should have warned you. I will go and tell them off now."

"It's okay, Solange," said Clare smiling. "I've given them thirty minutes to make good. I went into the room to find them sitting on the buckets and smoking."

"They are so stupid, Clare. But usually their girlfriends, Françoise and Yolen, keep them under control. I will go with you in half an hour and together we will check their work. But I suggest that we do not insist with their capacities for cleaning. Let us have some other work planned for them for after."

"Good idea. They can start loading the removal van, back at the gatehouse gîte. Frank's manning the office at the moment and Owen will take over from him this afternoon."

Owen, meanwhile, had elected to clean his own bedroom with, inevitably, Léa as cleaning companion. In fact they worked quite well, both happy just to be in each other's company, Léa doing the lion's share as Owen could only use one arm and Owen doing as much as he could to help her.

Clare went back to cleaning toilets, this time upstairs, making it obvious to Jean-Claude and Alain that she was just across the corridor. She chuckled to herself as she overheard them lamenting that Madame Hunter was a tough old nut, hard as nails... and perfectly unjust in her appreciation of their cleaning skills...

Thirty-five minutes later, Clare called a halt to the first round of cleaning as most of the teams had finished their designated rooms. Downstairs all the rooms were looking good and two out of four of the bedrooms had also been done. She called everyone into the kitchen where, over coffee or lemonade, she meted out the next round of chores. Solange and Marina would tackle the conservatory, not an easy task, and Logan and Audrey a bedroom, Yolen and Françoise the other, the two other girls Klara and Amelie would take the corridor upstairs and the hall downstairs plus the stairwell in-between and Jacky, the remaining boy, would help them. Léa, Owen and Clare would make a start on the kitchen.

Alain and Jean-Claude, once they had eventually finished the bedroom to Clare's satisfaction, were packed off to the gîtes to begin loading the van and setting up the barbeque. Clare made a quick call to Frank to warn him to supervise.

Another hour went past before Clare had time to realize it and shortly after mid-day she called a halt for lunch. She was pleased, and not a little surprised, to see the barbeque set up and ready in a corner of the garden, garden furniture table and chairs borrowed from the gatehouse gîte laid out under the big cherry-tree which had been bursting into fruit for some weeks now. Extra chairs and tables had been brought from the games-room and several large cooling boxes, two for food and one for drink, tucked well into the shade. What had started out as a rather dull morning for June in France had now become a scorcher of a day and cool drinks and shade were a welcome break from all the hard work.

"Good for you, Frank," said Clare, when she got her husband on his own. Everything's perfect. How did you get those two to have it all done in time?"

He chuckled. "Well, we had a short but fruitful discussion on the way some women are unreasonably tidy and make other people's lives difficult when they impose their will. Then another about how barbequing was a man's job and could not be entrusted to said fussy women." He looked at Clare knowingly. "And we took it from there. They're grand lads. I let them get on with it and I'm just as delighted as you are."

Beers and lemonades were handed round as Alain and Jean-Claude got to work with the barbeque. Clare had to admit they knew their stuff. No throwing on the meat and just waiting for it to cook. The chicken and pork had been marinated; the salmon steaks seasoned with dill and rolled in sorrel leaves, other herbs that Clare was not even aware were growing in the garden were picked and used in the marinade or on the salads. These boys might not know how to clean a room but when it came to cooking, they knew their stuff. She left them making three different kinds of vinaigrette sauce to take a welcome break herself.

About 2pm, they cleared up the remaining food and while the girls went back into the house to continue cleaning, all the boys headed off to the gatehouse gîte where Owen took over the manning of the office and everyone else helped to load up the van. It took five trips in all as the van was not very big and things like the office desk took up most of it. But by four pm they were done and Jacky, who happened to be taking a Masters in IT, volunteered to set up the computers in the new study and get them hooked up to the Internet there. For this, Frank was very grateful.

Once the gatehouse gîte had been emptied of all their possessions, four of the girls got stuck in to clean there too. At some point a large furniture van arrived and out came a double bed, two wardrobes and bedside tables for the gîte as the former office became a bedroom once more. Frank had negotiated with the furniture company to send men along to build the furniture, which came in kits, as he was purchasing a bedroom suite for the gîte, plus two double beds, a large fridge freezer and a washing-machine for the manor house, all from the same sales outlet.

By six o'clock, everything was finished, more or less. The manor house still looked quite huge and empty, even with their furniture, which admittedly was not a lot, but Clare reasoned with herself that she had months and years in which to fill it and never mind if the summer was spent in frugal surroundings.

Frank and Clare paid all the students cash in hand, invited them to fill plastic bags with as much fruit as they could take from the trees, and thanked them sincerely for their help. Clare particularly thanked the two pranksters, Alain and Jean-Claude, for their excellent barbeque and promised to get them back when she would have her house-warming party to be the caterers. This was high praise indeed, coming from Clare, and both boys left quite chuffed.

Solange and Léa had travelled together and invited Owen now to go back with them to Léa's house where Antoine would be coming later on, the idea being to get a take-away and chill out, nothing more. Some of the rest of the group might join them there too and even stay overnight. Owen did not need to be asked twice and by seven pm, Clare and Frank found themselves alone, locking up the gatehouse gîte after admiring the new bedroom there, and strolling hand in hand back to their new home for a welcome glass of wine and barbeque leftovers, happy, and too tired out for words.

-oOo-

Chapter Thirty-Seven

Going Further

Being back in Léa's house felt strange. It had only been ten days since Alex had turned that pleasant Sunday afternoon into a nightmare, and although Owen was well on the mend and pleased to be back, he could not help but shudder as he glanced into the guest bedroom on his way to Léa's studio and saw the brass bedstead where he had been tied up. Memories of Alex gripping his broken arm to make him divulge his pin number still rankled, as did his leather-clad accomplice taking advantage of Owen's helpless state to kiss him.

He was not surprised to learn from Solange that she had taken up residence here since the attack, not wanting Léa to be on her own again, just yet.

In the end it was only the four of them staying there that evening. Too tired to envisage cooking,

Solange and Antoine went off to buy pizzas. Owen went to his favourite window seat in the studio and Léa, inevitably, went back to her painting. He had been delighted to see that she had already made a start on the manor house one.

"Aren't you tired, Léa, after all the work you put in for my parents today?" he asked.

"No. I have never felt so good, Owen. I feel... I don't know... born again. I am happy, liberated."

"Because of today?"

"No. Not because of today. Today was fun. Hard work but fun. I enjoyed today. No, it is because I have at last freed myself from Alex, you know?"

"At least he's back in prison. He won't be bothering you for a long time."

"But, you see, that is what I am telling you. He will never bother me again. I am free from him. Even if he will come back in five or ten years' time, he will never have that psychological power he had over me before. All these years, even though I was... cured in that hospital... I still dreaded the fact that Alex might come back. I... I *gave* him that power over me. But now I have taken back my life. Now I am ready to live again... without fear of Alex. Perhaps it is the fact he has someone else in his life that has helped me. Or realizing just what a bad person he really is. I don't know..." she finished lamely.

"I suppose when you are living in a bad relationship you cannot always be objective. And now you have had the courage to see him as he really is. He's a no-body who uses his brute strength to get what he wants. He's just a bully."

"Exactly. And he does not deserve me to think about him anymore. I have given him too many years of my life already."

"Brave little Léa. You are brave, you know," said Owen fondly, coming over to the easel and putting his good arm around her.

"And so are you, Owen Hunter. You are my hero."

"Wow! That's something I've never been called before."

"It is true," she said putting down her paintbrush and turning to face him. "Solange says so too. She... she told me a little about you. We have talked a lot since Alex's attack. In the evening, when it is quiet, just the two of us."

"And what has Solange been telling you then?" said Owen smiling, intrigued, wishing he could take her in both his arms.

"That you have a reputation!" laughed Léa, determined not to tell him even a fraction of what the sisters had been discussing. "A reputation with girlfriends." She wagged her finger at him. "Solange says you should come with a warning notice : 'precautions for use' is what she said."

"Remind me to have a word with your sister, one of these days," said Owen, highly amused. Then he became serious. "Look Léa, I might have had a few girlfriends in the past but I was with my last girlfriend for over a year. Ask anyone. Ask my mum!"

"That was Judith?"

"Yep. That was Judith."

"And why did you break up with her?"

"I didn't! Well, yes, I suppose I did. But only because she had left me. She went off to America for a year."

"And you were not prepared to wait for her?"

"Yes... No... It was complicated," said Owen sighing, trying to put words on how he felt at the time. "I realized that Judith was starting a new chapter in her life, professionally and even personally. She had made friends out in America and I knew it was just a question of time before she met someone else. It was obvious that I was no longer very important in her life. Believe me, that hurt."

"That hurt your pride."

"Umm... yes, if you want to know the truth; that hurt my pride."

Pleased that he was honest with her, Léa went on: "And you are a very proud man. And stubborn, and courageous too. Solange told me all you did that afternoon with Alex. Thank you, Owen, for being courageous for us."

And she stood on tip-toe to plant a soft kiss on his cheek.

If ever there was a moment not to be missed it was now. But before Owen could take things further, they heard footsteps on the stairs and Solange came in to tell them that the pizzas were ready and waiting for them all downstairs.

After dinner they played *belote*. This very popular French card game is similar to whist but with some different rules that took a while to get the hang of. Solange partnered Owen and Antoine, Léa, so that the two teams would be balanced. Owen, who was actually good at card games, soon began to take initiatives and contribute his share and by the time they had reached 1,000 points, it was clear that Antoine and Léa would have their work cut out to beat him next time around.

Afterwards, Solange professed to be tired after the long day at the manor house and said goodnight. Antoine followed soon after. Léa and Owen, after clearing away the cards, found themselves looking at each other, unsure of where to go from here.

"Do you want to head up to bed, Léa? Or would you like to share a glass of wine with me?" said Owen, suddenly not knowing whether he was doing right or wrong.

"Let us not share a glass. Let us have a glass of wine each," said Léa, smiling.

"I… um… didn't mean it literally. One glass of wine… *each*… coming up," he said busy matching actions to words. They were in the sitting-room and Léa was curled up on the sofa. Owen sat down opposite her in a comfy armchair. He raised his glass.

"To you, Léa."

"Thank you, Owen, and to you too."

They sipped their wine in silence. Their eyes locked.

"Does it hurt you much now?" asked Léa.

"My arm you mean?"

"That, yes. And the rest."

"Well," said Owen smiling. "I'm furious with Alex for having broken my arm but I'm even more furious with him for chipping my tooth. Now I'm having to go for a crown. I mean, Léa, this is my very first crown. I don't think I'll ever be able to forgive Alex for that."

"There are a lot of things I will never be able to forgive Alex for," she said softly.

"I can't even imagine all the hurt he has caused you," said Owen, suddenly contrite. "My tooth is nothing in comparison."

"But I am grateful to him too, you know."

"Really? Why?"

"Because he has made me what I am today. He is a bad experience that has had… shall we say… unforeseen side effects on me?"

Owen chuckled. He moved over to the sofa and sat down beside Léa, putting his good arm around her and pulling her close. They sat like that for a long time, in silence, enjoying the comfort of each other. Léa lent her body back on his shoulder and Owen kissed the top of her head. He had never felt so much at peace. This was like… like… coming home.

It was strange to feel this way, just being happy to sit there. No rush. No urgency. No overpowering passion that clamoured for hungry kisses, and mutual exploring, and sex. Perhaps it was the warning Solange had given him when they had talked in the car. Perhaps it was Léa herself who was content just to take things step by step. But Owen found himself revelling in this waiting, savouring every moment they spent together, content to hold her, feel her body against his, smell her hair…

He awoke suddenly from a deep dream several hours later and it took him a few seconds to figure out where he was. Léa was asleep across his lap, her hair hiding most of her face. He tenderly pushed it out of her eyes and woke her gently.

"Léa. Léa! We've fallen asleep. Come on. Time to go to bed. *Aller! Reveille-toi*."

He took her by the hand and led her un-protesting and half-asleep up the stairs and to her room. In the darkness there she slipped out of her clothes and into her nightie, went past Owen to the loo and stopped at the door to his room on her way back.

"*Bonne nuit*," she whispered.

"*Bonne nuit, Léa*," said Owen, "*Dors bien*."

And she was gone, leaving Owen to reason with himself that he *would* get a good night's sleep, even if it *was* the bed he'd been tied to.

And even though his mind might want to take things slowly with Léa, his body had no such good intentions.

It was actually quite some time before he got back to sleep.

Clare awoke early the following day and stretched luxuriously in her new bed, in her new bedroom, in her new house. Frank was still asleep, breathing gently, so she took time to drink in her new surroundings. The sun was streaming in from the east window, quite bright really. They would have to purchase proper curtains, no doubt made-to-measure, or at least shut the shutters over. The room was dual aspect and the other widow, south-facing, gave out over the rear garden and the cherry tree that they had barbequed under only the day before. Clare could make out the top of it from where she lay.

It was strange lying in such a big bedroom. She wondered what the original owners actually *did* in bedrooms this size. Even their king-sized bed, a luxury Clare had not been able to see herself doing without, was dwarfed by the size and the height of the room. Just as well Owen had had all the walls insulated. It meant that the room was fresh and ready for decorating. They had put one of the two armoires in here but it sorely lacked company and they were using upturned boxes for bed-side tables. While this all had a certain rustic charm, it was difficult going back to student-type furniture at Clare's age and she resolved, as soon as their finances permitted, to make this room one of her priorities for redecoration.

Frank was going into Lorient that afternoon to take a few classes at the language school. She would get him to pick Owen up on his way home. Owen's stitches now needed to be removed and physiotherapy begun if he were to get back full use of his arm.

Thinking of Owen got Clare automatically thinking of Léa. She turned on her side to look at the sketch Léa had given her, now standing against the wall, framed and ready for hanging. It was really very good. She loved the way the girl had captured Owen's lazy, far-away look, his limbs relaxed, his head back resting against the window-frame. It was a natural pose, you could see that he was totally unaware of being sketched. Clare loved it.

And what about those two, then? Léa and Owen. Would they hit it off? The girl was special and Clare somehow felt protective towards her. Would she become just another girlfriend in the long line that had been courted by her fickle son? Clare did not want that to happen. From what she had gleaned from hearing about Alex's attack, Léa had had a very rough time of it some years back. She didn't need Owen toying with her affections before getting tired of her and moving on.

Yet they all seemed to think he'd been the hero of the day. And certainly he had the war wounds to show for it. So who knows? Perhaps her eternal teenager was growing up after all.

-oOo-

Chapter Thirty-Eight

Changes

The first Kieran knew of Beth having passed her driving test was when she drove up to his mother's house on the day of the big move. Her parents had lent her their car, she said, and she wanted to give a hand. Her pride at being able to drive was almost palpable and she went into the house to throw all her excitement into helping Sharon sort and pack. Kieran didn't know whether he was pleased or put out and stood there gawping until Paul told him to stop staring and get a move on.

It didn't seem worthwhile hiring a removal firm to move just up the road, so to speak, and Paul had enlisted the help of his father and Krzysztof too. He had hired a 12m3 van which he was insured to drive, although as a restricted driver Kieran wasn't, much to his disappointment. Paul's mother had volunteered to bring them all a picnic around half past one. It was a cool summer's day in July, blowy but not inclined to rain, which was the most they could really hope for.

Beth found Sharon in the spare room that Eileen had used when she first came to live in Kilmore. From not showing at all for months, Sharon now sported quite a tummy. She had been banned from lifting anything both by Paul and by Eileen and had grudgingly given in. She was standing now in the middle of the room looking rather bewildered.

"Sharon, you there? It's me, Beth."

"Oh, hi Beth. Come on in. I've just been going through some last minute boxes of stuff."

"Can I carry anything down for you?"

"Just those three boxes on the landing there. Yes, that's the ones. Two are for the house and that one with a cross on it is for the charity shop. All the charity shop stuff is to go in the garage and Eileen will get it lifted and do the sorting herself next time she's on duty there."

"Okay, Sharon. I can put the other boxes in my Dad's car. He's lent it to me for the day."

"Oh, I didn't know. Congratulations! You've passed your test then."

"Last Thursday. I'm chuffed to bits. I never said anything to Kieran. He would only have stressed me out."

"Good girl. I'm proud of you. And I'm sure your mum and dad are too."

"They are, Sharon. Mum's already got me ferrying Nina here and there. She's glad of a helping hand. And now I know how Kieran feels. It's great to be able to drive wherever I want."

"And it's good of your dad to lend you the car for today. I appreciate that. And your help."

When Beth had gone, Sharon sat down heavily on the unmade bed. Only two more boxes to sort but they were the hardest ones to do. It had been a long time since she had looked through Matt's stuff, her own little source of solace when he died. And as she well knew, it wouldn't be any easier to go through his belongings now than it had been ten years ago. She sighed and got to work. Out came his big cuddly jumper that she had slept in for weeks after the accident, clinging to the smell of him, burying her face in its folds. His wallet with her photo in it and one of Kieran and Sharon taken together when Kieran was eight. His driving license with a solemn-looking Matt staring back at the camera. *Why do official documents always make you look stern?* she thought. Matt was rarely solemn or stern. He loved to laugh. She shut her eyes, trying to recapture the way he laughed and suddenly there it was, just fleetingly, gone before she could fully enjoy it. The frustration was enormous.

She sat hugging his jumper on the bed, trying to pretend it was Matt, just like she had done so often in the years after his death. Tears rolled down her cheeks unchecked. She was so absorbed in her memories that she hadn't noticed she wasn't alone until suddenly Whisky jumped up onto the bed and licked her face. She turned and looked into the eyes of Eileen, who looked back at her full of love and compassion. She came over now and put her arms around Sharon, rocking her back and forth.

"There, there, love," she said, her own voice catching. "He'd be happy for you, you know he would. Remember how he liked to see you happy? How much fun he was?"

"I do," hiccupped Sharon. "He was always laughing."

"He loved his little family, you know. He was proud of you both. You gave him the happiest years of his life. And for that I'll always be grateful."

"Oh, Eileen! There are times when I still miss him so much. I'm happy with Paul, really, really happy, but I'll never be able to forget those lovely years I spent with Matt."

"You don't have to, sweetheart. He'll always be here, in your heart. Just like in mine."

"Would you like to help me sort out his things? It's time I gave away some of them but I can't bring myself to do it on my own. It's just too difficult."

"You don't mind me looking, then? You don't want to keep this for yourself?" said Eileen softly.

"I've looked at them all a million times over the years. Now it's time to move on. I only want to keep the things I treasure most, perhaps give some items to

Kieran, and anything else can go in the charity shop or if you see anything you would like yourself, please take it."

"Oh Sharon! There are things here that do take me back. Look, that's the scarf and gloves I bought him for the Christmas just before the accident. They were expensive too. Cashmere, so it was." And Eileen put the scarf tentatively to her cheek to feel its softness.

"Take them, Eileen. Please. Do what you wish with them. Look here's a small bag of stuff I had already sorted out ages ago. I'll not be keeping any of it. Why don't you take it home and go through it. You can then decide what to give away or what you'd like to keep."

"Yes, Sharon. I'll do that... and thank you. This means a lot to me," faltered Eileen.

"I know, Eileen, I know."

Downstairs, Paul and Krzysztof were just finished loading the first lot of furniture into the van and already the sitting-room was beginning to look very bare indeed. They headed off to the new house, with Paul's father, Kieran and Beth following, their cars filled to the brim with boxes and smaller bits of furniture.

The new house was looking splendid indeed. In size it was almost twice as big as Sharon's little house with two large reception rooms and four bedrooms, one with en-suite. The garden wasn't huge but it wrapped itself right round the house which was detached. A double garage, separate from the house, was situated to the rear. All in all, it was a well-proportioned, elegant property that would no doubt gain in value over the years. The view over the hills to the sea would see to that.

A second run with the van was completed before lunch and Mrs Harrison, Paul's mother, came along with her picnic. She 'oohed' and 'ahhed' at the new property which Eileen showed her round with as much pleasure as if it had been her own. With no garden furniture to speak of, lunch was taken outside on the kitchen table placed temporarily on the terrace decking, with an assortment of chairs, healthy appetites and good craic. By now, Krzysztof was well versed in the Irish sense of humour and laughed heartily at their jokes with the rest of them.

The breeze died down in the afternoon and the sun rained down on the little party with a vengeance. By the time all the furniture was in place and beds made and electrical appliances installed, they were quite worn out. Paul sent Kieran and Beth to purchase a huge Chinese take-away meal and the evening finished on a quieter note with Paul's parents leaving first, Eileen soon after, and Kieran & Beth giving Krzysztof a lift home around nine o'clock.

With the place to themselves, Paul and Sharon took a stroll outside to take in the last rays of sun. Grass had been sown and was showing through the soil in tiny, furry blades. A building firm would be coming in two weeks to fence in the gardens back and front but even now, as they stood looking up at the house, they were grinning in happiness and an overwhelming feeling of achievement.

"It's lovely, isn't it?" said Sharon for the umpteenth time since the building of the house had begun. "I can't wait to start decorating the baby's room."

"Kieran's already chosen which will be his room," said Paul ruefully. "It's the big double next to the main bathroom. I had kind of wanted that to be the guest room but I must admit, I didn't have the heart to tell him."

"You're a nice man, Paul Harrison. And anyway, we won't be having guests very often. And we won't be having Kieran very often either, if he gets into Queen's. God, I hope he *does* get into Queen's. It's what I worry most about at the moment."

"Hey," said Paul, making a 'T' with his hands. "Time out. No worrying. This is our big first night in the new house. I refuse to let thoughts of Kieran failing his exams tarnish our happiness. Now, which room for the baby, then? The small single next to ours or should we keep that as the study?"

"Oh I've always envisaged the baby there, Paul. Just next door. We can make the fourth bedroom into an office. There's plenty of room in there for two workstations and a double bed."

"Or we could even make part of the dining-room into a study and keep the fourth room as the guestroom."

"For all the times I kick you out of bed, then?"

"Exactly! For someone so calm and relaxed during the day, you do make up for it at night, my love. I'm battered and bruised most mornings."

They laughed.

"Talking of being bruised, do you remember when you were in that fight last year with Ian Maher and Kieran against those thugs Anita had sent to rough you up?"

"I do indeed. I'll never forget it. Thank God Kieran happened to be coming along and saw me dive in."

"Well, Eileen told me recently that Mrs O'Neill had it all around Kilmore that it was *me* that gave you that black eye. She gave me one hell of a reputation, you know."

Paul chuckled. "That scheming old busybody. She's been a thorn in our sides for years now, and before that in Clare's. She takes delight in making other people miserable. I remember Ian telling me that she spread rumours about Céline, who was, supposedly, having it off with Frank behind Clare's back. Jesus, the woman's sick. Ian said he had to take time off work to go to the school and prove to everyone that Céline was *his* girlfriend and that Frank was totally innocent. Can you *believe* it?"

"Actually, it was Kieran who let us know about that, or let Eileen know, to be precise. He was totally besotted by Céline in those days when she taught him. He was only fourteen. And when the rumour about Frank and her started up, fuelled by Mrs O'Neill and some sixth former who'd seen Céline go into Frank's house at four in the morning..."

"Hey! What was Céline doing in Frank's house at four in the morning? Now *I'm* curious," said Paul.

"A few weeks before the rumour took off, Ian and Céline had been to the south of Ireland and had had a car accident on the way back. Céline was only shaken but Ian had a bad gash to his head and was knocked unconscious. He spent five or six days in Daisy Hill hospital in Newry. And the night it happened, Céline had called Frank and Clare to tell them and they had immediately rushed to Newry to be with her."

"Oh! I didn't know. So Frank and Clare brought Céline home that night I suppose?"

"That's right. And Frank was helping Céline into the house, had his arm around her and was seen."

"Dear God! Doesn't take much to destroy a guy's reputation, does it?"

"Not with Mrs O'Neill around, it doesn't."

"So what happened then?"

"Kieran heard about it at school. He told Eileen. Eileen told me. I told Clare and Frank, who told Ian and Céline. So they concocted that little play-acting at the school gates to let everyone know who was dating who."

"And it all worked out in the end, didn't it? With or without Mrs O'Neill." Paul sighed. "God, Sharon, the day Anita had the nerve to come to Oak Lodge, you should've seen that old bat's face. She was practically jumping for joy, knowing that you would be just as upset as I was."

"I know. She had told me all about it before I'd even got my coat off. Sure we couldn't even keep our relationship a secret with her spreading nasty rumours. I'll not be regretting her, Paul. Not one bit."

"Imagine her stealing George's cheque-book, though. She went one step too far there. But at least it gave us a good reason to fire her. And I agree with you, I'll not be regretting her either. Life's sure going to be a lot quieter without her from now on."

"Let's not waste our breath talking about her again."

"Absolutely. This is *our* night. Our very first night in our very own home. And now Mrs Harrison, let's do this the right way."

They had reached the front door which they had left ajar. Paul swooped down and, before she could protest, had picked Sharon up to carry her neatly over the threshold.

-oOo-

Chapter Thirty-Nine

Summer

It was early July and Owen was sitting in front of his laptop, in the bedroom he was still getting used to, waiting for the results of his finals. The only other person aware of this fact was Léa; telling her had somehow seemed the right thing to do. His parents knew that the results were out sometime soon and took great pains, in Owen's eyes, never to bring the subject up in his presence. That in itself put him on edge and the thought of having to face them if he had failed was just beyond his powers at this point.

  The afternoon crawled on. At four pm he was due another session of physiotherapy so he would have to leave within the hour. Clare was still driving him everywhere these days which was another source of stress to add to all the other stress he was currently experiencing. Left to himself, he was finding it hard to control his temper on occasions, oscillating between fits of anger, often over the most trivial things, and shamefully making apologies afterwards. Only when he was with Léa did he feel at peace. She had the knack of diverting his attention away from his own worries and filling his thoughts with more pleasant things.

And yet it was not as if he could even call her his girlfriend. Their relationship was different. They were friends, good friends even, their shared experiences over the Alex episode having brought them close. But it all remained platonic. He had never even kissed her properly and she certainly wasn't encouraging him on that front. This was a first for Owen, who was wont to take things much further and much faster with the girls to whom he was attracted. Even with Judith he hadn't really taken his time, the difference being that he had remained faithful to her throughout their relationship and willingly agreed to set up home together when she had suggested it.

But Léa was different and Owen didn't really know why. Perhaps it was Solange's dire warnings about not messing her around that held him back. Perhaps it was having witnessed the cruelty of Alex that prevented him taking the risk of making Léa suffer again, should it not work out. Perhaps it was Léa herself who continued to surround herself with a multitude of friends while yet making him feel important to her. In what way exactly, he wasn't sure. But for now he surprised himself by being content to take things step by step, finding joy in her presence, knowing that Léa was not like the other girls... and that that made her very special indeed.

Lost in his thoughts, he hadn't realized that he had automatically refreshed the webpage once more and was startled to see that the results were out. At last! His heart thudding he scrolled down to 'H' and had to read what was written over and over again till it finally sunk in that he had passed. Then he gave a loud whoop of joy, punching the air with his good arm and jumping to his feet so quickly he knocked over the chair he had been sitting on which crashed to the floor, bringing an anxious Clare running up the stairs to his room within minutes.

"Owen, what's wrong? Are you alright?" she panted.

"I've passed, Mum! I got my results. I'm an architect. I passed!"

"Oh my God! Owen, that's wonderful. Oh, congratulations my darling. Well done!"

Mother and son hugged. Clare was trying hard not to cry. She felt she might burst with happiness and pride.

"Do you want to text your father with the good news? He'll be in class at the moment. You won't be able to call him."

"Yeah. I'll text him, no worries."

"Shall I make us both a cup of tea? I feel I need a cup right now. Oh, isn't this just great, Owen?"

"I'll be down in a few minutes, Mum. I just want to do something first."

"Okay, love."

And Clare left, her heart swelling with joy. Before she had got as far as the stairs she could hear Owen saying *"Léa? Léa, c'est bon!"*

He came downstairs some fifteen minutes later, dazed and happy, into the big old kitchen that Clare had already gone a long way into transforming. She put the kettle on again to make a fresh cup of tea and brought out the McVities chocolate biscuits that she had been pleased to find recently in the local supermarket, no less.

"You've texted your father then?"

"Oh, sorry, Mum, I forgot," said Owen, whipping out his phone.

"Typical! But I'll forgive you where thousands wouldn't." She let him text in peace.

"Now," she began, when he had finished. "When and where?"

"When and where for what?"

"When shall we go out and celebrate and where would you like to go?"

"Aw, Mum, that's nice. But you don't have to, you know."

"I *want* to. And so will your dad. We'll go out for a meal. Why don't you invite Solange and Léa and Solange's boyfriend, Antoine, isn't it? We'll invite Jean-Christophe and his wife too. After all, they're part of the set-up here and we've never really invited them before."

Owen gave his mother a knowing look.

"Léa's not part of the set-up, Mum. You trying to match-make again?" he said, smiling.

"Léa's very much part of the set-up, Owen. She's been coming every Saturday for the last three weeks, helping with the changeovers. She won't let me pay her. She says it's the least she can do after what you did for her. And this would be a nice way of saying thank you."

"Okay, Mum. That's a good idea. I'll contact the girls and see when it would suit. Then we can tell Jean-Christophe on Friday. I imagine it would have to be mid-week, wouldn't it?"

"Yes. Sorry, but week-ends are out. That's when we're most needed at the gîtes. Even Sundays are quite full, now that we're fully booked. But any weekday will do. Just let me know."

"Where shall we go then? Know any nice restaurants?"

"Actually," said Clare, who had the grace to look sheepish, "I've been having a look around. Just in case, you know? There's a nice little restaurant in Baud and that's about half-way between here and Lorient. It would mean that the girls have less travelling time…"

"So you've already booked a table for Monday next then?"

"Owen! That's not fair!"

"Just teasing you, Mum," said Owen, putting his arm around her and giving her a squeeze. "You're always so very organized; I quite expect you to have read everyone's minds, found out when they're free and decided on the menu. But it would appear that you are human after all."

"Umm… don't quite know whether you're teasing or insulting me, Owen Hunter." Clare thought for a moment. "Actually, Monday next would be quite good. It's the eve of the fourteenth of July – Bastille day and a bank holiday on the Tuesday. So anyone who is working, I'm thinking of Frank or Antoine or even Jean-Christophe, they wouldn't have to get up early the next day. What do you think?"

"I think you had it planned all along with Queen's University in Belfast so that the results would come out in time. That's what I think."

"You eejit, Owen. And stop taking the Mickey. I'm your mother, after all," said Clare primly.

"I might be an eejit, Mum, but now I'm an architect. Yahoo!" And he swung his mother round.

"Owen, stop! You'll hurt your arm. Away with you! Now you'll have a good excuse to call Léa again. But hurry up; we're leaving for your physiotherapy session in ten minutes."

She didn't have to tell him twice. Owen bounded up the stairs, speed-dialling Léa as he went.

Everyone came and the Auberge des Trois Pigeons at Baud provided a very good meal in delightful surroundings. Frank ordered champagne as an aperitif and Owen's success was toasted in style. Antoine got to meet Solange's bosses at long last and Nadège, Jean-Christophe's wife, soon lost her shyness once she realized that she would not have to listen to everyone talking English all evening. In fact, it was easier for them all to speak in French and Owen surprised everyone, including himself, at how quickly he had come on in that language. While it was true that the twins usually talked to him in English, this wasn't the case for any other of their friends, or even Antoine, who all preferred to speak French. Long summer evenings listening to and participating in endless discussions with them at Léa's house had given him confidence and he was getting to be quite fluent in that language when he wanted.

The meal over, Jean-Christophe and Nadège said their good-byes. The inn-keeper suggested to the others that they prolong their stay in Baud by making their way to the municipal town park where fireworks were being organized to celebrate Bastille day. Some towns like Baud, Owen learned, celebrated on the eve of Bastille day and some on the day itself. So it was quite possible to take in two firework displays if one knew where to go. Back to speaking English, they walked the short distance to the park. Here many townsfolk had turned out for the show and which proved to be really good and lasted for what seemed like ages before terminating in a fireworks finale that had them all gasping in admiration.

Then, as if by common agreement, the crowd moved off to another part of the park where a band was warming up. Here huge sections of wooden flooring had been laid out and within minutes people were getting up to dance. Frank and Antoine went off to buy beers and lemonade and Léa took Owen by the hand to join the dancers. Clare and Solange bagged a table and sat down.

"I am so very pleased for Owen, Clare. He will make a good architect. I have seen what he has accomplished at your manor house," said Solange.

"I still think it's a dream sometimes, Solange. But I'm so very happy for him. Now he can really start to think about his future."

Solange's face clouded. "Do you know what he intends to do now, Clare? What his plans are?"

"Umm… not really. I don't think he has decided anything definite yet. I know he intends to remain at the gîtes for the summer. To help us out, you know? But after that… I suppose he'll be wanting to apply for jobs."

"Jobs here in France… or jobs in Ireland perhaps?"

"I've no idea." Clare sighed. "I know what you're thinking, Solange. Believe me, I know my son. And I understand fully that you want to protect Léa… and you're very right to protect Léa, don't get me wrong."

"I don't want her to get hurt, Clare. I just want her to be happy, you know? She deserves to be happy after all she has been through."

"And I agree with you. Owen does not have the best reputation with girls. I found that out a long time ago. All I *can* say is that he is very fond of Léa. In fact, I have never seen him so… so at peace. That sounds silly, I know. But it's the truth."

"Thank you for telling me that, Clare. But… ah, here are Frank and Antoine. Lemonade for Clare and Léa; they are the drivers tonight."

On the dance-floor, Owen was beginning to use his left arm more and more as his physiotherapist had advised, taking care to stop if ever he felt pain. He could now stretch it fully and pick up objects that were not too heavy. He was even driving again which was encouraging.

But just now it was a slow dance and he had both arms around Léa. And that felt particularly good. Léa's eyes were closed and she had laid her head on his chest. Owen wished they could stay like that all night.

All too soon, the band changed their music to that of a waltz. Young couples faded from the floor as middle aged and even quite older couples got up to dance. After midnight a disk-jockey would be taking over to cater for the under-twenties and at two am sharp, it would all be over. Léa and Owen sat down with the others to a welcome drink.

"I think we'll be heading, Owen," said Clare. "I need to be up early tomorrow. There's always someone wanting fresh bread or croissants before eight am." She smiled at them all. "No rest for the wicked."

"Thank you both so much for the lovely meal," said Solange, with Antoine and Léa nodding their agreement. "Yes, thank you. It was delicious," added Léa.

"Yeah, it was great," said Owen. "Thank you both. Safe home now."

"You're not coming then?"

"Actually, no, Mum. The girls have invited me to stay and see the 14th July celebrations in Lorient. Apparently it's something else. So I'll be staying there tonight and tomorrow night, if that's okay. I've already put my bag in their car. Dad, could you call for me at Léa's house on Wednesday after work?"

"You girls willing to put up with this guy then?" said Frank, smiling. "Remember it's for two whole days."

"I think we can bear him for two days, Frank," said Solange. "He will be good."

"I'm *always* good," said Owen knowingly.

"Well, if you *can't* be good," said Frank laughing, "be careful."

"And if you cannot be careful?" said Antoine, joining in.

"Buy a pram!" said Léa, and laughed at the look on their faces.

-oOo-

Chapter Forty

More Results

Thursday August 13th. D-day. Kieran had not slept well. The results would be out by lunchtime and Tesco's was choc-a-bloc with no time to concentrate on what would happen if he didn't get his grades. But the nagging thought was there, jumping up to bite him every so often, no peace of mind possible.

Beth was not working that day and Kieran envied her heartily. He had tried, and failed, to get the day off, so it was doubly difficult to concentrate. Beth would be okay, Kieran just knew she would. And anyway, she never seemed to go overboard about anything really. She was steady. Hardworking, safe and steady. Oh! Why couldn't he be like Beth for once? Kieran berated himself for not having paid more attention to his studies. Now there was every possibility that he had not made the grades.

During his lunch-hour he tried to phone the university to see if he'd been accepted but could not get through, all the lines being permanently engaged. The frustration was almost more than he could bear and he still had the long afternoon ahead of him to get through before he could leave work, dash home and go online. He didn't even know his grades. God, what an awful day!

Six o'clock came slowly but inevitably around and Kieran left work with a heavy heart. He knew he'd done badly; there was just no other outcome possible. He put the key in the lock to Paul's flat, a flat he would have to give up at the end of the month whatever happened, and sat down in front of his lap-top to confront the inevitable.

And inevitably, he had not got the grades he needed for Queen's. Kieran put his head in his hands. He didn't often feel like crying but today, he did. After the frustration of having to work all day, now he'd gone down in his A levels.

After five minutes of undiluted self-pity, Kieran roused himself to go on the UCAS Track and check the status of his application. There was just a teeny chance Queen's would accept him anyway. He'd got the A levels but not the grades. Surely the university could see that he was worth taking a chance on, couldn't they?

But his UCAS Track status was still 'conditional'. That meant he would have to phone them and put his case forward. What could he say? That his AS grades were good? They were. That he had messed up his maths paper through nerves? That wasn't actually true. He had messed up his maths paper because he had read a question wrong... okay through nerves. But the physics paper, Jesus, there wasn't any excuse. He hadn't worked hard enough and that was the bottom line. Trembling he keyed in the number to phone.

The girl he spoke to was sympathetic but there was nothing she could do. The staff in the admissions office had just left. They had already worked overtime till half past six and now there was no-one to take his call. She suggested he ring back at nine the following day. Kieran could've wept. Damn bloody Tesco's! Damn them for not letting him have the day off. He flung himself on the bed, awash with anxiety.

Just then he heard a timid knocking on the door. Hoping to God it wasn't his mother, he went to answer it and there, standing on the doorstep, was Beth. One look at his face told her all she needed to know.

"Oh Kieran! It's bad, isn't it? Didn't you pass?"

"I did, Beth, but my grades are lower than expected. I really mucked up in Physics and Maths. And now the bloody admissions office is closed for the night and I'll have to wait till tomorrow to see if I'm in or not."

"What did the UCAS Track status say?"

"Conditional. I'm going to have to grovel. Oh Lord! I'm no good at this Beth. Why didn't I work harder?"

"Look, Kieran. All is not lost. We'll work out a speech that you can say tomorrow morning, putting forward your good points and minimizing the fact you didn't get the required grades. You've got the A levels after all. Let's do it now, right now. Okay?"

Kieran looked at Beth. She was so good, always backing him up. He didn't deserve her. He was a prat, a lazy prat, but she loved him anyway. Suddenly it occurred to him that he hadn't even asked her how she'd done.

"Beth," he said gently. "I'm so wrapped up in my own problems, I never even asked you. How did you do, yourself?"

"I'm in, Kieran. My results weren't quite as good as I'd hoped for too but my UCAS Track status says I'm accepted. Now all we have to do is concentrate on getting you in too. Remind me what your AS results were? We'll have this sorted out in no time."

The next morning Beth was there before nine, her face bright and encouraging. Between them, the night before, they had concocted a speech that was well-documented and sober. Kieran had read it over so many times, he now knew it off by heart.

At nine o'clock he rang but already the lines were engaged. He was put on hold. Beth went out to the kitchen to make them both a cup of tea. Suddenly she froze, as from the bedroom she could hear the sound of his voice, knew that he was launching into his speech and stood there praying that the Gods would let him get into Queen's. For Beth could not envisage going to Queen's without him. It was as simple as that.

Five minutes later he came out, his face beginning to relax.

"What did they say? Are you in?" said Beth anxiously.

"They didn't say. I've to watch my UCAS Track status and they'll give me a reply today. But the woman I spoke to was nice, Beth. She… she seemed encouraging. So I don't know…"

"If you don't get on that course, could you get on another one you'd like?"

"Probably," said Kieran, absentmindedly.

"What other course have you envisaged then?"

"What? Oh, I haven't really thought about that, to be honest. I've only ever wanted to get on this one particular course. It was the best in Queen's for what I'd like to do."

"You going into Tesco's today?" said Beth, handing him a cup of tea.

"No, actually. Thank God. Couldn't bear another day like yesterday." Kieran shuddered.

"I'll have to be going then. I'm on the ten-till-six shift. If you hear anything will you send me a text? I'll check my phone at tea-break."

"Okay, Beth."

"See you tonight, then. Don't give up, okay?"

"Yeah. And... and thanks, Beth. Thanks a million for your help and your support and... everything."

"Bye, Kieran." And she was off.

Kieran didn't have that long to wait. At half past eleven, his UCAS Track status suddenly changed from 'conditional' to 'accepted'. It took Kieran a few seconds to sink in. When it did, he jumped on the bed, jumped and jumped like a trampoline, shouting and whooping with joy. He eventually calmed down, went back on to UCAS Track to make sure they hadn't changed their minds, then he texted the good news to Beth, locked up the flat and headed out to Eileen's.

"Gran, gran, I've passed! I'm in! I've been accepted at Queen's," he shouted above the barking of Whisky who always set up a din whenever anyone came to visit.

"Oh my God! That's wonderful, Kieran. Whisky! Whisky, stop! I can't hear myself think! Stop now. Down, boy."

But Kieran had seized his gran to waltz her round the little sitting-room, sending Whisky into even further convulsions of excitement at seeing them dance.

"Kieran Murphy, would ye stop? I'm out of breath! What a to-do! Just as well my heart is strong. You'll be the death of me one of these days."

"Gran, aren't you happy for me? Aren't you proud of your grandson? Just think, Dad went to university and now I'll be going too."

"And so you will. Congratulations! Your mum must be over the moon. Did Beth get in too?"

"She did, Gran, but I haven't seen Mum yet. I'm heading over there now."

"I think she might be on duty. But try anyway. Now isn't that just the best news ever? You clever boy!"

"Thanks, Gran. Be seeing you." And off he went to run up the 200 yards or so to the new house. But there was no sign of Sharon or Paul. It must be the time of day when their shifts overlap, thought Kieran. Trust his luck. Well, he wouldn't wait till that evening. He'd go to Oak Lodge and give them the good news right away.

But when he let himself into Oak Lodge, he could see that something was wrong. Staff were agitated, talking in whispers. Further down the corridor, towards the back of the property, he could just make out Paul as he ran into one of the bedrooms, calling out something to another male nurse as he passed. An alarm was ringing, getting louder and louder as Kieran made his way down the corridor until suddenly it stopped and the silence was eerie. He slowly approached the room Paul had gone into and looked in through the door.

The room was full of people: his mother, her face clouded, as she pumped air into the old man's lungs using a sort of balloon; Paul, as he practiced a cardiac massage, beating out a strangely hypnotic rhythm, while shouting orders to have the room cleared; the other male nurse had come back with a hypodermic needle which he now carefully filled to a certain measure and injected something into the old man's arm; a lady of about seventy, small and thin, who was standing looking anxiously at the old man, tears streaming down her cheeks; a young girl with long black hair who comforted her in what sounded like French, and a care-worker called Geraldine whom Paul was exhorting to get the French people out.

Kieran stood back against the wall as they passed him, numbed by their misery. He watched as the care-worker, Geraldine, accompanied them down the corridor and handed them over to other staff with instructions to take them to the dining-room and give them a cup of tea. Then she fairly ran back to the bedroom, nodding as she recognized Kieran, went quickly in and shut the door behind her.

Kieran did not know how long he remained there. It seemed like a long, long time. It was a strange feeling to know that something urgent and terrible was going on behind that closed door, someone who was very ill, or even dying, whom Paul and his mother were trying hard to save. Kieran had never given much thought to their work, and if he did, he thought more along the lines of bedpans and medication and false teeth and senility rather than actually saving someone's life.

He suddenly felt humbled. And very, very proud.

The sound of a siren broke into these thoughts and within a few minutes an ambulance crew were racing to the room preceded by a member of staff. They seemed to be carrying a huge amount of equipment and a fold-up stretcher also. Their faces were grim.

From his viewpoint to the side of the now-open door, Kieran watched as Paul stopped the heart massage and the old man was quickly examined. Then one of the ambulance crew took over the massage while Paul helped set up a defibrillator, placing the pads one above and one below the old man's heart. Then everyone stood back, just like in the movies, as the old man was given electric shocks to get his heart beating once more. Again and again Kieran watched as his body jerked up and down. Again and again Paul listened with his stethoscope to a heart that was not beating of its own accord. Another injection; another electric shock. For twenty minutes more everyone worked hard, in perfect coordination, people who did not know each other but who knew exactly what to do. Until finally the dance was over, everything went silent, and the time of death was pronounced.

The first to leave were the ambulance crew, already making contact with their base to see where they would be sent to next. Then Kieran heard Paul telling Sharon to go have a cup of tea, that she must be tired after all their exertions, that he would inform Aurore and Angélique himself. He asked Geraldine to help Krzysztof clean up the body and the bed, telling them that he would send in Beatrice to give them a hand. Then he strode out of the room, taking off his glasses as he went, running his hand through his hair which Kieran knew was a sure sign of stress. He hadn't even noticed Kieran as he passed.

His mother came out more slowly. Kieran could sense her sadness. She looked up to see him standing there and gave him a wane smile.

"Kieran! I didn't know you were there. You've caught us at a bad time, I'm afraid. We've just lost George."

"I know, Mum. I've been here a while. I'm sorry about George. Isn't that the old man Clare was doing something in France for?"

"Yes, love. She found his daughter. Thank God she found her in time. Believe it or not, George was ninety-two. His daughter is seventy. She's here with *her* granddaughter. Paul's gone to tell them now." She sighed. "How about you and I having a cup of tea? I think I could do with one right now."

She had a quick word with one of the careworkers who was lingering in the corridor and beckoned Kieran to follow her up to the office.

Kieran had not been in Sharon's office since Clare's time and saw that the desk she used to occupy, as Clare's deputy, was now occupied by Paul. The oval table was still there and it was here that Sharon sat down heavily and motioned Kieran to take a seat. She looked worn out.

"Well, love, what brings you to Oak Lodge? Nothing wrong, I hope?"

"No, Mum, good news, actually. I know it's probably not the right time but I just wanted to let you and Paul know that I got into Queen's."

"Oh, sweetheart, that's wonderful. You've made my day! Congratulations!"

"It wasn't easy, Mum. I didn't get the grades I wanted. I didn't fail either," he added, seeing his mother's worried look, "but I went down in Maths and Physics and had to plead my cause to get on the course I wanted. But they've accepted me now. Beth helped me prepare my phone interview; she's been great."

"And did Beth get through also?"

"She did, Mum, no sweat."

"Come here. Let me give you a hug. I'm so happy for you." And Kieran was startled to see tears in his mother's eyes.

Just then there was a knock on the door and a care-worker entered with a tray of tea and biscuits. Sharon thanked her and poured out a cup for Kieran and for herself.

"You've made me proud, Kieran. Really proud. And if your dad had've been here today, he'd have been really proud of you too."

"Thanks, Mum. But, you know, when I watched you and Paul and all those other people trying to save that old man's life, even if he *was* ninety-two, well, I was proud of you too. You do a great job."

And he smiled.

Paul stood looking down at the shrunken body of the man he had been proud to call his friend. In a few minutes he would return to fetch Aurore and Angélique, but just now, he needed a minute alone to say good-bye. Geraldine and Krzysztof had done a good job. The old man looked clean and peaceful, the room smelt nice and through the partially open sash window, a gentle summer breeze filtered in, ruffling the old man's hair. He looked not dead, but asleep. Paul took his hand.

"Well, George," he said softly, "we lost the battle this time. What do you say about that, eh?"

Immediately the voice of George came into Paul's head telling him that it had been a good innings and why wasn't he toasting the future generations with a wee dram before the room was cleared out and some other unsuspecting soul came to live there? It was so real, so very like George, that Paul looked hard at the old man, as if he had spoken the words out loud. Then slowly he went to the wardrobe, fished out the bottle of whiskey and the glass that was stored with it, and poured himself out a small measure.

"To you, George. To your long and interesting life," he said. He raised his glass to the old man. "And to future generations, as you say."

-oOo-

Chapter Forty-One

The End of the Season

And so the summer wore on. Owen gradually got back full use of his arm and continued to do strengthening exercises long after the physiotherapy sessions had ended. Clare was genuinely saddened to learn of the death of George and grateful that she had had the time to find his family and to let them meet up. However, with it being the height of the season she could not go to Ireland for his funeral, but she did speak to Aurore on several occasions and for many weeks, George was never far from her thoughts.

Towards the end of September, she gave her housewarming party, inviting friends and family whom she lodged in the two biggest gîtes that had become available now that the season was nearly over. Ian and Céline were there, and so were Céline's parents.

Eammon and Brigit, Frank's brother and his wife, had come over from Ireland. Laura and Nathan had come up from Lanester and Owen had invited Léa, Solange and Antoine and all their friends, including Marina, Logan, Jean-Claude and Alain and their girlfriends Yolen and Françoise, who were collectively in charge of the catering. All the twin's friends had opted to bring tents and camp in the garden, the weather being extremely warm still, even for France.

Although the party was officially an evening do, many of the guests were already there for the week-end, so it actually got started on the Saturday lunch-time with Jean-Claude and Alain doing their famous barbeque, Yolen and Françoise concocting nibbles and salads and Céline, Solange and Léa looking after desserts. Then after a riotous lunch, the little troupe of changeover staff went off to see to the gîtes while those left behind either went for walks or a rest before tackling the preparations for the evening do.

By now Clare had got used to the French way of joyfully disorganized meals with everyone butting in to lend a hand. What was supposed to be an evening party was in fact a week-end marathon with no less than four meals to organize for an indeterminate number of people each time. So in the same haphazard spirit, she had prepared and frozen food throughout the month of September, bought ginormous quantities of fresh meat and sea-food and crudités the day before, given her 'official' caterers an almost totally free hand to plan the menus and on the day had let the girls pick fruit off the trees in the garden to make into flans and tarts.

In fact it was so warm that the evening do was also held outdoors with garden furniture drafted in from the gîtes and the garden illuminated by fairy lights and portable lamps. Frank and Ian took lots of photos and Clare, for once, shed her organization mode to relax and join in the fun.

She was taking a little tour of the garden, sipping her first drink of the day, when she bumped into Ian who was photographing the house from the front trying to get some nice views from an angle that did not show the presence of tents.

"Well, big Sis. You got your manor house. I always knew you would," he began.

"Mm... it's gorgeous, isn't it? I love the way the setting sun reflects on the conservatory at the back. Come round here. See for yourself." And she took him by the arm to show him her favourite spot.

"Stand there. Just there. I'll take a photo of you in front of it. Great! That's a nice one," said Ian.

"So how's it going for you and Céline, then? We haven't had much time to talk these last few weeks. We've just been so busy at the gîtes, you wouldn't believe it."

"Well, we're fine, actually. We still squabble from time to time, which is perfectly normal I'd say, but we've never had a bust-up like what happened in June. God, Clare, that was one of the worst weeks of my life."

"Let's say no more about it then. This is happy time. How's the hunt going for a house in Saint Aubert? Any luck?"

"Oh, Céline spends all her free time trawling the websites, looking at programmes for new-builds, and sussing out old houses too. She's totally obsessed about buying somewhere of our own now. Before it was me. But now she's taken over big style. There's not a week-end goes past without her dragging me off to visit something or other."

"And how's her new school going? Does she like it well?"

"Absolutely! She gets on well with the other teachers and is all into this new teaching method for foreign languages. She's so enthusiastic, she wears me out. You know what she's like, Clare. It's all or nothing with Céline. I'm running to keep up these days."

"But you're happy for her, aren't you?"

"I am. I wouldn't have it any other way," said Ian with conviction. "It's great to see her so motivated... and while she's so busy with school and house-hunting..."

"...our Ian can get away with blue murder and do whatever he likes!"

"Now, Clare, did I say that? But actually there's some truth in what you say. Good Lord! I'm just realizing that I'm definitely a hen-pecked husband now!"

"Welcome to the real world, Ian. But I know you wouldn't change your little Céline for all the tea in China.

Now, how about me getting you a drink? Oh, there's Frank calling to us."

And off they went arm in arm.

Frank was standing talking to Nathan and Laura, who together with Ian, had invested in the gîte project. Nathan, being a bank manager, was keeping an ever-watchful eye on Clare's projects but even he had to admit that the gîtes were doing well and that the season had been, if anything, better than the year before, the availability of the gatehouse gîte from July onwards being a serious contributing factor to the summer turnover.

"Clare, this is a great party. And this *maison de maître* house, it is wonderful. You have done it up so well," began Laura.

"That's thanks to Owen, Laura. He gave us great help and advice and kept all the artisans on track. We couldn't have done it without him… at least not at such a reasonable cost and in such a short time-frame."

"It is very elegant, I must admit," said Nathan. "A really nice property and it will gain value in time, I am quite convinced of that."

"Oh, Nathan," said Clare, teasing. "Once a banker, always a banker! Yes, it *has* been a big outlay but it'll be an investment too."

"Are you now organizing the IT and French language courses during the winter like you did last year?"

"Oh definitely! I intend to increase their number even," replied Clare. "Ian can't free up more time but hopefully Owen will take over there at least till we get a replacement person… I don't want to start organizing that until I know what Owen intends to do. But Ian has agreed to take the first course third week of October, when it's half-term for Céline, so she'll come too to give me a hand with the catering, and Frank will start his first French language course of the season just after that. Actually, they're already booked out."

"But you say Owen has not decided what to do yet?" said Laura, looking over to where he was playing *boules** with Léa, Solange and Antoine.

"He's staying till Christmas. That I *do* know. After that, well, I imagine he'll have to find a job in architecture. It's not worth his while studying all those years just to stay living with his parents."

"He speaks French now, does he not?" queried Nathan. "Quite well, I think?"

"He does, Nathan," said Frank. "A few mistakes as far as grammar is concerned but he's going to sit in on my French lessons this time. It will do him good to go over the basics. But as for fluency, he's not doing too bad."

"Well, I shall keep on the look-out for any companies that wish to hire an architect. I sometimes come across them in my job. Laura too."

"Oh yes!" agreed Laura. "We shall… how do you say… keep our ears stuck to the ground."

Frank said : "'Keep our ears to the ground' is all you need to say, Laura. But thank you very much. I'm sure Owen will appreciate that."

Owen was getting to be a dab hand at *boules* but still not as good as Antoine, nor even Solange. He could beat Léa though, much to her frustration. He was partnering Solange at the moment and they won by a hair's breadth. He high-fived her, grinning.

"Anyone fancy another beer?" he asked.

"*Oui, s'il te plait*,' said Antoine.

"*Pas pour moi*," said the twins in unison.

Owen went off to get two cold beers and when he came back the conversation was centred around the cottage on the Isle of Groix. The name rang a bell. Apparently they were all planning to go there the following week-end, as of the Friday night. Solange would no longer be needed at the gîtes, as the work-load had dropped spectacularly and Léa had already stopped helping out there now that Owen was able to take her place. The girls were planning to go to their parent's cottage and stay for the week-end at least, Léa perhaps even the whole week. They had not been since Easter. The place would need airing and cleaning. And apart from anything else, it was nice to return to the island, re-visit their childhood haunts. They described it to Owen in glowing terms, and took it for granted that he would be coming too.

"I'll have to see if my parents can spare me," he said, laughing at their enthusiasm.

"Go! Go ask them this very minute," said Léa, physically pushing him in the direction of Clare and Frank. He arrived in the circle they formed with Nathan, Laura and Ian much quicker than he had intended, spilling beer over himself in the process.

"Need a bib, Owen? Baby wipes?" said Ian, smirking.

"Lord, when those girls get a thing in their head..." began Owen. "Actually, I was sent over, Mum, to see if you could do without me next week-end. We're all heading over to the Isle of Groix. There's a cottage that belonged to Léa's parents and we're going to give the place an airing... um... or something."

"Oh, the Isle of Groix! It is really very pretty," said Laura. "Very few cars. Everywhere there are bicycles. Even at the supermarket, they prefer to deliver your goods. You can walk or cycle everywhere. You will enjoy it there, Owen."

"Thanks Laura. Good to know. But Mum, what's the bookings like for next week? Can you manage without me?"

"We'll manage," said Clare smiling. "I think I can let you off the hook this time, although if I'd known that by letting Solange go, I'd be letting three people go at once, I might have had second thoughts. Still, only four bookings for that week, Frank and I will manage it between us. And Eammon and Brigit will still be around if we need the extra help."

"Cheers, Mum. I'll tell the others." And Owen was off.

"So? So?" said Léa, tugging at his tee-shirt like a child.

"*C'est bon!* I'm free to go with you all next weekend to Groix. Happy days!" said Owen grinning.

"Great!" said Solange. She thought for a few seconds and said: "Now, Antoine has to work Saturday morning so I will wait and come with him. We will also bring Marina and Logan, who finish their jobs at 2pm. You, Owen, will go with Léa on Friday afternoon and get everything ready." She wagged her finger at them. "You may be getting out of the changeover at the gîtes but you two will be doing the changeover at the cottage. I expect it all to be perfect when we arrive on Saturday afternoon."

"Yes Ma'am!" said Owen saluting, secretly delighted to get Léa all to himself for a few hours.

"Now go and change your tee-shirt, Owen. You have got beer all down the front of it," said Léa.

"You two take the cake, you really do," said Owen wondering how he ever came to be bossed around so much by the twins.

"Cake? There is cake?" said Léa. "Where?"

"Aw… give me strength!" said Owen, laughing, as he headed off to his room to change.

The party ran on into the early hours, finishing up in the tents when the older generation headed off to bed. The next morning all was ominously quiet on that front so Clare and Frank began the preparations for lunch on their own. It was, inevitably, another barbeque, this time with salmon steaks that Clare had taken out of the freezer the night before. These would be cooked as the main course with an alternative of steaks or sausages for those who preferred. Baby boiled potatoes and broccoli would be the vegetables and a white sauce 'beurre blanc' laced with dill would be the accompaniment. There wouldn't be a starter but Clare had organized a host of nibbles to go with drinks, and banana-split for dessert. The evening meal that day, for those who remained, would simply be made up of left-overs supplemented by terrines of home-made pâté, salad and baguettes.

By the time the last of the revellers had headed home, or to the gîtes, that night, both Clare and Frank were numb with fatigue. But happy that everyone had had such a good time. Owen, who was already looking forward to the coming week-end on the Isle of Groix, did most of the clearing up alone and without even having to be asked.

And Clare wondered secretly, once again, where all this would lead.

-oOo-

Boules = French bowls

Chapter Forty-Two

L'île de Groix

Friday finally came around and it had been arranged that Frank drop Owen off at Larmor-Plage just before his first lesson at the language school which, that day, was programmed for 9:30 am. Various conversations with Léa since the party had lead him to believe they would be staying at the cottage for most of the week so Owen had packed a some extra clothes at her request in a rucksack and brought boots for walking and a waterproof coat just in case.

Léa greeted him with pleasure, kissing him on the cheek in that frustratingly sisterly manner. For once she was not dressed in an overall for painting, her habitual attire when at home.

She had prepared them coffee and Owen produced fresh croissants, having got Frank to stop off at the local *boulangerie* on the way. He was in high good spirits and even Léa was bubbly with excitement. They ate a happy breakfast, a second breakfast for Owen, with Léa chatting non-stop about the cottage and how lovely it was on Groix.

After this, Léa finished packing her own rucksack, then phoned a taxi to take them to the ferry terminal at Lorient.

"We're not taking the car, then?" said Owen, surprised at this.

"Oh no! It is far too expensive to take a car. And anyway, we do not need one. It is not a very big island. We can walk to the cottage once we leave the ferry; it is only about fifteen minutes."

The taxi took them back towards Lorient in good time to catch the 11 am ferry over to Groix. As they got out of the car, it began to rain, large fat drops that stirred up the dry soil, giving out an earthy smell. The sea looked rather choppy.

"Anyone would think that there's a storm brewing up," said Owen, looking at the sky. "There isn't, is there?"

"Um... there might be. Always at this time of year we have the *grandes marées,* very high tides, you know? If we have a storm on top of that, it can make the crossing difficult."

"How long does the crossing take, then?"

"Oh, only about forty-five minutes. It is not too long, the crossing."

The ferry was quite small with room for about sixteen cars; however the presence of two camper-vans reduced the space for cars to a maximum of twelve. Even then there were only two cars on this ferry, although there were quite a lot of foot-passengers, taking advantage of the last of the summer season's special offers to see the island.

The crossing was indeed choppy. Owen and Léa went to watch the coastline from the shelter of the foot-passenger lounge as the ferry worked its way down the Lorient estuary, past Larmor-Plage, and Léa's house, and turned its prow decidedly toward the isle of Groix.

What was not much more than a vague outline on the horizon now took on more definite forms, cliffs that got higher and higher as they neared, giving way to small stretches of white, sandy beaches and a huge promontory of a beach to their left that Léa told him was called the Plage des Grands Sables.

The island was only 8kms long, Owen learned, and 3kms wide. The cottage was situated just near Port Lay, less than a mile from where they were to land. They would take the coastal path to get there but not before going into the town of Groix to do some food shopping and have it delivered.

While Léa looked after the list of shopping she had made out with the help of Solange, Owen went to find a *boulangerie* and bought them sandwiches for lunch and bread for their evening meal. Then they set off together, dodging the rain that threatened from time to time, and made it to the cottage in twenty minutes, out of breath and rather damp. Léa proudly produced the key and in they went.

The cottage was made of stonework, dark grey stone that echoed many of the constructions on the island. The shutters were blue, the same blue that Léa's house had and the house itself was quite large, for a cottage, and built in a 'T' shape with a small building to the one side, separated from the main house.

"That is my studio," said Léa happily. "Solange had it built for me before I came out of hospital. Come, Owen, come with me and see it. We shall explore the house afterwards." And she took Owen by the hand, unlocked the studio and stood back proudly to let him see inside.

What looked like a large outhouse from the back now opened up into a well-lit room once Léa had opened all the shutters. French windows gave on to a tiny terrace to the front overlooking the sea. The view was lovely, even on a day as overcast as this. It was mainly just the one room, all set up for painting: easel, canvass, paints, rags and turpentine. And samples of Léa's work adorned the walls. To the back of the room was a large cupboard to one side and a toilet and shower-room to the other. Owen could see that it could easily be turned into a guest bedroom, if needed. There was even a top-quality bed-settee against one wall and a modern wood-burner standing ready for use on the opposite side.

"It's a... wonderful room, Léa," he said admiringly. "It must be a great place to work from."

"It was my life-line, Owen," she said simply, her face clouding for a second or two. Then she brightened. "Now I will show you the rest of the cottage. Come!"

They left the studio with the shutters open, Léa locking the door behind her. A few quick steps brought them to the main house.

To say it was a cottage was something of an understatement. They entered directly into a large kitchen-cum-diner-cum-sitting-room in an 'L' shape. From this lead off a bed-room with en-suite that Léa said was Solange's room. Upstairs there were two bedrooms in the eves and a toilet and shower-room also. Everywhere were signs of a recent renovation and a quality renovation at that: aluminium-framed double glazing, stone-rendered walls in the sitting-room, which sported a large open fireplace, state-of-the-art kitchen with all mod-cons, grey slate floor-tiling throughout the ground floor and wooden flooring above.

Léa told him to put his rucksack in one of the upstairs bedrooms, the one with two single beds. The other room sported a double bed and he wondered tentatively if Léa would be sleeping there.

"So, you will be sharing with Logan," she announced to him happily, dashing his hopes before he had time to build them up. "And Marina will have the other room," she concluded.

"But you, Léa, where will you sleep?" he asked.

"Why, in my studio, of course! That is where I always sleep." She came up to him and said. "Sometimes I paint all night. Then I forget to sleep!"

"But don't you get cold? I mean that's quite a storm gathering. Perhaps we should get your wood-burner lit and a fire in here too."

"Yes, we shall. That is what we shall do first of all. Come, I will show you where we keep the wood. No! Before we do that we must plug in the fridge and turn the water and electricity on. Then we will light the fires."

Some twenty-five minutes later, the studio wood-burner was throwing out a steady heat and Owen had a good fire going in the sitting-room. They sat in front of it to eat their sandwiches. All around the cottage the wind was beginning to howl.

"You think the ferries will be running tomorrow, then?" said Owen getting up to look out at the dark, murky landscape towards the sea.

"Oh, they usually run in all weathers. It will take more than a little storm to stop them, I am sure," she replied.

Their lunch over, it was not easy to envisage doing anything outdoors as the rain was now lashing against the window-panes. Léa suggested a game of chess.

An hour and a half and two games later, in her favour much to Owen's disgust, he went to put more logs on the fire.

"Now we must clean the house and make the beds," she sighed. "If we don't Solange will tell us off." She pulled a face.

"Okay for making beds but I don't see any point in doing a spring-clean today, Léa. Let's leave that till tomorrow, just before they come. That way it will all be perfect for your perfect sister."

Léa giggled. "You are right, Owen. My sister is too perfect at times."

It took them nearly an hour to make up the five beds, including the bed-settee in the studio. Once there, they built up the wood-burner with logs and Owen could see that Léa was itching to get at her painting. He went to the cupboard, found an overall there and held it out to her.

"Off you go. Don't mind me. I'll just lie down here in front of the fire and feel left out."

"Poor left-out Owen!" said Léa, mocking him. "Are you trying to make me pity you? Because if you are, it is not working, not working one little bit! Now I shall paint," she declared.

Owen lay down on the bed-settee and watched the breakers as they crashed on the harbour wall of Port Lay in the distance. It was strangely hypnotic. The wood-burner gave out a good heat and in the far corner of the room, Léa was working away. He soon fell asleep.

It was getting dark when he woke, puzzled to find himself in unfamiliar surroundings. The rain had stopped and all was quiet. Léa was still painting using a halogen lamp to see by. She didn't even notice him until he came up behind her.

"Why that's me, Léa!" he said startled.

"I know," she replied simply.

"But… but I'm naked!"

"Not quite naked. Almost naked," she specified, quite unperturbed.

She had sketched Owen asleep, lying on his front, one arm flung out, his head turned to the side. She had drawn him naked to the waist, even further as he could see, a sheet covering his backside… just. The pose was one of total abandon, deftly done. Owen privately thought he looked quite good in it.

But being around Léa was disconcerting, to say the least. That was twice now she had drawn him when he wasn't looking.

"Umm… how do you know I look like that?" he asked, puzzled.

"You're tee-shirt was all wet with beer last week at Clare's party. I saw you then. And you forget I have seen you swimming in the sea. But even so, I can imagine you naked, Owen. I do that from time to time."

Owen was not at all sure where this conversation was leading. He wanted to say, '*me too. I imagine you naked all the time, Léa,*' but was far from certain that that was what she wanted to hear.

The girl was driving him nuts. Was this about art or about sex? He wished fervently that he could read her mind. He *had* to know. All summer he'd been gravitating around her; they'd danced together, slow dances, with Léa leaning on him and him holding her tight; they'd laughed and talked well into the night; Christ, they'd even fallen asleep together on more than one occasion. Now they were alone with a full 24 hours before the others arrived. What more did the girl want?

What on earth *did* she want?

"Léa," said Owen softly, taking away her paintbrush and turning her round to face him. "I think of you naked, too, you know. Often. Because I like you very much. In fact... in fact, I sometimes think ..."

"What do you think, Owen?" she said, her head tilted upwards, her face inches from his.

Owen took a deep breath to reply just as a loud hammering on the French windows startled them both.

"Christ Almighty! *What*?" he expostulated.

"Oh! It is the man from the shop. He has brought us our food. We must go over to the kitchen with him."

"Yeah... wonderful. Great timing!" said Owen, angrily. And he stomped out to give the man a hand.

And of course, the moment was lost. By the time he had helped to carry in the groceries and stock the fridge and the cupboards, their closeness had evaporated into domesticity, much to Owen's frustration.

But he had glimpsed something in Léa that had given him encouragement and he was determined to continue their intimacy at the first possible opportunity.

-oOo-

Chapter Forty-Three

The Storm

A little later that evening, Léa made them a meal of cooked chicory wrapped in ham with a béchamel sauce and grated cheese on top. Owen was doubly surprised, not only because the meal was delicious, it was the first time he had tasted cooked chicory, but also because it was Léa doing the cooking. At Larmor-Plage it was always Solange who took on that particular task; she seemed to like cooking. It kind of went with her motherly, bossy ways.

"Hey, this is good, Léa," said Owen, "I didn't know you could cook."

"I like cooking for other people. For myself, it is a waste of time. Cooking for one person is boring, I think."

"Shall we have some wine? Or would you like a beer or something else?"

"Wine, please. There is some Rosé d'Anjou. Do you like Rosé wine?"

"Yeah. Fine by me." Owen uncorked the bottle and poured them both out a glass.

Outside the wind, which had almost abated earlier on, now began to get stronger. Through the dull evening light they could see the trees and bushes in the garden swaying and bending.

"Looks like we're in for a hefty storm tonight after all," said Owen.

"Umm… we shall have to make sure all the shutters are closed before we sleep."

"Are you really going to sleep out in your studio, then?"

"Of course. Where else would I sleep?"

"In here. With me. Keep me company…" said Owen.

"But you only have a single bed and you are big. There is not room for two people in a single bed," said Léa logically.

Owen wanted to shout that there were at least two double beds not in use that night and that wasn't counting the studio; that beds were not the problem here! But in an effort of understatement, he smiled, took another bite, and snapped a piece of baguette off with rather more force than necessary.

Léa took 'playing hard to get' to quite another level indeed.

After their meal, at Owen's suggestion, they took the rest of the bottle of Rosé and went into the sitting-room. Léa put on some classical music. Chopin, Debussy and Mozart all vied with each other and other composers in soothing, gentle melodies. Owen refilled their glasses.

"Come here," he said, holding out his arm. Léa came and sat with him, putting her head on his chest as she had done so often before. He gave her a hug.

"We have to talk, you know that Léa, don't you?"

"Do we, Owen? Can we not just sit here together like we usually do? I always feel good when we sit together."

"And so do I! But... God, Léa, I've been fighting this all summer! The truth is I want to be more than just good friends with you. I like you so much. You're lovely, beautiful, funny, brave, witty... you drive me crazy just looking at you. When I take you in my arms, I want to kiss you... properly..."

"Like this?" And she turned her head, reached up and kissed him full on the lips.

"No," said Owen, turning her round so that she was facing him on his lap and he could enfold her in both his arms, "like this."

Much later, Owen picked her up and, crossing the sitting-room and the dining-room, kicked open the ground-floor bedroom door and laid Léa softly on the bed. Gently, he undressed her, took off his own clothes and lay down beside her. She clung to him, trembling.

Slowly, ever so slowly, he took her through the art of making love which did not involve domination or violence. Hungry as he was for her, he knew he couldn't mess this up or Léa would be in an even worse place than before. And once she had got over her fear, she gradually became his equal, generous and giving, clearly enjoying it as much as he did.

When they finally broke apart, he turned back to take her in his arms and was startled to feel tears on her cheeks.

"Léa, you alright? I didn't hurt you, did I?"

"Oh no, Owen. I am very happy. I did not know it could be like that... so passionate, yet so gentle..."

"It was wonderful," said Owen, and meant it. Yes, it had been truly wonderful.

Suddenly Léa laughed and buried her face in his chest.

"What's so funny?"

"We have been naughty to make love in Solange's bed. We shall have to change the sheets now or she will know."

"I agree," said Owen, envisaging the scowl on Solange's face if she knew, and smiling at the thought. "But not till tomorrow morning. We've still got all night..."

At some point they did have to get up and shut the shutters, the storm having reached paroxysms of strength. Owen braved the elements in order to dash across to the studio and shut the shutters there. He came back into bed his hair wet and his body cold making Léa squeal and laugh as he turned to her for warmth.

And in the early morning, when the storm still raged, they made love a second time and it was wonderful, all over again.

They slept late and were woken by the sound of Léa's phone calling out to them from the sitting-room. She dashed out of bed to catch it. Owen could hear her speak in rapid French, saw her gesticulating as she spoke.

"They don't know when the ferries will be running," she told Owen afterwards. "The storm is so bad still that so far they are all cancelled."

"Oh... shame!" said Owen, a wide grin lighting up his face.

They breakfasted in bed, making the most of the treat, before stripping it and changing the sheets and the duvet cover just in case Solange and the others did arrive. Then after showering and changing, they set about doing a clean-up of the house, Owen hoovering and Léa dusting until they decided that even Solange could not complain. All about them the storm, which had raged all morning, was dying down, the wind still quite strong but the rain had stopped some time ago.

Braving the elements, they went out to the local *boulangerie* to buy bread for lunch and for dinner, the intention being to freeze the extra baguettes should Solange & Co. not be able to make it. Owen transferred his rucksack surreptitiously to the studio which had Léa giggling in pleasure when she found out.

Later that day they put on music to dance, slow dances at first, arms wrapped around each other. Then Léa put on some rock n' roll music and they pushed back the settee to make room as she put him through some specific routines and showed him how to signal to her when to do what. They got entangled together more than once as Owen missed his cue or turned the wrong way and it was on one of these occasions, with Owen's arms wrapped around her, taking advantage of the situation to tickle her mercilessly, making her wriggle and scream, that the door suddenly opened and Solange burst into the room, breathless.

"*Léa! Léa, ça va?*" she cried, her eyes wide with fear. She stopped dead in her tracks as she saw Léa caught in Owen's arms.

"*Mais oui, mais oui, je vais bien. Regarde!* " cried Léa. "*Owen me chatouille. Il me fait guili-guili. Nous dansions, c'est tout!*"

"We heard Léa scream," said Solange to Owen, her voice coming down an octave. "We… I thought she was in danger… again."

Owen smiled. "No, Solange. The only person in danger was me. I keep getting the steps wrong and Léa tells me off each time."

"That is alright then," said Solange rather haughtily. "But you both gave me a scare."

"Sorry, Solange," said Owen in his most placating tone. "Now, how was the crossing? It must've been rough. Let me help you all with your bags."

Antoine, Logan and Marina all came forward then to kiss Léa and Owen hello. They had remained silent throughout the exchange between Solange and her sister but now that the danger was past, they made up for it with noisy greetings and tales of a horrendous crossing in very rough seas.

Late that afternoon the wind had abated sufficiently for the twins to suggest an outing to a nearby beach, not to swim, that would have been dangerous, but as a first step to exploring the island. Antoine had obviously seen it all before but was, if anything, more eager than anyone else to get outside again.

In fact, they took in a good 4km trek that started out along the local beach, the wind whipping their faces and making conversation difficult; then they turned inland to criss-cross the island along pretty lanes lined with yellow-flowered gorse bushes and glimpses of the sea in the distance through small clusters of pine trees. They took in the Grand Menhir of Kermario, a large solitary upright *menhir** surrounded and protected from the elements by high fern hedges, and ended up in Port Tudy to have a welcome beer in a little bar overlooking the harbour.

That evening, Solange and Léa buried themselves in the kitchen, ostentatiously to cook dinner, but in fact to have one of those sister conversations in low voices that excluded everyone else. Antoine took over as host to make sure everyone had a pre-dinner drink and Marina set the table with help from Owen. Logan, finding himself at a loss for something to do, brought in some wood and Owen then did the same for the wood-burner in Léa's studio which had almost gone out.

It was while he was doing this particular task that the studio door opened and in came Solange. One look at her face told Owen that she now knew about him and Léa but he couldn't quite gauge whether she was pleased about this or not.

"I see you have brought your rucksack to the studio, Owen," she said without preamble. "So you will be spending the night with Léa here." It was a statement, not a question.

Owen decided that pussyfooting around Solange would only make things worse so he said frankly:

"I will, Solange. Léa and I are an item. And before you ask, no, I don't know where it will lead, I don't know what the future holds for this relationship. All I do know is that we're very happy together."

"You remember what I told you, Owen. I do not want you to play with Léa's feelings. She does not deserve to be hurt like that. She has suffered enough."

"I agree. But Léa needs to live again, really live, in a life that is not always pleasant and protected, where she will find her place, on her own terms. Perhaps that will be with me. Perhaps it won't. But I do know one thing. Neither you, nor I, can shield Léa from reality all our lives. She'll get hurt, Solange, it's inevitable. We all do. That doesn't mean her life will fall apart. And she'll know joy and frustration, and happiness and fear. That's *living*, Solange."

Owen hadn't realized he was shouting. He lowered his voice.

"I'm very fond of Léa," he said intently, "and I want only the best for her."

"And so do I," said Solange, in a strange, little-girl-lost voice. "You don't know what it has been like, Owen, seeing her suffer, watching her bravely trying to get her life back, being… being mother and father and sister to her… all together…"

Owen was stricken to see tears start into Solange's eyes, to hear her hiccup in an effort not to cry. He suddenly realized that she had been through a lot with the loss of her parents and a sister who had counted on her perhaps too much over the years; that she was only human after all. With a flash of understanding, he could see that the burden had been great and that Solange was afraid to let go. He strode over to her and took her in his arms.

"Here, come here," he said. "Shush, it's going to be alright. Léa's a big girl now. She can look after herself. Everyone needs a helping hand at some point in their lives. You've done that for Léa all these years. Now it's time to let her try her wings and fly, to think of yourself, Solange. You're allowed to, you know."

He turned her round to face him.

"Let go, Solange. Have fun. You deserve it. And don't worry about Léa. She doesn't need you to, anymore."

"I think you are a good man, Owen," said Solange, visibly brightening, "even if you do have a terrible reputation with girlfriends. My sister will be good for you. You will be good for each other," she affirmed.

"I'll drink to that," said Owen. "Now shall we go back with the others... before Antoine kills me?"

The rest of the evening passed off in a relaxed and rather boozy atmosphere over a nice meal of roast duck and duchesse potatoes with stuffed mushrooms to start with and a tarte Tatin for dessert. Then they played a game of Monopoly well into the night, with Owen tickled to see the streets of Paris replace those of London, but the boot, the iron and the ship remain the same.

Later that night, as he lay in the studio with Léa at his side, feeling on top of the world, he remembered to ask her a French word that had been bothering him all evening.

"Léa, what's *'guili-guili'*?"

And had the breath knocked out of him when she pounced.

-oOo-

Menhir = a prehistoric stone usually standing upright
Guili-guili = a child's way of saying 'to tickle'.

Chapter Forty-Four

Discoveries

It was Sunday evening and Léa and Owen were saying a reluctant good-bye to the others. Reluctant in the sense that the others didn't want to leave. For Léa and Owen, they couldn't wait to be on their own again.

They had accompanied them all to the ferry, Owen helping to carry Marina's and Solange's baggage. But soon the ferry had swallowed them up as the light faded and evening turned to night, and Owen and Léa headed back to the cottage, hand in hand.

Léa intended to stay for the week and Owen had no intention of leaving her. Solange had left them strict instructions about leaving the cottage clean and tidy with bedclothes washed and the fridge emptied and the power turned off. But the rest of the time was theirs to do with as they liked: for Léa to paint, for Owen to read or use his lap-top, for long walks or bike rides around the island, or even a swim or two in the sea, for nights spent making love in blissful abandon, for getting to know each other and falling in love.

The fact that he had fallen in love hit Owen sometime round about Wednesday afternoon when he again sat in the studio watching Léa paint, concentrating so intently that she was not even aware of his presence. He had brought his lap-top out there, had played a few games of Spider patience, then just sat watching Léa, loving everything about her, knowing that he never wanted this week to end.

He tried to remember if he'd felt this way about Judith and, on reflexion, thought not. Judith had been great fun, a perfect sparring partner, his equal in more ways than one. Setting up home together had been her idea and it's true that they had shared some great times. But Judith had never really needed him all that much. She had made room in her life for him but had never given herself up to him totally. There was always a part of Judith that he would never share. Up till now he hadn't realized just how big that part of her had been.

Whereas Léa, funny little Léa, made him feel so special, so wanted. When he looked into her eyes, he saw her love for him there. Now that she had got over her fear, she was proving to be a wonderful lover and a joy to be with. Suddenly it had occurred to Owen that he could not now envisage being without her. He wanted to be with her forever, to love and protect her, to grow old together.

For someone who rarely gave a thought to what he would be doing the following week, let alone next year or in twenty years' time, this was a new sensation for Owen to experience. He sat there, on the sofa-bed, thinking hard about his future.

He suddenly realized that for the moment he didn't have one.

His time from now to Christmas would be taken up at the gîtes, that was certain. There was always work to be done there and now he would be helping out with the IT courses also, perhaps even taking over from Ian from time to time. But that wasn't what he'd been trained to do. And he was hardly going to get into architecture by teaching sixty-five-year-olds how to use a search engine or deal with a virus, or spending his afternoons mowing the lawns at the gîtes. Nathan and Laura had said they would look out for a job in architecture for him but it was early days yet and there was no word from them so far. And he hadn't even applied for anything in that line... anywhere.

Did he really want to go back to Ireland, or England even? That would be the sensible option. Get a few years' training under his belt in a good firm, then possibly branch out on his own. But Owen was realizing that he didn't want that sensible option. He wanted to stay in France, with Léa, and something told him that Léa, even though she spoke English perfectly, would be loath to leave her country, her home in Larmor-Plage, her sister. So he would just have to find work in France, give it a year or two, see how things went. A sort of gap year... yeah, a gap year to see how he would cope professionally as an architect in France. And if it *did* work out, then he could ask Léa to marry him...

God in Heaven, said Owen to himself, as this thought came home. *I'm actually thinking of marriage. What on earth's come over me?*

Back at the gîtes, Clare was getting ready for the first IT course to be held third week of October, when it was mid-term for Céline, and she would be coming too before they both left for Ireland where Ian had a series of meetings to attend at his head office in Belfast. This was to be followed by Sharon giving not one, but two surprise birthday parties on the same day for both Kieran and Paul. She had invited Clare and Frank but Frank would be in the middle of a two-week French course for English-speaking people and Clare would have her work cut out with all the catering, and she had had to decline. On reflexion, she decided to give the catering school in Lorient a call. She had had a student on work placement from them earlier in the year and it had been a most satisfactory arrangement. Now she could be doing with the help for the coming three weeks and it was a bonus for the student to have to use English as well as French, apart from putting into practice their culinary skills and earning a small wage besides.

After the phone call, where her contact at the catering school had promised to send her two or three CV's, Clare set about making out menus and writing out lists. She was a great believer in lists, telling herself that it was a perfectly natural and efficient way of organizing herself and had strictly nothing to do with the fact that her memory was not quite as good as it was before. Having worked for over twenty years running a home for the Elderly Mentally Infirm and dealing with Alzheimer's on a daily basis, Clare refused to entertain the idea that she could one day become a victim of the disease herself. No, lists were necessary and always had been and she was not going to change now.

It felt strange being on her own at the gîtes. Frank was at school, only four of the gîtes were rented out this week and their occupants were relatively quiet, older couples, compared to the summer guests who tended to be mostly parents with a hoard of children. She didn't mind the squeals and laughter and occasional tears. It all went with doing business. But when the season was over, like now, the silence, though not unwelcome, was deafening.

And to compound matters, even Owen was away, he that had come unexpectedly after his exams in April and had stayed to help out with the manor house and the running of the gîtes. He'd proved to be indispensable and Clare knew she would miss him when he went for good. She wondered how he was getting on in Groix. From what she had gathered, Solange and Antoine and their friends were all back at university, or at work. So that meant that Owen and Léa were on their own?

And Clare wondered, not for the first time, where all this would lead.

Over in Saint-Aubert des Loges, on that Wednesday afternoon, Céline was making the most of her free time to get all her school work up-to-date so that when Ian got home, and he'd promised to get home early that night, they could head off without delay to see the latest house she had found for them and keep their appointment with the estate agent which was for half-past six. Any later and the evenings were getting darker, not the best time of day to visit a property. But this particular property looked really special and Céline had been looking forward to seeing it all day.

It was strange, thought Céline, how Ian had gone from harping on about buying a house to taking a back-seat when they actually came to finding it. He was quite happy to let her do the hunting, fine-tuning their requirements with each visit. They'd poured over plans for new-builds on housing estates and rejected them, not enough character. And Ian already possessed a glass-and-chrome apartment in Belfast. They'd visited large upside-down houses dating from the sixties and seventies with living accommodation above and huge workshops, garages and empty rooms below and rejected them on the grounds of bad insulation... and not enough character. They'd been out to the countryside to visit stone-built farmhouses and longères* with lots of land and outbuildings, too far from amenities... and still not enough character. Time and time again their thoughts would come back to Clare's manor house, and every house they visited seemed pale in comparison.

So Céline was quietly excited about this latest find which looked like it had bags of character although with a price tag that low, it was probably in need of more than just a touch of TLC.

The house itself was situated in quite a large village about fifteen minutes south of Saint Aubert and within thirty minutes of Ian's job. That was always something Céline checked on first. The village itself had a smattering of shops: a bakery, a chemist and a small grocery shop. There was also a bar-cum-newsagents-cum-tobacconist, a church and a tiny village school. A little stream ran through the village and had been made into a small lake with a play area and walkways. Nothing elaborate, just pretty and tranquil. Céline liked the sound of the place. She was hoping against hope that she would not be disappointed in the house itself.

Ian was on time, even a little early, so they had a quick coffee and then set out. The estate agent was to meet them at the village church and was waiting for them when they got there, just finishing a hectic conversation on his mobile phone. He greeted them pleasantly and they set off following him in Ian's car.

The house which Céline had found was something along the lines of a Victorian villa, tall and angular and oozing character. Céline watched her husband anxiously to see his reaction. So far, so good, she gauged, he wasn't against the idea. It was situated in the centre of the village, with a fairly decent-sized garden to the front and a larger, mature one to the rear. There were neighbours but no-one overlooking them directly. Before they went inside, the estate agent warned them that it was a house that needed refurbishing from top to bottom, hence the low asking price, but he was certain that they would be charmed by its size and layout and some of the original features like marble fireplaces and tiled floors and big bow windows. It had actually been lived in, he explained, up till about a year ago, when the current owner, a widow, had needed to concede defeat and downsize. Since then there had been a lot of interest but so far, no takers. He suggested quietly that the price was most likely negotiable, should they be interested in making an offer.

After going through most of the house and pointing out its singularities, the estate agent's phone started ringing persistently and he suggested they continue on their own and take their time to revisit it all while he took this call. He would catch up with them as soon as he could. Just as soon as his footsteps echoed down the wide wooden staircase, Céline turned to Ian and whispered:

"What do you think, Ian? Isn't it lovely?"

"It *is* lovely, Céline. I really like the place but I'm just worried that it'll cost and arm and a leg to refurbish."

"There are some wonderful features though. Just look at that staircase and it is in good repair. And I love the bow windows. It's so very English, is it not? And the ornamental ceilings, and the height of the rooms."

"I think we shouldn't get our hopes built up, darling. Let's get an architect in to see what needs doing and get an estimate of the cost."

"I know. Let's get Owen!"

"But is Owen going to stay in France, then? He hasn't said anything to me."

"But he hasn't said anything about moving away either. I do know he is staying at the gîtes till Christmas. He could find time from now till then to draw up plans for us, couldn't he, Ian?"

"Well, I suppose he'll have a few weeks free between the courses and there'll not be that many guests in the gîtes at this time of the year. It might work out. Yeah. It might at that," said Ian pensively. "We could pay him for his time and expertise. At least we'd know he would do his best to keep costs to a minimum."

"And we could negotiate a good price for the house, of that I am sure. The estate agent was hinting that and if the owner has left it over a year ago, she must want to get it sold very much by now."

"Let's go back outside for a quick scoot around the garden before it gets too dark. Then I want to see down in the cellars and up in the attics. We haven't looked there yet. Don't worry. I've got a torch with me."

And Ian took her hand to carry on with the tour.

It was nearly eight pm when they finally said good-bye to the estate agent. He promised to have the *'diagnostiques'** brought up to date and supply them with the result. Ian knew that Owen would need this information in order to gauge the amount of work that needing doing. He was quietly optimistic about the property but could not let Céline see just how enthusiastic he was or she would be just too excited for words and he didn't want to see her disappointed if it didn't work out. He resolved, though, to send an email to Owen that very evening with a link to the website where the house could be seen.

The following day, Thursday, when Léa went off as usual to her studio to paint, Owen picked up the email from Ian. The house, though different from his parent's house, probably had the same sorts of features and pitfalls. He was actually quite interested in seeing it and the possibility of another architectural project was quite appealing. He brought his lap-top over to the studio to show it to Léa.

"Oh, Owen. It is a very pretty house. So much character! It has similarities to my own house in Larmor-Plage. Don't you see?"

"Yeah. You're right. They *are* similar. Similar construction periods, anyway."

"And now you have experience of what is needed. You can do this for your uncle and aunt."

"My who? Oh you mean Ian! He's not my uncle," said Owen, laughing at the idea.

"Is he not your mother's brother?"

"Well, yes he is. But I've never considered him to be my uncle. And I'd never in a million years consider Céline to be my aunt. We're the same age! But yes, they're family. My very close family. Ian is my big brother, really."

"And now he is giving you a chance to use your skills in architecture again!"

"Well, yes. I suppose he is."

"And that is good, no?"

"Yes. Yes it is. Actually, I was thinking about that yesterday. About architecture. About getting a job."

"So you must reply immediately to Ian and tell him you will come and see this house for yourself. Tell him you will come next week, when we finish our stay here in Groix," she said with finality and faced with her urgency, Owen did just that.

-oOo-

Longères = long, low farmhouses, one story with attics lit by tiny windows

Diagnostiques = the obligatory controls (electricity, termites, asbestos, energy performance etc that have to be carried out when a property is being sold in France)

Chapter Forty-Five

Birthdays

Kieran and Beth had settled into Queen's university quite quickly with that adaptability that goes with being eighteen, or nearly. Kieran's birthday was at the beginning of November and as it so happened, Paul's was towards the end of October, his fortieth. Sharon had planned a surprise birthday party for them both on the Saturday 31st, Hallowe'en night. That way, Kieran could have a separate party with his friends on his birthday, and Paul would not know she was planning a party if she took him out for a meal on the actual day he turned forty.

      She had long since manipulated the work rotas so that Paul was on duty that Hallowe'en till eight pm. That way, she could have the whole day free to prepare food with the help of Eileen and Paul's parents. Kieran and Beth were coming home for the event, Kieran thinking it was Paul's do, and Sharon had invited some of *their* closest friends, with a little help from Beth, to surprise Kieran. In the same way, with the help of Paul's mother, she had contacted some of Paul's friends from school-days as a surprise and needless to say, a lot of the staff from Oak Lodge would also be there.

Ian and Céline were flying in from France, Ian having organized a trip to his head-office in Belfast for the last week in October and bringing Céline with him who was on half-term from school. They would be staying in Ian's old flat which was, by pre-arrangement with the exclusive letting agency, free that week, although they would be heading back to France on the Sunday, as Céline had school the next day. They were both quite excited at having found a house of their own, as Sharon had learned when she spoke to Clare, and Owen was going to get another chance at playing architect. Clare confided that she was pleased for him and secretly hoping that he would consider finding work in France and staying there for good. But she sincerely regretted that she couldn't make it to Sharon's party. Frank was giving a course, apparently, and it was all hands to the breech.

Time flew by and the day of the party approached. Sharon was doubly glad to have a bigger house in which to host the event as they would be quite a few people coming and it wasn't as if she could hold it outdoors. Trying to keep everything a secret from Paul was a job in itself and she was by now eight months pregnant and getting the odd twinge of labour pains from time to time. This, as she knew perfectly well, was only natural, but she would be glad to put her feet up once the party was over.

Everyone had been told to be there by 8pm, and cars were to be parked as far away from the house as possible. Lights were kept down low and when Paul's car was spotted, everyone went quiet, apart from a little giggling and nudging. They all heard him put his key in the door and open it.

Then the lights went on and everyone cheered, giving poor Paul a shock. But he recovered quickly and Sharon could see that he was really pleased, greeting everyone in turn. He finally came to her and gave her a huge hug. All her hard work evaporated and she knew he was really happy.

Then it was Kieran's turn. His friends had been asked to come as a group around half past eight, so when the knock came on the door and Sharon sent him to open it, it was his turn to gasp in shock and pleasure as a large portion of the previous year's sixth form, and one or two friends from Tesco's, stood there grinning.

The night was a roaring success. Sharon had decorated the rooms with a Hallowe'en theme, lights were low and the food was good and plentiful. Guests spilled out from the dining and sitting-rooms into the hall and the kitchen and a lot of the younger ones ended up in Kieran's room upstairs. Beth spent her time helping

Sharon as much as she could and so did Eileen, Paul's mother, and even Céline. Staff from Oak Lodge also helped and Ian and Krzysztof did drinks.

By midnight Mr and Mrs Harrison, Eileen and a lot of the staff and friends had left for home and by two am, Céline decided that it was time she left with Ian, who was rather the worse for wear, as was Paul, and Sharon suggested calling a few taxis to take Kieran's friends back home. By 3am there was just Paul and Sharon and Kieran and Beth. Sharon had never been so tired and Paul was falling asleep on the settee. Somehow or other it seemed normal for Beth to stay the night and Sharon suddenly realized that if ever she had doubts about what her son had got up to in Paul's old flat, she knew for definite now.

That night the baby had a field day, kicking and wriggling for all it was worth. That plus Paul, who was snoring loudly, he that never snored usually, meant that Sharon only got a few hours' sleep. Catriona was holding the fort at Oak Lodge which meant that neither Paul nor Sharon had to go into work the next day, but as she made her way slowly down the stairs sometime after nine, Sharon realized that she might need to take a few extra days off to recover. Having a baby at nearly forty was not as easy as at twenty-two and throwing surprise birthday parties for not one but two people was almost akin to biting off more than she could chew.

Beth was already up and clearing away plates and glasses and loading the dish-washer. She had made coffee and was now boiling up the kettle to make tea. Between them they managed to clear a space in the kitchen to sit down.

"I must look terrible, Beth," said Sharon, "I didn't get much sleep last night."

"The baby?"

"Still kicking away at five am and Paul snoring didn't help."

"Umm... I think Paul and Ian hit the whiskey at some point. They weren't very coherent after that."

"So I noticed! But I'll forgive my husband just this once. I doubt if we'll see him this morning. He never lets himself go like that."

"He was funny," said Beth giggling, "they both were."

"Hanging on to each other to do an Irish jig, yeah," laughed Sharon. "The eejits!"

Just then there was a knock on the back door and in came Eileen.

"Oh Lordy, Lord, what a good night we all had, Sharon! It was great craic," she began.

"And you didn't see the worst of it, Eileen. I was just saying to Beth here what a pair of eejits Paul and Ian were, dancing a jig at two in the morning. Thank God all the Oak Lodge staff had already left or Paul's credibility stakes would have taken a battering."

"You do look tired, love," said Eileen, "Why don't you go and lie down again? Beth and I will clear up here. It won't take us that long."

"Actually, Eileen, I might just do that. I'm exhausted. Forgive me, both of you, if I let you down for an hour or two. It's so good of you to help me out."

"No problem, Sharon," said Beth.

"Away with you, now," added Eileen.

When Paul arrived downstairs towards midday, it was to see the kitchen tidied, the sitting-room and dining-room cleared, the decorations taken down and only a good hoovering left to do. Kieran had woken up soon after Sharon had returned to bed and had been press-ganged into helping out too. He was sitting now having a coffee in the kitchen, as Eileen had just left and Beth was upstairs having a shower.

"Morning, Paul," he stated.

"Shush..." said Paul, holding his head, "Where's the paracetamol?"

"Here. And here's some water. Want a coffee?"

"Please... God, I feel awful. I'm never going to let that Ian Maher talk me into drinking whiskey with him again. I'd been on beer all night. Why couldn't I be reasonable?"

"You don't look forty, you know."

"Don't I?" said Paul, looking up, pleased.

"You look fifty plus... easily... this morning."

"Just you wait till I'm rid of this hangover, Kieran Murphy," growled Paul.

"Yeah. Want to go for a run?"

"I *suggest* you just shut up. Right now. And anyway, I saw you drinking last night. Why don't you have a hangover then?"

"Difference in age, I suppose. That's what happens when you get on in years."

Before Paul could make a retort, the door opened and Sharon came in. This time she was wide awake, showered and dressed, and feeling much better.

"And how are the two men of my life, the birthday boys, then?" she said brightly.

"I'm fine, Mum. Can't say the same for your old man."

"Sharon, get him out of here before I commit murder, will you?"

"Now, Kieran, don't bait a bear with a sore head. Umm... a very sore head by the looks of things."

"Sure, Mum. I'll go upstairs and see if Beth's finished in the shower. Perhaps I should put on some fiddle-dee-dee music? Liven things up with a jig or two? What'd ya say, Paul?"

"GET *OUT*!"

"Go-*ING*..." And off went Kieran, whistling as loud as he could.

Sharon did take a few days off after the party, putting her feet up whenever she could. The contractions she had been feeling before were now becoming frequent and stronger but a visit to the mid-wife showed no signs of alarm. She still had three weeks to go and to Sharon, that meant she could still work for another week or two yet.

In fact, she began to feel much better indeed as the baby started its slow journey downwards, giving her less heartburn and more energy. From being tired and a little dispirited, Sharon now felt so well she could not envisage sitting at home, watching telly and getting bored, and showed up at Oak Lodge for a few hours' work most days. Paul had given up trying to make her take things easy and confided his fears to Catriona one afternoon.

"I know, Paul, I know," came her soothing reply. "But Sharon's already had a baby, you haven't, so it's only natural you're more worried than she is. She looks fine to me, healthy and happy. Let her potter about the place for another few days, then put your foot down once and for all and make her stay at home."

"Easier said than done, Catriona," said Paul ruefully. "She's still the boss here and being pregnant has put extra pressure on her, obviously. I'm running around like a headless chicken trying to make things easier for her but she doesn't seem to notice. I caught her lifting a resident the other day... by herself! I mean, what can you do?"

"Oh dear! You poor thing. And it's not as if you can tell her off, at least not in front of staff. Look, if it's any consolation to you, I worked in midwifery for several years, out in Bangladesh. Oh, I know it was a long time ago, but the things I saw there, the cases I had to deal with, sometimes in the most rudimentary conditions, gave me good experience." She chuckled. "So, if Sharon decides to go into labour here at Oak Lodge, I'll be able to help out, at least till we get her into hospital."

"That's good to know, Catriona," said Paul sighing. "Here's hoping we won't need it."

"When's her next maternity visit?"

"In three days' time, on Friday, mid-morning. I'll take an hour or two off, as it's a visit to the hospital, and drive her there."

"Sure, no problem. I'll be here to cover for you. Just say the word."

Over the next two days, Sharon's contractions began getting more frequent, sometimes quite intense. They kept her awake at night and she stopped spending time at Oak Lodge.

Catriona and Paul breathed a sigh of relief.

On the Friday morning, around half-past nine, Sharon arrived at Oak Lodge where Paul was already on duty. It was getting nigh on impossible for her to get behind the wheel of a car these days, and as the day was sunny, though cold, and she felt quite well, she had made the journey on foot. But as she climbed the stairs to the office, she was assailed by a series of heavy contractions which made her glad that she was actually on her way to the hospital that morning for a check-up.

She opened the door of the office to find it empty. Obviously Paul was still doing his rounds. She sat down heavily to wait for him, then got up quickly as hot liquid coursed down her legs. Perhaps it hadn't been such a good idea to walk to Oak Lodge. Now her waters had broken and were causing a mess on the office floor. Oh Lord!

Sharon pulled out her phone from her coat pocket with difficulty and phoned Paul's mobile. He answered almost at once.

"Nearly finished, love. Won't be more than a few minutes. Where are you?" he said.

"In the office, Paul. Can you come as soon as possible?" she panted as she was gripped in the worst contraction yet.

"Okay. Won't be long. I'll be there in five minutes maximum." And he rang off.

Sharon debated whether to call him back but decided that there was no use panicking. Even if she were having the baby now, it had been over twelve hours of labour before Kieran had been born. They would have plenty of time before this one would come and the hospital was only 30 minutes away by car. She decided to make her way over to the toilet situated just outside the small room that Paul used when on night duty. At least she wouldn't be inundating the office.

By the time she heard Paul's footsteps, Sharon was sweating with the intensity and rapidity of the contractions. For the first time, it began to enter her head that she was giving birth now, right now, and that she might not make it to the hospital in time.

After a few minutes searching, he found her in the toilets, her faced screwed up in pain, her clothes all wet.

"Sharon, God, Sharon, what's happened?" he cried, his eyes wide with fear.

"Waters... broke," she panted. "Baby coming... I think, Paul. Contractions."

After a second or two of sheer panic, Paul whipped out his phone and called Catriona, asking her to come up to the sleep-over room urgently. Then he gently lifted Sharon to her feet, guided her out of the toilets and across the landing where he laid her down on the bed. Between contractions, he managed to get her coat off and the maternity trousers which were soaking wet and had begun to wipe the sweat from her face and neck.

Then he called the hospital to send out an ambulance.

By the time he had completed this task, Catriona had arrived and was already assessing the situation and putting on surgical gloves. She asked Sharon's permission to examine her and did so quickly and very professionally to Paul's practiced eye. His own stint in a maternity ward during his training as a nurse was possibly more recent than Catriona's, but he'd only ever helped with an actual birth once or twice. And always under supervision.

"Well, Sharon," said Catriona, standing up. "The baby's on its way. Your cervix is dilated to nearly 10cms and I can feel its head. I don't think we're going to have time to wait for the ambulance."

"Oh, Catriona!"

"I know, dear. But it's looking very much like it. Now, we've a bit of work ahead of us, so we may as well get started. Paul, go and tell Beatrice to take charge. We're going to be tied up here for a wee while. And while you're at it, get Geraldine to bring us some clean sheets and towels and ask her if she wouldn't mind cleaning up the mess. Now, Sharon, I can see another contraction on its way. Here grip my hands, that's right, breathe now, there you go. You're doing fine."

Over the next twenty minutes, Catriona talked Sharon through the contractions, got the bed as clean and sterile as possible, got Paul organized to help his wife find the most comfortable position for childbirth and when the minutes of intense labour gave way to the actual birth, she gently eased the baby out, head first, then a shoulder, then the rest of its little body in a slippery heap. While Sharon looked on, her face red with the effort, her hair damp with sweat, Paul proceeded to cut the umbilical cord and wrapped his little daughter tenderly in a clean towel to present her to Sharon. His eyes were bright with unshed tears.

"Look, Sharon, she's perfect. Perfect in every way," he said simply.

"She's lovely, Paul. Really lovely," said Sharon. "Look at her move! No wonder she kept me awake at night, wriggling like that. Oh Catriona, thank you! Thank you so much."

"Think nothing of it, Sharon," said Catriona reassuringly. Then she chuckled: "Well, that's a first, and no mistake!"

"A first time you delivered a baby?" said Sharon surprised. "You were so professional!"

"No, dear. The first time I've delivered a baby in an old people's home!"

And they all laughed.

Just then the baby decided to let them know that her lungs were working perfectly too and her little cries made them all smile in relief that everything had gone so well.

After a few minutes, the placenta having come away, Catriona decided that it was time for the baby to be cleaned properly and set Paul to do this task with the help of Geraldine. Then she began cleaning up Sharon herself. She had just finished this when a knock on the door announced the arrival of the ambulance crew and fifteen minutes later, Sharon was being whisked away to the hospital, tired and happy, with Paul at her side and their little baby in his arms.

-oOo-

Chapter Forty-Six

Future Plans

"Eileen, Eileen, isn't it wonderful news about the baby?"

"Oh, Margaret! I'm so pleased. It's a wee dote. And guess what?"

"What?"

"They've called it after me!"

"Oh how lovely for you!"

"Emily Eileen Harrison!"

"E.E.H. – with initials like that she'll grow up to be famous. A writer or a doctor or something!"

"Well, all I know is that she's the most loveliest little creature you ever saw."

"And how's Sharon?"

"She's doing well. It was a quick birth. A bit too quick, really. The baby was born in Oak Lodge, with Paul and Catriona and Geraldine helping."

"Yes. I'd heard about that. It's all over Kilmore. The first baby ever to be born in an old people's home!"

"Indeed," chuckled Eileen. "Well, Sharon will be home in a couple of days. Then the fun will start. Paul's walking on air at the moment but after a month or two of sleepless nights, he might not be quite so enthusiastic."

"I'm sure he's very happy to be a dad, a real dad I mean."

"Oh, he's been a real dad to Kieran too, you know, these last few years. A sort of good friend kind of dad. They've always got on well together."

"And what about Kieran? I'm sure he's over the moon."

"He is, Margaret, he is. And Beth too. When I was at the hospital this afternoon, they were both cuddling the baby. Well, Beth was actually holding it. Kieran's too afraid he'll drop it or break it or something."

"Only natural. He'll get over that."

"And now we'll be able to take your David and our Emily out for walks together, just like we said we would. Just think. You and me with our very own grandchildren."

Margaret laughed. "Yes, we'll do that but let's wait till the spring, till the weather gets a bit warmer. It's very wet and cold and the moment for the wee mites."

"Oh isn't this all just wonderful, Margaret? I'm so happy I could cry."

It's true what they say, thought Owen, as he drove Clare's car to Saint Aubert for the third time in as many weeks, *it never rains but it pours*. Here he was, quite busy actually, up to his eyes in another architectural project and a really interesting one at that.

The house that Céline and Ian were intending to buy was in a much worse state than his parents' manor house had been. So they had given him a free hand to bring it back into the twenty-first century and they needed an estimation of the cost before putting in an offer to purchase. His first set of ideas had met with their approval and apart from taking into account Céline's wish for an en-suite and Ian's for a bigger kitchen, he really had carte blanche to do as he liked.

He had first been to see it just after returning from Groix. Léa had declined his invitation to accompany him, stressing that this was business, not pleasure, that she would come to see it some other time. Owen had stayed that night in the little flat that Céline and Ian rented temporarily, sleeping on the futon in the bedroom they used as a study. Ian was working from home the following day which meant he could accompany Owen for a second visit to the house and help out with measuring the rooms and supplying other information that Owen now needed.

A few days after that, they had all met up at the gîtes where Owen was acting as Ian's assistant for the IT class, with a view to taking one of his own before Christmas. This gave them a chance to discuss his suggestions at length. And then when Ian and Céline took a week off to go to Ireland, he sat in on some of Frank's French classes to brush up on the basics and worked on revised plans for the house in his spare time.

And with all that, he was constantly trying to make time to see Léa, so much so that his mother was starting to hint broadly that he should think of buying a car of his own.

She was right of course. Living rent-free at his parents, no bills, no food to pay for, and having earned a modest wage from them for helping out at the gîtes and supervising the work to the manor house, all meant that Owen now had some money in the bank. Years of student living had made him naturally economical and he did now have enough to buy a second-hand car.

So that was something else to eat into his time.

But just now, as he drove into Saint Aubert with the final plans, he was confident that this branch of architecture was something he really wanted to do. And not only drawing up the plans, supervising the work was interesting and rewarding too. It meant he got away from the drawing board and out into the real world, getting his hands dirty, dealing with potential problems before they arose. The experience he'd got from overseeing the manor house refurbishment more than made up for the small remuneration he had received in return. And the same went here. If Ian and Céline decided to purchase the villa, given that the project was twice as complicated as the previous one, it would stand him in good stead for future employment and the makings of a very good CV.

"And that's it in a nutshell, Léa," said Owen as they sat together on the settee in Larmor-Plage one evening a week later. "Ian and Céline are happy with the plans. I've collected quotes from local, and some not so local, firms to carry out what they want and they've negotiated an even lower price for the house so it's full-steam ahead. I'll be supervising the renovations just as soon as they exchange contracts, sometime after Christmas."

"I am sure that they are very excited about this house. It looks very elegant from the photos."

"Well, Céline's up to high doh and Ian is going round with a big grin on his face all the time. I'm pleased for them."

"And so am I! Now, tell me, when do you get your new car?"

"On Friday. I can't wait. But it's not a new car, Léa. It's a second-hand car but in quite good shape. Dad helped me pick it. Not that he knows a great deal about cars but his technical French is better than mine. At least for cars, anyway."

"Shall I come with you to collect it?"

"Would you?"

"Of course. I shall come to the gîtes and pick you up. Then we will collect your car and come back here. I have not seen you very often this last week or two. I want to make up for lost time."

"I love making up for lost time with you, Léa. Shall we make up for lost time now?"

"I thought you would never suggest it," said Léa giggling.

It was towards the end of November that Owen got a call from Nathan asking him to call into the bank when he got a chance.

Owen's first reaction was to wonder if his account was in the red, which in the past had been the only reason he ever got calls from the bank. But some rapid mental arithmetic quickly reassured him on that point and it was arranged that he would call in to see Nathan on the following Saturday morning.

Owen wasn't free before then as he was taking his first IT course without Ian and wanted to give his pupils, for want of a better word, his full attention throughout the week. In fact, he was enjoying the teaching side of things, taking his cue from Ian who goofed around and made everything look easy. And no-one ever felt ashamed or put down for asking even the silliest of questions. Everyone in his class, all eight of them, were well over sixty, and most of them were recently retired and finding it hard to come to grips with technology that their grandchildren seemed to master from the cradle up. And Frank, hearing the sound of laughter on more than one occasion when preparing the last French course of the year in the adjoining class-room, knew that Owen was a natural and that things were going well.

On Saturday morning, then, after seeing his pupils off, Owen drove into Lorient and parked his car in the car-park set aside for the bank's customers and gave his name to the girl on reception. He didn't have to wait long. Nathan was just finishing with a customer and showing him out and came over to greet Owen on his way back. They settled into Nathan's office and got down to work.

It appeared that Nathan was already aware that Owen was doing a second architectural project and had been spreading the word. He now had two firms that might be interested in taking Owen on, on a trial basis, and gave him the low-down on these companies as Nathan, in true banker's style, generally made it his business to know his clients well. Owen left the bank with contact numbers and email addresses and instructions to send off his CV to the Managing Directors, mentioning Nathan's name, and be ready to sustain interviews in French. Frank could help him out there. And even though he would be expected to work on a daily basis in French, Nathan reassured him that speaking English would be a bonus, not a hindrance, to an up-and-coming architect in this world of globalisation.

Clare, when Owen told her about his interview with Nathan, was touched by this show of trust. Finding work in France in these difficult times was hard enough. For someone who was not French, it could be very hard indeed. Nathan putting in a good word for him might not guarantee Owen a job but it would certainly be good experience of doing interviews and she knew Frank would help him prepare for that as best he could.

And the very fact that Owen was willing to apply for jobs in France was wonderful. That meant he was now intending to stay in the country, at least in the short or even medium term. Having her son within hugging distance was nice, very nice indeed, and Clare was pleased. Perhaps the fact that he was now going out with Léa had made him take that decision? It was all too obvious that they were an item. And now that he had his own car, he was forever escaping to Larmor-Plage. Every spare minute he had he was staying over at Léa's. Clare's matchmaking instincts were on full alert these days but she knew better than to meddle in Owen's love life. That was much too close to home.

And when she thought about it, she realized that she liked Léa very much indeed.

The first week in December saw all the gîtes empty and Frank's French course was not due to start till the following week. Clare decided that the time was right to pay that long overdue visit to Marcel and his wife in Saint Avit and call in on Aurore to see how she was faring also. Unfortunately, as Frank was taking the following two weeks off from the language school, he was not free to go with her and Clare faced the long six-hour car journey once more on her own.

She spent a pleasant evening with the Jouberts, bringing them up-to-date with all that had happened in Ireland since they had found Aurore. Marcel had not known that George was now dead and Clare felt remiss about having forgotten to tell him. Her only excuse was that it had been in the middle of August, the height of her season at the gîtes, and that she regretted not having been able to attend the funeral herself, either. She suggested to Marcel that he accompany her the following day to see Aurore. She was expecting Clare, and had said on the phone that her daughter Catherine and granddaughter Angélique would be present also.

So after lunch in a tiny restaurant that Marcel was fond of, and where the food was wholesome and quite delicious, they both headed to Rion des Landes to Aurore's house. She opened the door to them herself and to Clare's practised eye looked a lot healthier than when they had first met earlier that year. She said as much.

"Thank you Clare, I do feel stronger. It has been good to find my father even if it were only for a short while. But thank you, thank you for giving me that. And thank you also Monsieur Joubert. Without help from you both I would never have known he was still alive."

"And what are your plans, now, Aurore?" said Clare gently, after greeting Catherine and Angélique with kisses. "Are you going back to Ireland or will you stay in France? Have you given it any thought?"

"Oh, I have, Clare. I have thought of nothing else. And with Angélique, here, we have made plans. I have wanted to talk to you about them. To see what you think. Damien, you remember Damien...?"

"Damien Murray, the solicitor? Yes he's a good friend. It was Damien that asked me to find you, Aurore. He was the reason I set out on this quest in the first place."

"Well, Damien, he has suggested to me to come back to Ireland from time to time. To sit on the Board of Governors at Oak Lodge and take the place that should have been my father's. I have talked it over with Angélique and she has agreed to be my assistant, my help, and interpret for me." She sighed. "I am rich, Clare, apparently. And I have no need for the money but at least I can pay Angélique a good salary and it will mean that she will use her English and it will be a professional experience for her for as long as she wishes to stay with me. We will lodge at my father's house and Madame Curran will look after us. She has agreed to remain. We get on very well, even if we do need Angélique sometimes to explain words we have not understood, either of us."

"Oh, I *am* glad, Aurore. I'm sure you will do very well on the Board of Governors. I spent twenty years on it as a small shareholder when I ran Oak Lodge. They are a nice bunch of people and you now have Sharon and Paul running the home. It could not be in better hands."

"I do agree. And they were so very kind to me when I was in Ireland. They have just had a baby girl, so I hear. Madame Curran told us."

"They have indeed. Born in Oak Lodge."

"Oh, how wonderful! And rather unusual…"

"Not actually planned. But they're very happy."

Aurore beamed. Then she looked from Clare to Marcel and her face clouded.

"Clare, Monsieur Joubert, I have something I wish to do and I have waited for you to be with us because I feel it is only fitting that you be there. Without you, none of these good things could have happened to me and I know my father would have wanted you to be there at the end. Catherine and Angélique will come too."

She got up and went to a small cupboard at the back of the room and took out an urn. "My father had left instructions with Damien that he was to be cremated and I got permission to take the ashes to France. If you agree, I would like us to go to Mont de Marsan, all of us. My adoptive mother was from Mont de Marsan and that is where her family had Meira buried. I have visited her grave many times with Maman, ever since I was a little girl." She sighed. "They could not be together in life but it would be good and right if my birth parents could be together in death."

An hour and a half later, Clare stood looking down at Meira's grave in the Jewish cemetery in Mont de Marsan as Aurore scattered the ashes that once made up George upon it. Catherine and Angélique were there and Serge, Aurore's son, was also present with his wife. Aurore had had the headstone changed and now the names of both her birth parents were indicated along with their dates of birth and death. Clare could not help remembering the George she had known so well in the home, the sweet-natured gentleman who had remained faithful to his only love, who had lost her not once, but twice, in the aftermath of that horrible war, and who had carried the burden of that loss all his life.

Amid the sorrowful, poignant thoughts that clouded her brain, she was nonetheless quietly pleased and proud that she had been able to bring this family together before he died.

-oOo-

Chapter Forty-Seven

Future Perfect

"So? So? How did it go?" said Léa, fairly bouncing in excitement. They were sitting in a café on the seafront at Larmor-Plage and Owen had just come from the second of his interviews. Léa privately thought that he looked so glamorous dressed in a suit, so different, so adult and professional, like the *publicité* on television for aftershave. He leaned over now to kiss her before replying.

"Actually, it went quite well. I like this firm better than the first one, but I'd be quite happy working for either."

"That is good news" said Léa smiling.

"Yeah. Although there'd be more chance here to work on houses, new builds or even refurbishing old houses, which is what I'd like to specialize in one day. It's a smaller, cosier kind of firm. But the company I was with the other day was fine too. And it would give me experience in working on some larger projects, constructions for industry or sales outlets, that type of thing. When you come down to it, Léa, it's all a question of experience, especially when you're only starting out."

"I am glad it went well. They would be stupid not to employ you, Owen."

"Says the lady in her most objective manner."

"Where you are concerned, I will never be objective. It is not in my power to be objective anymore," she answered.

"Me neither. Lost the will to be objective ages ago," he agreed, looking into her eyes and losing himself there. He suddenly wanted to tell her the words that kept coming into his head, wanted to ask her what she thought, but he had promised himself that he would find work first and take that step after; a question of pride, he realized, of stubborn Irish pride.

Or pig-headedness, he thought ruefully, take your pick.

The days went past and Christmas approached. Clare was planning, as usual, to have all the family over to the gîtes for the celebrations and had sent out her invitations some weeks previously. Céline's parents had had to decline, with regret, as Jean-Luc's mother was not very well and it was generally accepted that this might be one of her last Christmases. They were going over for a quiet meal on Christmas Eve with the old lady before organizing a bigger meal for the extended family on Christmas day. This meant that Ian and Céline would also be absent on Christmas day but they would spend Christmas Eve with Clare and Frank and be back to the gîtes on Boxing Day evening. It also meant that there would be no untimely gate-crashing by Céline's Aunt Maryse, which had caused them all so much mirth the previous year, much to Ian's disgust, as that good lady always made a bee-line for him, with or without the presence of Céline. Clare knew that he would be dreading Christmas day in La Méaugon for that very reason and could not help but chuckle to herself. It was Ian's annual comeuppance and Maryse had a *very* soft spot for him and was wont to show it with such brazenness that it actually made him blush.

This year though, Clare was also inviting Solange and Antoine and, of course, Léa. This had been Owen's request and Clare was more than happy to comply. She could see that Owen was... dare she mention it...in love with Léa? And Solange, of course, had been a true and trusted employee, a friend really, ever since the gîtes had had to cope with that first hectic summer.

Nathan and Laura would be coming on Boxing Day, as usual, with a meeting of all those who had invested in the gîtes, which included Ian of course, scheduled for the day after. It was the perfect opportunity for them all to discuss the year past and plan for the future. Nathan's expertise as a banker meant that he naturally took the lead on these occasions and this annual get-together, before the year-end accounts were handed in and forecasts for the coming year finalized, was a good opportunity to take stock. To all intents and purposes, it had, once again, been a good year at the gîtes, in spite of the purchase of the manor house which had put a strain on Clare and Frank's personal equity, but the gatehouse gîte being available for rental from July onwards had brought in quite a bit of extra income, which went a long way to consolidating the business per se.

Clare was also inviting her parents, which was always a source of mixed blessings, with her mother managing to get everyone's back up within hours of arrival and her dear dad spending his life smoothing things over because of her. Still, she was glad they were coming, even her mother, as when you came down to it, what was Christmas without family?

Christmas Eve came around quicker than Clare had expected in a flurry of shopping, cooking, planning, cleaning and Christmas card writing. Why was it that in Britain and Ireland, Christmas cards had to be sent so early when in France you had all of the month of January to acquit this task? It only put extra pressure on everyone, thought Clare crossly, who was convinced she wasn't the only person with this problem; but time-old traditions were hardly going to change, she reasoned, because she, personally, was running late.

She softened. This year, though, Christmas would be extra special as it was the first time she would be holding it in the manor house. This had taken quite a bit of organizing and ferrying of extra chairs and other necessary items from the gîtes as Clare and Frank's finances had not yet run to furnishing the place as she wished. Only her parents would be staying in the house itself, in Owen's room, and all the other guests would use the gîtes as in the past.

By six o'clock on Christmas Eve, most of the preparations were done and only the nibbles for the aperitif remained. This was a job she usually roped her mother into helping with as it kept that good lady's thoughts occupied and away from complaining. In fact, Mrs Maher seemed quite pleased to be back in France and said as much to Clare, complimenting her daughter on the way she had decorated her new home, with its new three-piece suite and the huge Christmas tree that took centre stage by the drawing-room window and the lovely welcome she always received.

Clare had frowned, seriously worried, as this was not in her mother's *modus operandi* at all but it was early days yet and Clare reassured herself that her mother would no doubt get into full stride before long. She thanked the Gods, not for the first time, that her mother didn't speak French.

Then panicked when she remembered that, this year, all her guests spoke English!

She would have to have a word with Frank.

"Now, young man, you must tell me why you are not capable of keeping the same girlfriend from one year to the next," said Mrs Maher to Owen in a deafening whisper. "I mean your new little lady friend looks very sweet and all that but does she know you were almost engaged to Judith?"

"Gran..." began Owen, blushing to the roots of his hair, hoping Léa couldn't hear. "Judith and I were never engaged. It wasn't like that, honestly!"

"Well, it certainly looked like that to me. In my opinion, you're as much to blame as anyone, Owen. Too flighty for your own good. And Judith was nice. We used to have such interesting conversations on the plane when we travelled together."

Owen cringed even further, remembering the grilling Judith got every time his gran was around. Mrs Maher always managed to wrangle it so that she was sitting beside Owen's ex-girlfriend and their time spent together was something of a trial for the poor girl.

"And this new lassie, she's French, isn't she? I mean, she's not even *Irish*, Owen. It's bad enough for Ian to have married a French girl, although Céline is very nice, don't get me wrong, but are you intending to do the same?"

"Gran..."

"I had *thought* you would find a job with a good architect firm in Belfast, there's lots of them around, you know, and settle down and start a family with some nice girl from Northern Ireland."

"But Gran..."

"Now it looks like the whole family's come to live in France. What is wrong with you people? Isn't Ireland good enough for you?"

"It isn't *like* that, Gran..."

"Don't know what the world's coming to, Owen. In my day, things were a lot less complicated. Why, I remember when your Grandfather and I began walking out, he went to my parents immediately to ask their permission to date me and it was very clear from the start that we were intending to marry. None of this changing girlfriends from one year to the next. Now if you ask my opinion..."

"Mary, could you spare a minute?" came the unmistakable voice Frank was wont to use to command attention in class. "We really would appreciate your help in the kitchen. Clare always says that you make excellent suggestions and between you and me, I think she could be doing with a helping hand."

"Oh, Frank, why, yes of course. I'd be delighted to help you out. Here, help me up. Just show me the way. Our Clare's an excellent cook but there are always last minute disasters. I know how complicated it all can be."

As Frank helped his mother-in-law to her feet, Owen looked over her head to give his father a grateful smile and got a look of understanding in return. His grandmother was, if anything, getting worse as the years went on. He should've warned Léa what she was like. He hoped against hope that she hadn't heard this last conversation. He went over to her now where she was talking to Céline.

"Léa," he broke in rather awkwardly, "I must apologize for my grandmother. She tends to say the most outrageous things…"

"Does she? What does she say? Tell me!"

"You didn't hear her then? I was sure everyone had heard her from here to Lorient."

"We were talking in French, Owen," said Céline. "I don't think either of us heard what my mother-in-law was saying."

"Thank God for small mercies, then."

"But I can imagine. I remember when Ian introduced me to her. He got very angry."

"Angry? Me? I'm never angry. Who's says I'm angry, then?" came a voice from over Céline's shoulder.

"We're talking about Gran."

"Ah. That explains it. She's impossible. What's she gone and said now? Who has my mother managed to upset this time?"

"Me, actually. But dad came to the rescue before she went too far."

"What is Mrs Maher saying, Owen, that makes you want to apologise to me?" said a rather baffled Léa.

"You'll see…" came a chorus from the other three.

It was midnight on Christmas Eve and present-opening time. The meal, as always, had been delicious thanks to Clare's forward planning and culinary skills, despite a serious dose of interference from her mother all evening. But good food and good wine always help to mellow even the most virulent critics and but the time midnight came around, even Mrs Maher was enjoying herself and looking forward to what *Papa Noël* might bring.

Solange had been quietly pleased all evening, watching this funny little mixed-up family try to marry the traditions of France and Ireland. If anything, she now felt quite at home here, part of the family almost, made especially welcome, with Antoine, by Clare and Frank.

For many years Christmas had been a sorrowful time for the twins, first in the aftermath of the loss of their parents and then when Alex had wormed his way into Léa's life, with his domineering ways and the fear and tension it had created. Now all that was over and thanks to Owen, Solange could at last let go, sensing that

Léa was happy and fulfilled, no longer needing her sister to hold her hand.

While Frank took a video recording and Ian photographed away, Owen handed out the presents under the Christmas tree to exclamations of joy, amazement or even mystification.

Léa found herself with a bottle of her favourite perfume from Solange and Antoine, a large, colourful cookery book in English from Clare and Frank, a box of whiskey-flavoured Irish fudge from Mr and Mrs Maher and a leather-backed diary and pen-set from Ian and Céline.

Suddenly, she looked up to see Owen waiting for her as he hauled out the painting she had completed of the manor house for Clare and Frank, now wrapped up in yards of shiny Xmas paper. He carried it over to present it to his parents.

"Mum, Dad, Happy Christmas!" he said, holding the painting upright while they beamed at him in happiness. As Léa watched somewhat anxiously, Clare gently removed the wrapping paper and gasped as she realized just what the painting was of. Even from where she sat, Léa could see just how pleased she was. Frank too, by the look of joy and awe on his face. They both turned to her to express their thanks and compliment her on all her hard work and give her a hug. Léa was at pains to explain that it was a commission that Owen had paid her for but it made no difference. Owen was thanked but Léa was acclaimed. He looked on in amusement as she tried, and failed, to put things right. In the end, he came over to hug her too.

Then everyone was crowding round to get a look and Léa found herself blushing at their praise. Someone was saying she should put her work on display, open a gallery said someone else, the general consensus being that she should sell her pictures. Solange and Antoine were confirming that she now had more than enough paintings done to start a small business of her own. Céline and Ian were already commissioning one for their new house.

Léa listened in awe. It had never occurred to her to paint for a living. She had never considered herself good enough, nor did she think she had the confidence. Living and working at home had kept her happy and secure... and away from all but a few close friends. But so much had changed in these last few months. Alex, her all-consuming terror, no longer had the power to terrorize her. She was free to live her life as she chose, was learning to accept that fact and let herself go.

And she was very much in love.

Now, with Owen's arm around her and so much praise for just one painting, she didn't know what to say. Seeing Clare wipe away a tear of happiness when she looked at it, had ensured that this one of the best Christmases Léa had ever had.

When the fuss and excitement of the presents had died down, it was time to wind up the evening and the six young people headed back on foot to the biggest gîte where they were all staying the night, no doubt to continue the revelries for an hour or two more.

Sometime after two am, Owen and Léa found themselves at last on their own, in the sitting-room, the others having just left to go to bed. Léa was still flushed and excited at all the praise she had received and her head was buzzing with ideas. Owen gave her a hug. Then he slipped his hand into his jacket pocket and brought out a letter which he handed to Léa to read. It was from the second of the firms that he had had an interview with, offering him a six-month contract there with a view to a permanent post if things worked out.

"Owen," she squeaked. "The job! You've got the job you wanted! Oh this is wonderful."

"It's only for six months, Léa. I still have to prove myself before they offer me a permanent post. "

"They will offer you a permanent post, Owen. I know they will."

"Oh Léa! You've more confidence in me than I have in myself."

He smiled and looked into her eyes. Then he pulled her to him and kissed her long and passionately. When at last they broke away, he put his hand back into his jacket pocket and rummaged around till he found what he wanted, finally bringing out a tiny box with an oversized bow on top of it. He handed it, somewhat shyly, to Léa. She looked at him in awe.

"Oh, Owen, it's beautiful," she cried when she opened it and saw the silver ring inside. It showed two hands holding a heart on top of which was a tiny crown studded with diamonds. Owen smiled, took the ring from its box and put it on the third finger of Léa's left-hand, the heart facing inwards towards her body.

"It's a traditional Irish ring, called a Claddagh ring, Léa," he said, "I bought it via the Internet. Does it fit okay? I had to guess."

"It is a little too big but we will get a jeweller's to fix that. It will not be a problem," said Léa. "Oh, I do love it, very much."

"It has a meaning... symbols... look," said Owen. "The hands are for friendship, and the crown is for loyalty, and the heart..."

"... is for love," whispered Léa.

"I love you, little Léa," said Owen softly.

"Oh! Me too! Me too! I love you too, Owen," she replied, her enthusiasm making him laugh.

"Look, when you wear the heart facing inwards, like that, it means you are with someone, you love somebody, your heart is taken."

"And if I change it so that the heart if facing outwards?"

"It means your heart is free."

"My heart is not free, Owen."

"Neither is mine, Léa." He chuckled. "Never thought I'd ever say that. Wow! If Pete could see me now..."

"Who is Pete? A friend?"

"A friend from university, yes."

"You must let me meet this Pete."

"Oh no! No way! Much too soon. I know how dangerous Pete can be when there is a beautiful girl around. But when we're married, we'll…"

"Owen, wait! Did you say '*married*'?"

"Léa… I've wanted to marry you practically from the first day I ever set eyes on you," said Owen softly.

"You are asking me to *marry* you, Owen?" she whispered.

"I am," he said, smiling at her look of disbelief, "Léa Duval. Will you be my wife? For ever and ever? *Pour toujours*? " And he took both of her hands in his.

Léa was silent for a few seconds.

"*Oh, oui, Owen*," she said, catching her breath, "*Oh, oui, pour toujours*."

He picked her up then in a huge hug and swung her round.

"*On va se marier!*" he shouted, loud enough to wake the dead. "*Elle a dit OUI!*"

Then he ran upstairs to hammer on bedroom doors.

"Solange! Antoine! Ian! Céline! We're getting married!"

Within thirty seconds, and in various stages of undress, Owen and Léa found themselves surrounded by their friends.

And he kissed Léa again, roundly, in front of them all, to the sound of cheers and wolf-whistles and applause.

Chapter Forty-Eight

Post-Scriptum

It was Tuesday afternoon and shortly before two pm Eileen pushed open the door of the charity shop where she now worked the equivalent of two days a week. Not that she got paid or anything, but it was a way for her to do good works and she loved getting out of the house and meeting people. And Phoebe, who ran the shop, liked dogs and Whisky was allowed to stay, so long as he didn't get in the way.

Eileen was particularly proud of the work she had done in the shop, especially the range of clothes for larger women which she had set up all on her own. She had built it up into a popular, well-stocked additive to the normal range of clothes and was happy to see that a lot of the older women made a bee line for it when they came into the shop.

"Hi, Phoebe, it's only me," she called out. "Just getting my coat off and then I'm ready."

"Oh, good, Eileen, I'm glad to see you," said Phoebe, coming out from the storeroom at the back of the shop. "It's been hectic in here all morning. In the run-up to Christmas, you understand."

"Of course I do. I don't know how you manage sometimes, all on your own."

"Well, actually, I wanted to talk to you about that. Do you think you'd be free to do an extra day from time to time? Just over the holiday period, you understand. Once Christmas is out of the way, I'll be able to cope. Especially now that Father McGonagall has found me an assistant at long last."

"Oh, that's excellent news! You really did need someone to help you out on a daily basis, Phoebe."

"I do, Eileen, I do. I'm not getting any younger, myself."

"Well, don't you worry. I'll come in for an extra day whenever I can. I only wish I could do more, but now that Sharon's home, I go in there and clean the place for her now and then and make a dinner for them from time to time. She's up to her eyes with the baby, as you can imagine, and she's grateful for my help."

"Aw... having a wee baby around the place must be lovely for you."

"It is. Oh it *is*! Sometimes, I encourage Sharon to have a wee nap to herself of an afternoon and she lets me take Emily out for a walk in the pram. Not when it's wet or too cold, mind, but there are days when a wee outing does her good. And Sharon's so grateful to catch up on an hour's sleep here and there."

"And what about Paul? I'm sure he's so pleased to have a daughter. He just turned forty, didn't he?"

"He did indeed. Oh, he's *nuts* about her. Calls her his little princess. Takes her in his arms as soon as he gets home from work. And he feeds her and changes her. He's a really good dad."

"Sharon not breastfeeding then?"

"No. It didn't work out and she didn't insist," said Eileen. She lowered her voice. "Between you and me, it's just as well. She won't be on maternity leave forever and it'll be easier for her to hand the baby over to the nanny, if she's not breast-feeding."

"So they're getting a *nanny*, then, are they?"

"They are indeed. Someone who is free to fit in with their working hours and that they can turn to in an emergency. You might know her. She's one of Beatrice's daughters. Beatrice Kearney, you know? Who works as a nurse at Oak Lodge? Well, her daughter Mandy is a fully-trained crèche assistant, that's one of those people who work in a childcare centre. But she doesn't like commuting to Belfast every day and hasn't found work nearer home. So she's going to look after the baby! She's already been round for a few hours here and there and according to Sharon, she's a natural!"

"Now isn't that just wonderful? But you won't mind that they have a nanny, Eileen? It'll mean you won't get to look after the baby as much as you wanted to."

"No. Really, I don't mind. Looking after Emily is a big job, and I'm not getting any younger. Just like yourself, Phoebe. I'll always be there for them whenever they need me, if Mandy needs a day off or if they both have to work an evening shift. Believe me, there'll be plenty of opportunities for me to look after the wee mite. Oh, she's *gorgeous*, Phoebe. I'll have to get Sharon to bring her into the shop one day so you can see her for yourself."

"I'll look forward to that. Now, we'll have to get a move on, Eileen. There's loads to unpack. People seem to give in a lot of stuff at Christmas, don't they? And I haven't had a chance to get at it this last couple of days."

"When did Father McGonagall say he'd be bringing the new assistant?" said Eileen as she began emptying a huge tea-chest of clothes. "We could be doing with her right away."

"Well, he said he would probably bring her round this afternoon, actually," said Phoebe. "So that she could meet both of us at once." She lowered her voice. "We'll be doing her a good turn, or so he told me. The poor woman was wrongly accused of something in her last job and got the sack. He didn't say what it was exactly and I didn't like to ask. But it's obvious that she could be doing with the money and it's Christmastime, after all."

"Oh how awful! That's so unfair!" said Eileen, appalled. "I'll do my very best to make her feel at home, Phoebe. You can count on me. Some employers think they can get away with anything. Turning the poor woman out of a job and Christmas just round the corner. A crying shame, so it is."

"Indeed it is. Thank you, Eileen. I knew I could trust you to show her the ropes and make her feel part of the team. Ah! Our first customers of the afternoon. Looks like we're in for another busy one."

The afternoon was indeed busy, busier than Eileen had ever known it to be in the charity shop. People deposited boxes of stuff in amazing quantities and other people came in to browse and buy. The till never seemed to stop as Phoebe rang up sale after sale and Eileen had her work cut out trying to replenish the racks of clothes and the shelves of books and trinkets as fast as they were being depleted. The time just flew by.

Shortly before closing time at half-past five, there was a lull that took both women by surprise. Just then, as if he had been waiting his cue, the door opened and Father McGonagall came in.

"Well, ladies, how's it going? Been a busy day, then, has it?" he beamed.

"Oh Father, the busiest yet! Thank God Eileen was here to help me. I'd never have managed without her."

"Well, at least you'll have help from tomorrow onwards, Phoebe. Your new assistant should be here any minute now. I asked her to come along at closing time. I thought it would be best. Ah, here she is now. Come in. Come in. Let me introduce you to Phoebe Giles and Eileen Murphy, two angels straight out of heaven. I don't know what we'd do without them."

He turned back to the po-faced, middle-aged woman who stood defiantly behind him.

"Phoebe, Eileen… meet your new co-worker… Agnes O'Neill!"

The End

Printed in France by Amazon
Brétigny-sur-Orge, FR